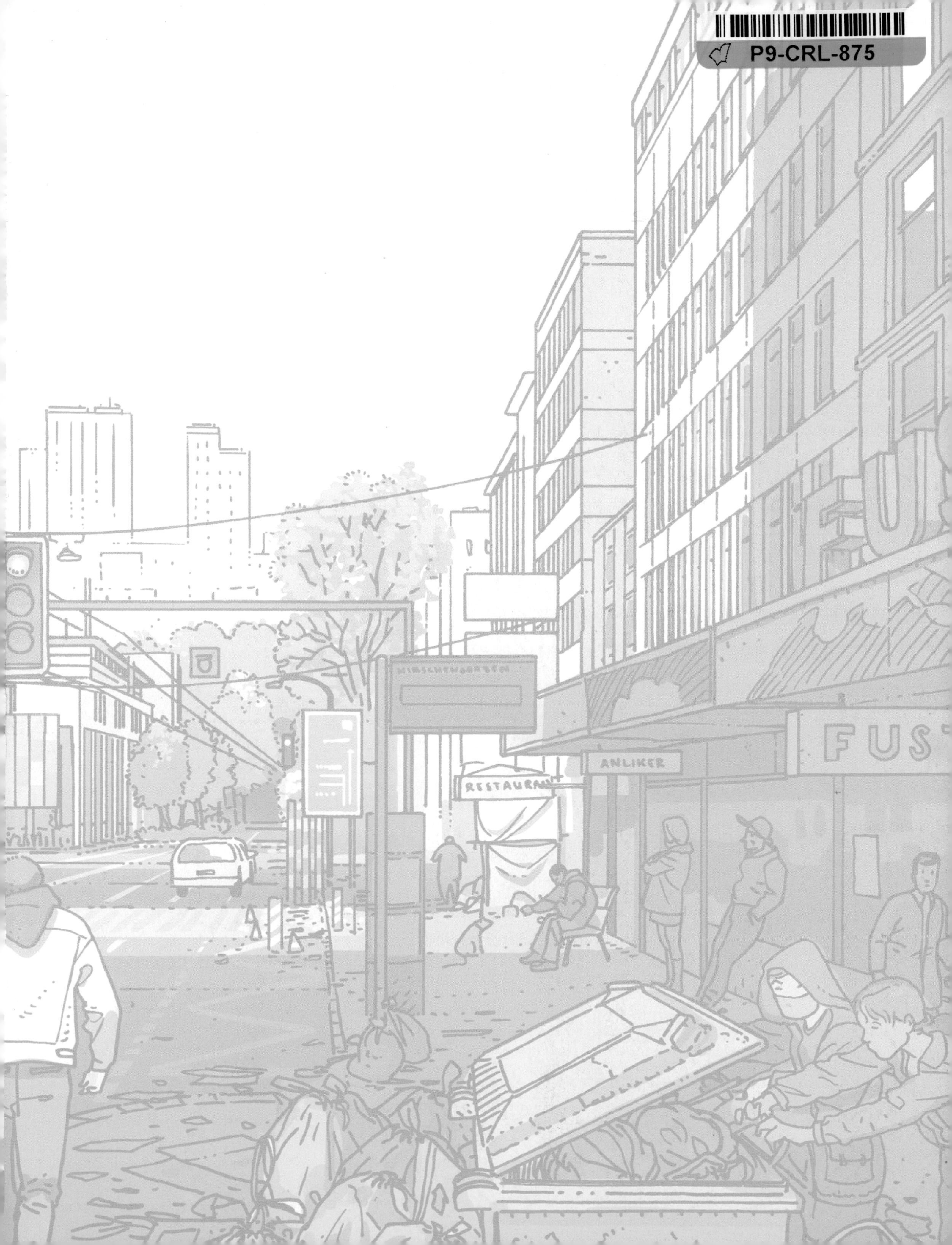
ANLIKER

THE FALL, VOL. I.
First printing. March 2021.
Published by Image Comics, Inc. Office of publication:
PO BOX I4457, Portland, OR 97293.

Copyright © 2021 Jared Muralt.
All rights reserved.
Contains material originally published in single magazine
form as THE FALL #I-6.

Translated from German into English by Franz He &
Christoph Studer-Harper.

Printed in the USA.
For international rights, contact:
foreignlicensing@imagecomics.com.

ISBN: 978-I-5343-I838-0

VOLUME ONE

—

WRITTEN AND DRAWN BY
JARED MURALT

Thanks to:
Silvio for the layout and The Fall title logo.
Eliane & Sandro for the valuable feedback
on the dialogues.
Samuel Rassy for flatting.
Pädu for the administrative assistance.

Christian & Philipp
for their support and wise
words of advice.
Yvonne and everyone
who believes in The Fall series.

All my patrons on Patreon, especially
Ian Carnevale, Julien Combot
Karin Rudin, Ariadne Papadakis,
Matthias Schrader, Adam Jefford, Harry Murr,
Marion Kamper, Johan Lindberg Brusewitz,
Jerome Ng Xin Hao, Alisdair Gordon, Miguel Bustos,
Davide Musmeci, Levi Cooke.

—

www.blackyard.ch
www.patreon.com/jaredmuralt

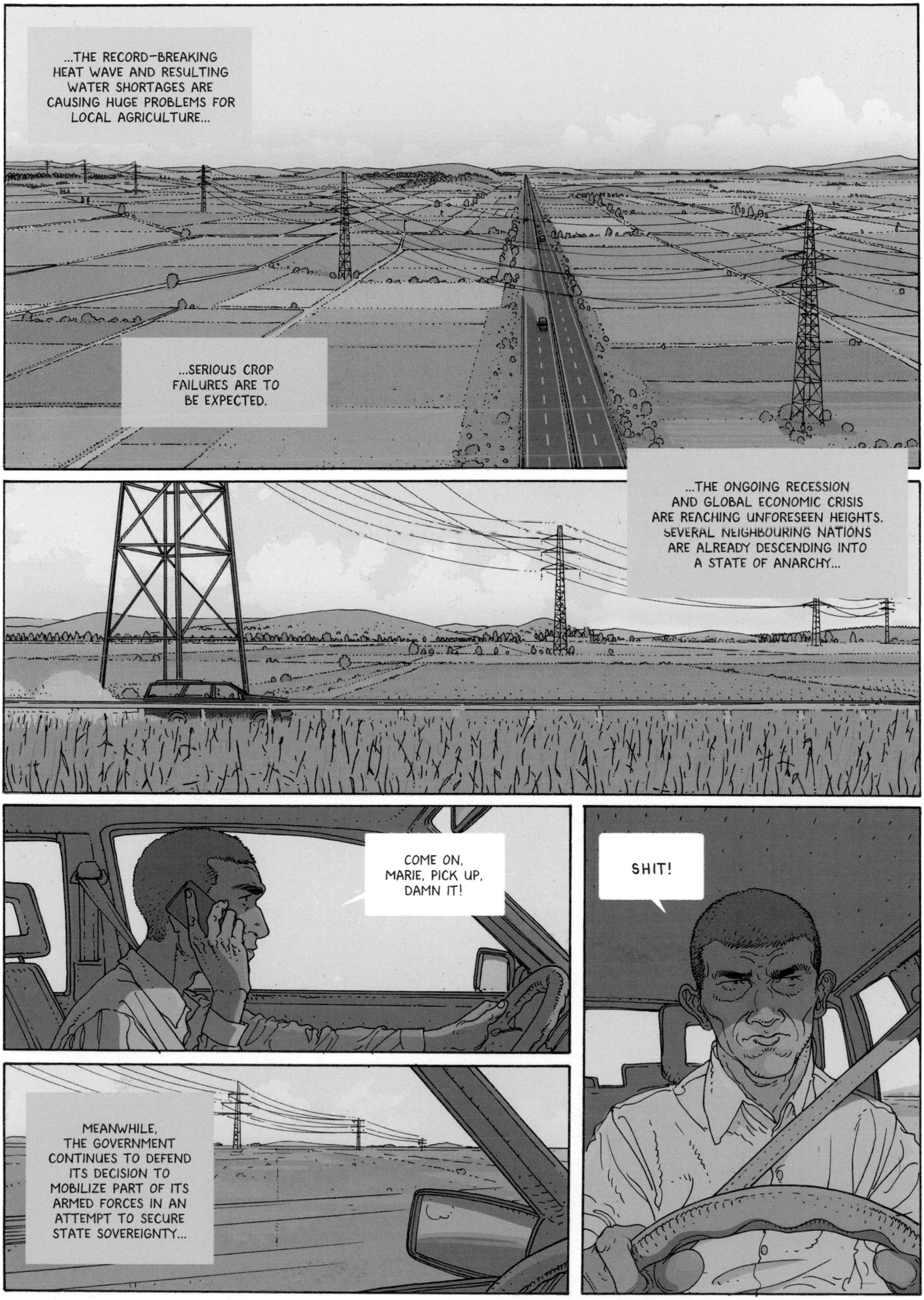
...THE RECORD-BREAKING HEAT WAVE AND RESULTING WATER SHORTAGES ARE CAUSING HUGE PROBLEMS FOR LOCAL AGRICULTURE...
...SERIOUS CROP FAILURES ARE TO BE EXPECTED.
...THE ONGOING RECESSION AND GLOBAL ECONOMIC CRISIS ARE REACHING UNFORESEEN HEIGHTS. SEVERAL NEIGHBOURING NATIONS ARE ALREADY DESCENDING INTO A STATE OF ANARCHY...
COME ON, MARIE, PICK UP, DAMN IT!
MEANWHILE, THE GOVERNMENT CONTINUES TO DEFEND ITS DECISION TO MOBILIZE PART OF ITS ARMED FORCES IN AN ATTEMPT TO SECURE STATE SOVEREIGNTY...
SHIT!

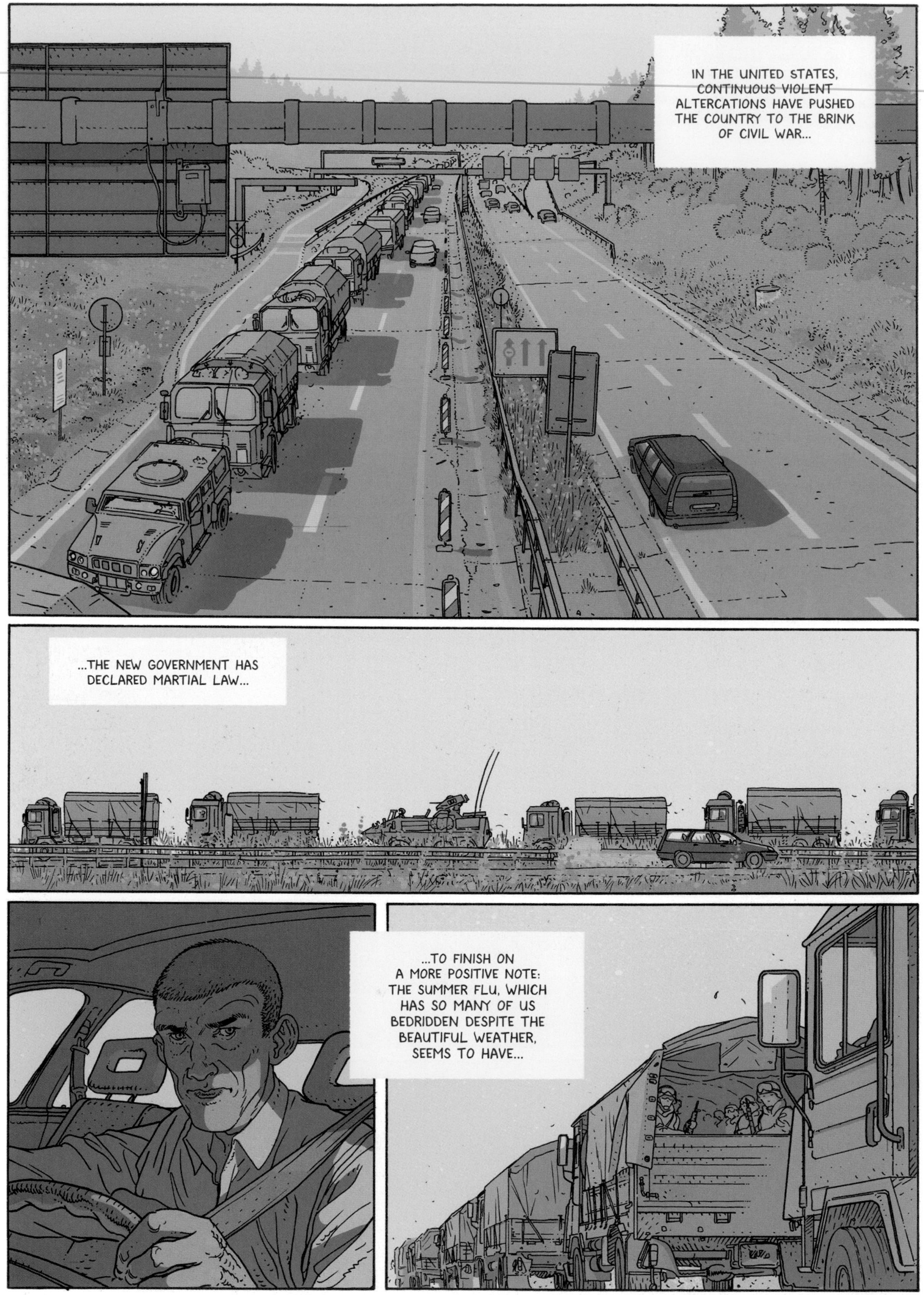
IN THE UNITED STATES, CONTINUOUS VIOLENT ALTERCATIONS HAVE PUSHED THE COUNTRY TO THE BRINK OF CIVIL WAR...
...THE NEW GOVERNMENT HAS DECLARED MARTIAL LAW...
...TO FINISH ON A MORE POSITIVE NOTE: THE SUMMER FLU, WHICH HAS SO MANY OF US BEDRIDDEN DESPITE THE BEAUTIFUL WEATHER, SEEMS TO HAVE...

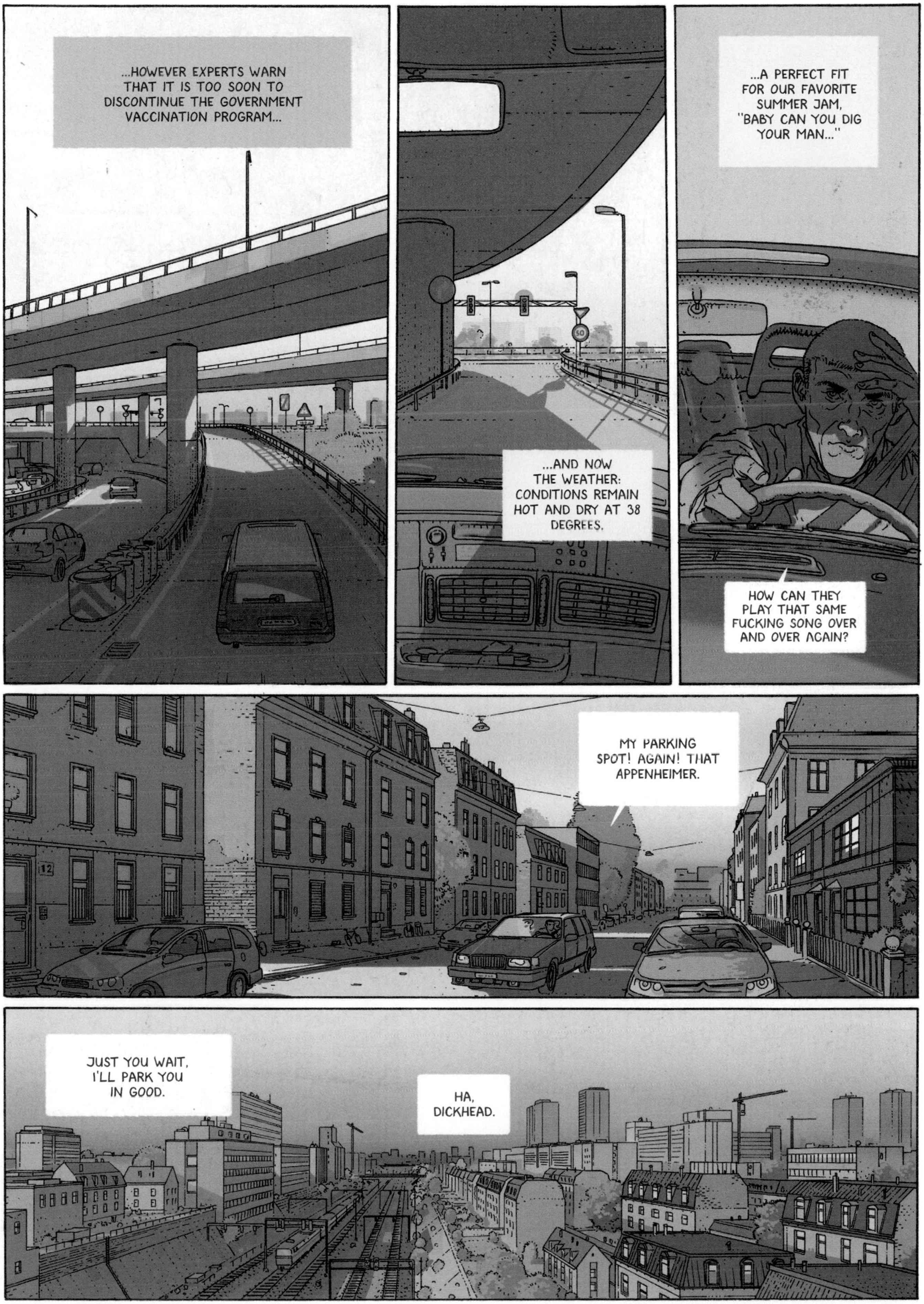
...HOWEVER EXPERTS WARN THAT IT IS TOO SOON TO DISCONTINUE THE GOVERNMENT VACCINATION PROGRAM...
...AND NOW THE WEATHER: CONDITIONS REMAIN HOT AND DRY AT 38 DEGREES.
...A PERFECT FIT FOR OUR FAVORITE SUMMER JAM, "BABY CAN YOU DIG YOUR MAN..."
HOW CAN THEY PLAY THAT SAME FUCKING SONG OVER AND OVER AGAIN?
MY PARKING SPOT! AGAIN! THAT APPENHEIMER.
JUST YOU WAIT, I'LL PARK YOU IN GOOD.
HA, DICKHEAD.

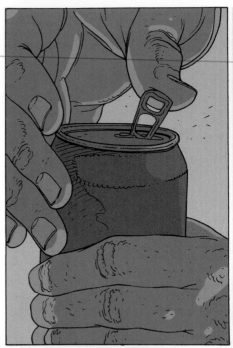

WE'RE SCREWED!

DAD? HOME ALREADY?

LOOK WHO WE BROUGHT!

HEY LIAM.

YOU'LL NEVER BELIEVE WHAT HAPPENED TO ME TODAY...

I'M NOT IN THE MOOD, THIERRY.

COME ON. LISTEN TO ME. THE BUTCHER. AT MATTENHOF. YOU KNOW THE ONE. THEY SELL OFFAL AT A GOOD PRICE.

WHO ARE YOU TEXTING?

NONE OF YOUR BUSINESS, DUMBO!

8

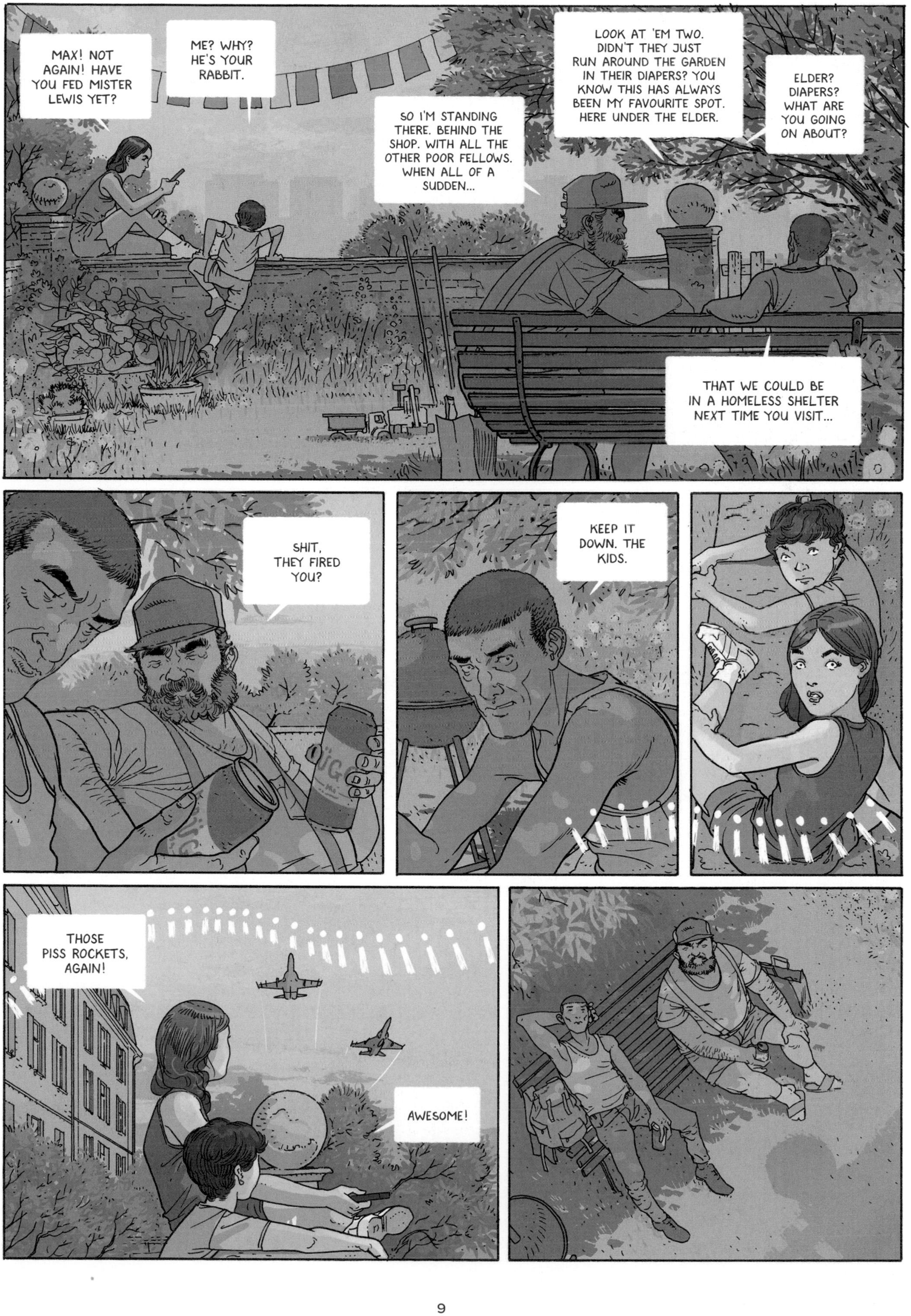
MAX! NOT AGAIN! HAVE YOU FED MISTER LEWIS YET?
ME? WHY? HE'S YOUR RABBIT.
SO I'M STANDING THERE. BEHIND THE SHOP. WITH ALL THE OTHER POOR FELLOWS. WHEN ALL OF A SUDDEN...
LOOK AT 'EM TWO. DIDN'T THEY JUST RUN AROUND THE GARDEN IN THEIR DIAPERS? YOU KNOW THIS HAS ALWAYS BEEN MY FAVOURITE SPOT. HERE UNDER THE ELDER.
ELDER? DIAPERS? WHAT ARE YOU GOING ON ABOUT?
THAT WE COULD BE IN A HOMELESS SHELTER NEXT TIME YOU VISIT...
SHIT, THEY FIRED YOU?
KEEP IT DOWN. THE KIDS.
THOSE PISS ROCKETS, AGAIN!
AWESOME!

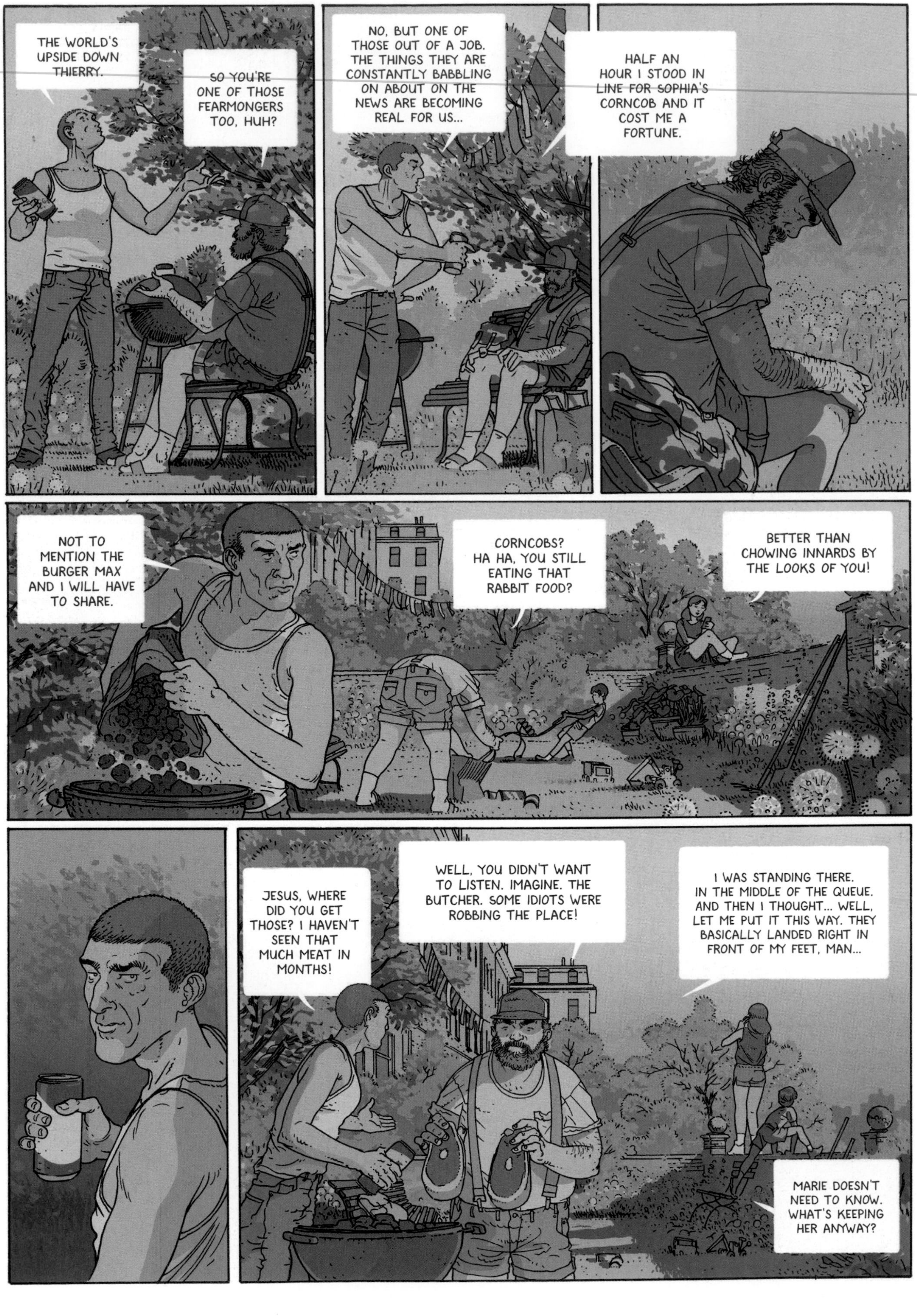
THE WORLD'S UPSIDE DOWN THIERRY.
SO YOU'RE ONE OF THOSE FEARMONGERS TOO, HUH?
NO, BUT ONE OF THOSE OUT OF A JOB. THE THINGS THEY ARE CONSTANTLY BABBLING ON ABOUT ON THE NEWS ARE BECOMING REAL FOR US...
HALF AN HOUR I STOOD IN LINE FOR SOPHIA'S CORNCOB AND IT COST ME A FORTUNE.
NOT TO MENTION THE BURGER MAX AND I WILL HAVE TO SHARE.
CORNCOBS? HA HA, YOU STILL EATING THAT RABBIT FOOD?
BETTER THAN CHOWING INNARDS BY THE LOOKS OF YOU!
JESUS, WHERE DID YOU GET THOSE? I HAVEN'T SEEN THAT MUCH MEAT IN MONTHS!
WELL, YOU DIDN'T WANT TO LISTEN. IMAGINE. THE BUTCHER. SOME IDIOTS WERE ROBBING THE PLACE!
I WAS STANDING THERE. IN THE MIDDLE OF THE QUEUE. AND THEN I THOUGHT... WELL, LET ME PUT IT THIS WAY. THEY BASICALLY LANDED RIGHT IN FRONT OF MY FEET, MAN...
MARIE DOESN'T NEED TO KNOW. WHAT'S KEEPING HER ANYWAY?

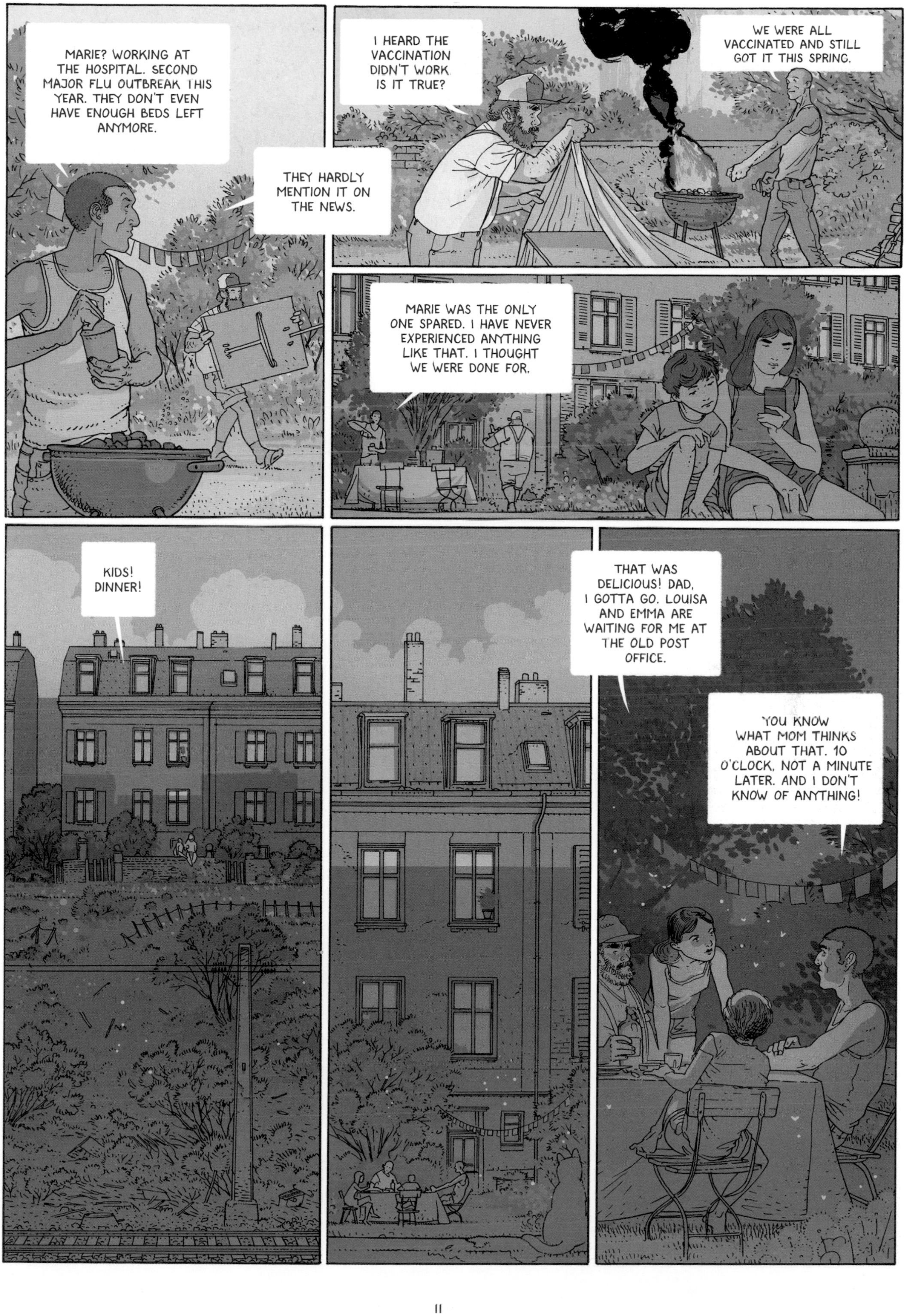

MARIE? WORKING AT THE HOSPITAL. SECOND MAJOR FLU OUTBREAK THIS YEAR. THEY DON'T EVEN HAVE ENOUGH BEDS LEFT ANYMORE.
THEY HARDLY MENTION IT ON THE NEWS.
I HEARD THE VACCINATION DIDN'T WORK. IS IT TRUE?
WE WERE ALL VACCINATED AND STILL GOT IT THIS SPRING.
MARIE WAS THE ONLY ONE SPARED. I HAVE NEVER EXPERIENCED ANYTHING LIKE THAT. I THOUGHT WE WERE DONE FOR.
KIDS! DINNER!
THAT WAS DELICIOUS! DAD, I GOTTA GO. LOUISA AND EMMA ARE WAITING FOR ME AT THE OLD POST OFFICE.
YOU KNOW WHAT MOM THINKS ABOUT THAT. 10 O'CLOCK, NOT A MINUTE LATER. AND I DON'T KNOW OF ANYTHING!

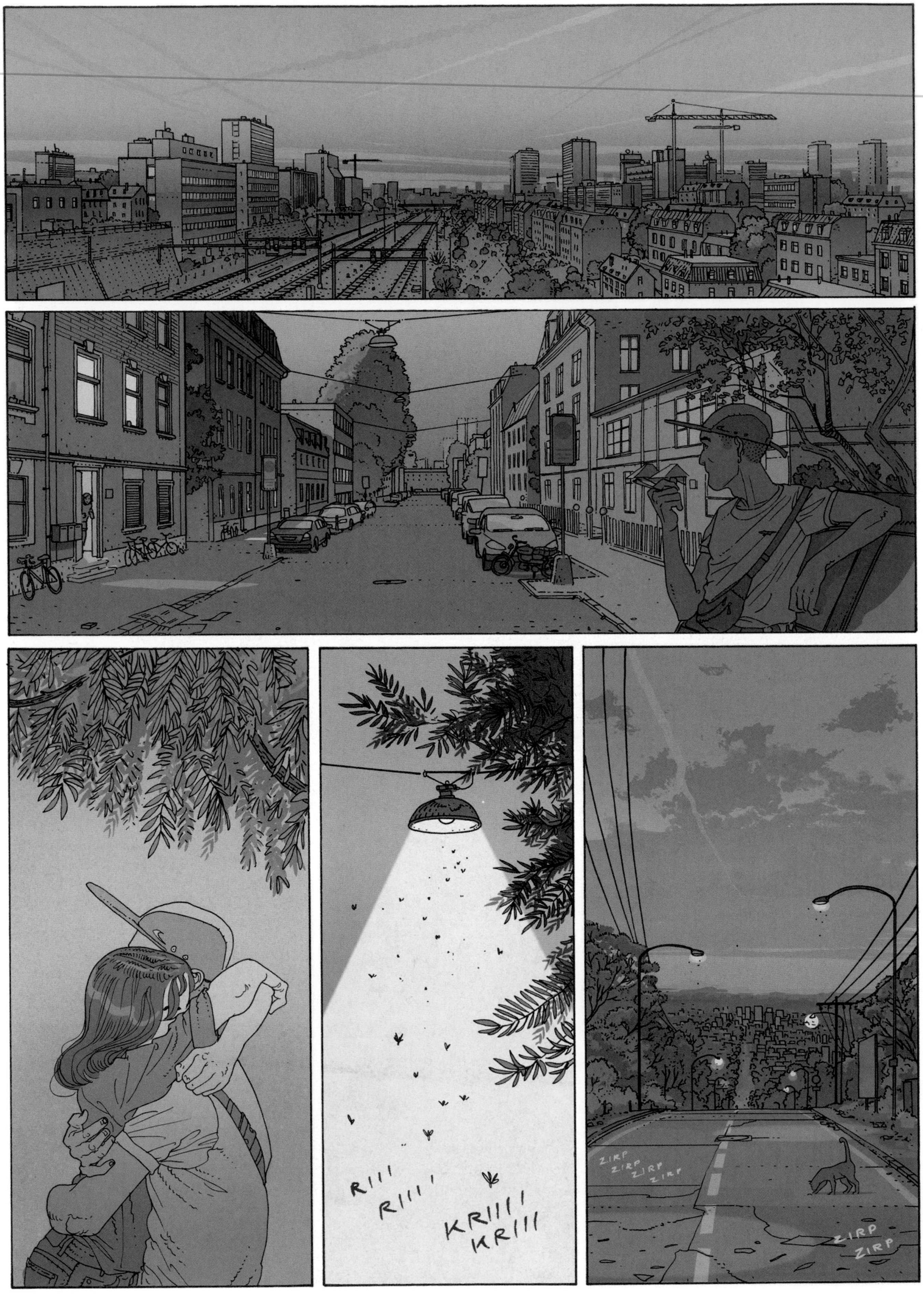
RIII
RIII
KRIIII
KRIII
ZIRP
ZIRP
ZIRP
ZIRP
ZIRP
ZIRP

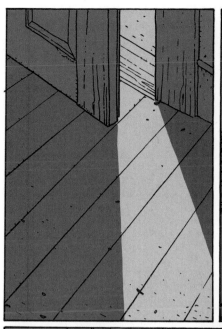

DAD?

WHERE'S MOM?

WHAT? NO IDEA. WHAT TIME IS IT?

HALF PAST MIDNIGHT?! AND YOU'RE STILL UP?! WHAT THE...

MOM'S NOT HOME YET?

ALSO, YOU GOT ANOTHER PARKING TICKET!

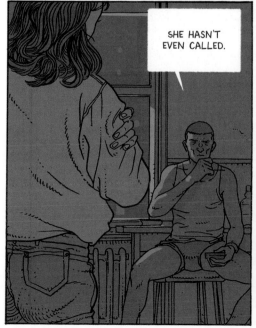

SHE HASN'T EVEN CALLED.

ALL LINES ARE BUSY. PROBABLY BECAUSE OF THE FLU.

...PLEASE LEAVE A MESSAGE AFTER THE TONE.

IT'S ME. CALL ME WHEN YOU GET A MINUTE. WHAT'S GOING ON? THE KIDS ARE GETTING WORRIED. LOVE YOU...

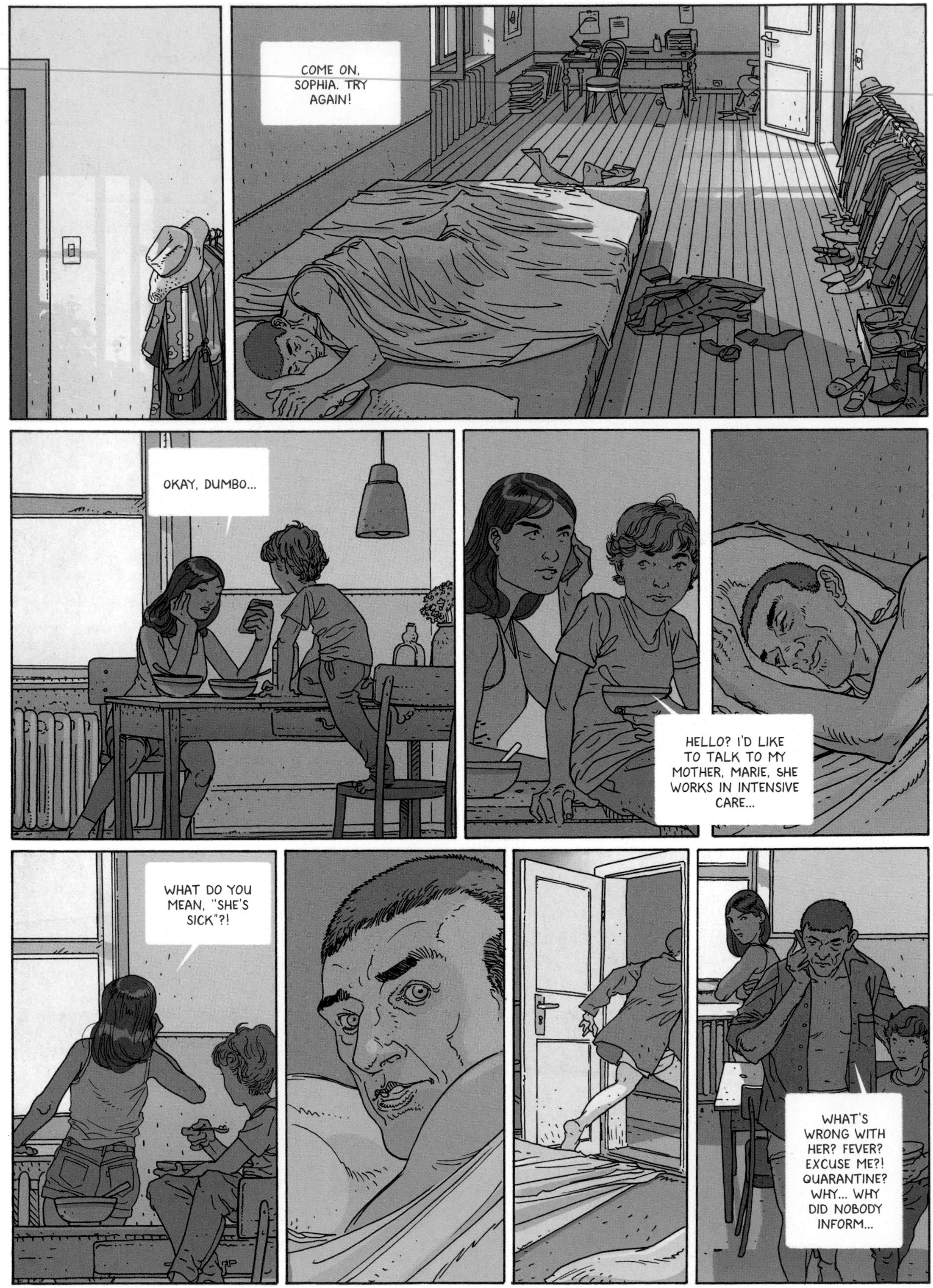
COME ON, SOPHIA. TRY AGAIN!
OKAY, DUMBO...
HELLO? I'D LIKE TO TALK TO MY MOTHER, MARIE, SHE WORKS IN INTENSIVE CARE...
WHAT DO YOU MEAN, "SHE'S SICK"?!
WHAT'S WRONG WITH HER? FEVER? EXCUSE ME?! QUARANTINE? WHY... WHY DID NOBODY INFORM...

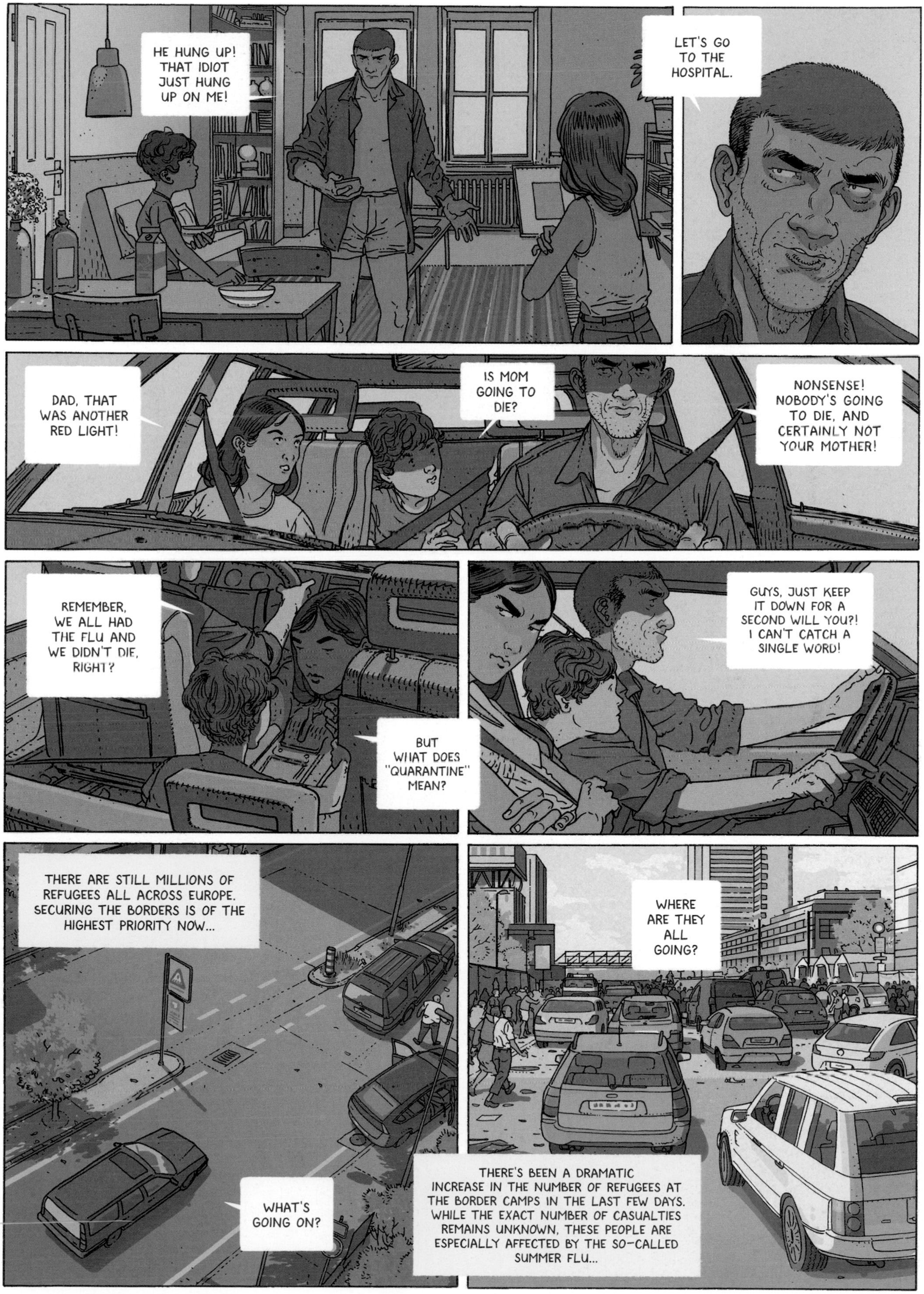
HE HUNG UP! THAT IDIOT JUST HUNG UP ON ME!
LET'S GO TO THE HOSPITAL.
DAD, THAT WAS ANOTHER RED LIGHT!
IS MOM GOING TO DIE?
NONSENSE! NOBODY'S GOING TO DIE, AND CERTAINLY NOT YOUR MOTHER!
REMEMBER, WE ALL HAD THE FLU AND WE DIDN'T DIE, RIGHT?
BUT WHAT DOES "QUARANTINE" MEAN?
GUYS, JUST KEEP IT DOWN FOR A SECOND WILL YOU?! I CAN'T CATCH A SINGLE WORD!
THERE ARE STILL MILLIONS OF REFUGEES ALL ACROSS EUROPE. SECURING THE BORDERS IS OF THE HIGHEST PRIORITY NOW...
WHAT'S GOING ON?
WHERE ARE THEY ALL GOING?
THERE'S BEEN A DRAMATIC INCREASE IN THE NUMBER OF REFUGEES AT THE BORDER CAMPS IN THE LAST FEW DAYS. WHILE THE EXACT NUMBER OF CASUALTIES REMAINS UNKNOWN, THESE PEOPLE ARE ESPECIALLY AFFECTED BY THE SO-CALLED SUMMER FLU...

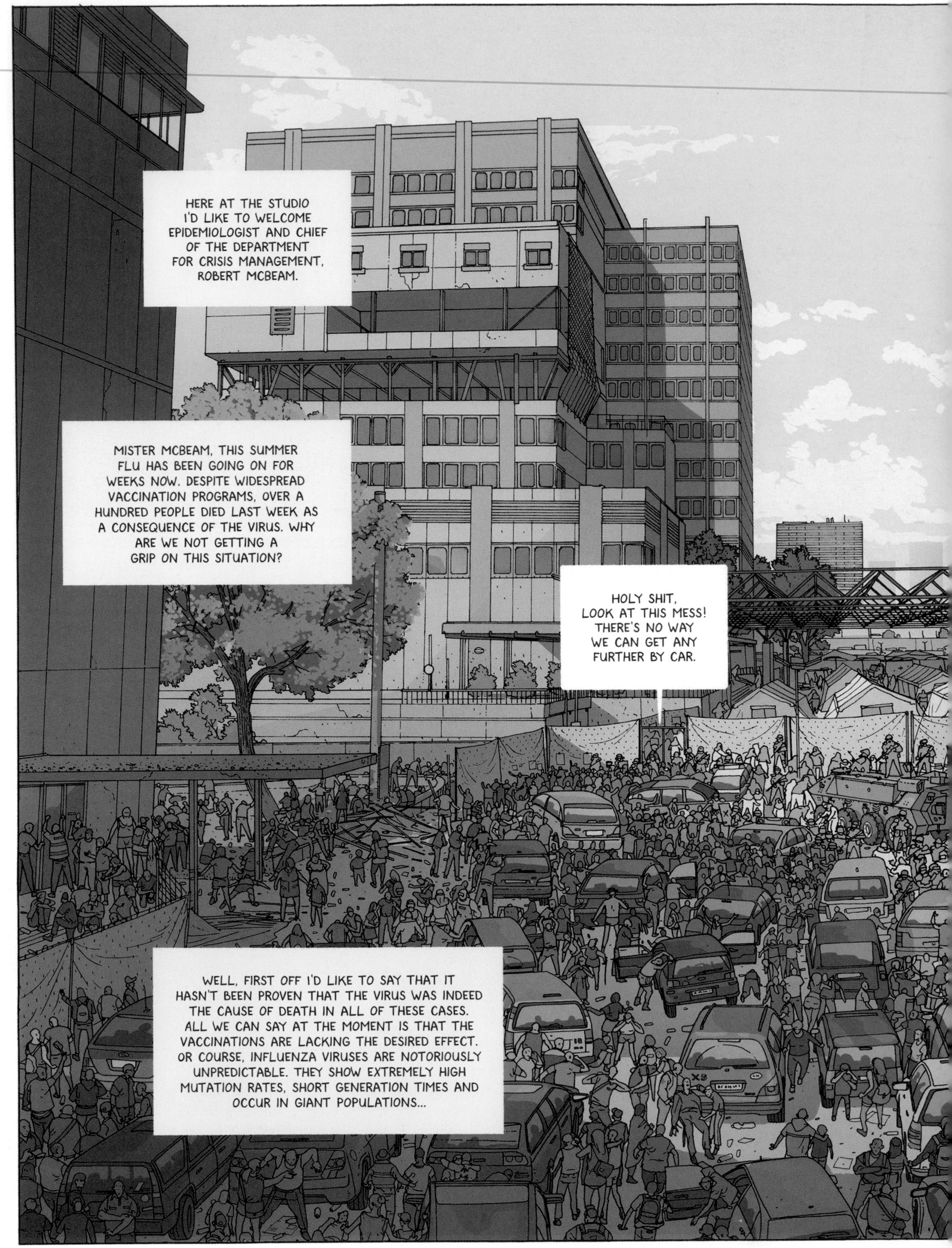
HERE AT THE STUDIO I'D LIKE TO WELCOME EPIDEMIOLOGIST AND CHIEF OF THE DEPARTMENT FOR CRISIS MANAGEMENT, ROBERT MCBEAM.
MISTER MCBEAM, THIS SUMMER FLU HAS BEEN GOING ON FOR WEEKS NOW. DESPITE WIDESPREAD VACCINATION PROGRAMS, OVER A HUNDRED PEOPLE DIED LAST WEEK AS A CONSEQUENCE OF THE VIRUS. WHY ARE WE NOT GETTING A GRIP ON THIS SITUATION?
HOLY SHIT, LOOK AT THIS MESS! THERE'S NO WAY WE CAN GET ANY FURTHER BY CAR.
WELL, FIRST OFF I'D LIKE TO SAY THAT IT HASN'T BEEN PROVEN THAT THE VIRUS WAS INDEED THE CAUSE OF DEATH IN ALL OF THESE CASES. ALL WE CAN SAY AT THE MOMENT IS THAT THE VACCINATIONS ARE LACKING THE DESIRED EFFECT. OR COURSE, INFLUENZA VIRUSES ARE NOTORIOUSLY UNPREDICTABLE. THEY SHOW EXTREMELY HIGH MUTATION RATES, SHORT GENERATION TIMES AND OCCUR IN GIANT POPULATIONS...

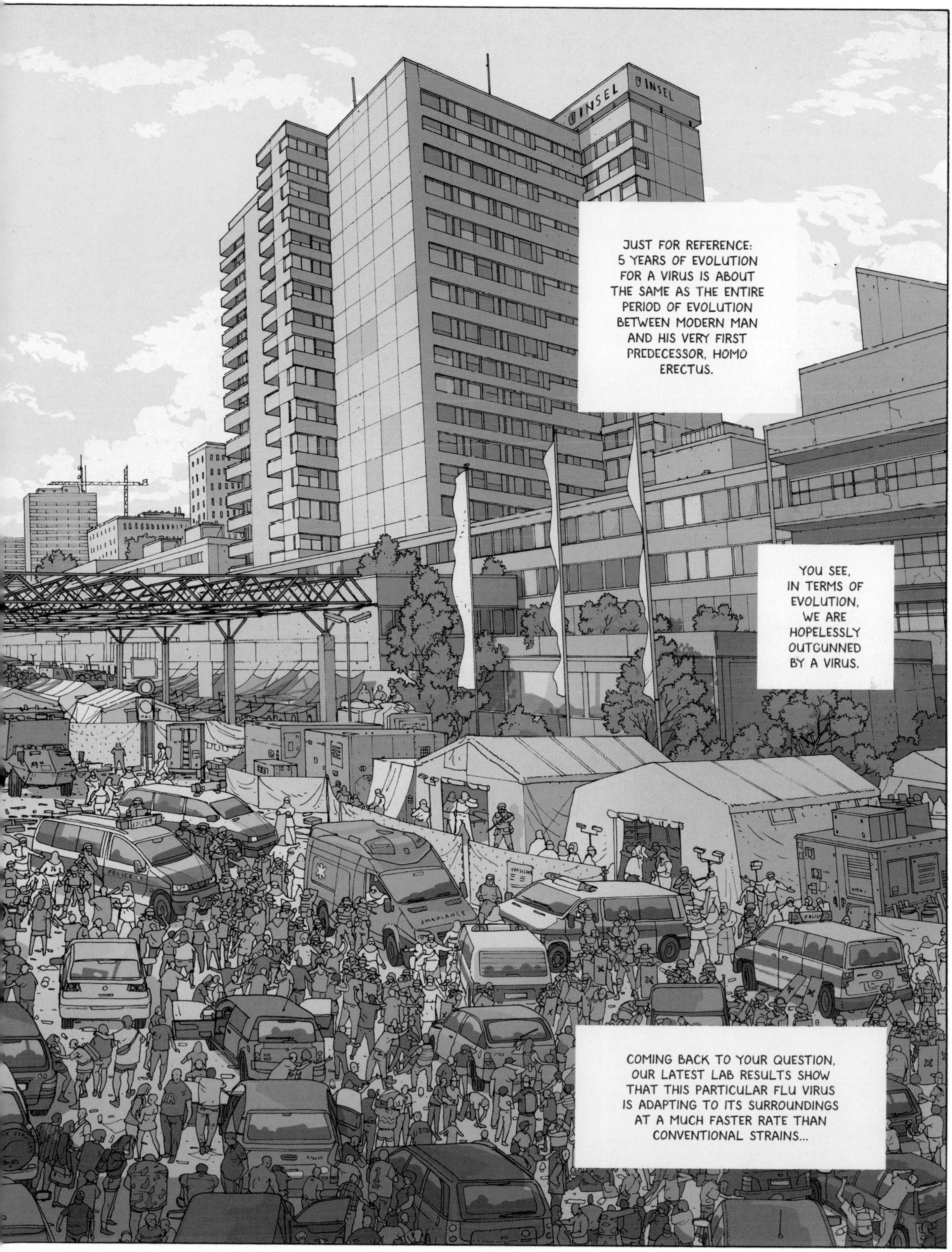
INSEL
JUST FOR REFERENCE: 5 YEARS OF EVOLUTION FOR A VIRUS IS ABOUT THE SAME AS THE ENTIRE PERIOD OF EVOLUTION BETWEEN MODERN MAN AND HIS VERY FIRST PREDECESSOR, HOMO ERECTUS.
YOU SEE, IN TERMS OF EVOLUTION, WE ARE HOPELESSLY OUTGUNNED BY A VIRUS.
COMING BACK TO YOUR QUESTION, OUR LATEST LAB RESULTS SHOW THAT THIS PARTICULAR FLU VIRUS IS ADAPTING TO ITS SURROUNDINGS AT A MUCH FASTER RATE THAN CONVENTIONAL STRAINS...

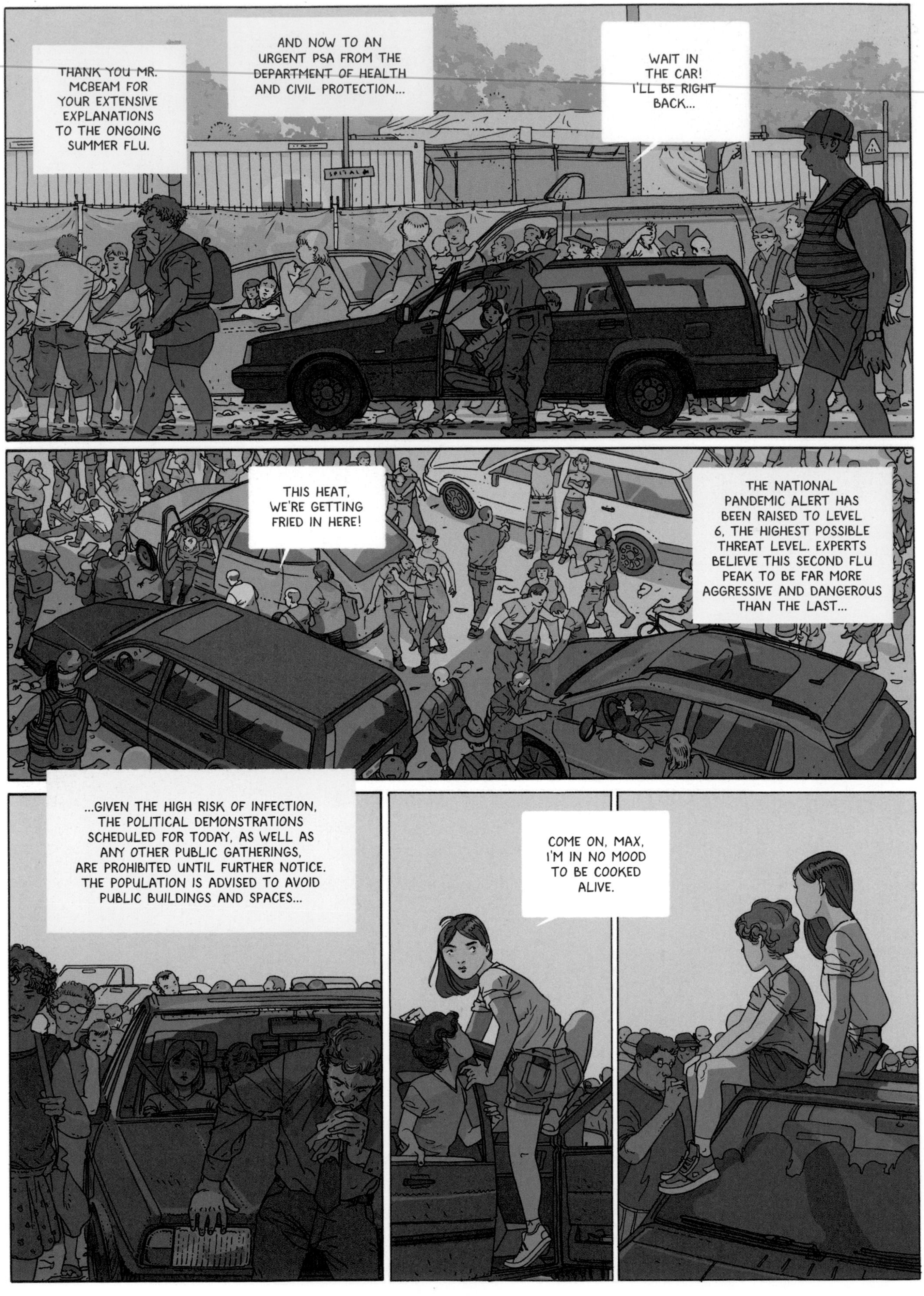
THANK YOU MR. MCBEAM FOR YOUR EXTENSIVE EXPLANATIONS TO THE ONGOING SUMMER FLU.
AND NOW TO AN URGENT PSA FROM THE DEPARTMENT OF HEALTH AND CIVIL PROTECTION...
WAIT IN THE CAR! I'LL BE RIGHT BACK...
THIS HEAT, WE'RE GETTING FRIED IN HERE!
THE NATIONAL PANDEMIC ALERT HAS BEEN RAISED TO LEVEL 6, THE HIGHEST POSSIBLE THREAT LEVEL. EXPERTS BELIEVE THIS SECOND FLU PEAK TO BE FAR MORE AGGRESSIVE AND DANGEROUS THAN THE LAST...
...GIVEN THE HIGH RISK OF INFECTION, THE POLITICAL DEMONSTRATIONS SCHEDULED FOR TODAY, AS WELL AS ANY OTHER PUBLIC GATHERINGS, ARE PROHIBITED UNTIL FURTHER NOTICE. THE POPULATION IS ADVISED TO AVOID PUBLIC BUILDINGS AND SPACES...
COME ON, MAX, I'M IN NO MOOD TO BE COOKED ALIVE.

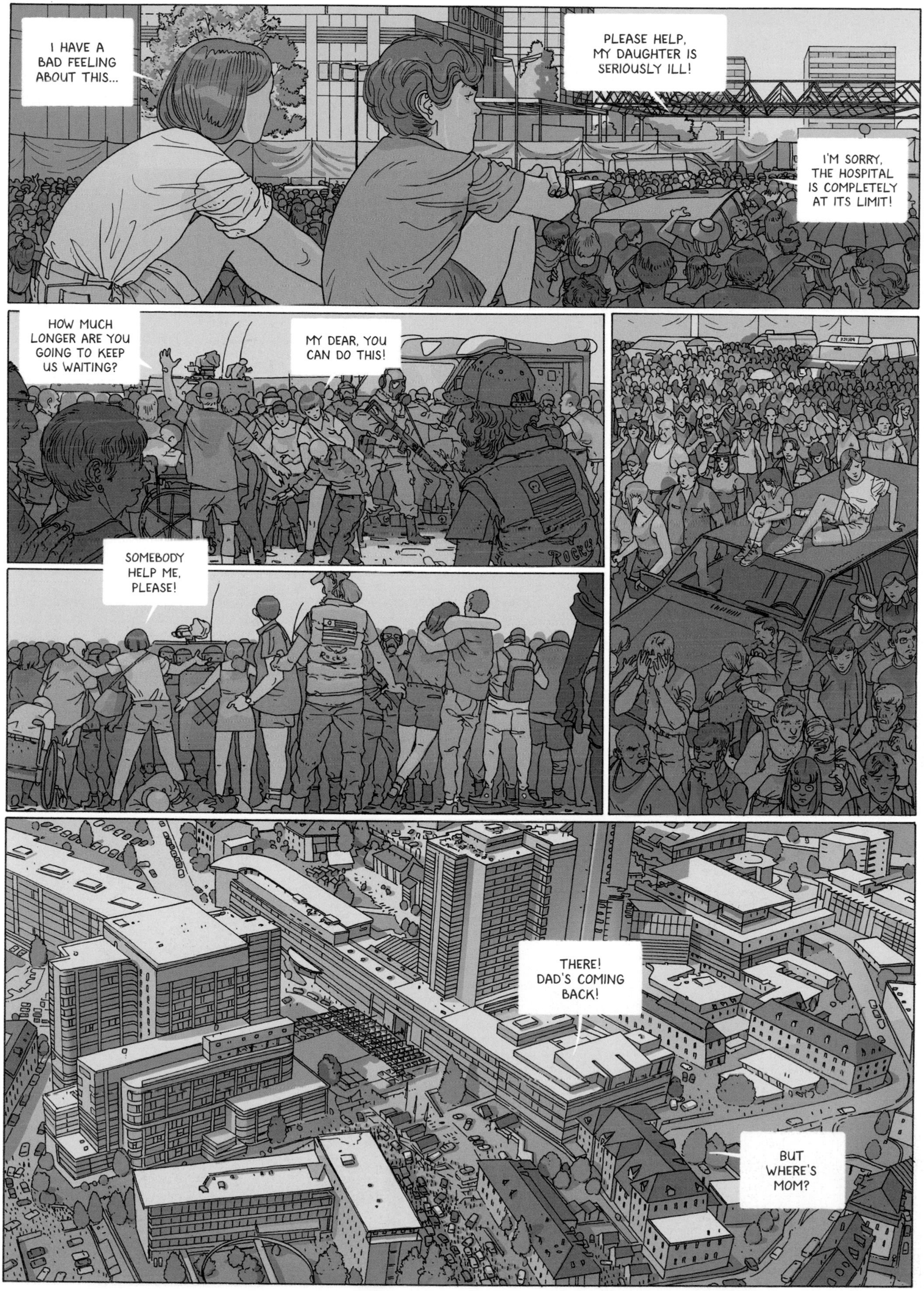
I HAVE A BAD FEELING ABOUT THIS...
PLEASE HELP, MY DAUGHTER IS SERIOUSLY ILL!
I'M SORRY, THE HOSPITAL IS COMPLETELY AT ITS LIMIT!
HOW MUCH LONGER ARE YOU GOING TO KEEP US WAITING?
MY DEAR, YOU CAN DO THIS!
SOMEBODY HELP ME, PLEASE!
THERE! DAD'S COMING BACK!
BUT WHERE'S MOM?

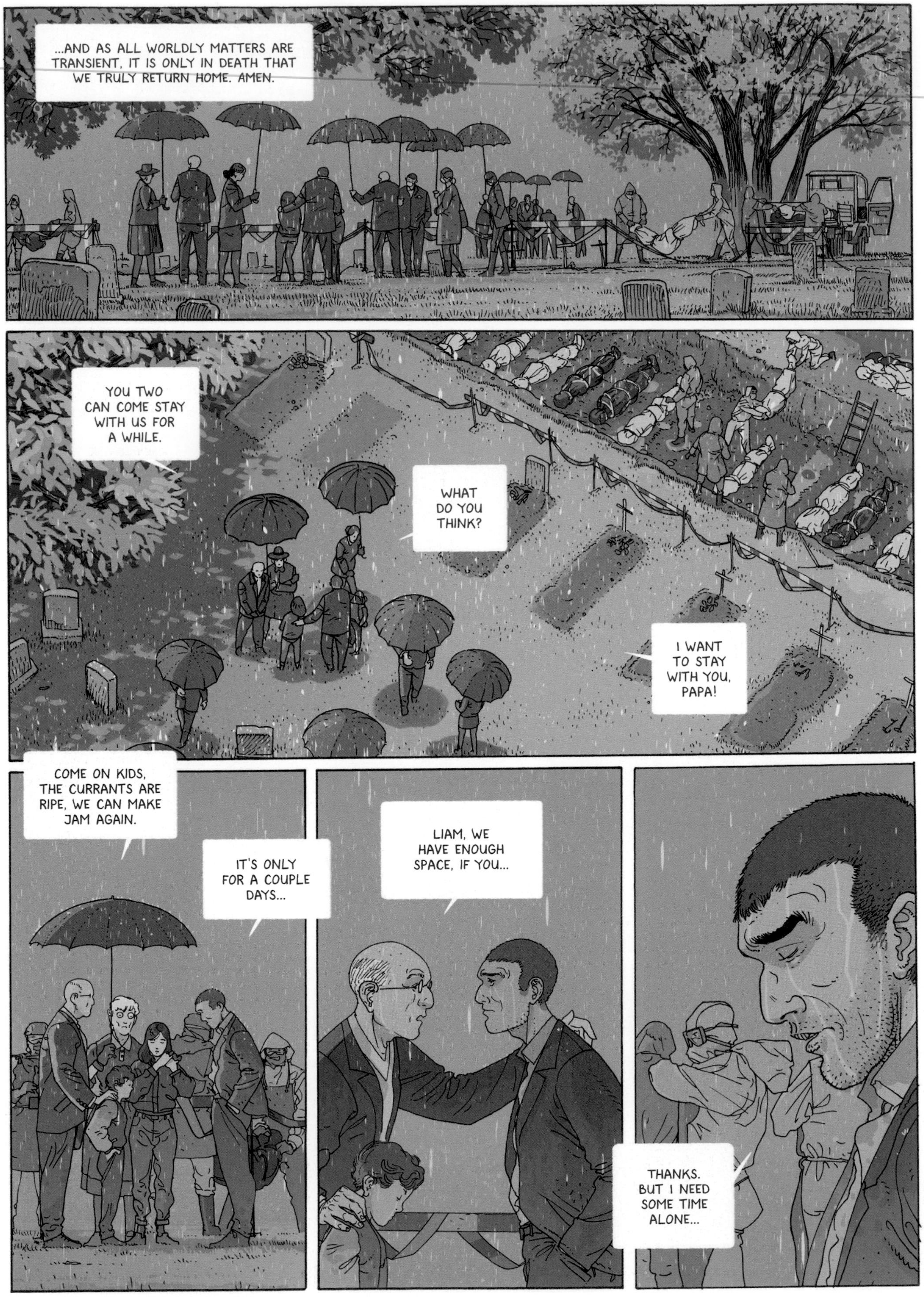

...AND AS ALL WORLDLY MATTERS ARE TRANSIENT, IT IS ONLY IN DEATH THAT WE TRULY RETURN HOME. AMEN.
YOU TWO CAN COME STAY WITH US FOR A WHILE.
WHAT DO YOU THINK?
I WANT TO STAY WITH YOU, PAPA!
COME ON KIDS, THE CURRANTS ARE RIPE, WE CAN MAKE JAM AGAIN.
IT'S ONLY FOR A COUPLE DAYS...
LIAM, WE HAVE ENOUGH SPACE, IF YOU...
THANKS. BUT I NEED SOME TIME ALONE...

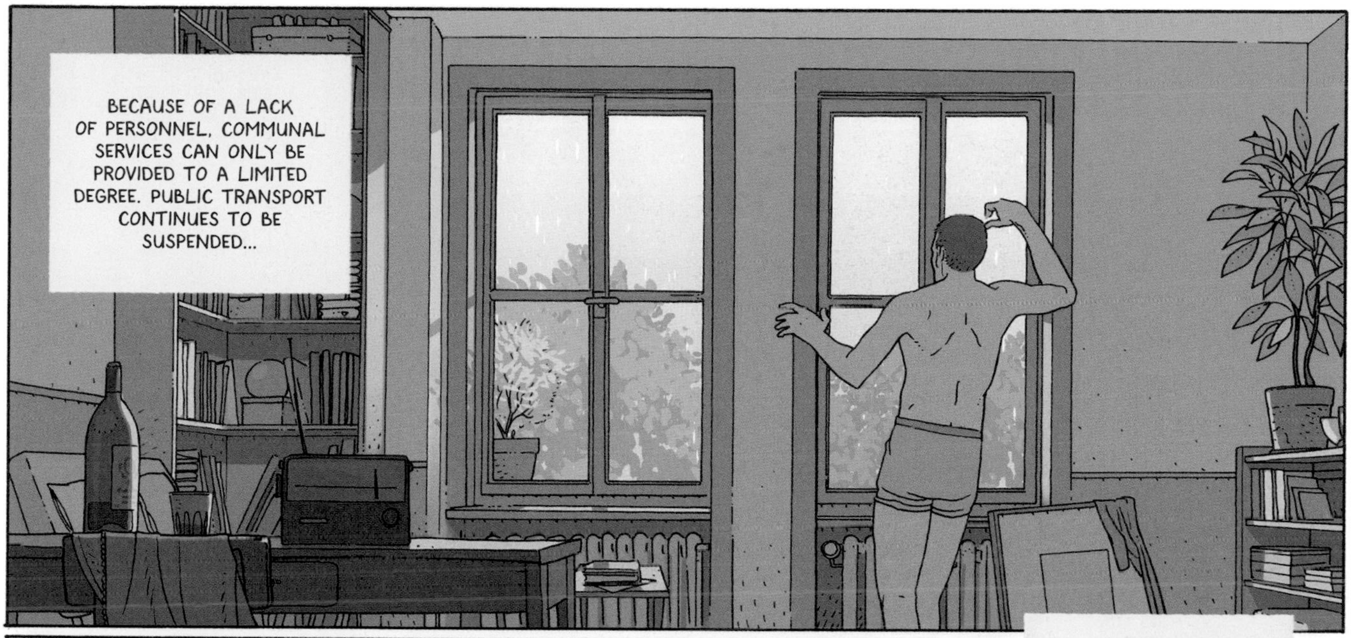
BECAUSE OF A LACK OF PERSONNEL, COMMUNAL SERVICES CAN ONLY BE PROVIDED TO A LIMITED DEGREE. PUBLIC TRANSPORT CONTINUES TO BE SUSPENDED...
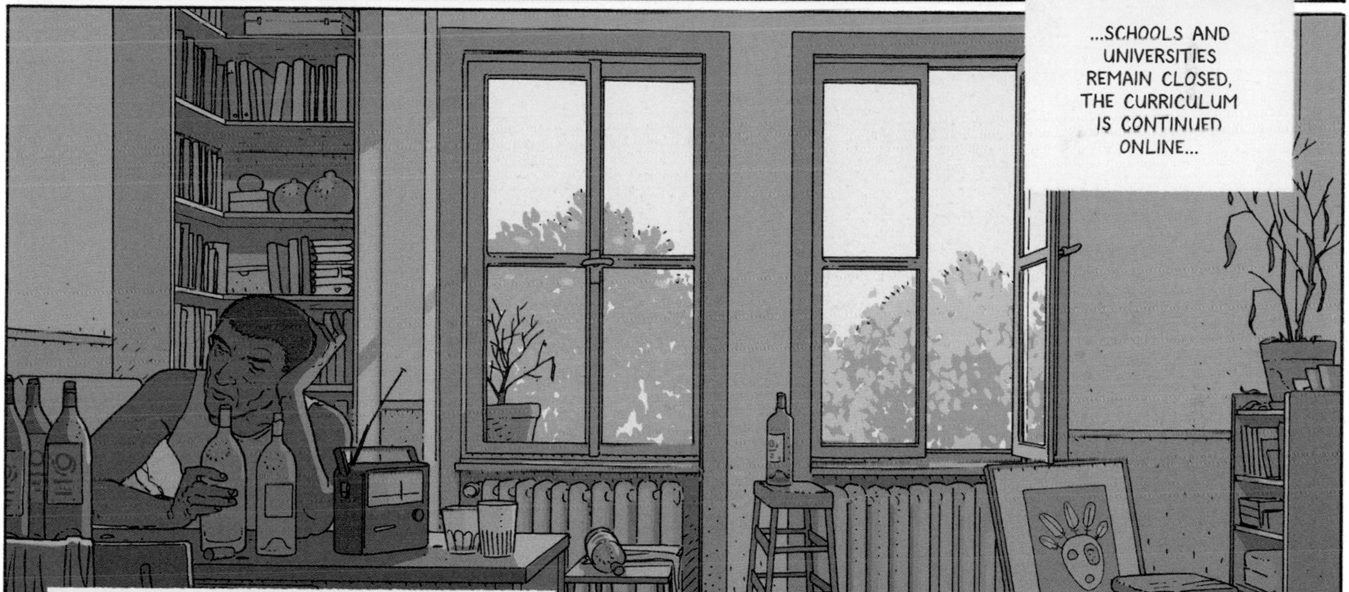
...SCHOOLS AND UNIVERSITIES REMAIN CLOSED, THE CURRICULUM IS CONTINUED ONLINE...
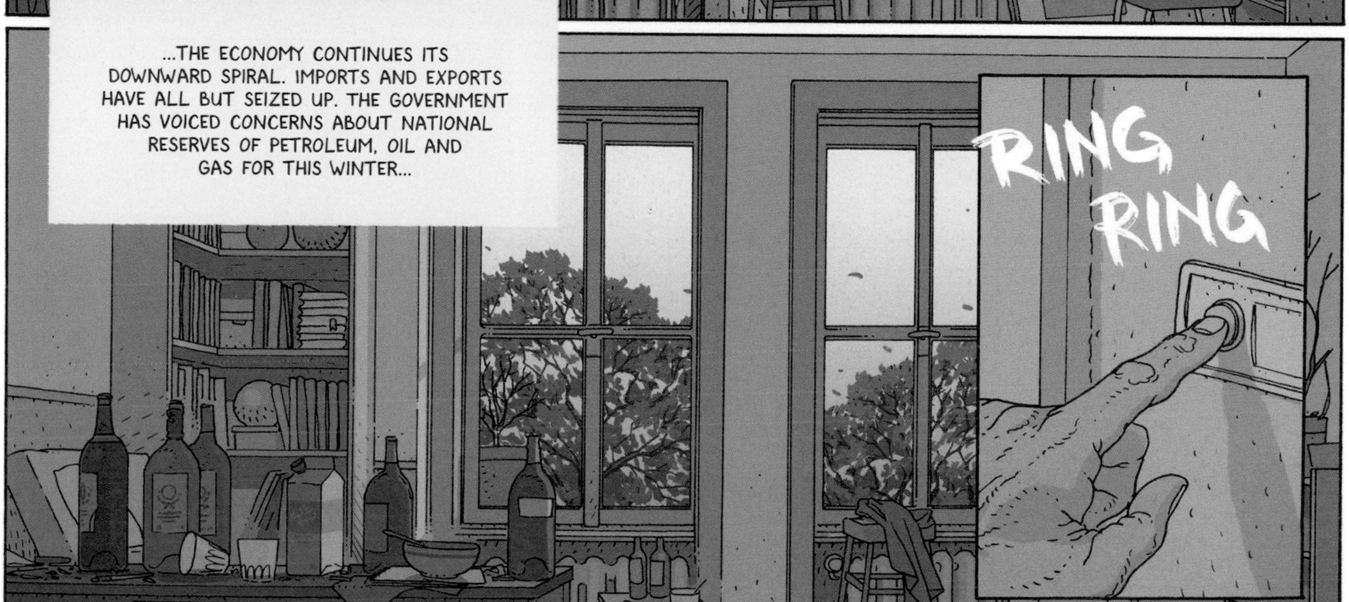
...THE ECONOMY CONTINUES ITS DOWNWARD SPIRAL. IMPORTS AND EXPORTS HAVE ALL BUT SEIZED UP. THE GOVERNMENT HAS VOICED CONCERNS ABOUT NATIONAL RESERVES OF PETROLEUM, OIL AND GAS FOR THIS WINTER...
RING
RING

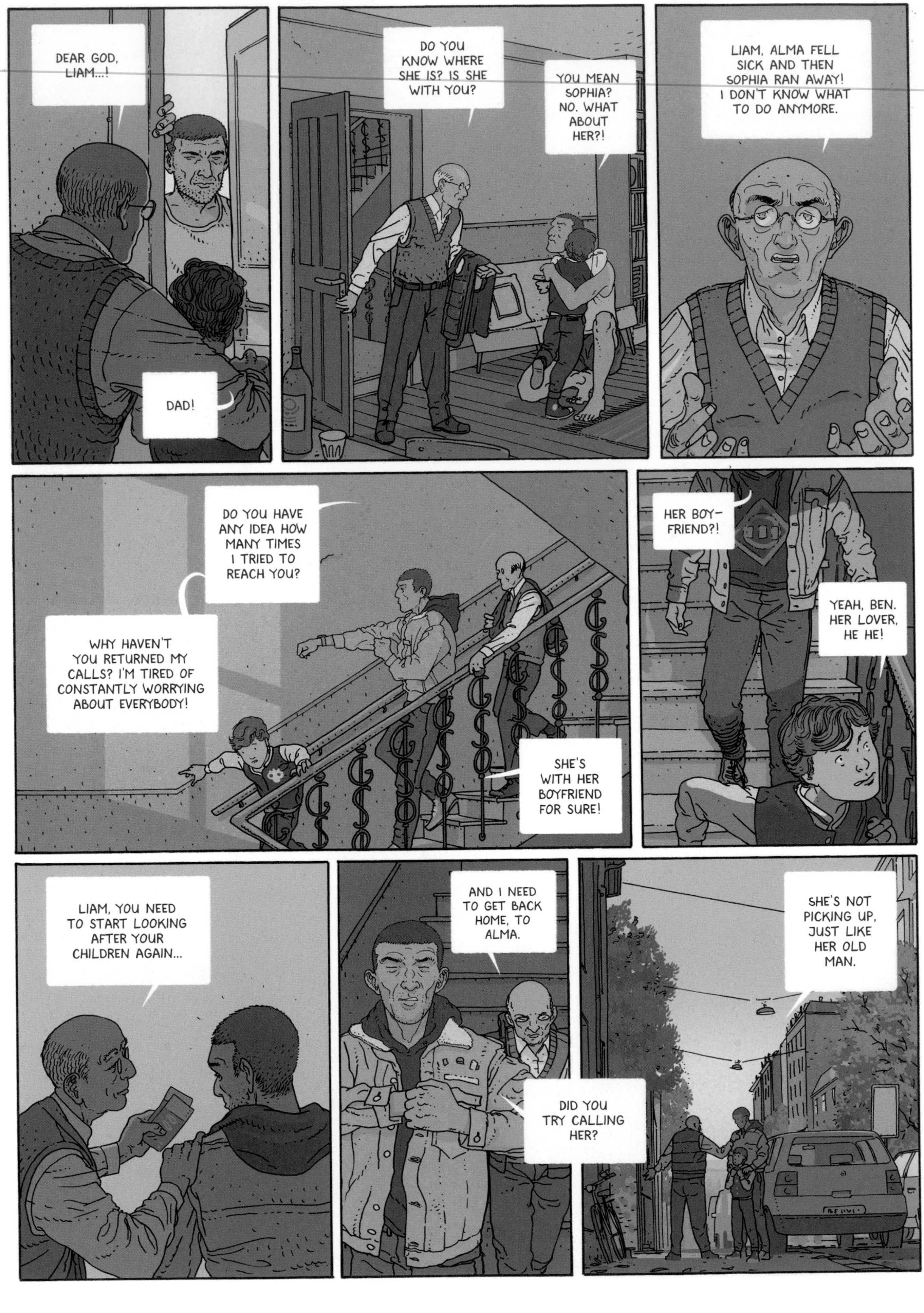
DEAR GOD, LIAM...!
DAD!
DO YOU KNOW WHERE SHE IS? IS SHE WITH YOU?
YOU MEAN SOPHIA? NO. WHAT ABOUT HER?!
LIAM, ALMA FELL SICK AND THEN SOPHIA RAN AWAY! I DON'T KNOW WHAT TO DO ANYMORE.
DO YOU HAVE ANY IDEA HOW MANY TIMES I TRIED TO REACH YOU?
WHY HAVEN'T YOU RETURNED MY CALLS? I'M TIRED OF CONSTANTLY WORRYING ABOUT EVERYBODY!
SHE'S WITH HER BOYFRIEND FOR SURE!
HER BOY-FRIEND?!
YEAH, BEN. HER LOVER, HE HE!
LIAM, YOU NEED TO START LOOKING AFTER YOUR CHILDREN AGAIN...
AND I NEED TO GET BACK HOME, TO ALMA.
DID YOU TRY CALLING HER?
SHE'S NOT PICKING UP, JUST LIKE HER OLD MAN.

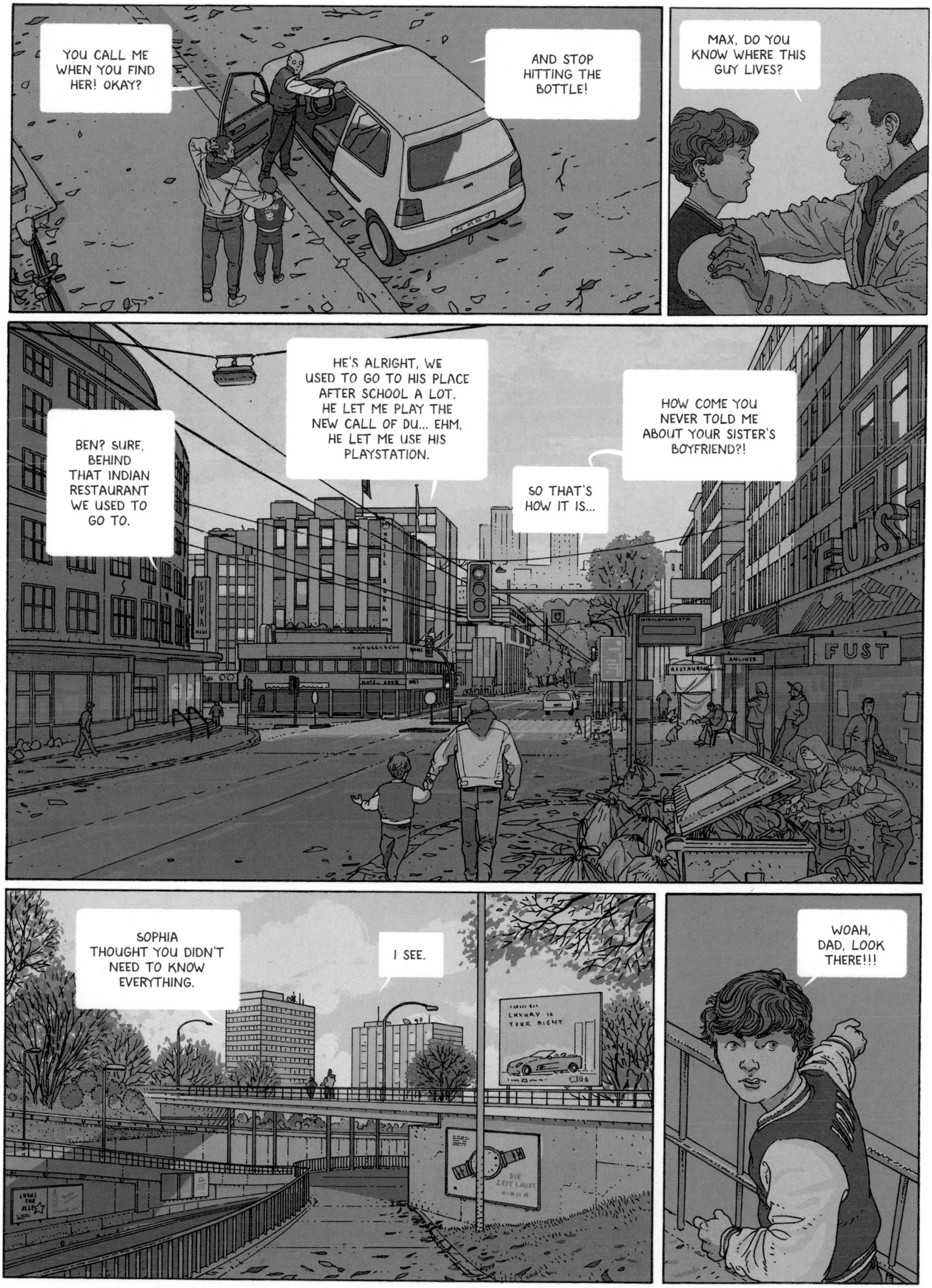
YOU CALL ME WHEN YOU FIND HER! OKAY?
AND STOP HITTING THE BOTTLE!
MAX, DO YOU KNOW WHERE THIS GUY LIVES?
BEN? SURE, BEHIND THAT INDIAN RESTAURANT WE USED TO GO TO.
HE'S ALRIGHT, WE USED TO GO TO HIS PLACE AFTER SCHOOL A LOT. HE LET ME PLAY THE NEW CALL OF DU... EHM, HE LET ME USE HIS PLAYSTATION.
SO THAT'S HOW IT IS...
HOW COME YOU NEVER TOLD ME ABOUT YOUR SISTER'S BOYFRIEND?!
FUST
FUST
SOPHIA THOUGHT YOU DIDN'T NEED TO KNOW EVERYTHING.
I SEE.
LUXURY IS YOUR RIGHT
DIE ZEIT LAUFT
WOAH, DAD, LOOK THERE!!!

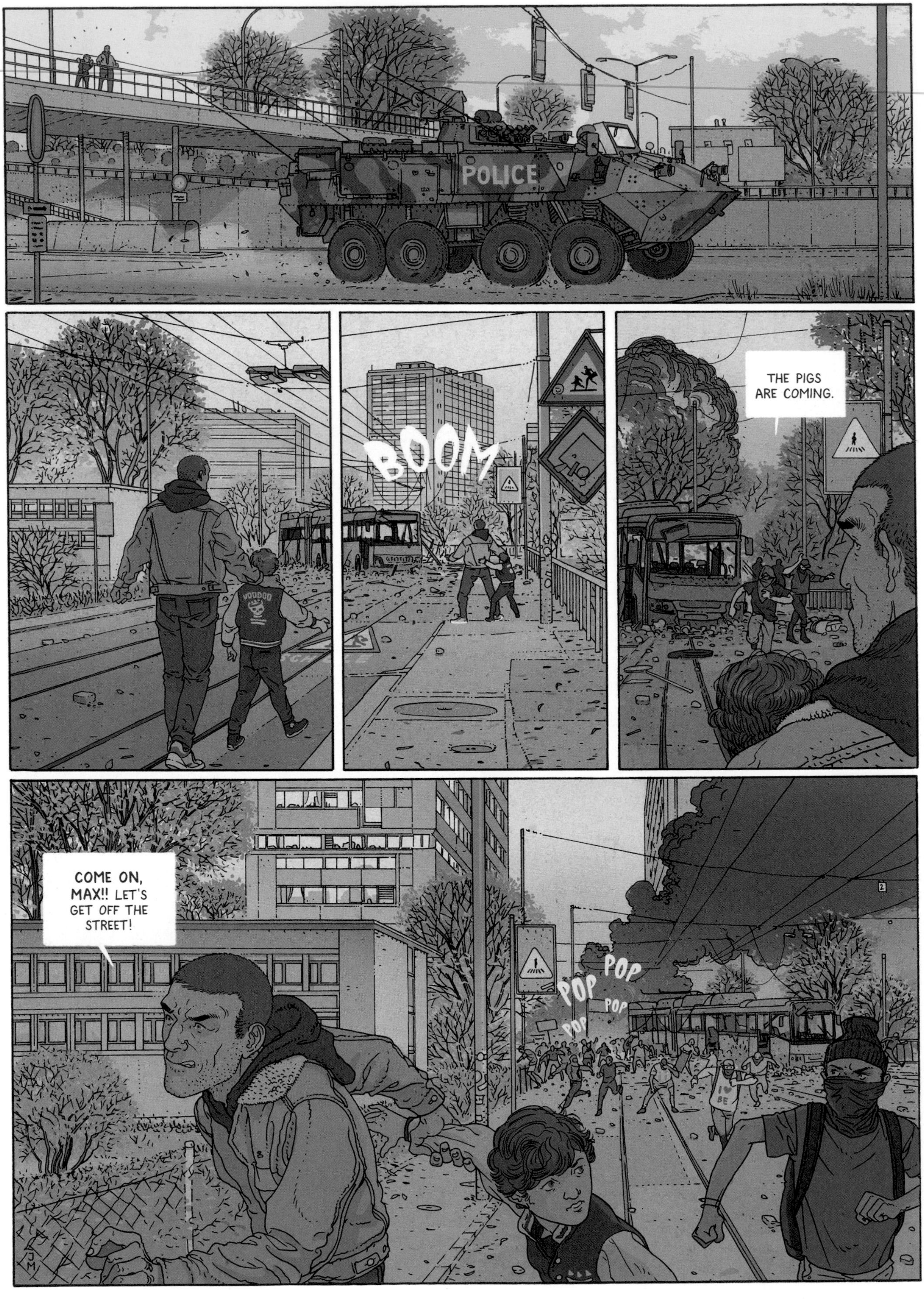
POLICE
BOOM
THE PIGS ARE COMING.
COME ON, MAX!! LET'S GET OFF THE STREET!
POP
POP
POP
POP

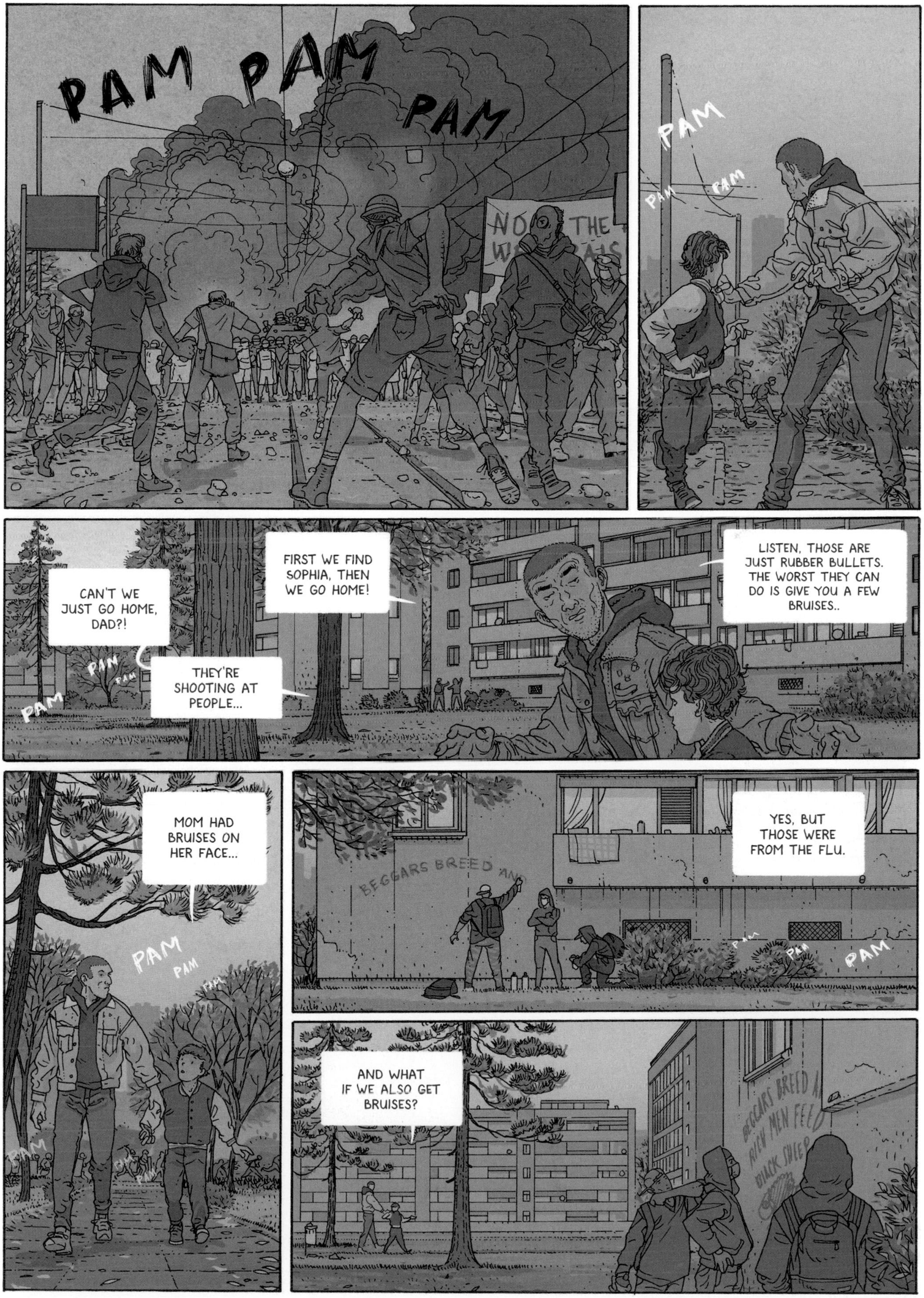
PAM PAM PAM
PAM
PAM PAM
CAN'T WE JUST GO HOME, DAD?!
PAM PAM PAM
THEY'RE SHOOTING AT PEOPLE...
FIRST WE FIND SOPHIA, THEN WE GO HOME!
LISTEN, THOSE ARE JUST RUBBER BULLETS. THE WORST THEY CAN DO IS GIVE YOU A FEW BRUISES..
MOM HAD BRUISES ON HER FACE...
PAM PAM PAM
YES, BUT THOSE WERE FROM THE FLU.
PAM PAM PAM
AND WHAT IF WE ALSO GET BRUISES?

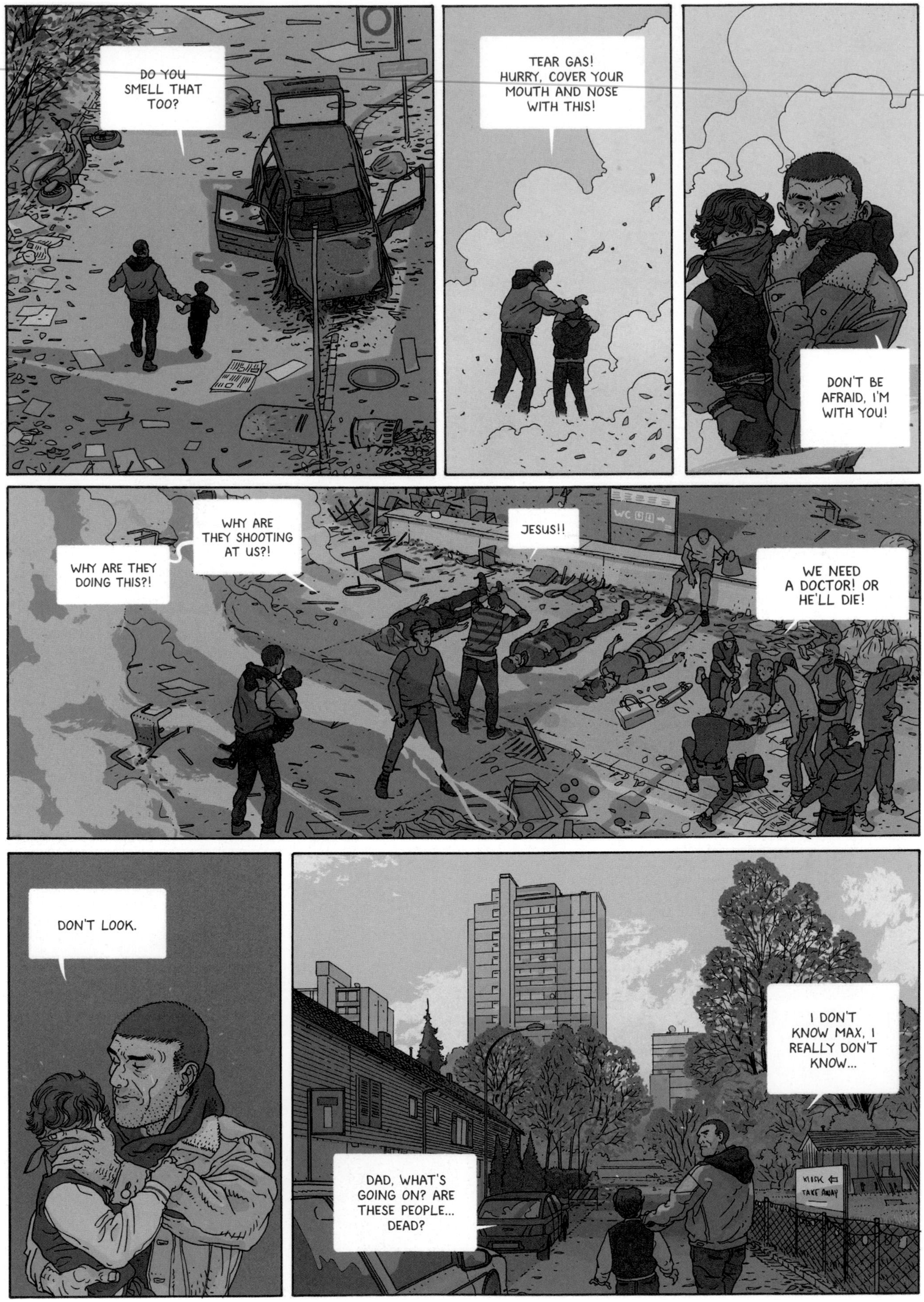
DO YOU SMELL THAT TOO?
TEAR GAS! HURRY, COVER YOUR MOUTH AND NOSE WITH THIS!
DON'T BE AFRAID, I'M WITH YOU!
WHY ARE THEY DOING THIS?!
WHY ARE THEY SHOOTING AT US?!
JESUS!!
WC
WE NEED A DOCTOR! OR HE'LL DIE!
DON'T LOOK.
I DON'T KNOW MAX, I REALLY DON'T KNOW...
DAD, WHAT'S GOING ON? ARE THESE PEOPLE... DEAD?
KIOSK
TAKE AWAY

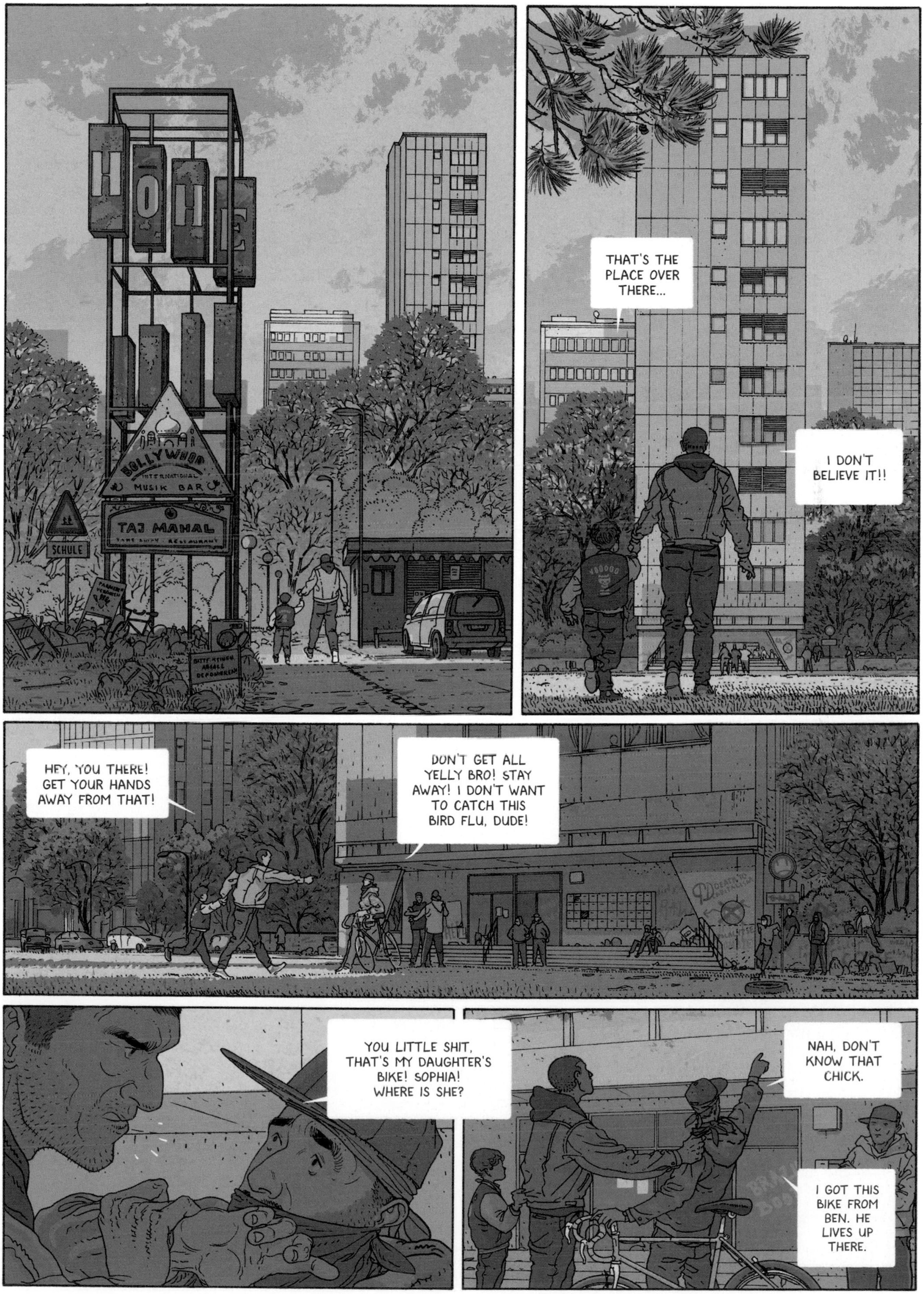

SCHULE
MUSIK BAR
TAJ MAHAL
THAT'S THE PLACE OVER THERE...
I DON'T BELIEVE IT!!
HEY, YOU THERE! GET YOUR HANDS AWAY FROM THAT!
DON'T GET ALL YELLY BRO! STAY AWAY! I DON'T WANT TO CATCH THIS BIRD FLU, DUDE!
YOU LITTLE SHIT, THAT'S MY DAUGHTER'S BIKE! SOPHIA! WHERE IS SHE?
NAH, DON'T KNOW THAT CHICK.
I GOT THIS BIKE FROM BEN. HE LIVES UP THERE.

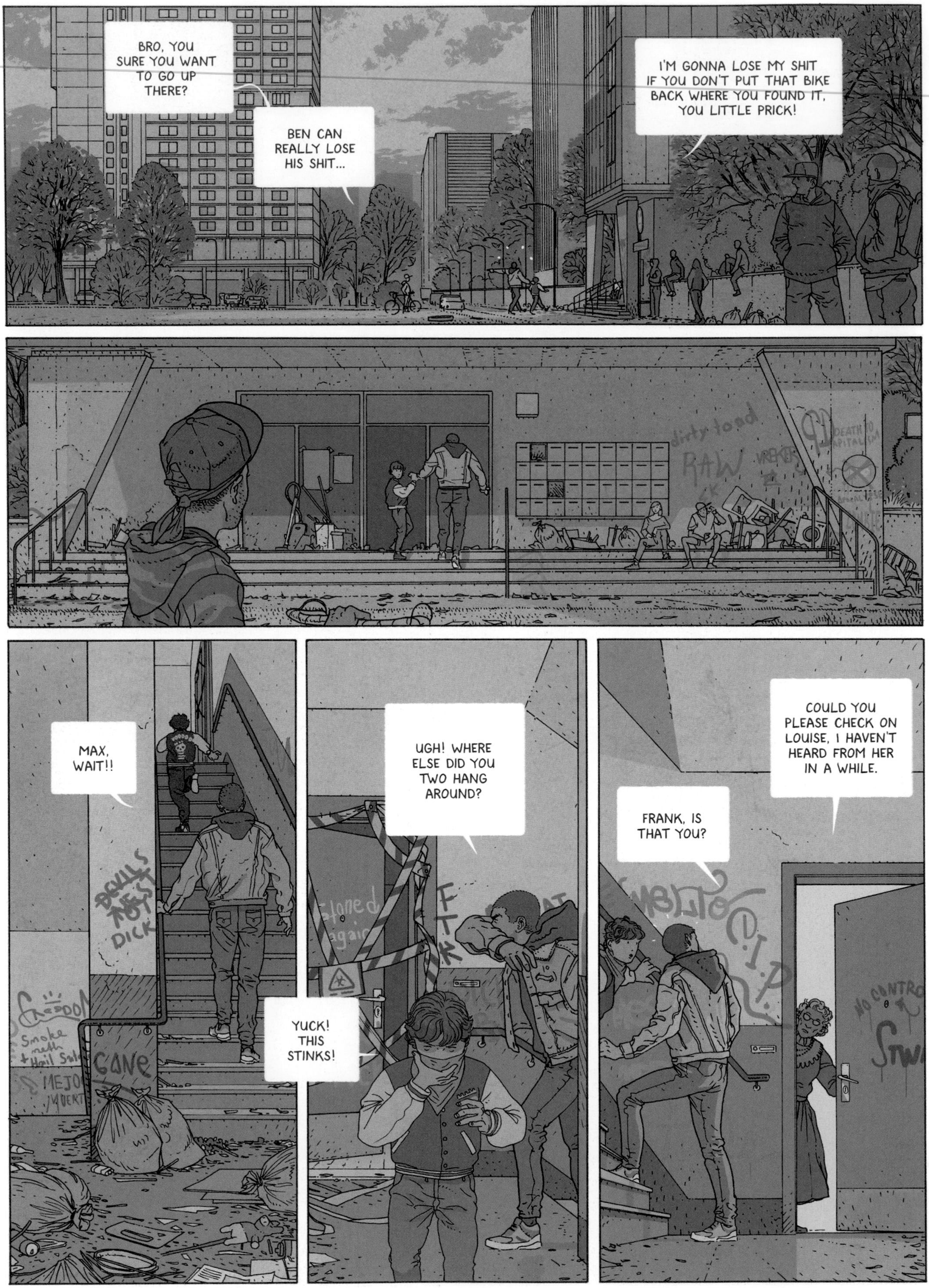
BRO, YOU SURE YOU WANT TO GO UP THERE?
BEN CAN REALLY LOSE HIS SHIT...
I'M GONNA LOSE MY SHIT IF YOU DON'T PUT THAT BIKE BACK WHERE YOU FOUND IT, YOU LITTLE PRICK!
dirty toad
RAW
DEATH TO CAPITALISM
MAX, WAIT!!
UGH! WHERE ELSE DID YOU TWO HANG AROUND?
YUCK! THIS STINKS!
FRANK, IS THAT YOU?
COULD YOU PLEASE CHECK ON LOUISE, I HAVEN'T HEARD FROM HER IN A WHILE.

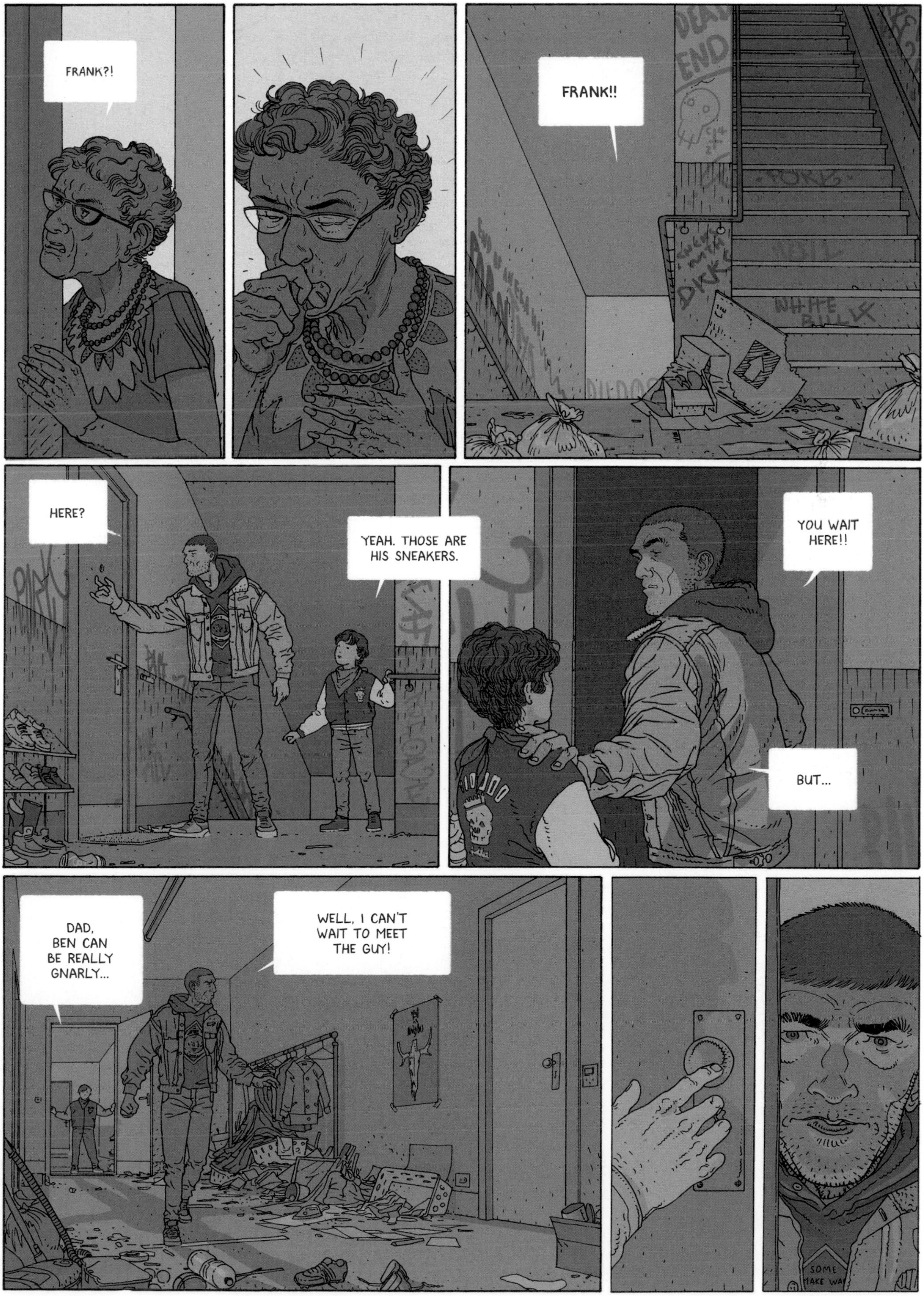
FRANK?!
FRANK!!
HERE?
YEAH. THOSE ARE HIS SNEAKERS.
YOU WAIT HERE!!
BUT...
DAD, BEN CAN BE REALLY GNARLY...
WELL, I CAN'T WAIT TO MEET THE GUY!

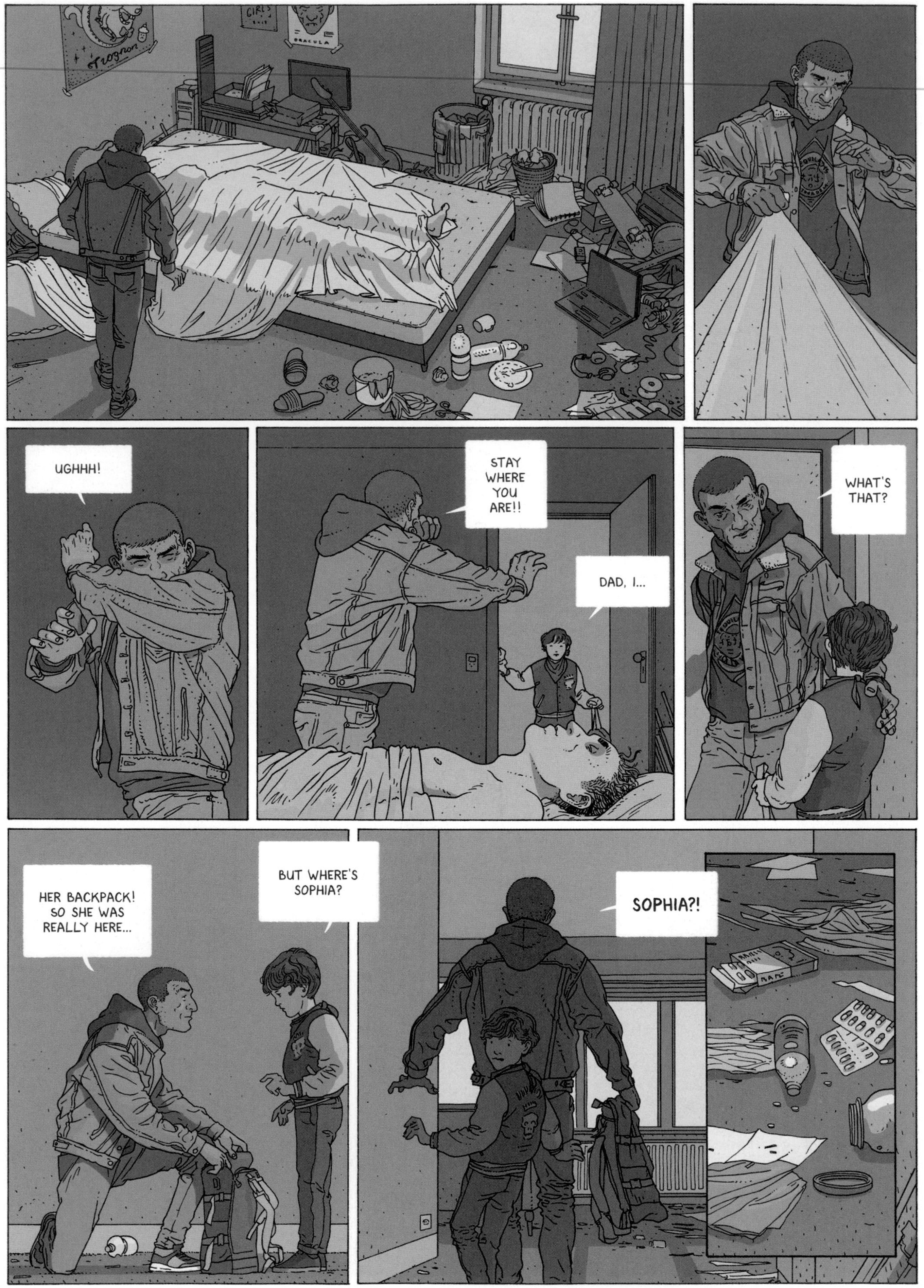
UGHHH!
STAY WHERE YOU ARE!!
DAD, I...
WHAT'S THAT?
HER BACKPACK! SO SHE WAS REALLY HERE...
BUT WHERE'S SOPHIA?
SOPHIA?!

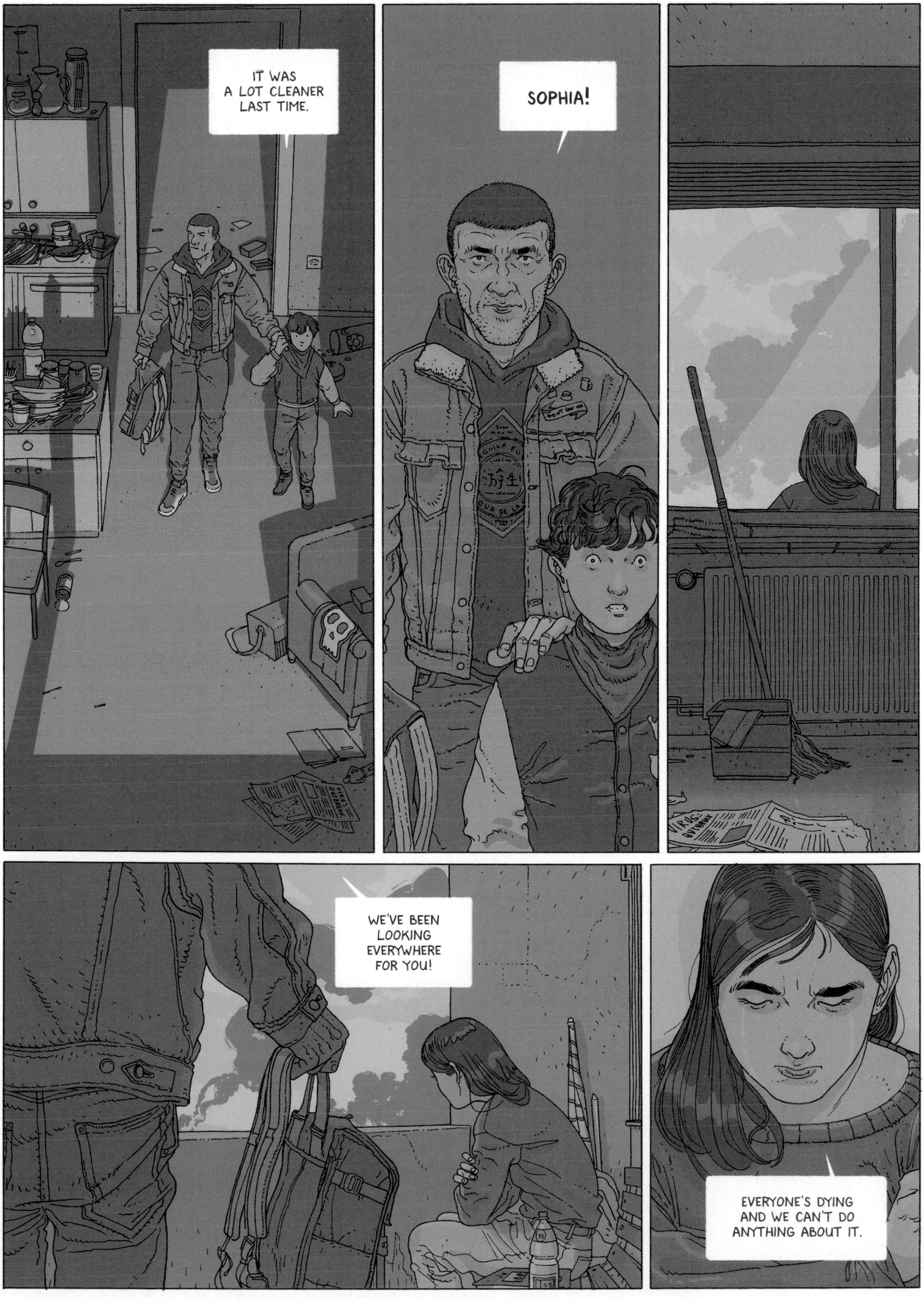
IT WAS A LOT CLEANER LAST TIME.
SOPHIA!
WE'VE BEEN LOOKING EVERYWHERE FOR YOU!
EVERYONE'S DYING AND WE CAN'T DO ANYTHING ABOUT IT.

AND YOU! YOU SENT US AWAY! YOU JUST SENT US AWAY AFTER MOM DIED!!

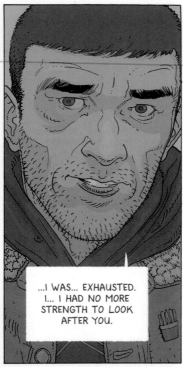

...I WAS... EXHAUSTED. I... I HAD NO MORE STRENGTH TO LOOK AFTER YOU.

I MISSED YOU SO MUCH...

I MISS HER SO MUCH!!

I WILL NEVER LEAVE YOU AGAIN, EVER! I'LL DO EVERYTHING POSSIBLE TO MAKE SURE YOU GET THROUGH THIS MESS. FROM NOW ON I'LL BE THERE FOR YOU, I PROMISE.

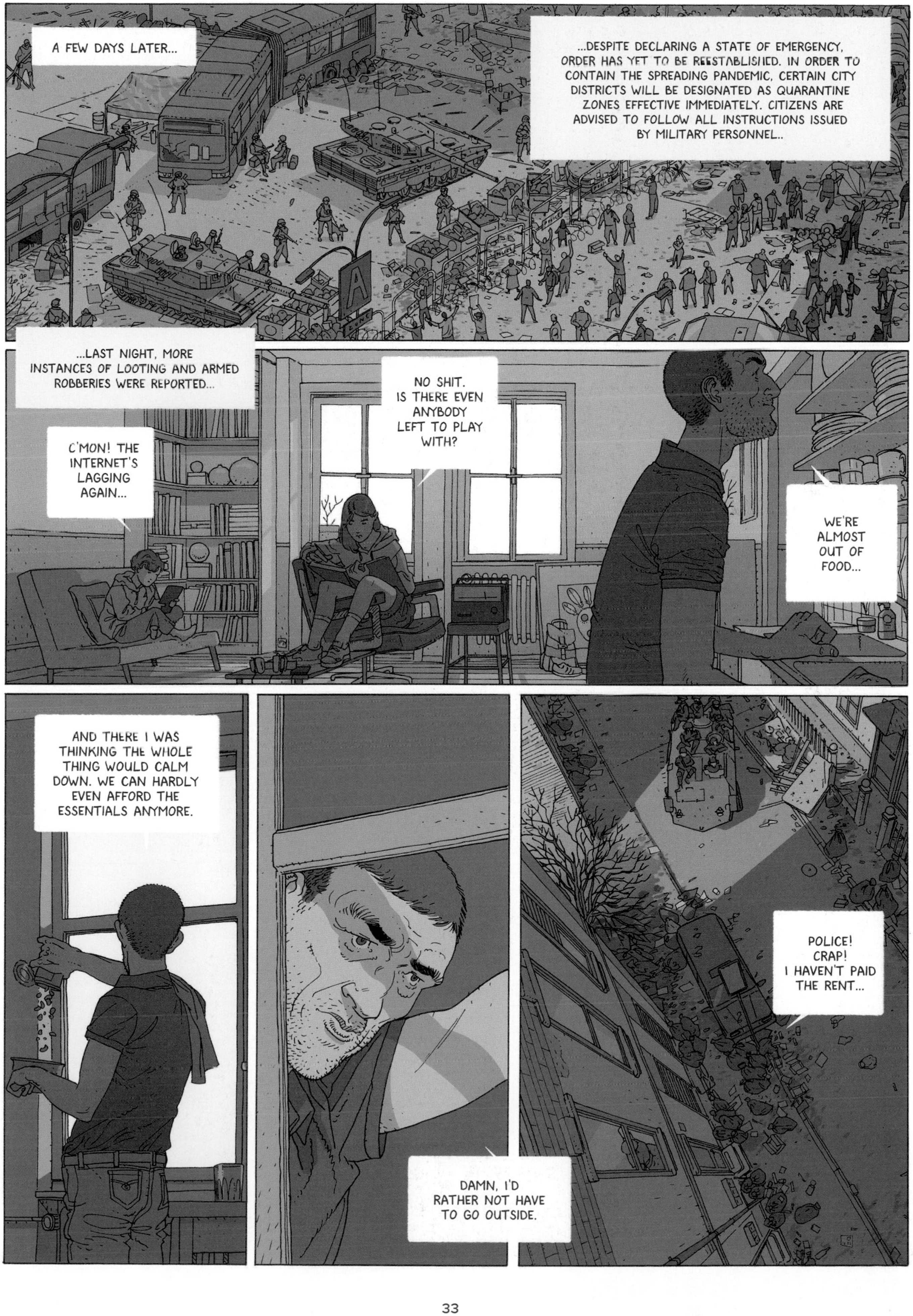

A FEW DAYS LATER...
...DESPITE DECLARING A STATE OF EMERGENCY, ORDER HAS YET TO BE REESTABLISHED. IN ORDER TO CONTAIN THE SPREADING PANDEMIC, CERTAIN CITY DISTRICTS WILL BE DESIGNATED AS QUARANTINE ZONES EFFECTIVE IMMEDIATELY. CITIZENS ARE ADVISED TO FOLLOW ALL INSTRUCTIONS ISSUED BY MILITARY PERSONNEL..
...LAST NIGHT, MORE INSTANCES OF LOOTING AND ARMED ROBBERIES WERE REPORTED...
C'MON! THE INTERNET'S LAGGING AGAIN...
NO SHIT. IS THERE EVEN ANYBODY LEFT TO PLAY WITH?
WE'RE ALMOST OUT OF FOOD...
AND THERE I WAS THINKING THE WHOLE THING WOULD CALM DOWN. WE CAN HARDLY EVEN AFFORD THE ESSENTIALS ANYMORE.
DAMN, I'D RATHER NOT HAVE TO GO OUTSIDE.
POLICE! CRAP! I HAVEN'T PAID THE RENT...

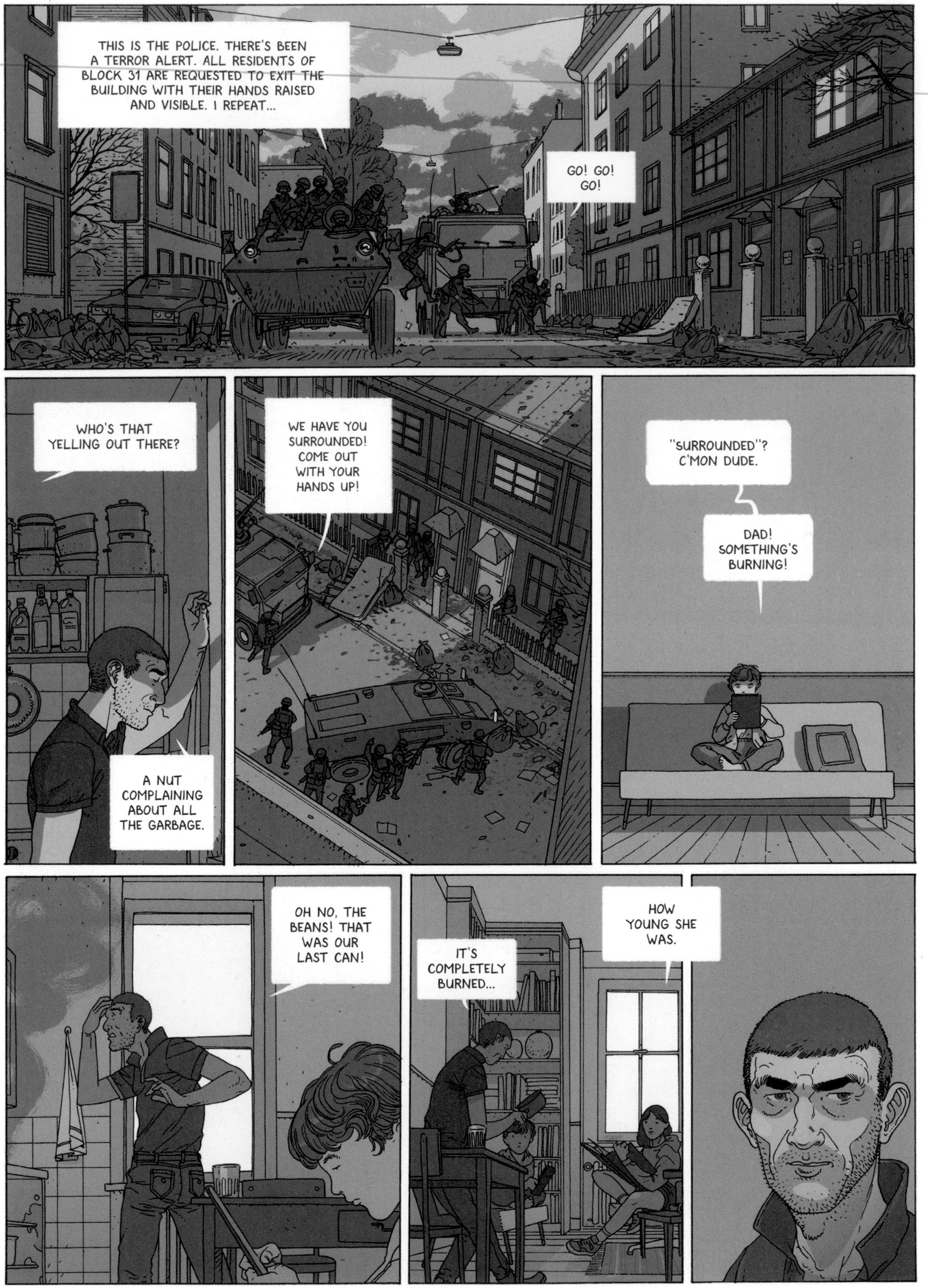
THIS IS THE POLICE. THERE'S BEEN A TERROR ALERT. ALL RESIDENTS OF BLOCK 31 ARE REQUESTED TO EXIT THE BUILDING WITH THEIR HANDS RAISED AND VISIBLE. I REPEAT...
GO! GO! GO!
WHO'S THAT YELLING OUT THERE?
A NUT COMPLAINING ABOUT ALL THE GARBAGE.
WE HAVE YOU SURROUNDED! COME OUT WITH YOUR HANDS UP!
"SURROUNDED"? C'MON DUDE.
DAD! SOMETHING'S BURNING!
OH NO, THE BEANS! THAT WAS OUR LAST CAN!
IT'S COMPLETELY BURNED...
HOW YOUNG SHE WAS.

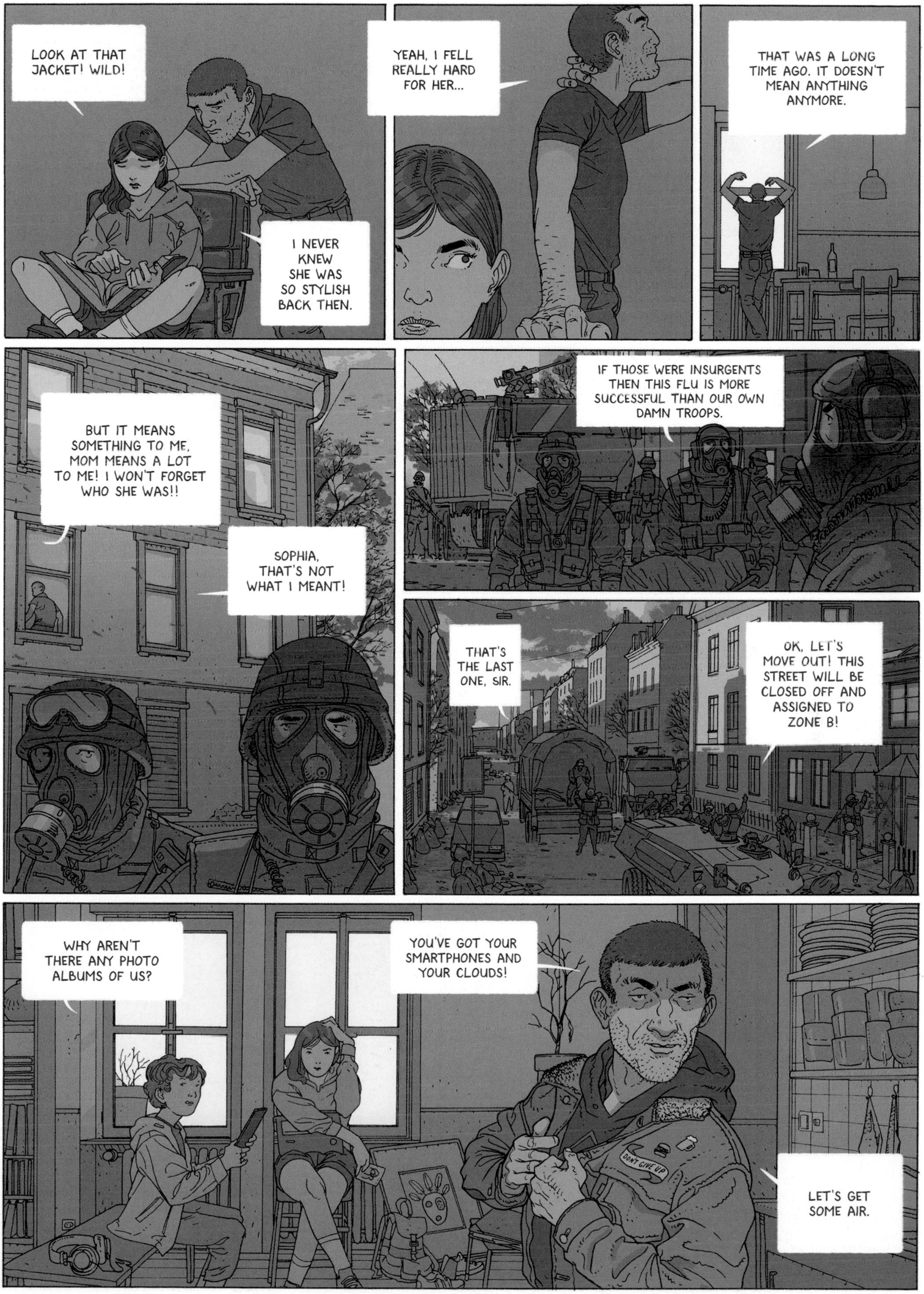

LOOK AT THAT JACKET! WILD!
I NEVER KNEW SHE WAS SO STYLISH BACK THEN.
YEAH, I FELL REALLY HARD FOR HER...
THAT WAS A LONG TIME AGO. IT DOESN'T MEAN ANYTHING ANYMORE.
BUT IT MEANS SOMETHING TO ME, MOM MEANS A LOT TO ME! I WON'T FORGET WHO SHE WAS!!
SOPHIA, THAT'S NOT WHAT I MEANT!
IF THOSE WERE INSURGENTS THEN THIS FLU IS MORE SUCCESSFUL THAN OUR OWN DAMN TROOPS.
THAT'S THE LAST ONE, SIR.
OK, LET'S MOVE OUT! THIS STREET WILL BE CLOSED OFF AND ASSIGNED TO ZONE B!
WHY AREN'T THERE ANY PHOTO ALBUMS OF US?
YOU'VE GOT YOUR SMARTPHONES AND YOUR CLOUDS!
DON'T GIVE UP
LET'S GET SOME AIR.

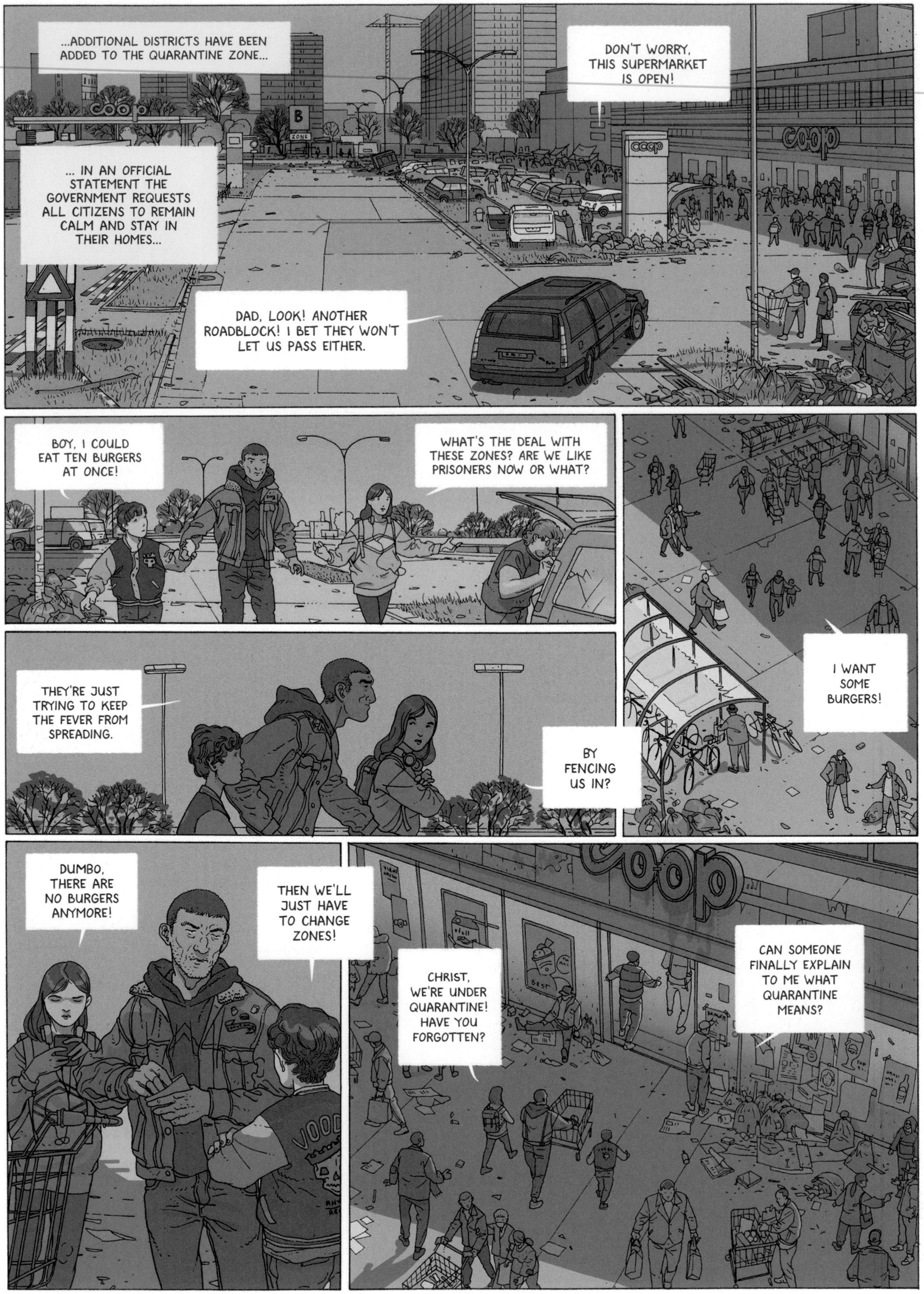
...ADDITIONAL DISTRICTS HAVE BEEN ADDED TO THE QUARANTINE ZONE...
... IN AN OFFICIAL STATEMENT THE GOVERNMENT REQUESTS ALL CITIZENS TO REMAIN CALM AND STAY IN THEIR HOMES...
DON'T WORRY, THIS SUPERMARKET IS OPEN!
DAD, LOOK! ANOTHER ROADBLOCK! I BET THEY WON'T LET US PASS EITHER.
BOY, I COULD EAT TEN BURGERS AT ONCE!
WHAT'S THE DEAL WITH THESE ZONES? ARE WE LIKE PRISONERS NOW OR WHAT?
THEY'RE JUST TRYING TO KEEP THE FEVER FROM SPREADING.
BY FENCING US IN?
I WANT SOME BURGERS!
DUMBO, THERE ARE NO BURGERS ANYMORE!
THEN WE'LL JUST HAVE TO CHANGE ZONES!
CHRIST, WE'RE UNDER QUARANTINE! HAVE YOU FORGOTTEN?
CAN SOMEONE FINALLY EXPLAIN TO ME WHAT QUARANTINE MEANS?

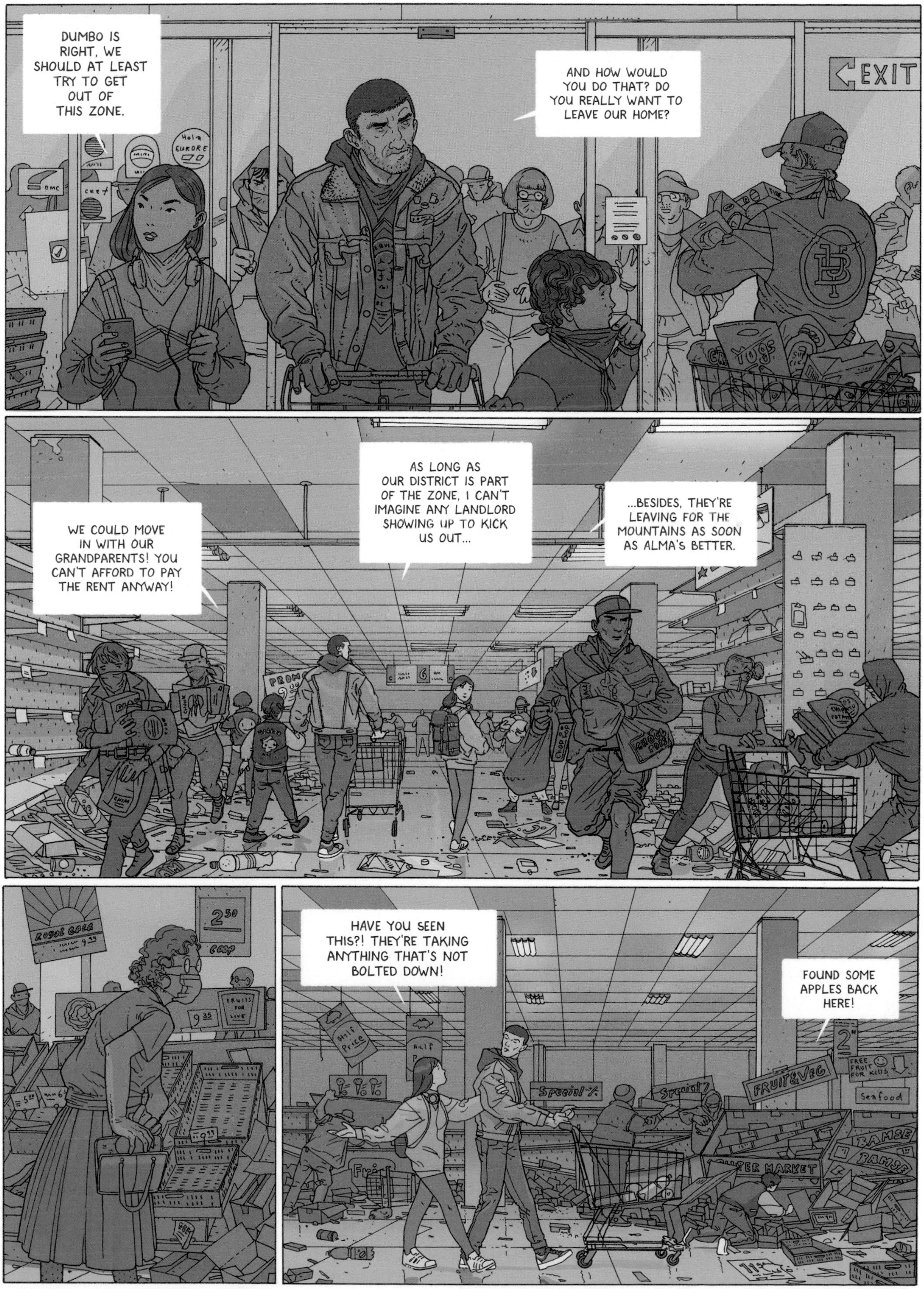

DUMBO IS RIGHT, WE SHOULD AT LEAST TRY TO GET OUT OF THIS ZONE.
AND HOW WOULD YOU DO THAT? DO YOU REALLY WANT TO LEAVE OUR HOME?
EXIT
WE COULD MOVE IN WITH OUR GRANDPARENTS! YOU CAN'T AFFORD TO PAY THE RENT ANYWAY!
AS LONG AS OUR DISTRICT IS PART OF THE ZONE, I CAN'T IMAGINE ANY LANDLORD SHOWING UP TO KICK US OUT...
...BESIDES, THEY'RE LEAVING FOR THE MOUNTAINS AS SOON AS ALMA'S BETTER.
HAVE YOU SEEN THIS?! THEY'RE TAKING ANYTHING THAT'S NOT BOLTED DOWN!
FOUND SOME APPLES BACK HERE!
FRUIT&VEG
Seafood

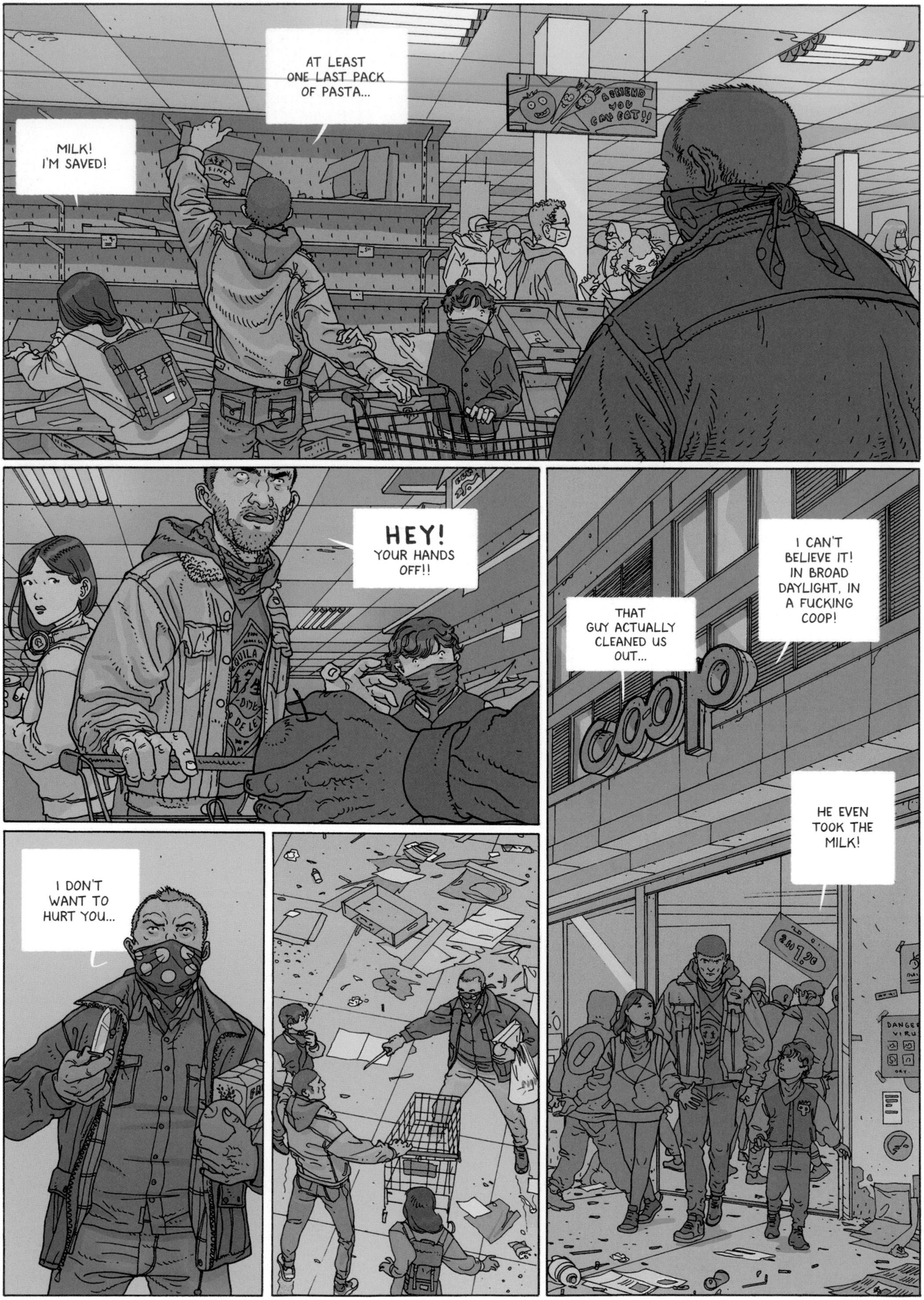
MILK! I'M SAVED!
AT LEAST ONE LAST PACK OF PASTA...
A FRIEND YOU CAN EAT!!
HEY! YOUR HANDS OFF!!
THAT GUY ACTUALLY CLEANED US OUT...
I CAN'T BELIEVE IT! IN BROAD DAYLIGHT, IN A FUCKING COOP!
coop
I DON'T WANT TO HURT YOU...
HE EVEN TOOK THE MILK!

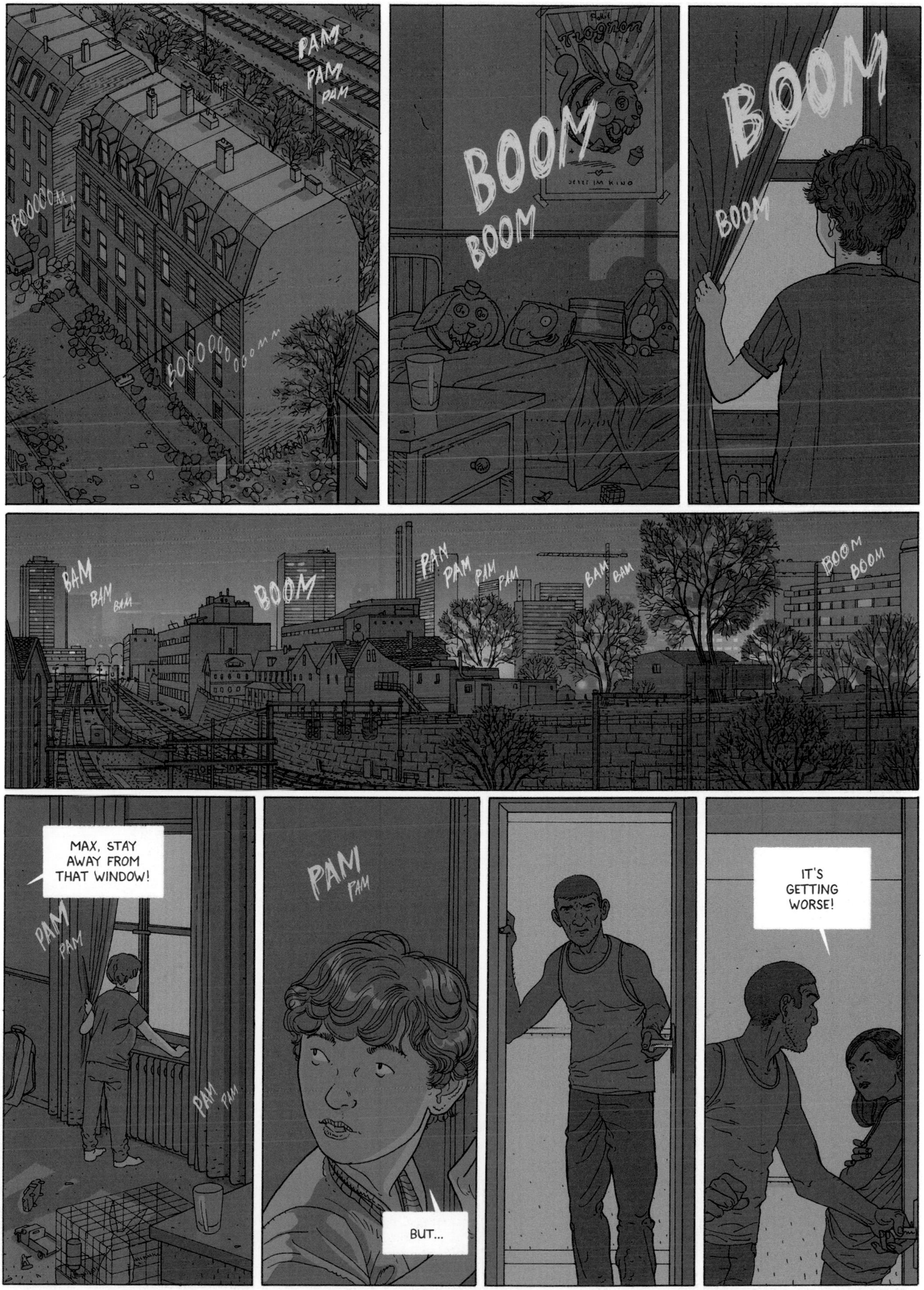
PAM
PAM
PAM
BOOOOOM
BOOOOOOOOOMM
BOOM
BOOM
BOOM
BOOM
BAM
BAM
BAM
BOOM
PAM
PAM
PAM
PAM
BAM
BAM
BOOM
BOOM
MAX, STAY AWAY FROM THAT WINDOW!
PAM
PAM
PAM
PAM
PAM
PAM
BUT...
IT'S GETTING WORSE!

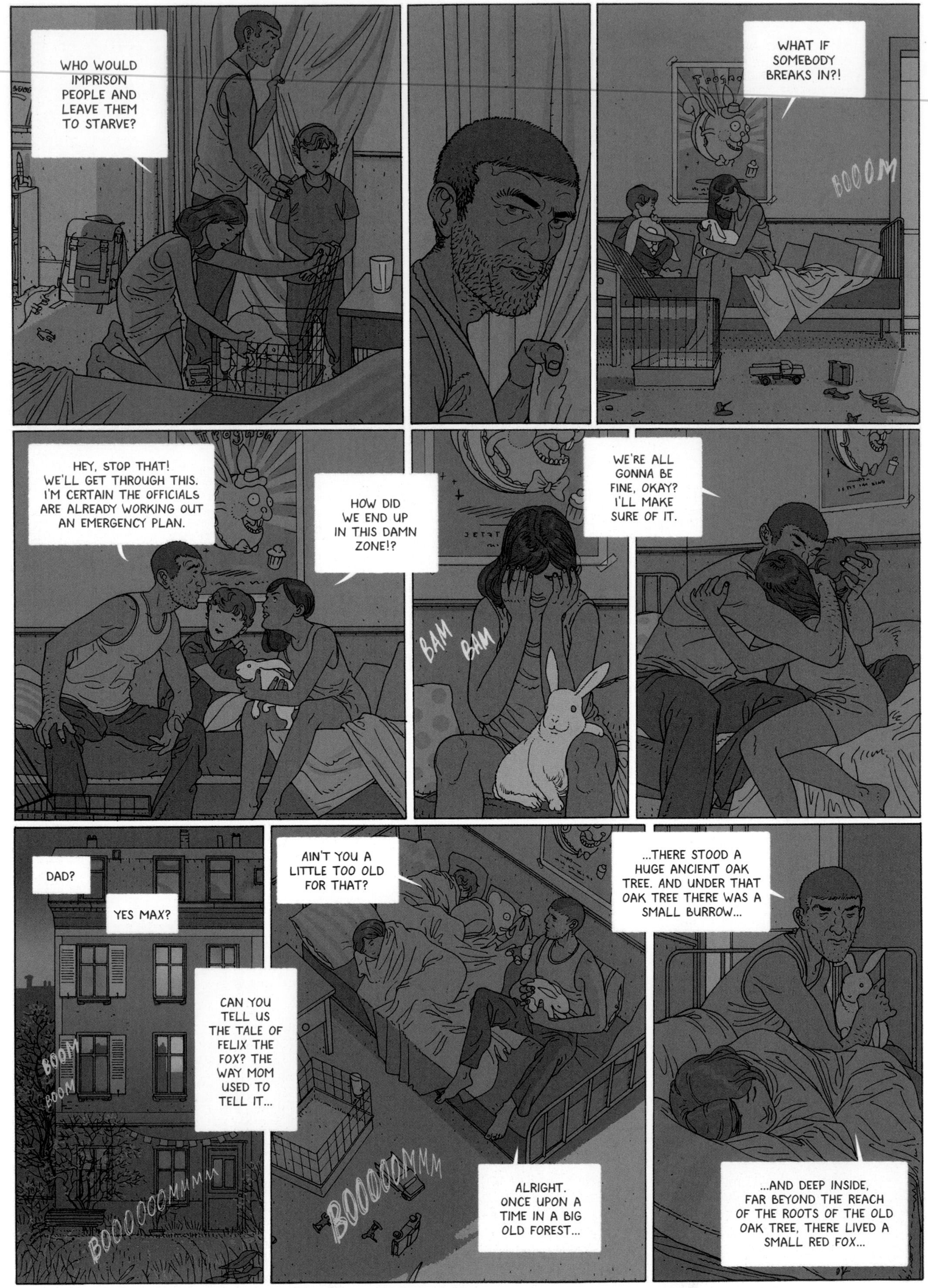
WHO WOULD IMPRISON PEOPLE AND LEAVE THEM TO STARVE?
WHAT IF SOMEBODY BREAKS IN?!
BOOOM
HEY, STOP THAT! WE'LL GET THROUGH THIS. I'M CERTAIN THE OFFICIALS ARE ALREADY WORKING OUT AN EMERGENCY PLAN.
HOW DID WE END UP IN THIS DAMN ZONE!?
BAM BAM
WE'RE ALL GONNA BE FINE, OKAY? I'LL MAKE SURE OF IT.
DAD?
YES MAX?
CAN YOU TELL US THE TALE OF FELIX THE FOX? THE WAY MOM USED TO TELL IT...
BOOM BOOM
BOOOOOOMMMM
AIN'T YOU A LITTLE TOO OLD FOR THAT?
BOOOOOMMM
ALRIGHT. ONCE UPON A TIME IN A BIG OLD FOREST...
...THERE STOOD A HUGE ANCIENT OAK TREE. AND UNDER THAT OAK TREE THERE WAS A SMALL BURROW...
...AND DEEP INSIDE, FAR BEYOND THE REACH OF THE ROOTS OF THE OLD OAK TREE, THERE LIVED A SMALL RED FOX...

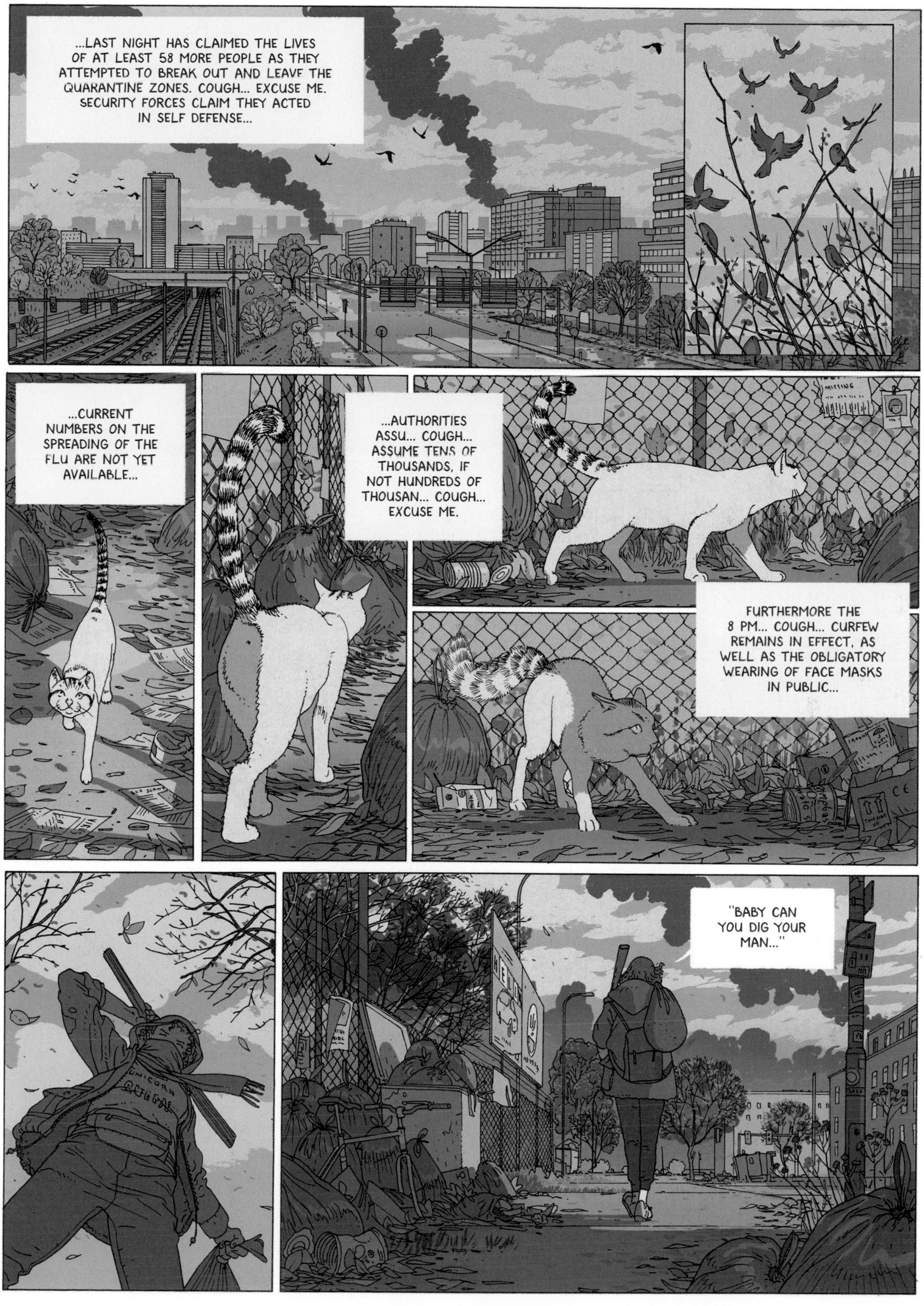
...LAST NIGHT HAS CLAIMED THE LIVES OF AT LEAST 58 MORE PEOPLE AS THEY ATTEMPTED TO BREAK OUT AND LEAVE THE QUARANTINE ZONES. COUGH... EXCUSE ME. SECURITY FORCES CLAIM THEY ACTED IN SELF DEFENSE...
...CURRENT NUMBERS ON THE SPREADING OF THE FLU ARE NOT YET AVAILABLE...
...AUTHORITIES ASSU... COUGH... ASSUME TENS OF THOUSANDS, IF NOT HUNDREDS OF THOUSAN... COUGH... EXCUSE ME.
FURTHERMORE THE 8 PM... COUGH... CURFEW REMAINS IN EFFECT, AS WELL AS THE OBLIGATORY WEARING OF FACE MASKS IN PUBLIC...
UNICORN QUEEN
"BABY CAN YOU DIG YOUR MAN..."

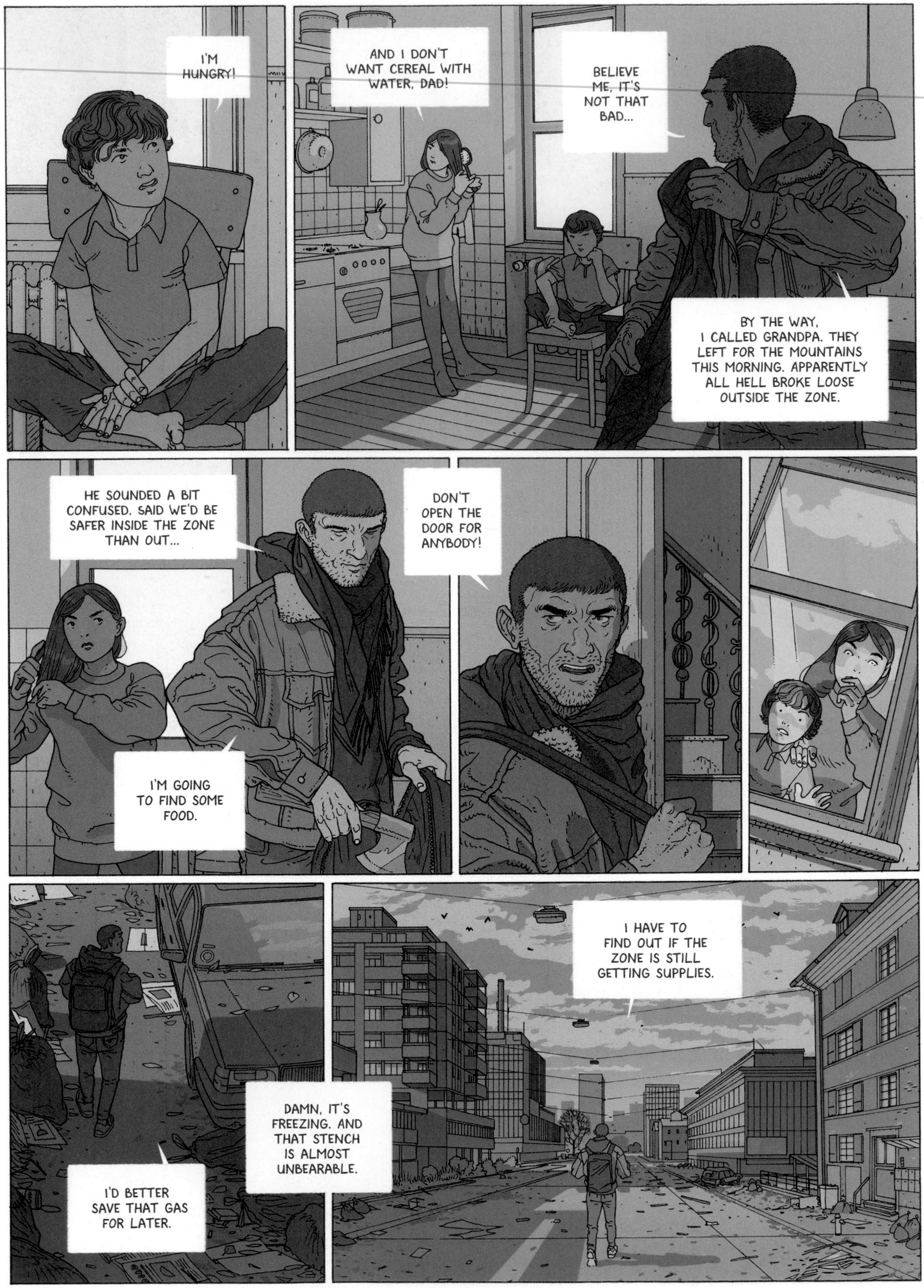
I'M HUNGRY!
AND I DON'T WANT CEREAL WITH WATER, DAD!
BELIEVE ME, IT'S NOT THAT BAD...
BY THE WAY, I CALLED GRANDPA. THEY LEFT FOR THE MOUNTAINS THIS MORNING. APPARENTLY ALL HELL BROKE LOOSE OUTSIDE THE ZONE.
HE SOUNDED A BIT CONFUSED. SAID WE'D BE SAFER INSIDE THE ZONE THAN OUT...
I'M GOING TO FIND SOME FOOD.
DON'T OPEN THE DOOR FOR ANYBODY!
I'D BETTER SAVE THAT GAS FOR LATER.
DAMN, IT'S FREEZING. AND THAT STENCH IS ALMOST UNBEARABLE.
I HAVE TO FIND OUT IF THE ZONE IS STILL GETTING SUPPLIES.

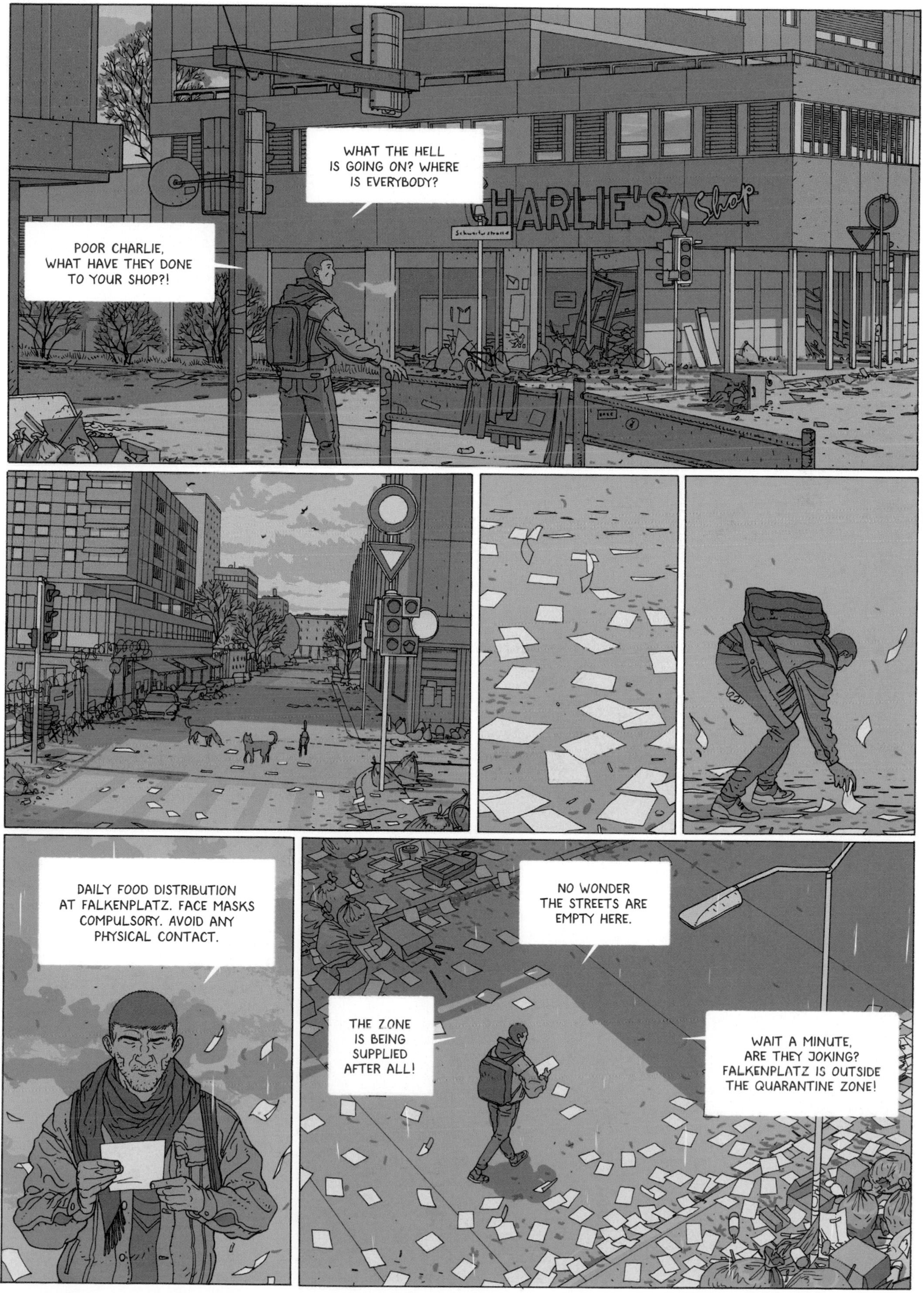
WHAT THE HELL IS GOING ON? WHERE IS EVERYBODY?
CHARLIE'S Shop
POOR CHARLIE, WHAT HAVE THEY DONE TO YOUR SHOP?!
DAILY FOOD DISTRIBUTION AT FALKENPLATZ. FACE MASKS COMPULSORY. AVOID ANY PHYSICAL CONTACT.
NO WONDER THE STREETS ARE EMPTY HERE.
THE ZONE IS BEING SUPPLIED AFTER ALL!
WAIT A MINUTE, ARE THEY JOKING? FALKENPLATZ IS OUTSIDE THE QUARANTINE ZONE!

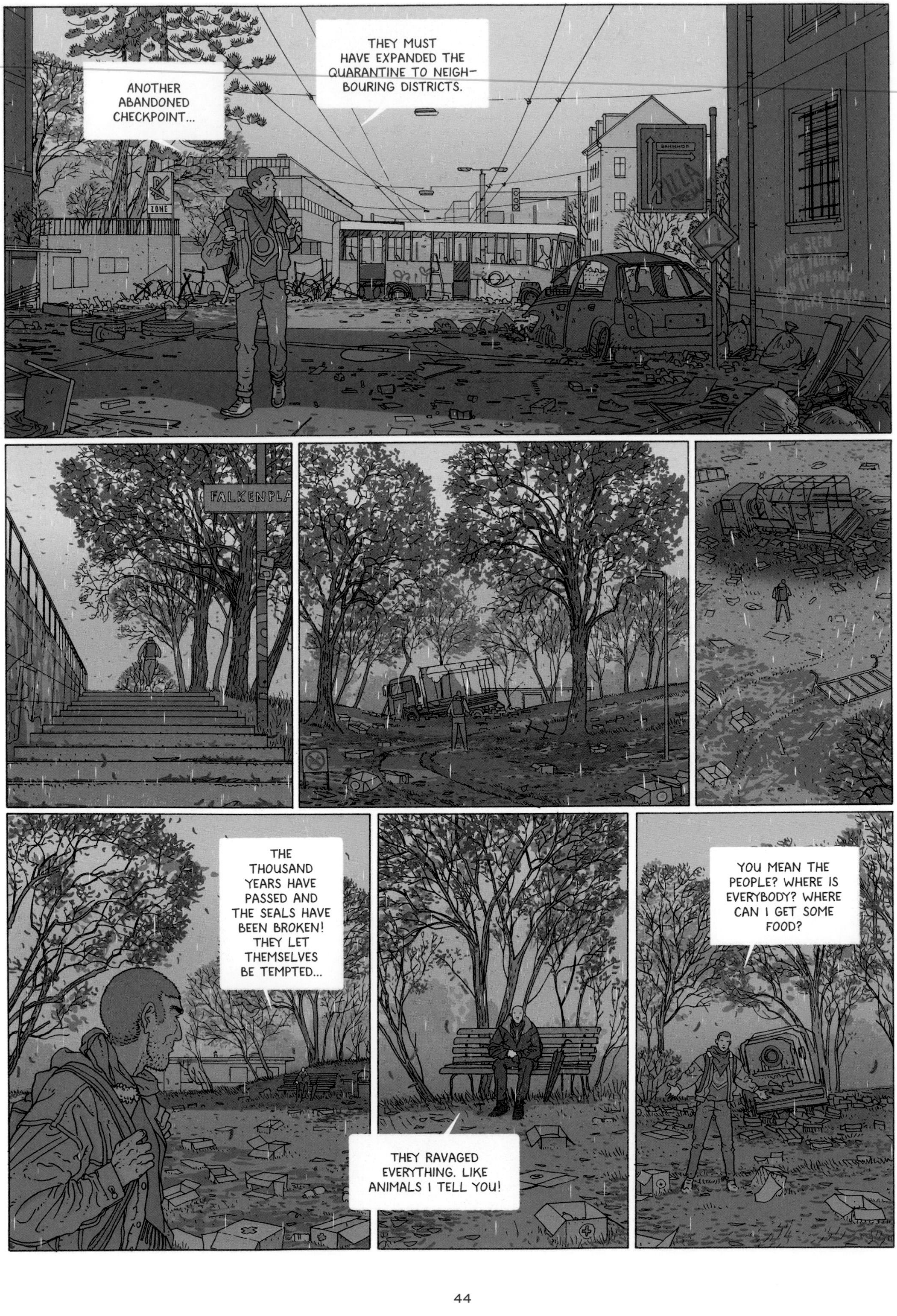
THEY MUST HAVE EXPANDED THE QUARANTINE TO NEIGH-BOURING DISTRICTS.
ANOTHER ABANDONED CHECKPOINT...
FALKENPLA
THE THOUSAND YEARS HAVE PASSED AND THE SEALS HAVE BEEN BROKEN! THEY LET THEMSELVES BE TEMPTED...
THEY RAVAGED EVERYTHING. LIKE ANIMALS I TELL YOU!
YOU MEAN THE PEOPLE? WHERE IS EVERYBODY? WHERE CAN I GET SOME FOOD?

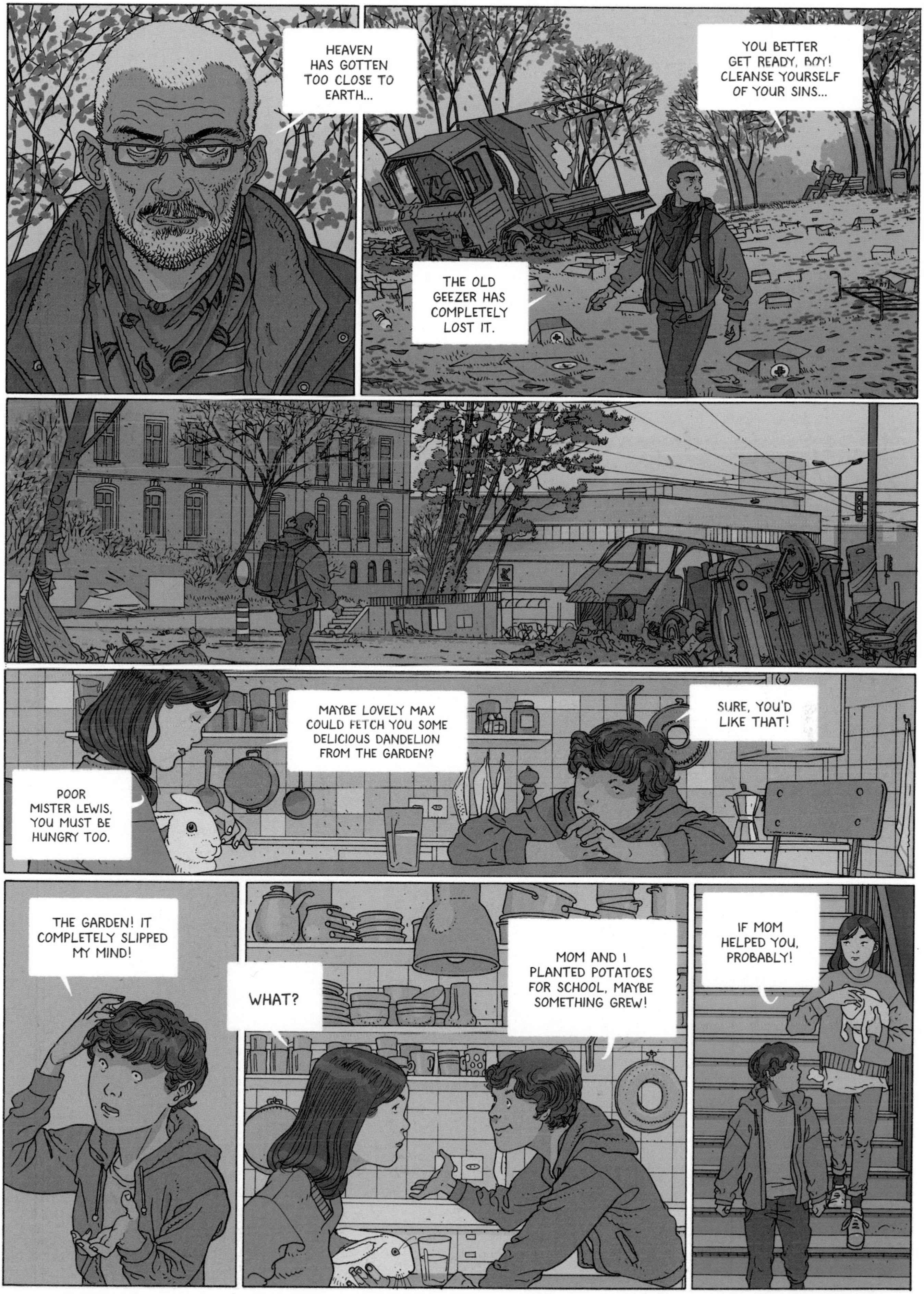
HEAVEN HAS GOTTEN TOO CLOSE TO EARTH...
YOU BETTER GET READY, BOY! CLEANSE YOURSELF OF YOUR SINS...
THE OLD GEEZER HAS COMPLETELY LOST IT.
MAYBE LOVELY MAX COULD FETCH YOU SOME DELICIOUS DANDELION FROM THE GARDEN?
SURE, YOU'D LIKE THAT!
POOR MISTER LEWIS, YOU MUST BE HUNGRY TOO.
THE GARDEN! IT COMPLETELY SLIPPED MY MIND!
WHAT?
MOM AND I PLANTED POTATOES FOR SCHOOL, MAYBE SOMETHING GREW!
IF MOM HELPED YOU, PROBABLY!

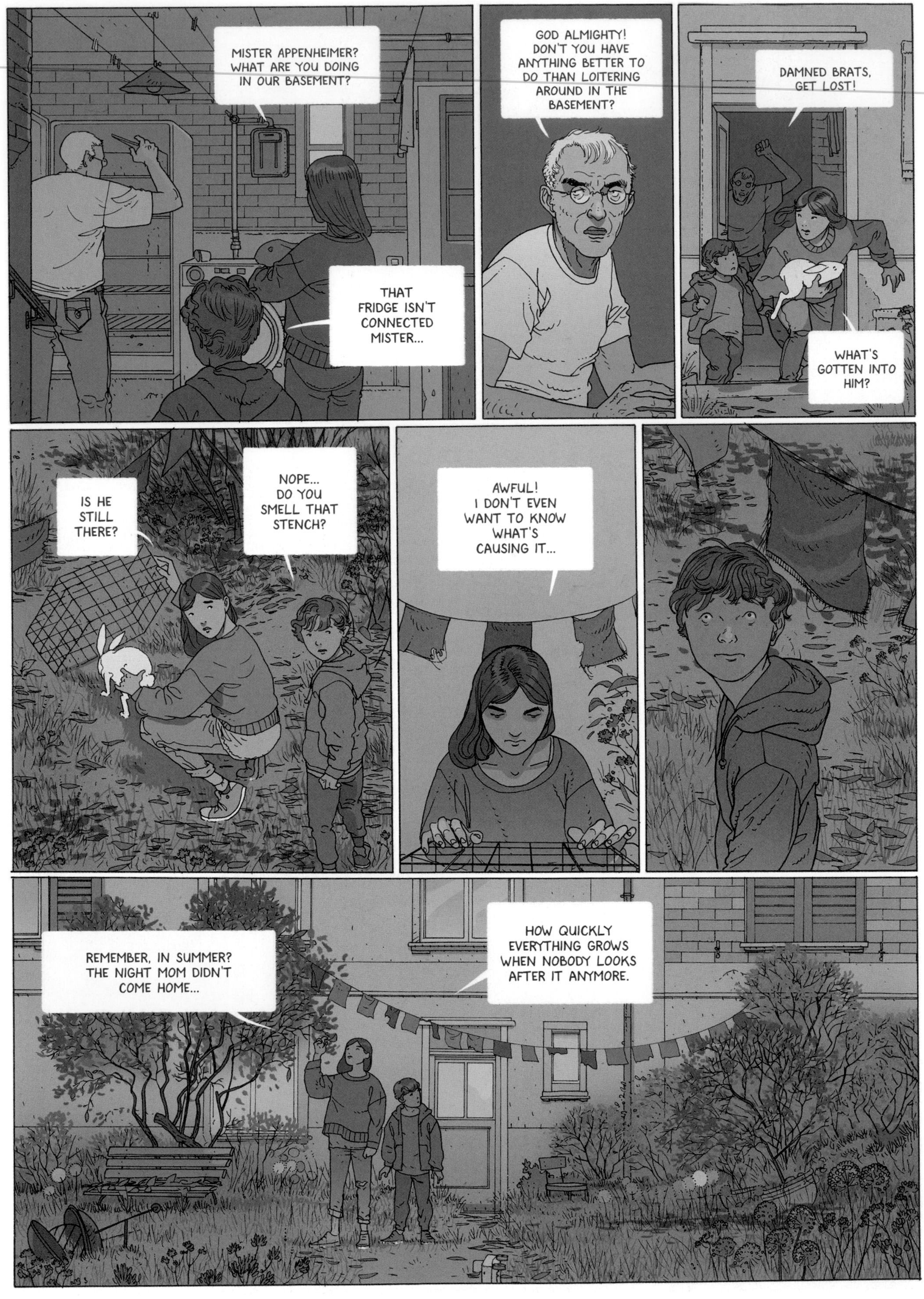
MISTER APPENHEIMER? WHAT ARE YOU DOING IN OUR BASEMENT?
THAT FRIDGE ISN'T CONNECTED MISTER...
GOD ALMIGHTY! DON'T YOU HAVE ANYTHING BETTER TO DO THAN LOITERING AROUND IN THE BASEMENT?
DAMNED BRATS, GET LOST!
WHAT'S GOTTEN INTO HIM?
IS HE STILL THERE?
NOPE... DO YOU SMELL THAT STENCH?
AWFUL! I DON'T EVEN WANT TO KNOW WHAT'S CAUSING IT...
REMEMBER, IN SUMMER? THE NIGHT MOM DIDN'T COME HOME...
HOW QUICKLY EVERYTHING GROWS WHEN NOBODY LOOKS AFTER IT ANYMORE.

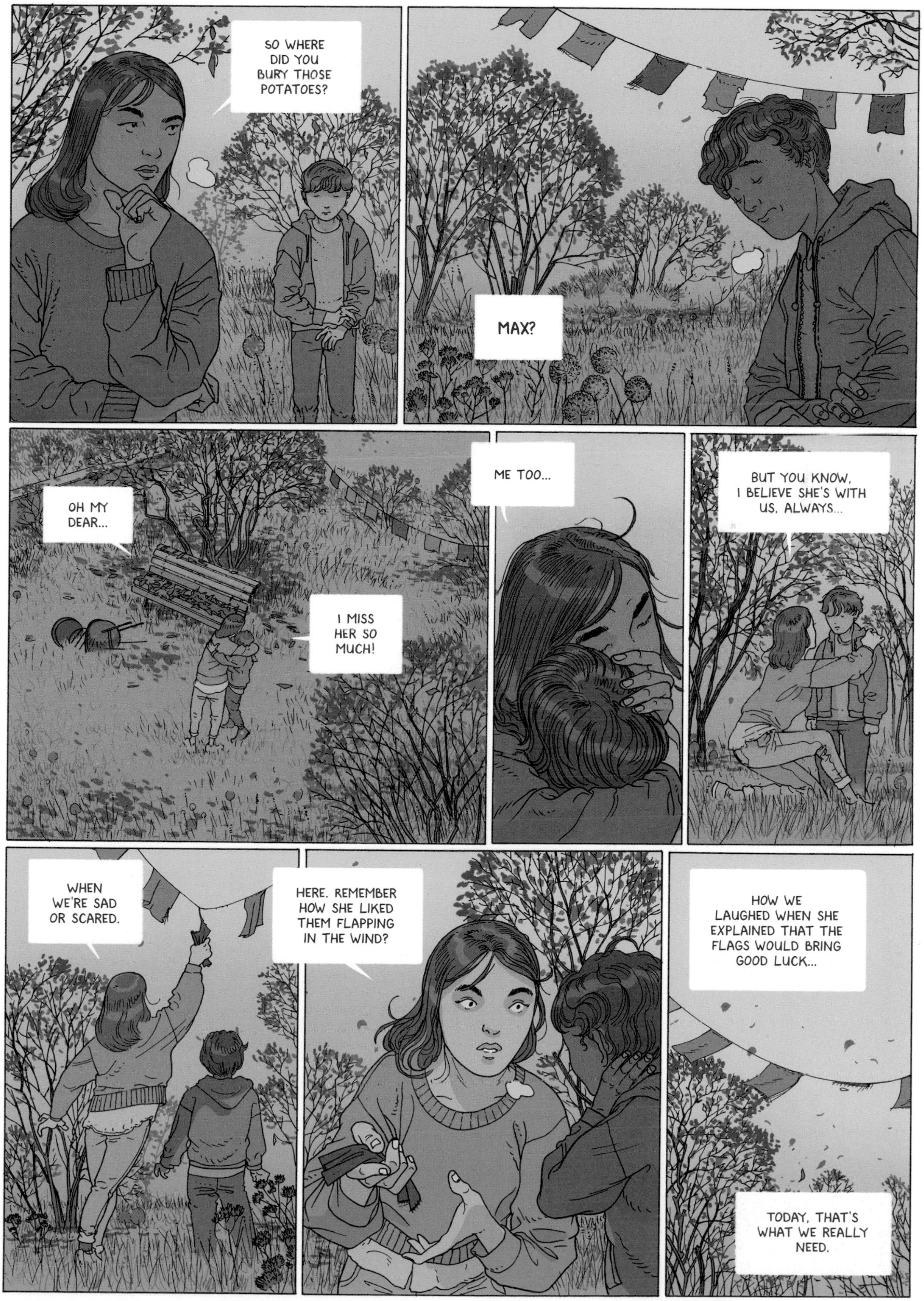
SO WHERE DID YOU BURY THOSE POTATOES?
MAX?
OH MY DEAR...
I MISS HER SO MUCH!
ME TOO...
BUT YOU KNOW, I BELIEVE SHE'S WITH US, ALWAYS...
WHEN WE'RE SAD OR SCARED.
HERE. REMEMBER HOW SHE LIKED THEM FLAPPING IN THE WIND?
HOW WE LAUGHED WHEN SHE EXPLAINED THAT THE FLAGS WOULD BRING GOOD LUCK...
TODAY, THAT'S WHAT WE REALLY NEED.

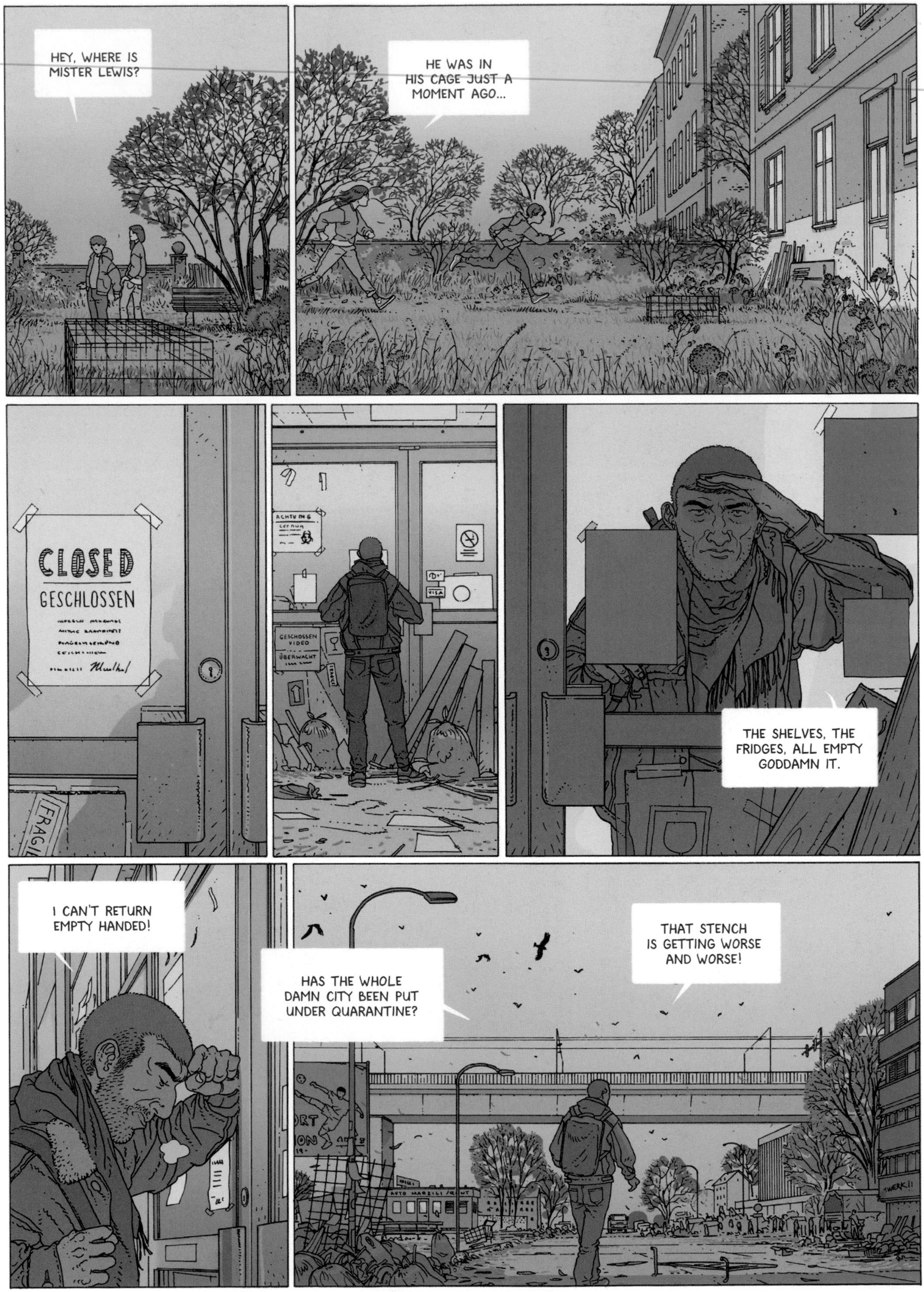
HEY, WHERE IS MISTER LEWIS?
HE WAS IN HIS CAGE JUST A MOMENT AGO...
CLOSED
GESCHLOSSEN
ACHTUNG
GESCHLOSSEN VIDEO ÜBERWACHT
VISA
THE SHELVES, THE FRIDGES, ALL EMPTY GODDAMN IT.
I CAN'T RETURN EMPTY HANDED!
HAS THE WHOLE DAMN CITY BEEN PUT UNDER QUARANTINE?
THAT STENCH IS GETTING WORSE AND WORSE!

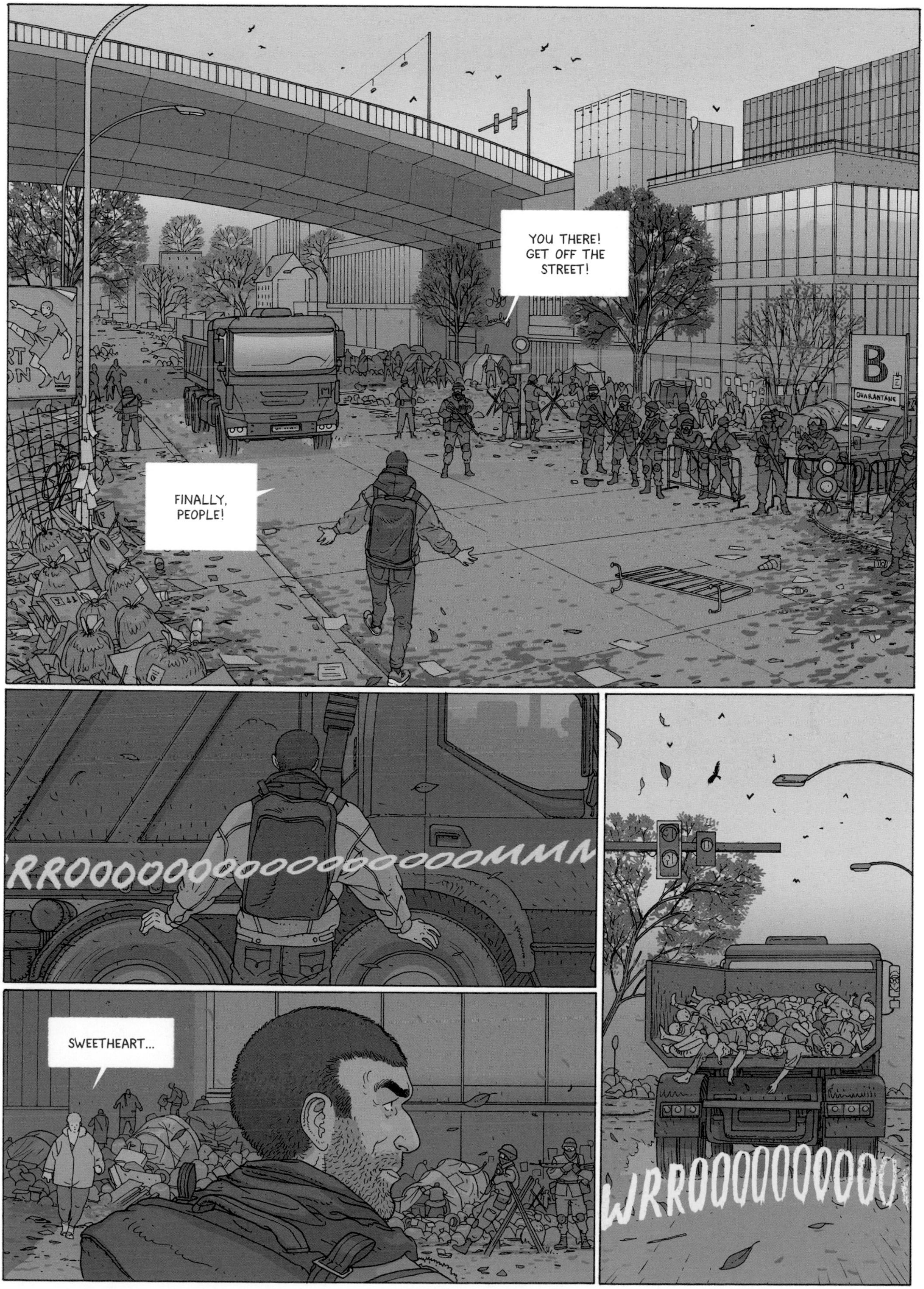
YOU THERE! GET OFF THE STREET!
FINALLY, PEOPLE!
QUARANTÄNE
WRROOOOOOOOOOOOOOOOOOOOMMM
SWEETHEART...
WRROOOOOOOOOOO

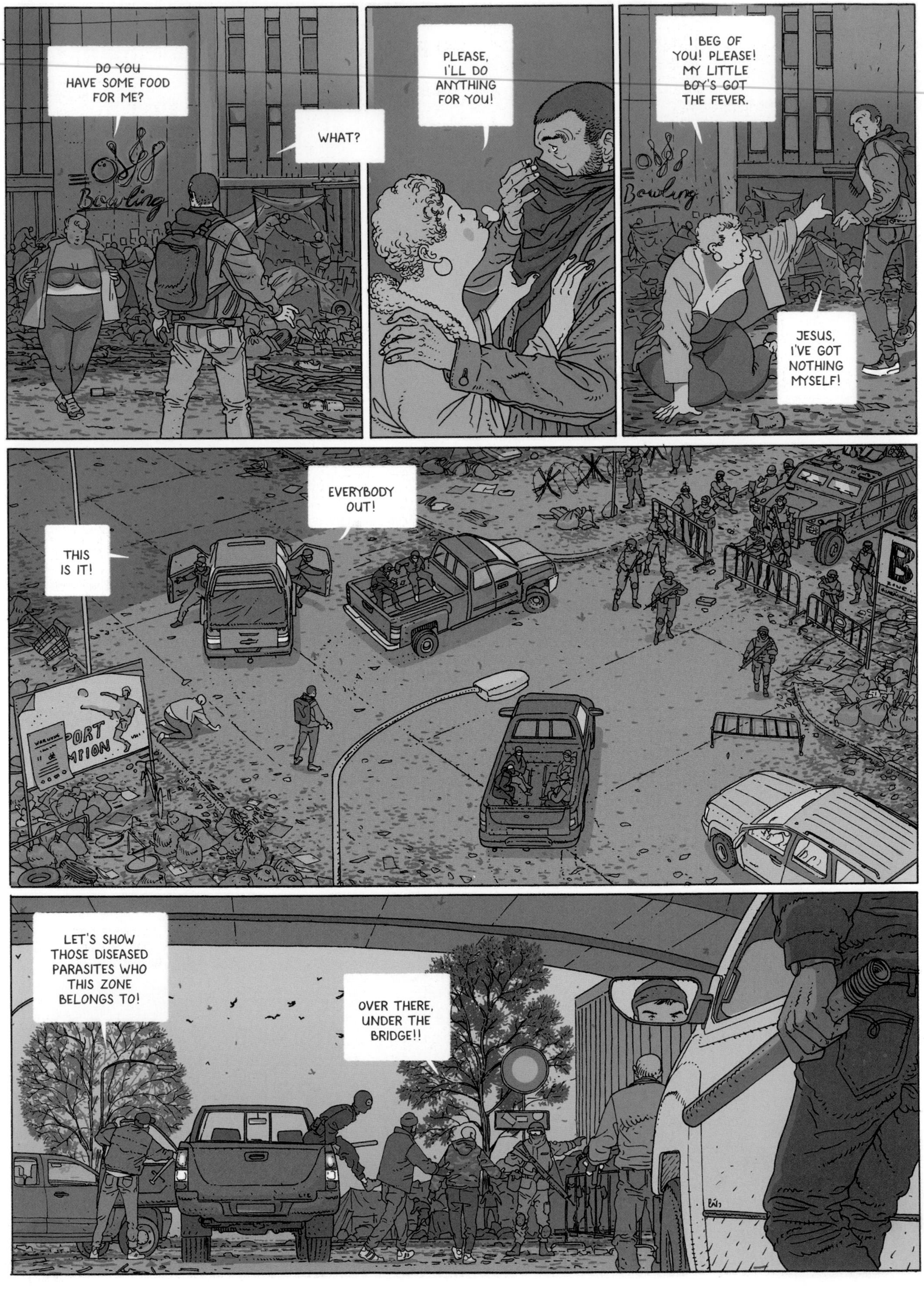
DO YOU HAVE SOME FOOD FOR ME?
WHAT?
PLEASE, I'LL DO ANYTHING FOR YOU!
I BEG OF YOU! PLEASE! MY LITTLE BOY'S GOT THE FEVER.
JESUS, I'VE GOT NOTHING MYSELF!
THIS IS IT!
EVERYBODY OUT!
LET'S SHOW THOSE DISEASED PARASITES WHO THIS ZONE BELONGS TO!
OVER THERE, UNDER THE BRIDGE!!

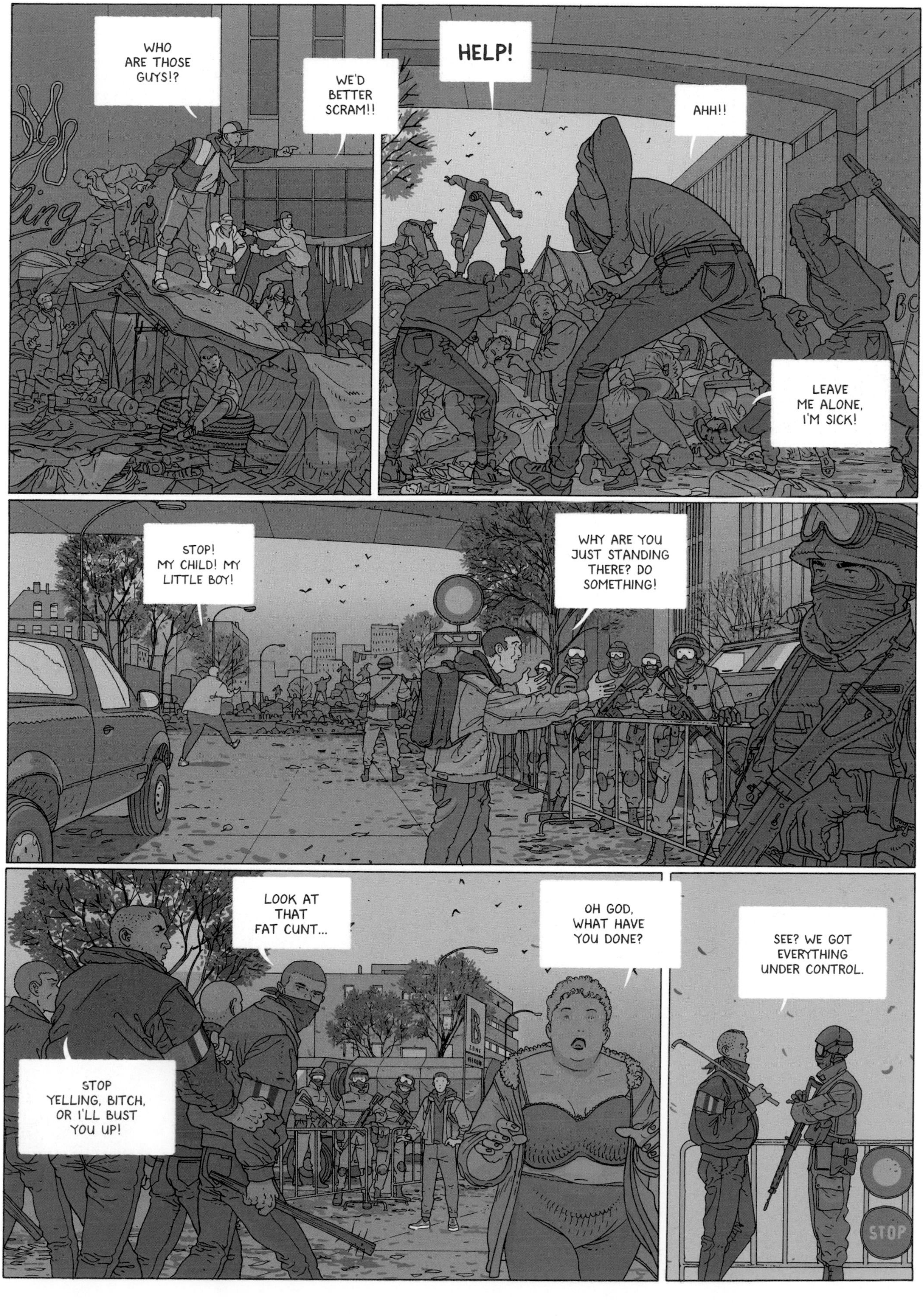
WHO ARE THOSE GUYS!?
WE'D BETTER SCRAM!!
HELP!
AHH!!
LEAVE ME ALONE, I'M SICK!
STOP! MY CHILD! MY LITTLE BOY!
WHY ARE YOU JUST STANDING THERE? DO SOMETHING!
LOOK AT THAT FAT CUNT...
STOP YELLING, BITCH, OR I'LL BUST YOU UP!
OH GOD, WHAT HAVE YOU DONE?
SEE? WE GOT EVERYTHING UNDER CONTROL.
STOP

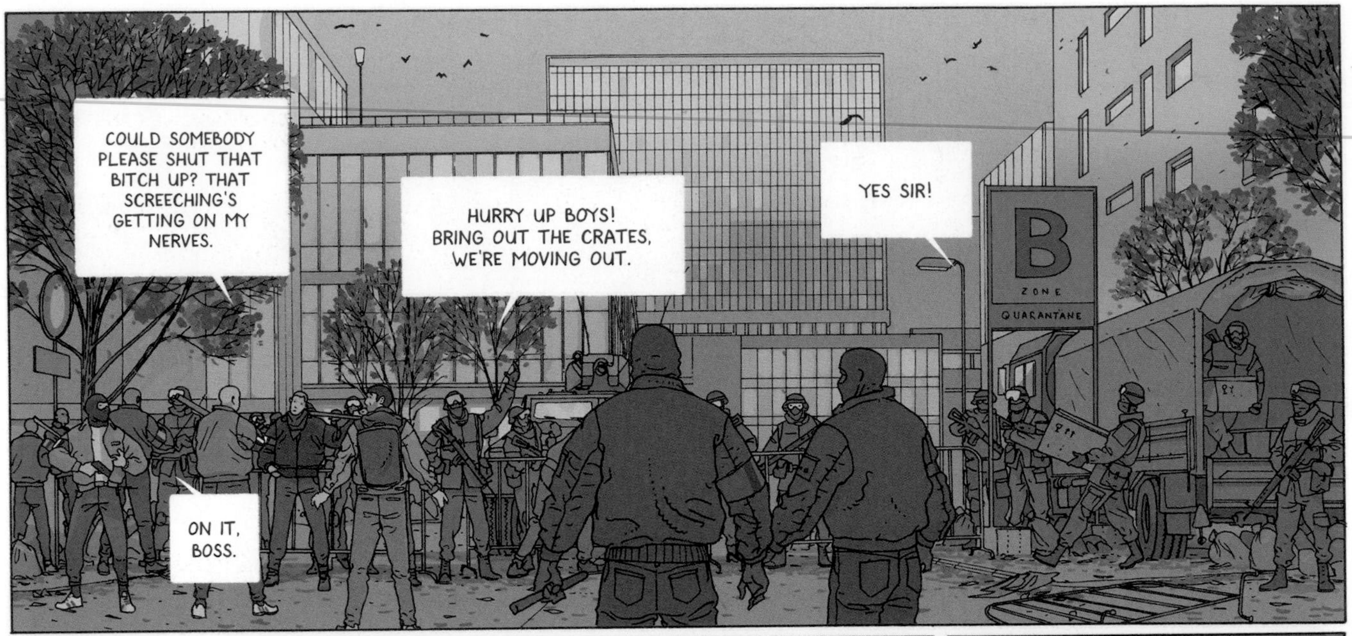
COULD SOMEBODY PLEASE SHUT THAT BITCH UP? THAT SCREECHING'S GETTING ON MY NERVES.
HURRY UP BOYS! BRING OUT THE CRATES, WE'RE MOVING OUT.
YES SIR!
B
ZONE
QUARANTAINE
ON IT, BOSS.

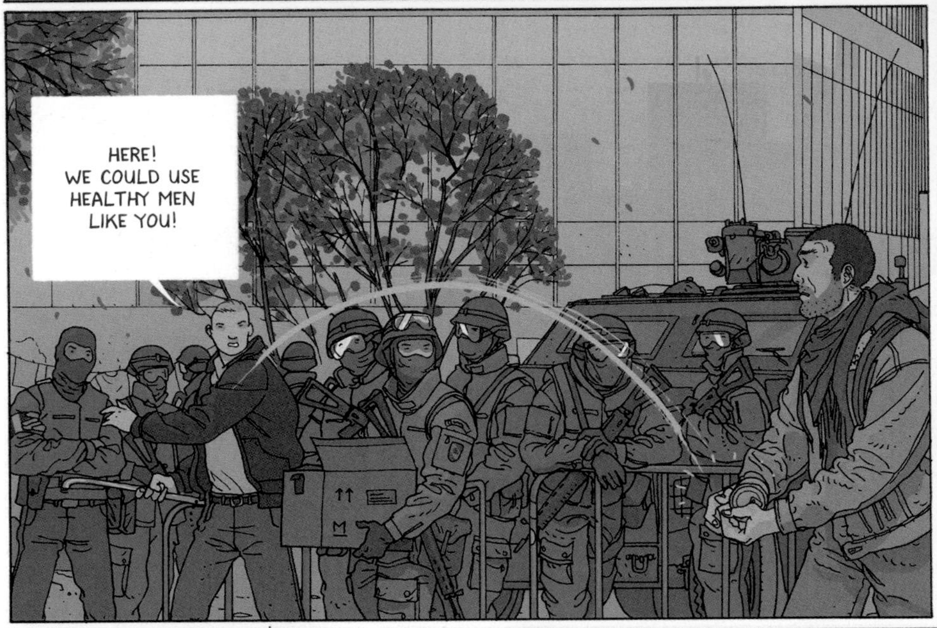
HERE! WE COULD USE HEALTHY MEN LIKE YOU!

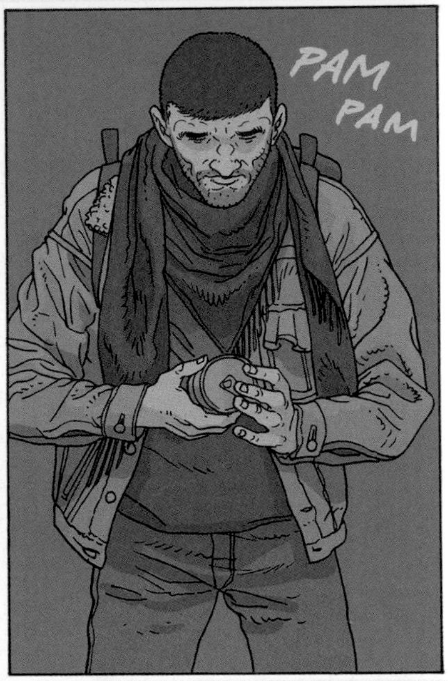
PAM
PAM

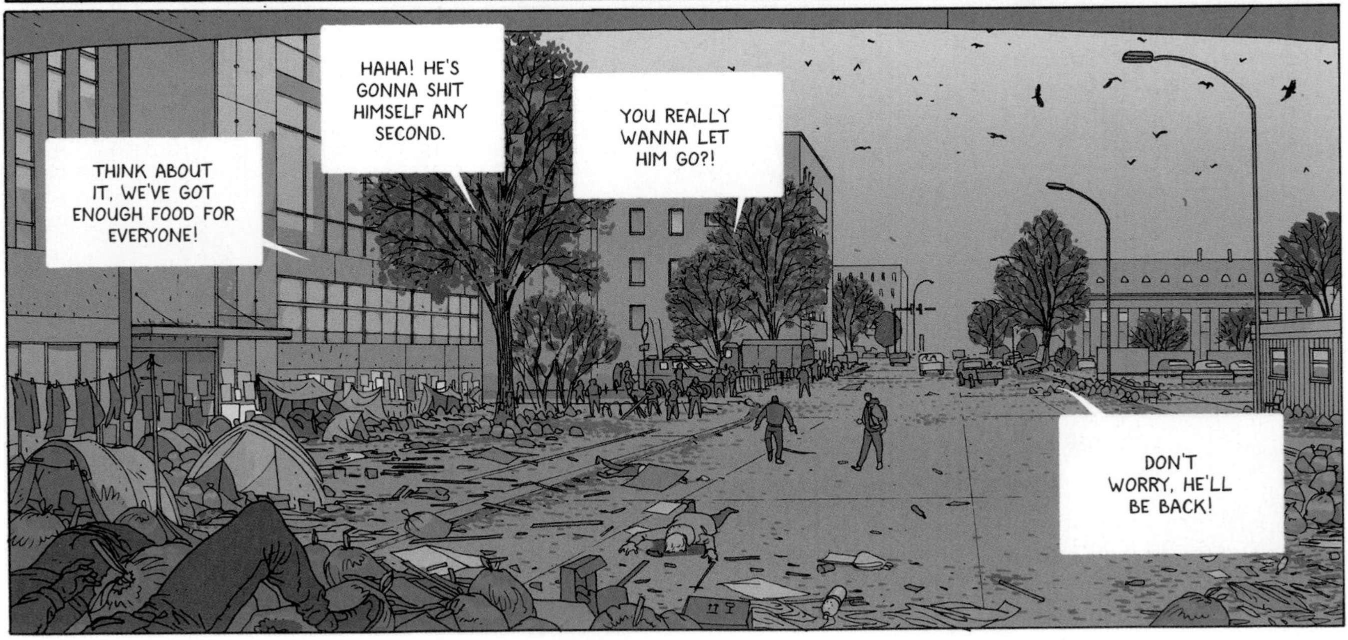
THINK ABOUT IT, WE'VE GOT ENOUGH FOOD FOR EVERYONE!
HAHA! HE'S GONNA SHIT HIMSELF ANY SECOND.
YOU REALLY WANNA LET HIM GO?!
DON'T WORRY, HE'LL BE BACK!

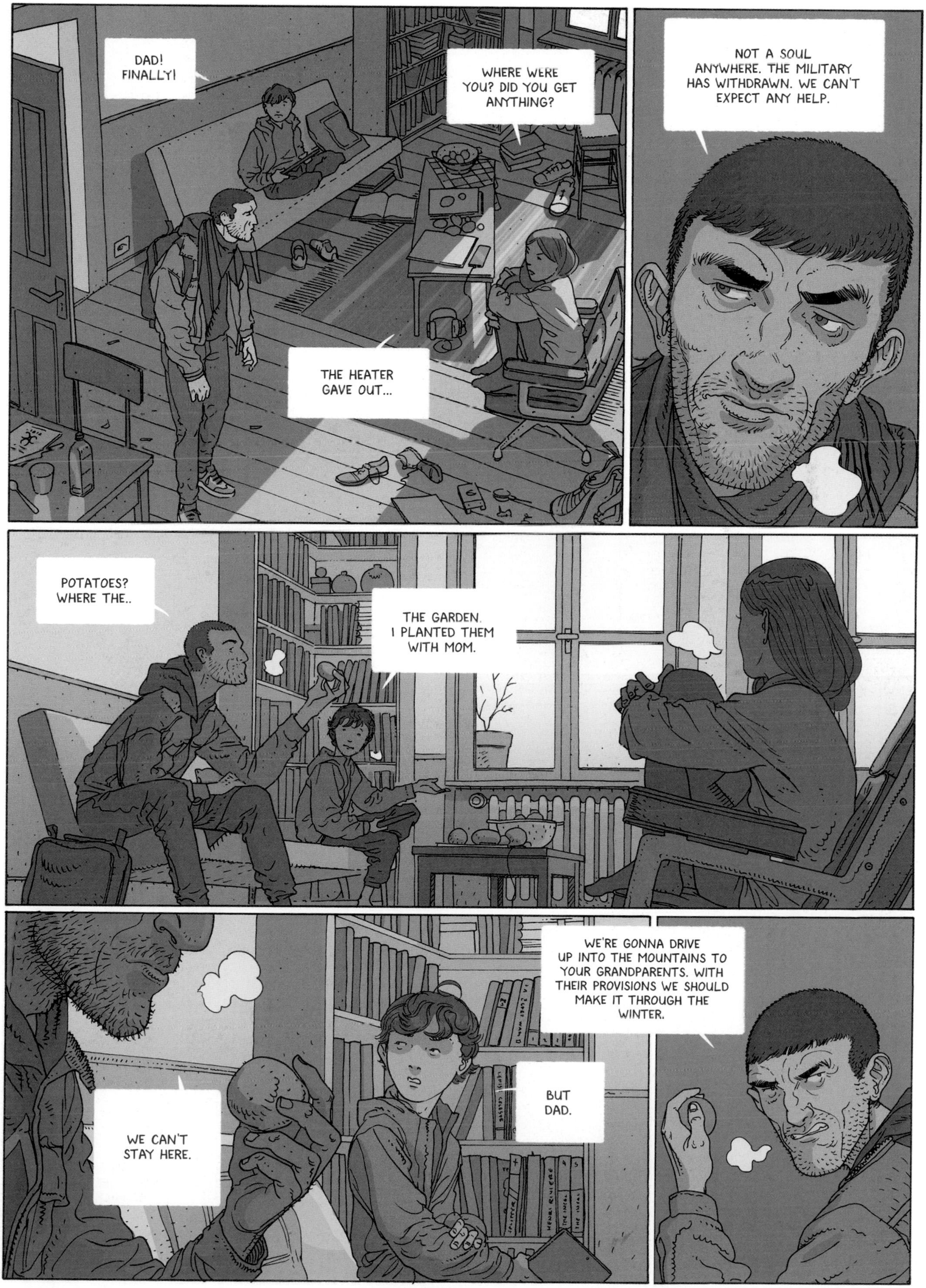
DAD! FINALLY!
WHERE WERE YOU? DID YOU GET ANYTHING?
THE HEATER GAVE OUT...
NOT A SOUL ANYWHERE. THE MILITARY HAS WITHDRAWN. WE CAN'T EXPECT ANY HELP.
POTATOES? WHERE THE..
THE GARDEN. I PLANTED THEM WITH MOM.
WE CAN'T STAY HERE.
BUT DAD.
WE'RE GONNA DRIVE UP INTO THE MOUNTAINS TO YOUR GRANDPARENTS. WITH THEIR PROVISIONS WE SHOULD MAKE IT THROUGH THE WINTER.

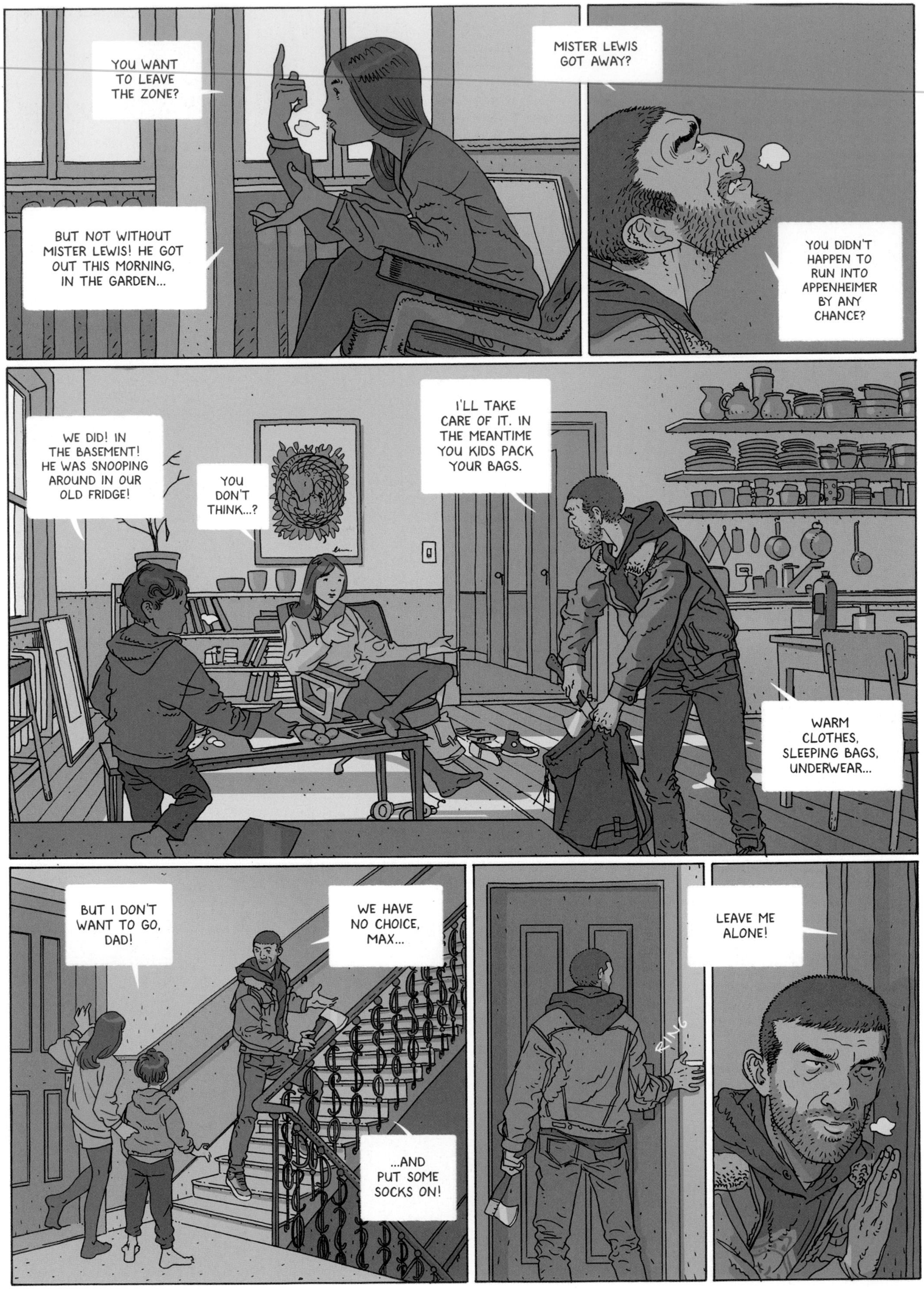
YOU WANT TO LEAVE THE ZONE?
BUT NOT WITHOUT MISTER LEWIS! HE GOT OUT THIS MORNING, IN THE GARDEN...
MISTER LEWIS GOT AWAY?
YOU DIDN'T HAPPEN TO RUN INTO APPENHEIMER BY ANY CHANCE?
WE DID! IN THE BASEMENT! HE WAS SNOOPING AROUND IN OUR OLD FRIDGE!
YOU DON'T THINK...?
I'LL TAKE CARE OF IT. IN THE MEANTIME YOU KIDS PACK YOUR BAGS.
WARM CLOTHES, SLEEPING BAGS, UNDERWEAR...
BUT I DON'T WANT TO GO, DAD!
WE HAVE NO CHOICE, MAX...
...AND PUT SOME SOCKS ON!
RING
LEAVE ME ALONE!

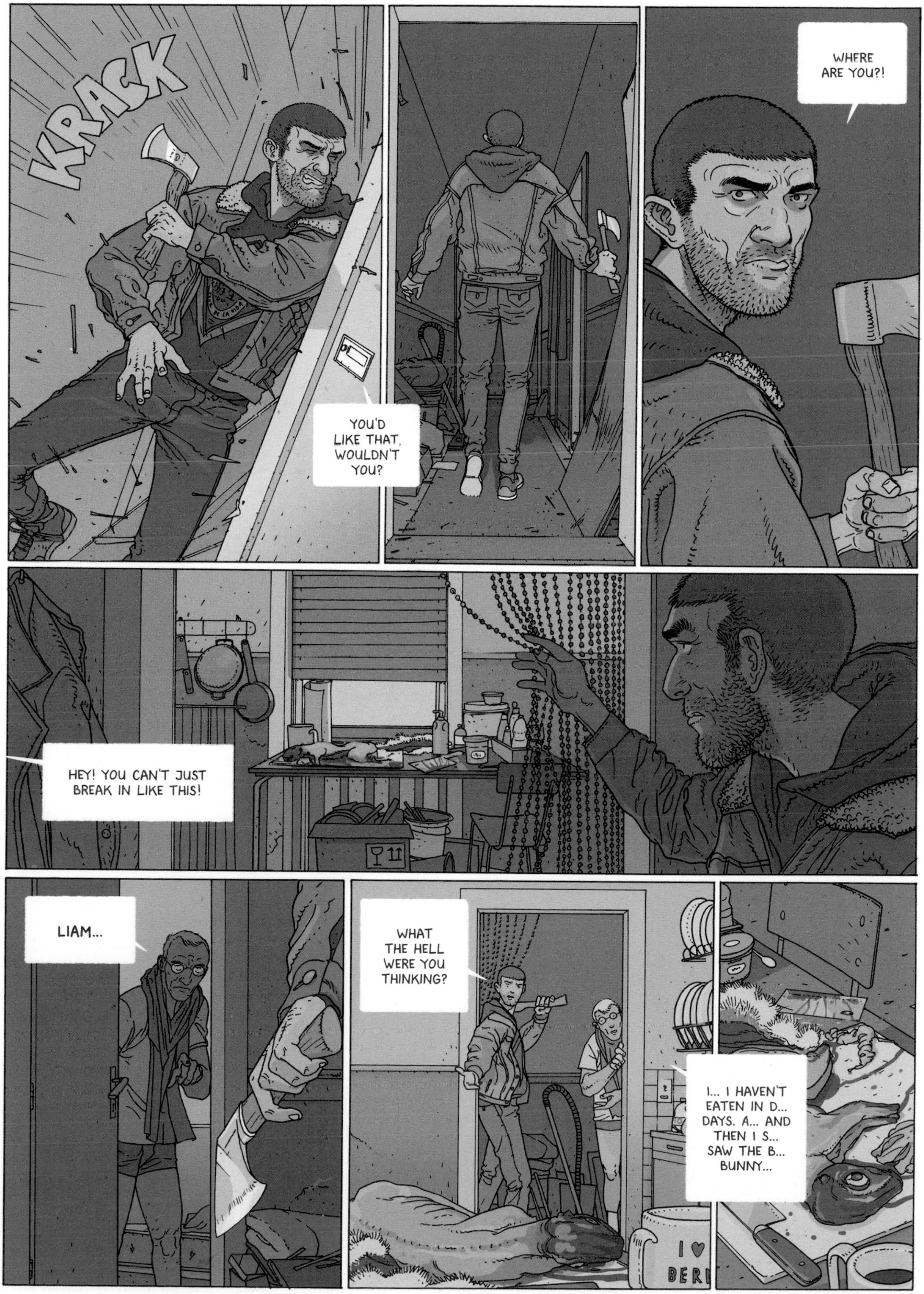
KRACK
YOU'D LIKE THAT, WOULDN'T YOU?
WHERE ARE YOU?!
HEY! YOU CAN'T JUST BREAK IN LIKE THIS!
LIAM...
WHAT THE HELL WERE YOU THINKING?
I... I HAVEN'T EATEN IN D... DAYS. A... AND THEN I S... SAW THE B... BUNNY...

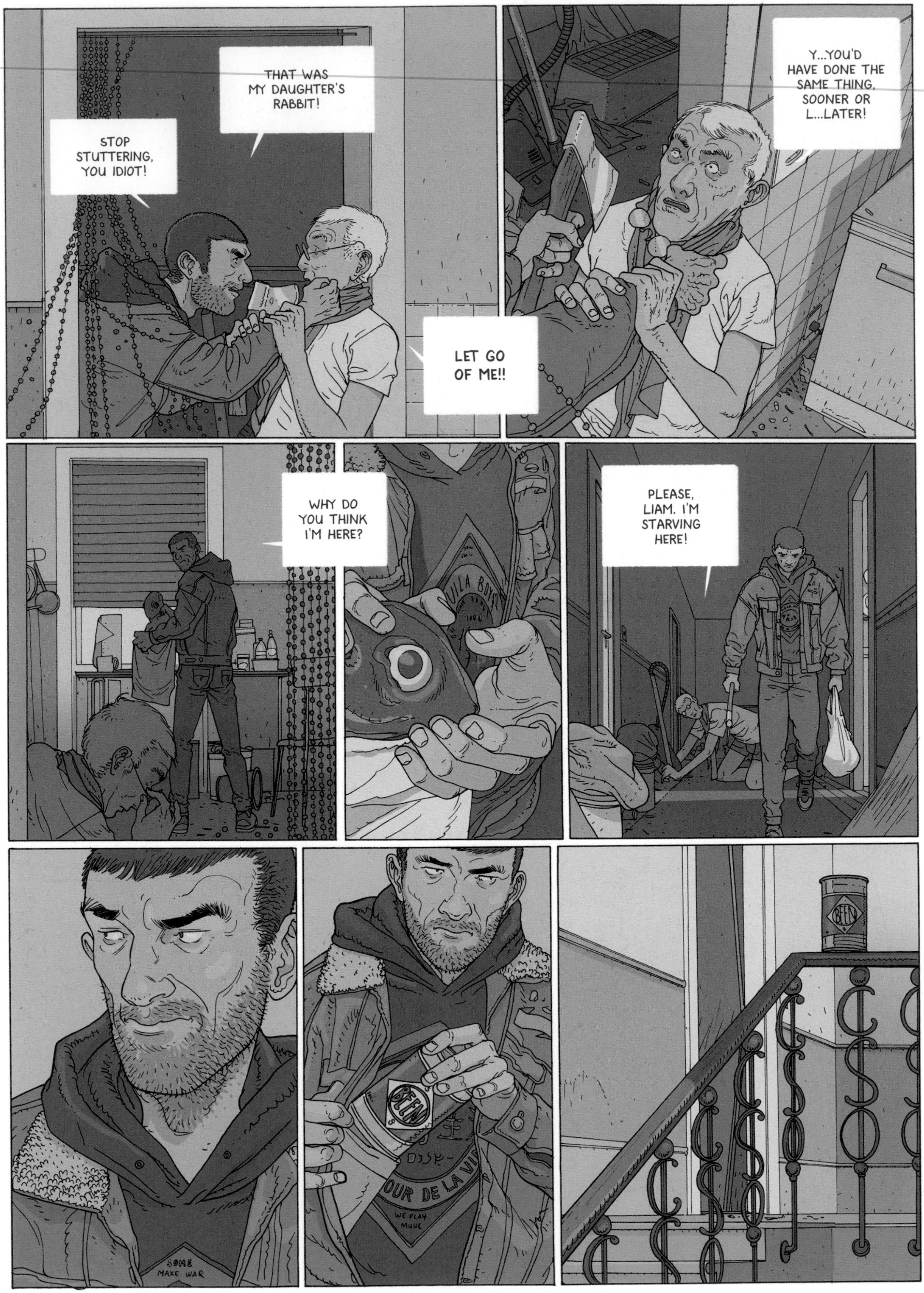
THAT WAS MY DAUGHTER'S RABBIT!
STOP STUTTERING, YOU IDIOT!
LET GO OF ME!!
Y...YOU'D HAVE DONE THE SAME THING, SOONER OR L...LATER!
WHY DO YOU THINK I'M HERE?
PLEASE, LIAM. I'M STARVING HERE!
OUR DE LA VI
WE PLAY MUSIC
MAKE WAR

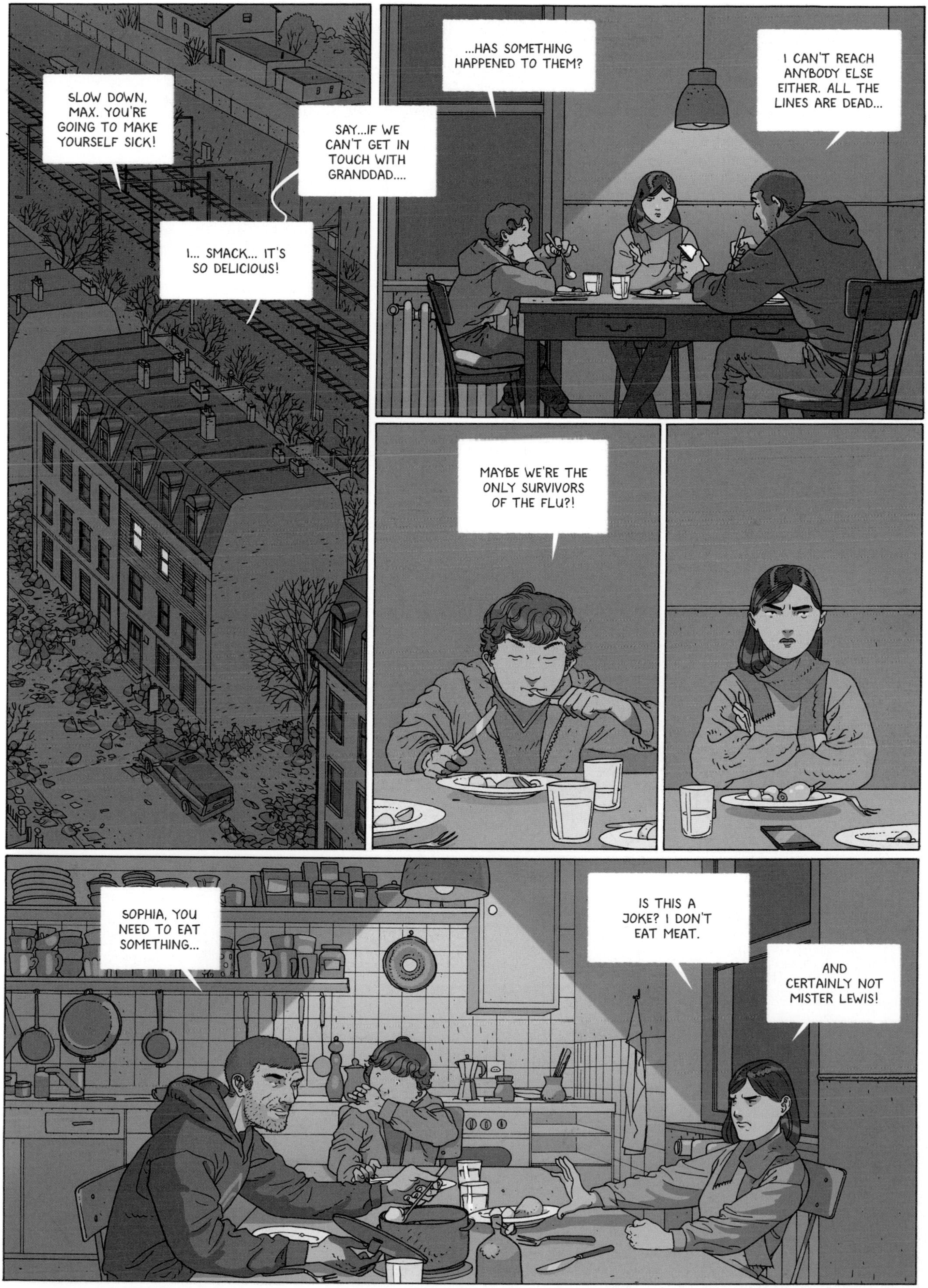
SLOW DOWN, MAX. YOU'RE GOING TO MAKE YOURSELF SICK!
I... SMACK... IT'S SO DELICIOUS!
SAY...IF WE CAN'T GET IN TOUCH WITH GRANDDAD....
...HAS SOMETHING HAPPENED TO THEM?
I CAN'T REACH ANYBODY ELSE EITHER. ALL THE LINES ARE DEAD...
MAYBE WE'RE THE ONLY SURVIVORS OF THE FLU?!
SOPHIA, YOU NEED TO EAT SOMETHING...
IS THIS A JOKE? I DON'T EAT MEAT.
AND CERTAINLY NOT MISTER LEWIS!

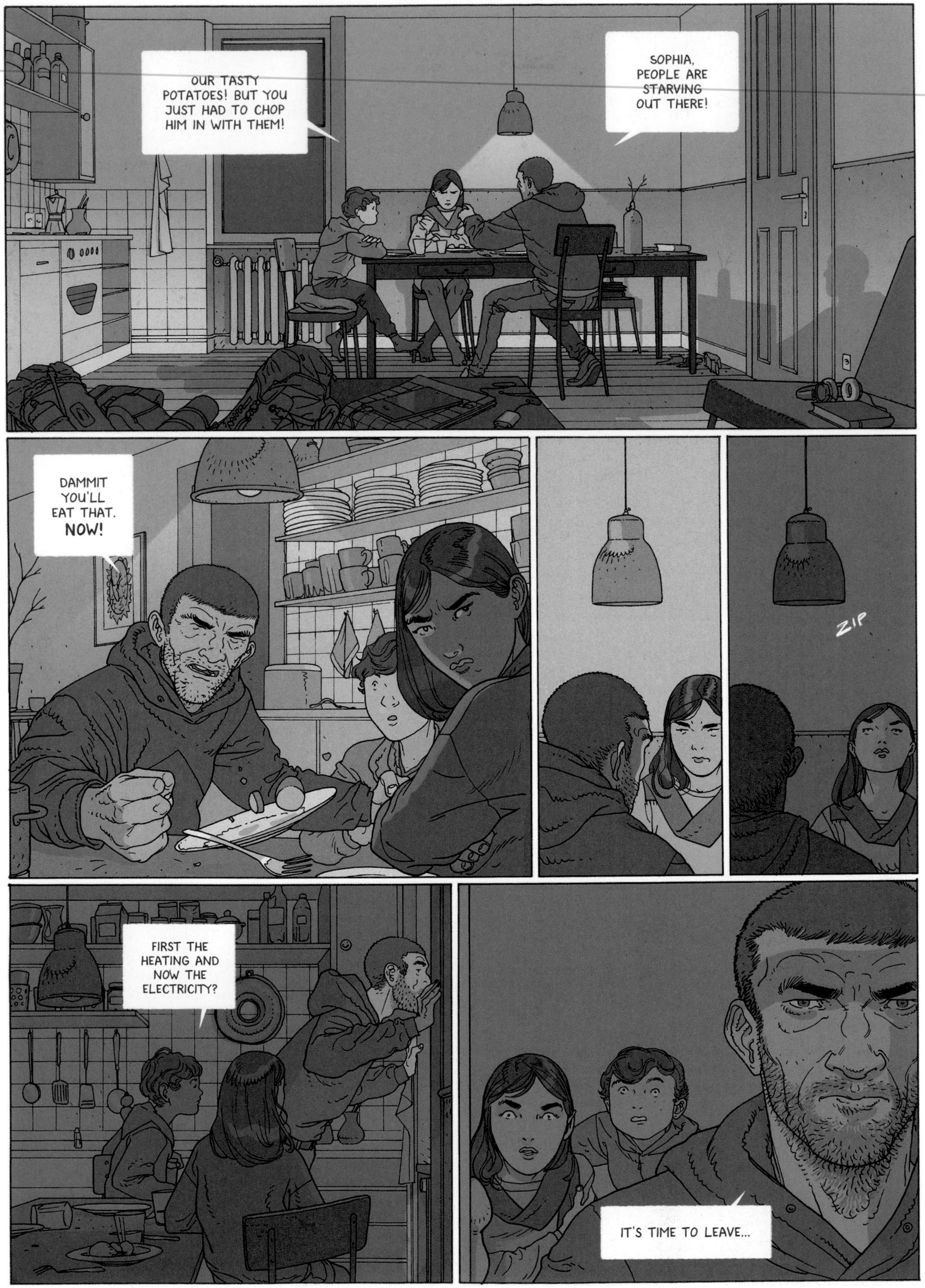

OUR TASTY POTATOES! BUT YOU JUST HAD TO CHOP HIM IN WITH THEM!
SOPHIA, PEOPLE ARE STARVING OUT THERE!
DAMMIT YOU'LL EAT THAT. **NOW!**
ZIP
FIRST THE HEATING AND NOW THE ELECTRICITY?
IT'S TIME TO LEAVE...

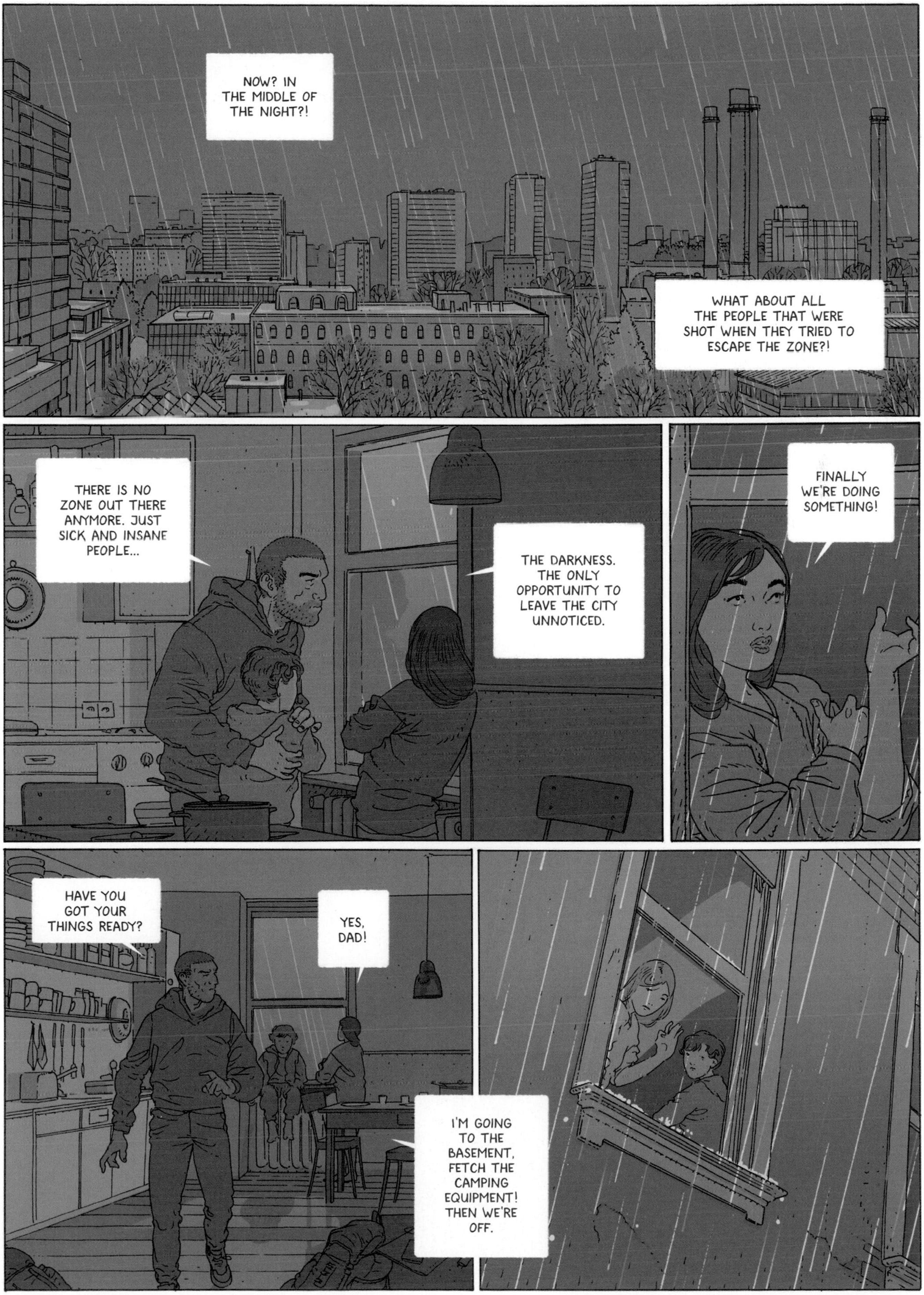
NOW? IN THE MIDDLE OF THE NIGHT?!
WHAT ABOUT ALL THE PEOPLE THAT WERE SHOT WHEN THEY TRIED TO ESCAPE THE ZONE?!
THERE IS NO ZONE OUT THERE ANYMORE. JUST SICK AND INSANE PEOPLE...
THE DARKNESS. THE ONLY OPPORTUNITY TO LEAVE THE CITY UNNOTICED.
FINALLY WE'RE DOING SOMETHING!
HAVE YOU GOT YOUR THINGS READY?
YES, DAD!
I'M GOING TO THE BASEMENT, FETCH THE CAMPING EQUIPMENT! THEN WE'RE OFF.

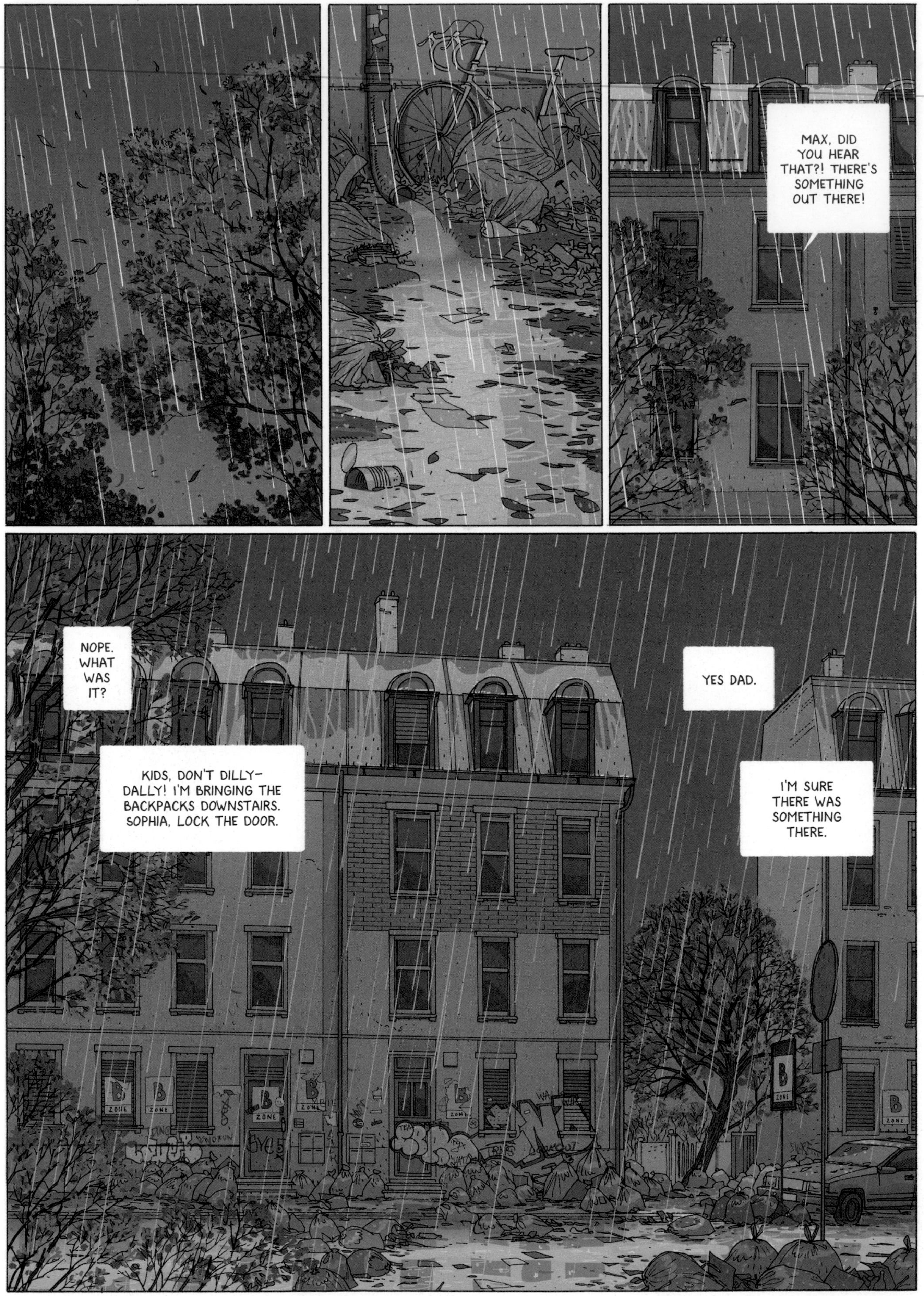
MAX, DID YOU HEAR THAT?! THERE'S SOMETHING OUT THERE!
NOPE. WHAT WAS IT?
YES DAD.
KIDS, DON'T DILLY-DALLY! I'M BRINGING THE BACKPACKS DOWNSTAIRS. SOPHIA, LOCK THE DOOR.
I'M SURE THERE WAS SOMETHING THERE.

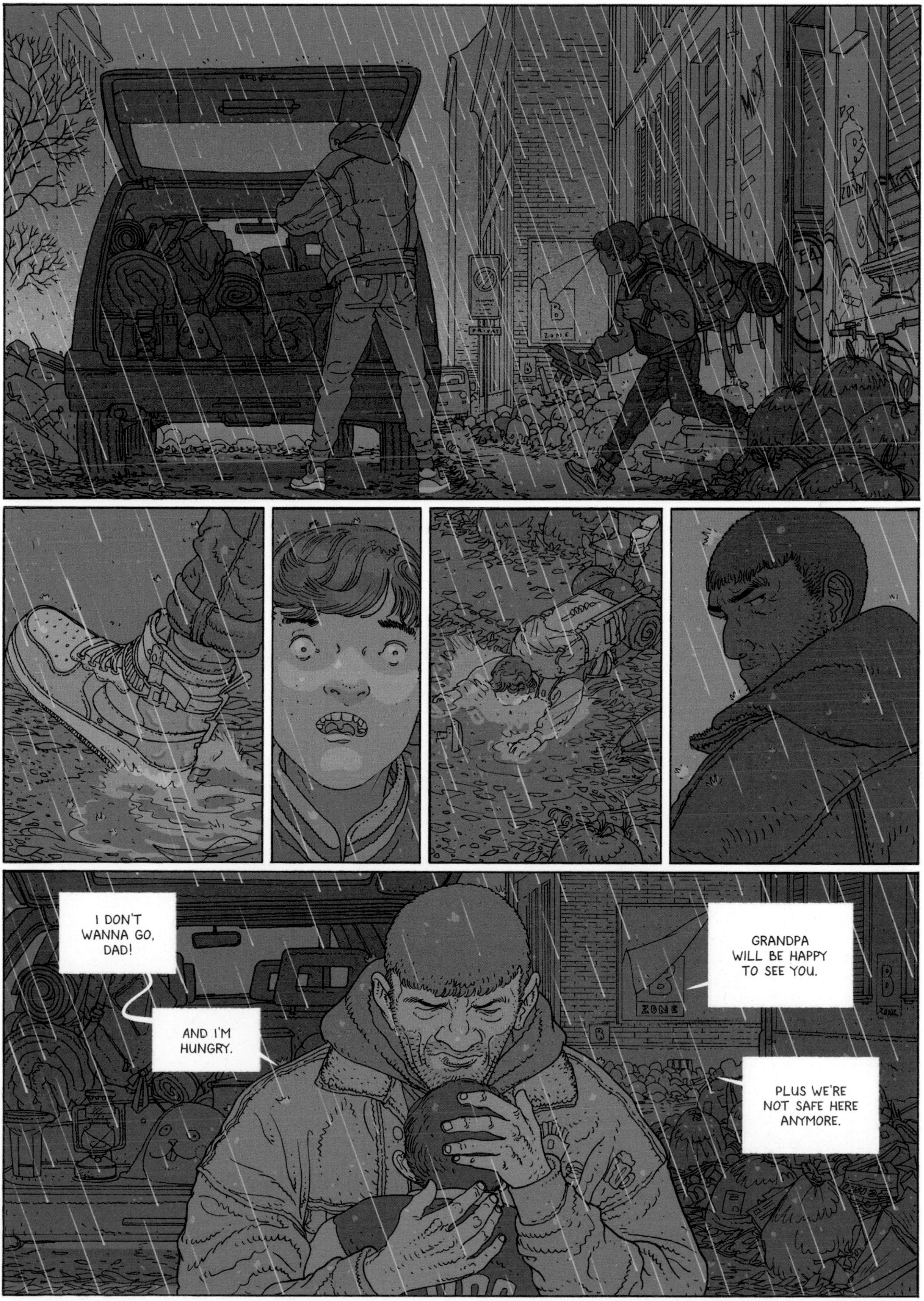
I DON'T WANNA GO, DAD!
AND I'M HUNGRY.
GRANDPA WILL BE HAPPY TO SEE YOU.
PLUS WE'RE NOT SAFE HERE ANYMORE.

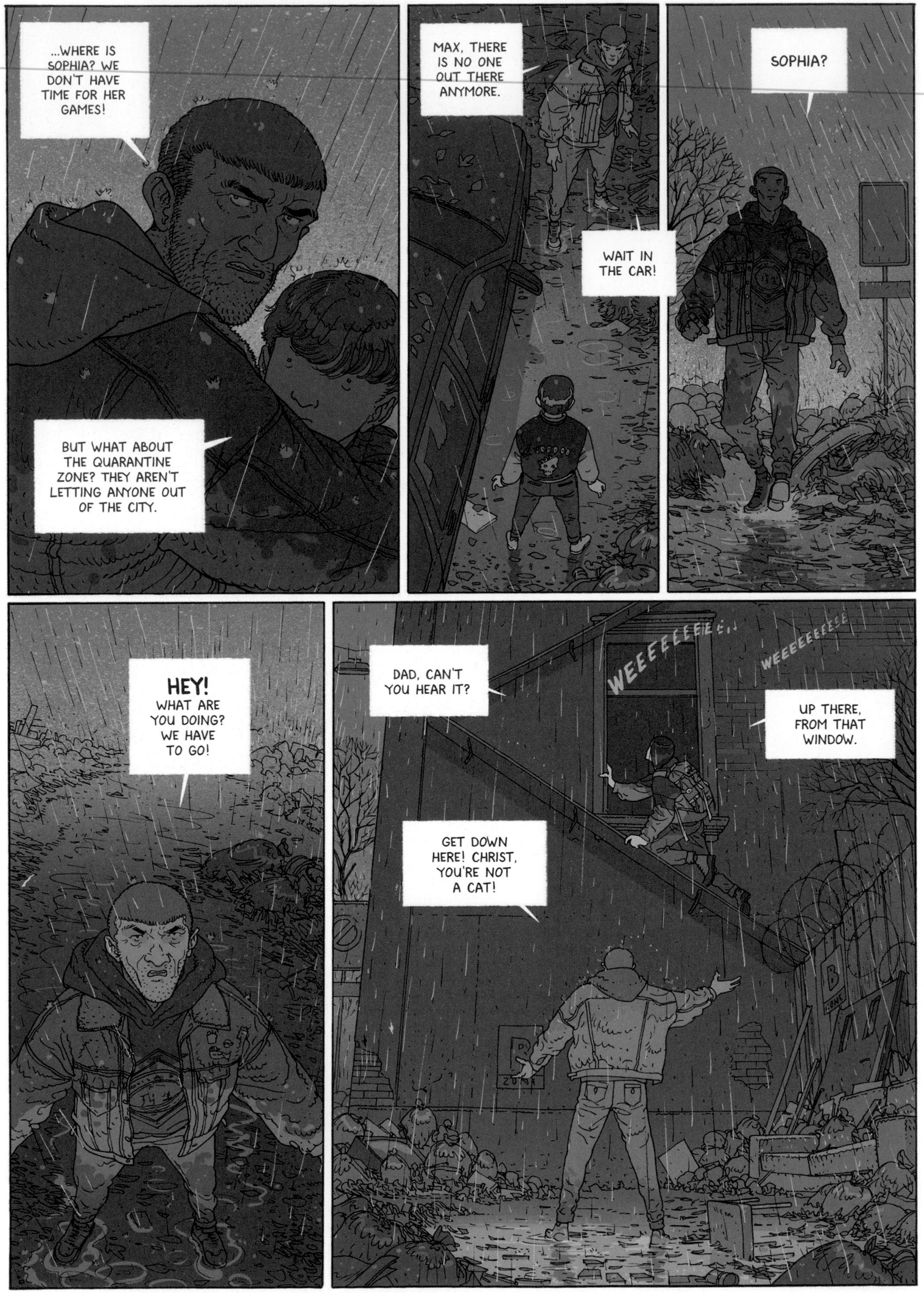
...WHERE IS SOPHIA? WE DON'T HAVE TIME FOR HER GAMES!
BUT WHAT ABOUT THE QUARANTINE ZONE? THEY AREN'T LETTING ANYONE OUT OF THE CITY.
MAX, THERE IS NO ONE OUT THERE ANYMORE.
WAIT IN THE CAR!
SOPHIA?
HEY! WHAT ARE YOU DOING? WE HAVE TO GO!
DAD, CAN'T YOU HEAR IT?
WEEEEEEEEE
WEEEEEEEEEE
UP THERE, FROM THAT WINDOW.
GET DOWN HERE! CHRIST, YOU'RE NOT A CAT!

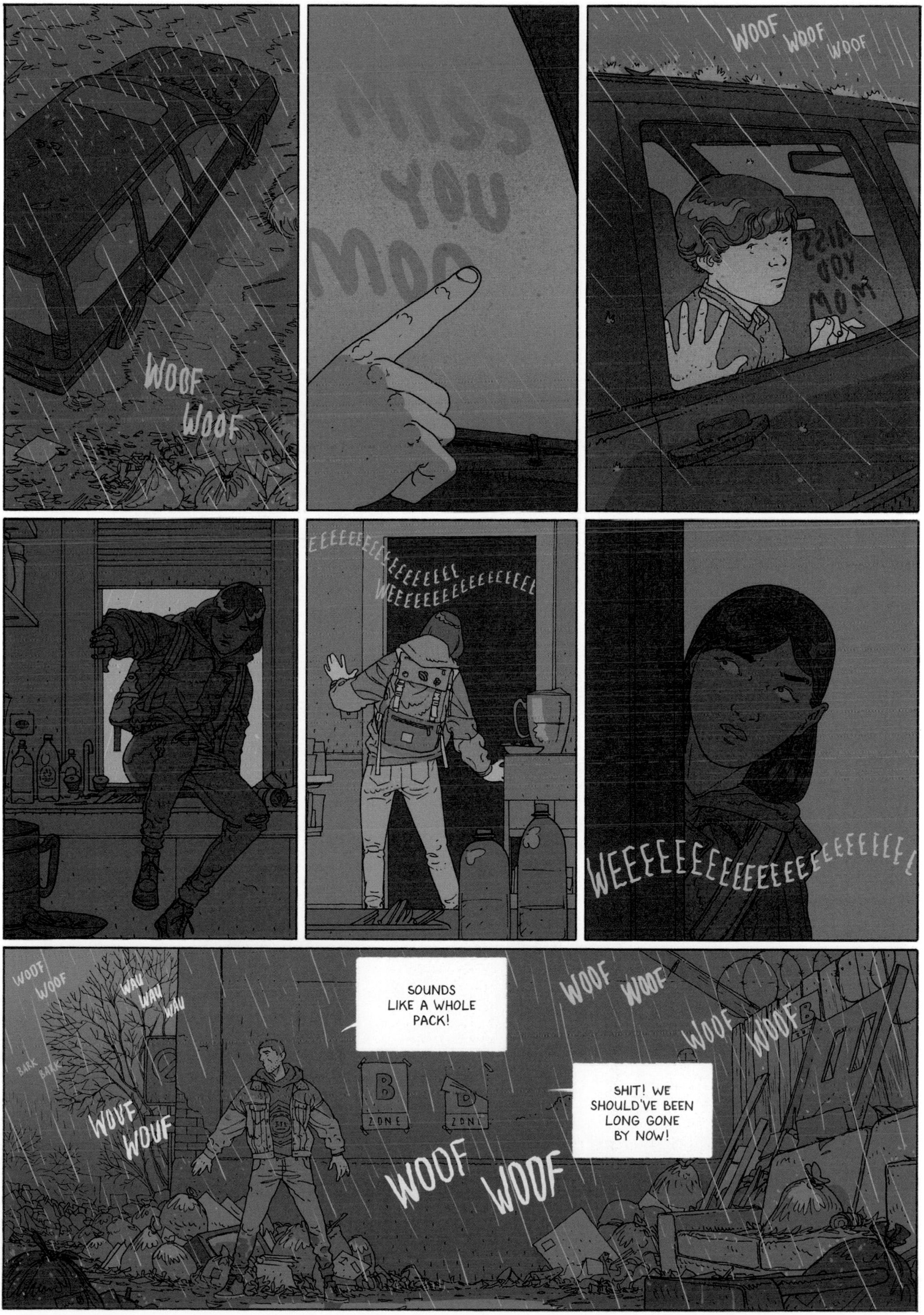
WOOF
WOOF
MISS YOU MOM
WOOF WOOF WOOF
MISS YOU MOM
EEEEEEEEEEEEEEE
WEEEEEEEEEEEEEEEEE
WEEEEEEEEEEEEEEEEEEEEEE
WOOF WOOF
WAU WAU WAU
BARK BARK
WOOF WOOF
SOUNDS LIKE A WHOLE PACK!
WOOF WOOF
WOOF WOOF
B ZONE
SHIT! WE SHOULD'VE BEEN LONG GONE BY NOW!
WOOF WOOF

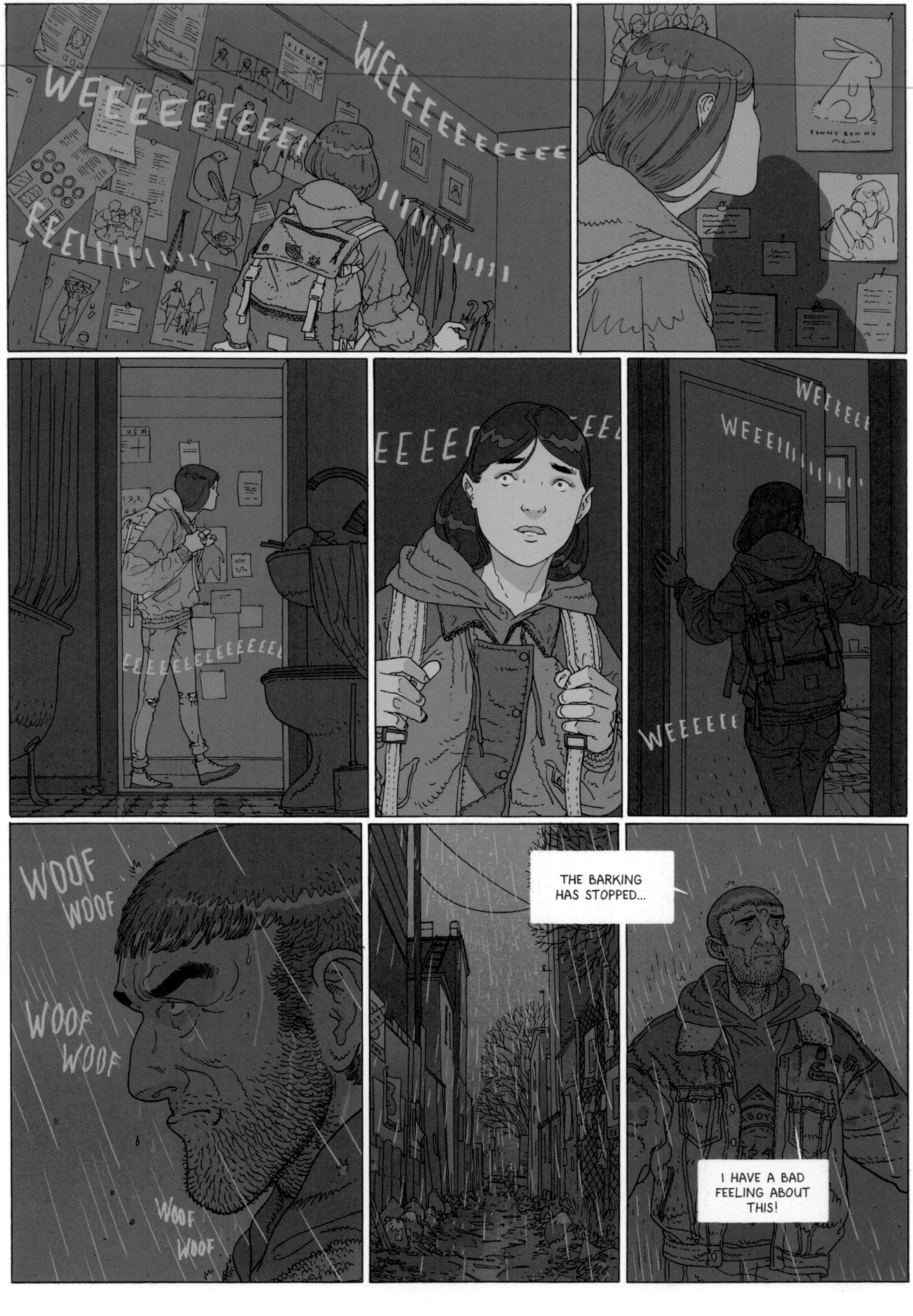
WEEEEEEEEEEEEEEEEIIIIIIIII
WEEEEEEEEEEEEEEEEEIIIIIIII
EEEEEEEEEEEEEEEL
EEEEEEEEL
WEEEEEEE
WEEEIIIIIIIIII
WEEEEEL
WOOF WOOF
WOOF WOOF
WOOF WOOF
THE BARKING HAS STOPPED...
I HAVE A BAD FEELING ABOUT THIS!

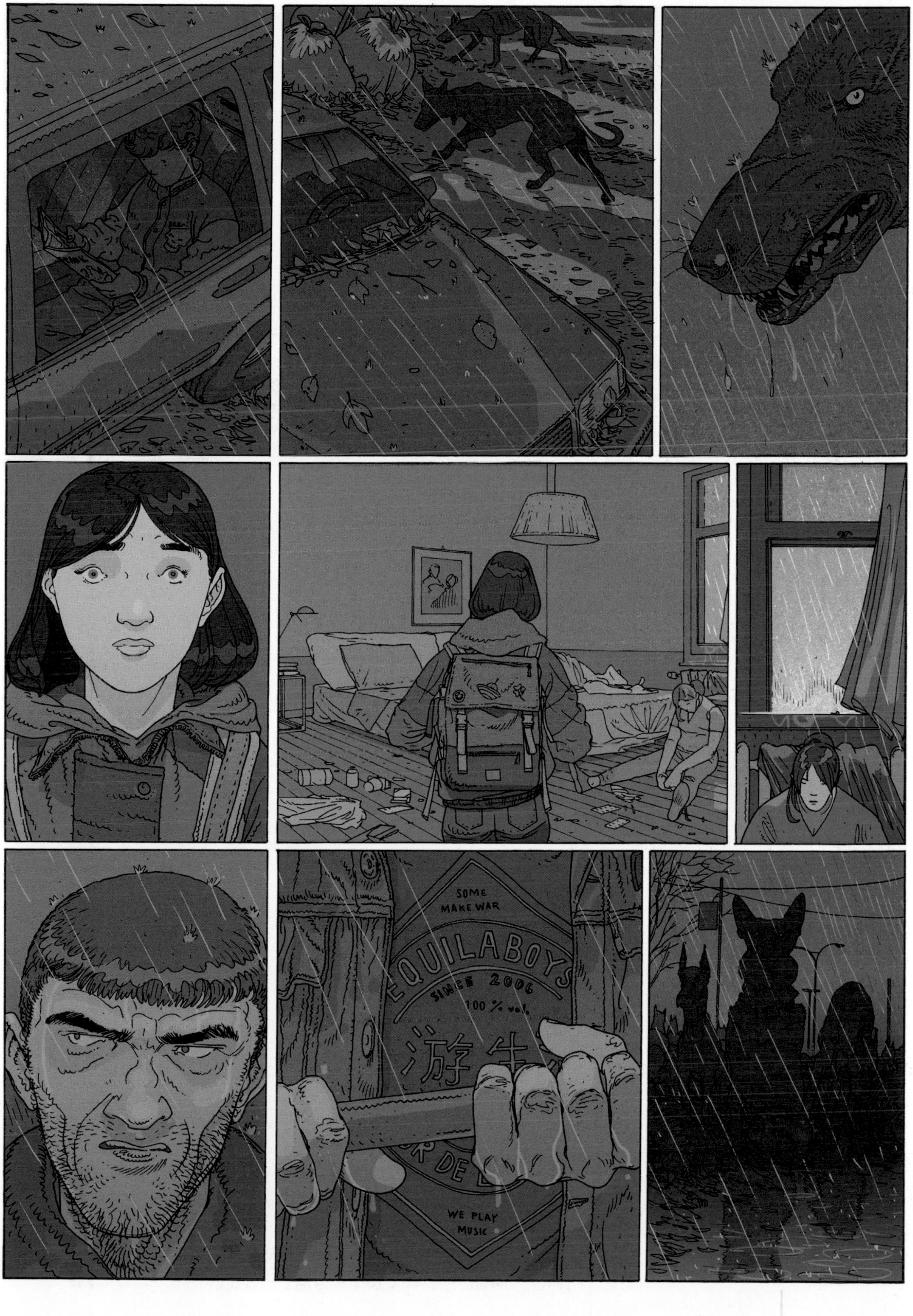
SOME MAKE WAR
EQUILABOYS
SINCE 2006
100 % vol.
WE PLAY MUSIC

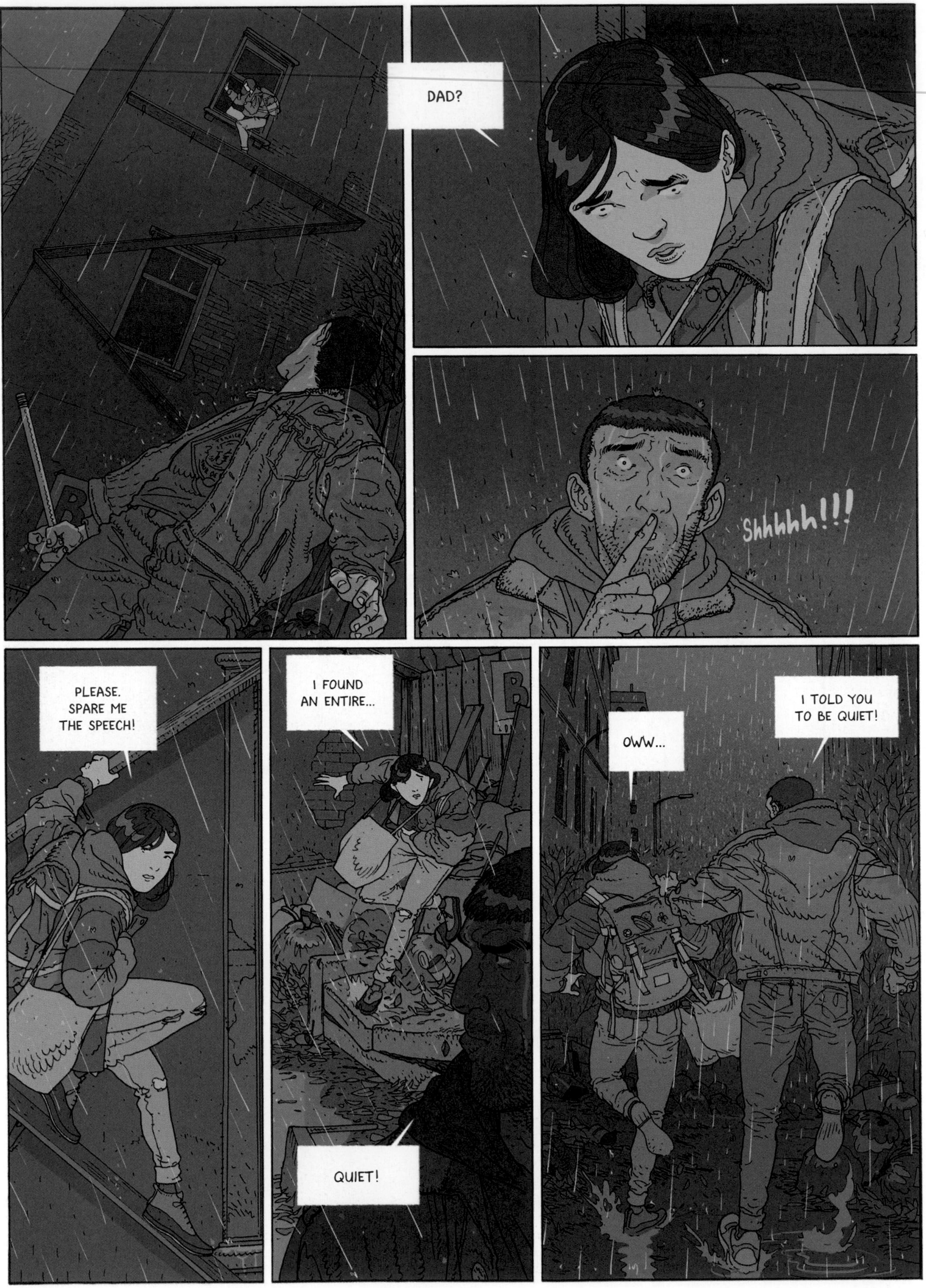
DAD?
Shhhhh!!!
PLEASE. SPARE ME THE SPEECH!
I FOUND AN ENTIRE...
QUIET!
OWW...
I TOLD YOU TO BE QUIET!

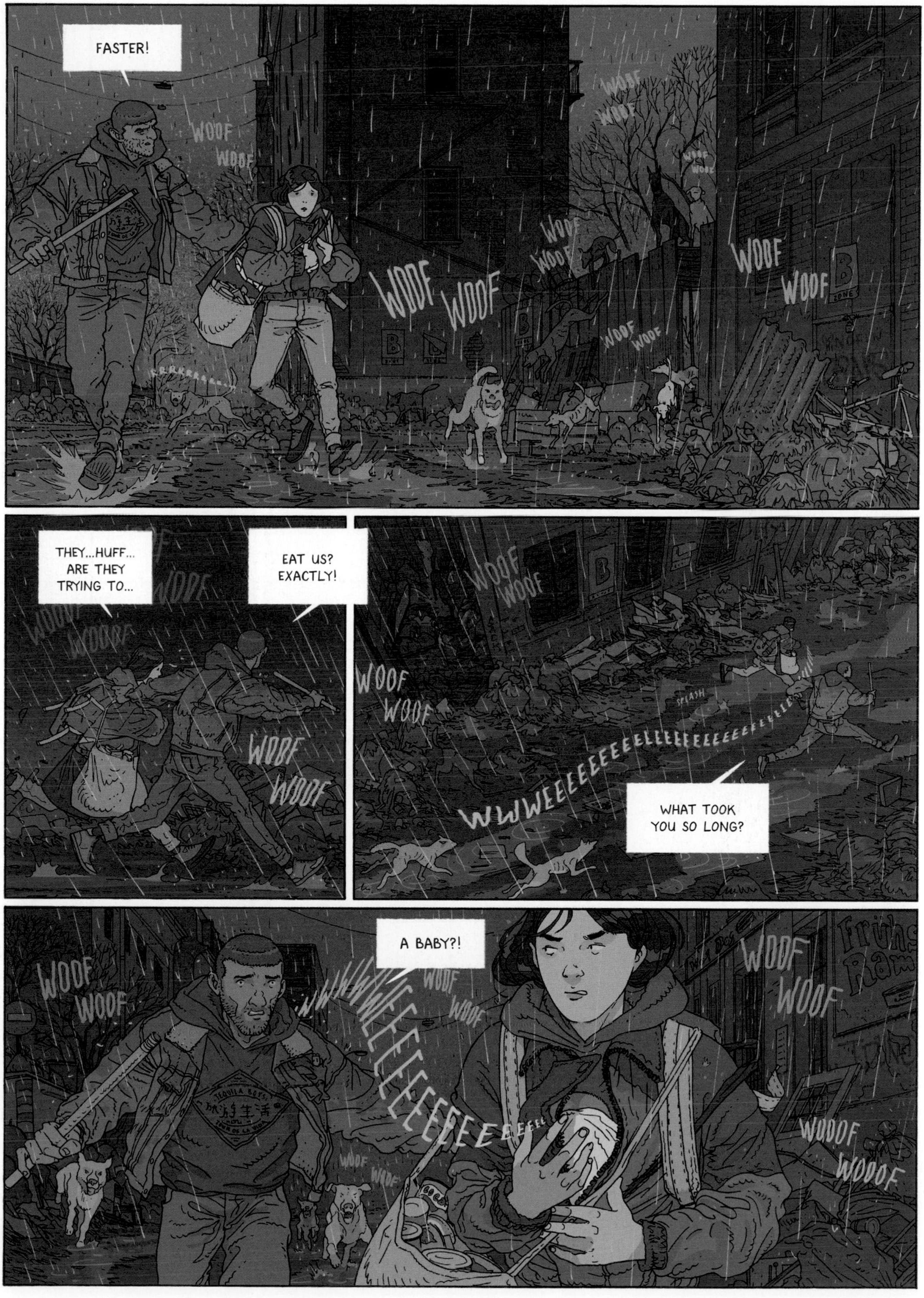

FASTER!
WOOF WOOF
WOOF WOOF
WOOF WOOF
WOOF WOOF
WOOF WOOF
WOOF WOOF
WOOF WOOF
THEY...HUFF... ARE THEY TRYING TO...
EAT US? EXACTLY!
WOOF WOOF
WOOF WOOF
WOOF WOOF
WOOF WOOF
SPLASH
WWWEEEEEEEEEEEEEEEEEEEEEE
WHAT TOOK YOU SO LONG?
A BABY?!
WOOF WOOF
WWWWWEEEEEEEEEEEEEEE
WOOF WOOF
WOOF WOOF
WOOOF WOOOF
WOOF WOOF

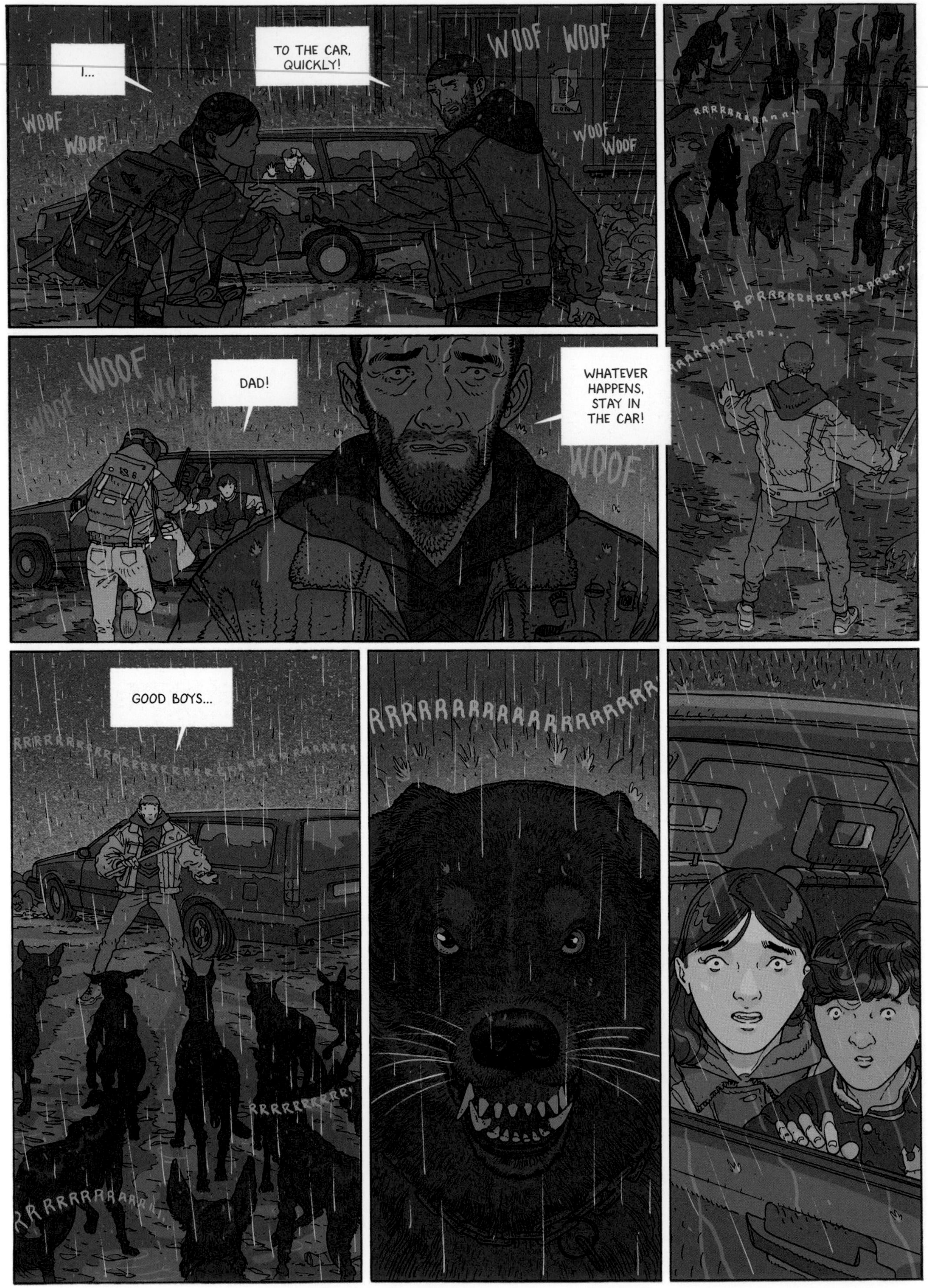
I...
TO THE CAR, QUICKLY!
WOOF WOOF
WOOF
WOOF
WOOF
WOOF
DAD!
WOOF
WHATEVER HAPPENS, STAY IN THE CAR!
WOOF
GOOD BOYS...
RRRRRRRRRRRRRRRRRRRR

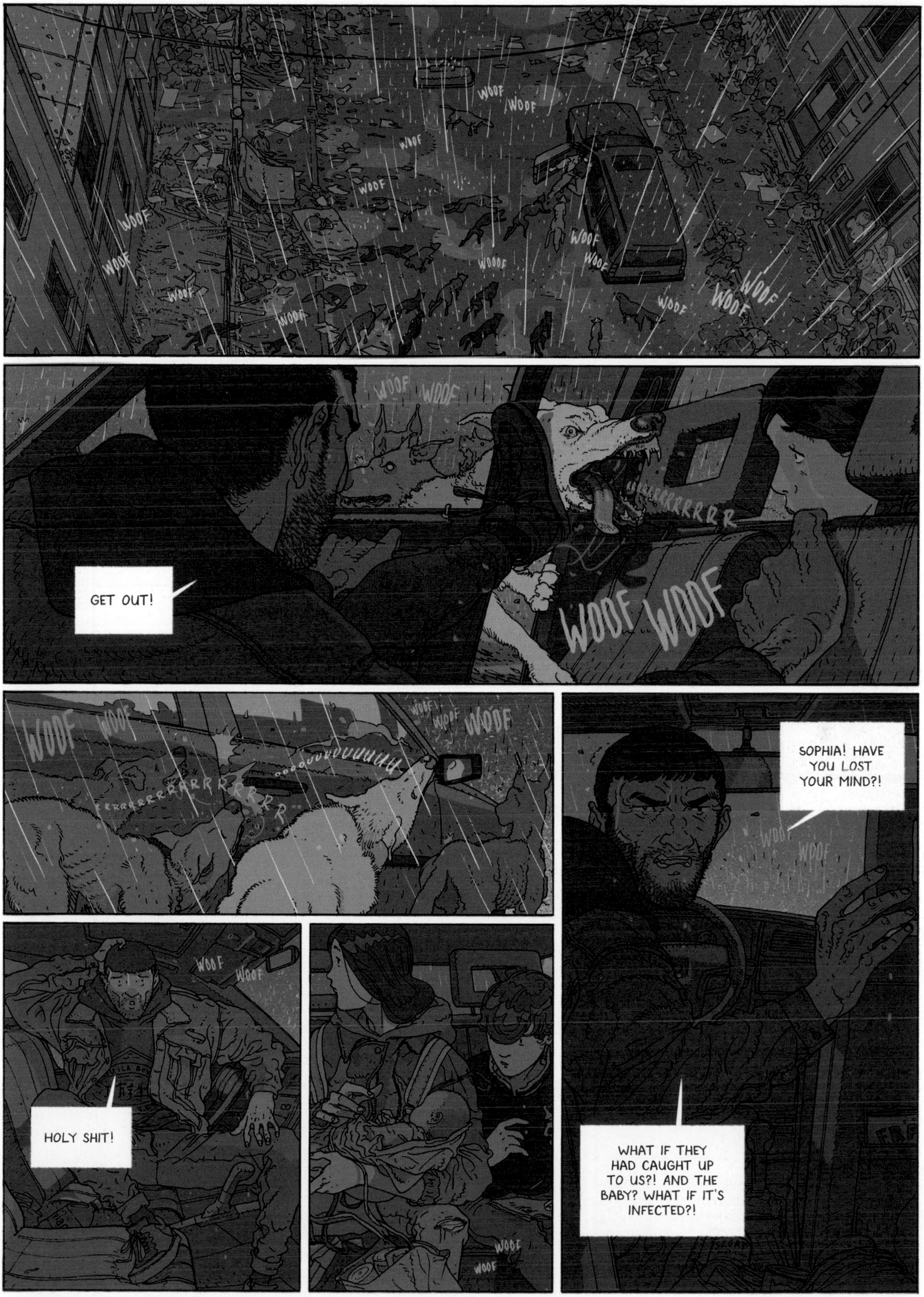
WOOF
WOOF
WOOF
WOOF
WOOF
WOOF
WOOF
WOOF
WOOF
WOOF WOOF
WOOF
WOOF
WOOF WOOF
GET OUT!
WOOF WOOF
WOOF WOOF
SOPHIA! HAVE YOU LOST YOUR MIND?!
WHAT IF THEY HAD CAUGHT UP TO US?! AND THE BABY? WHAT IF IT'S INFECTED?!
HOLY SHIT!
WOOF
WOOF
WOOF
WOOF

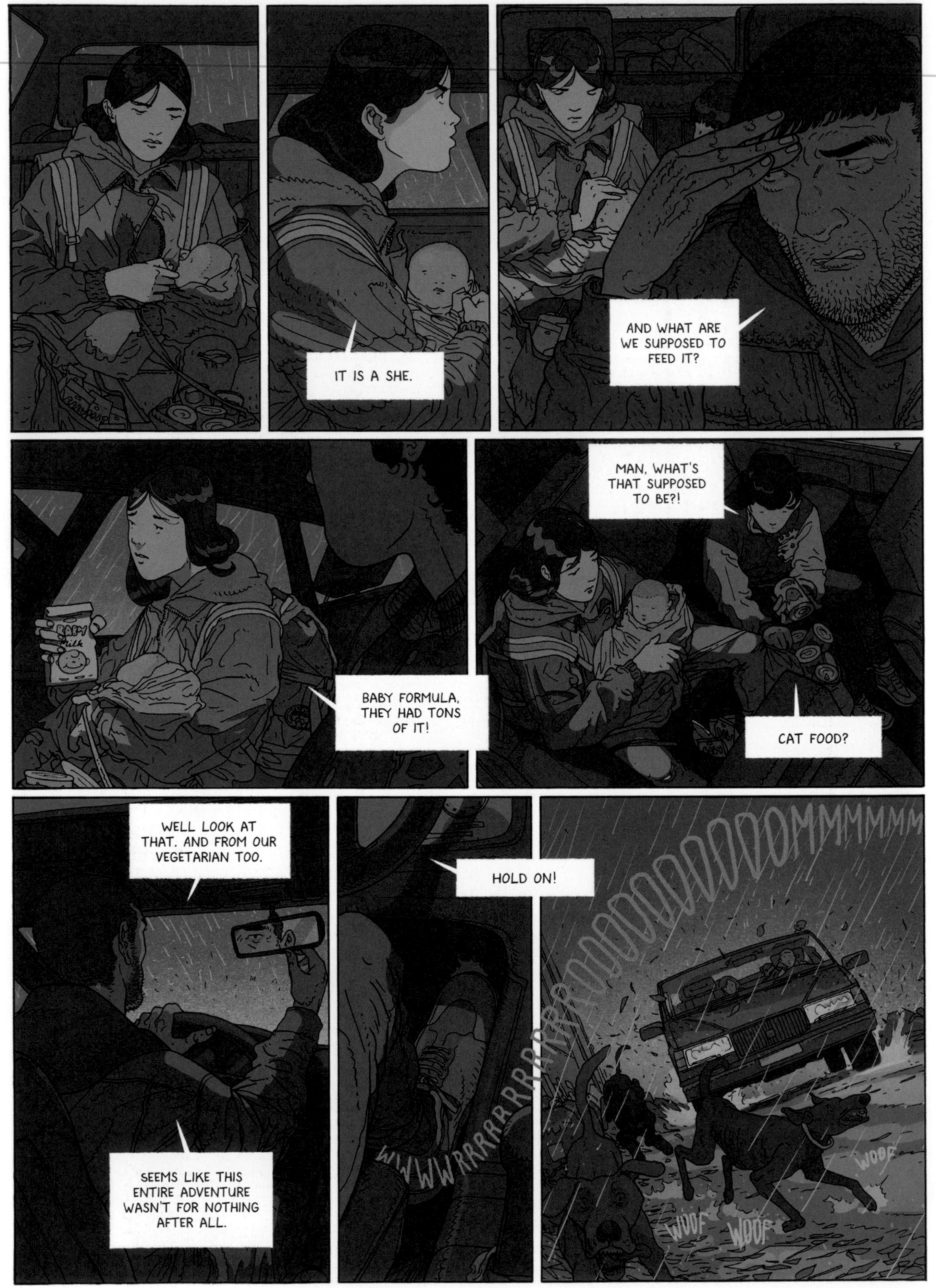
IT IS A SHE.
AND WHAT ARE WE SUPPOSED TO FEED IT?
BABY FORMULA, THEY HAD TONS OF IT!
MAN, WHAT'S THAT SUPPOSED TO BE?!
CAT FOOD?
WELL LOOK AT THAT. AND FROM OUR VEGETARIAN TOO.
SEEMS LIKE THIS ENTIRE ADVENTURE WASN'T FOR NOTHING AFTER ALL.
HOLD ON!
WWWWWRRRRRRRRRRRRROOOOOOOOOOOOOMMMMMM
WOOF
WOOF
WOOF

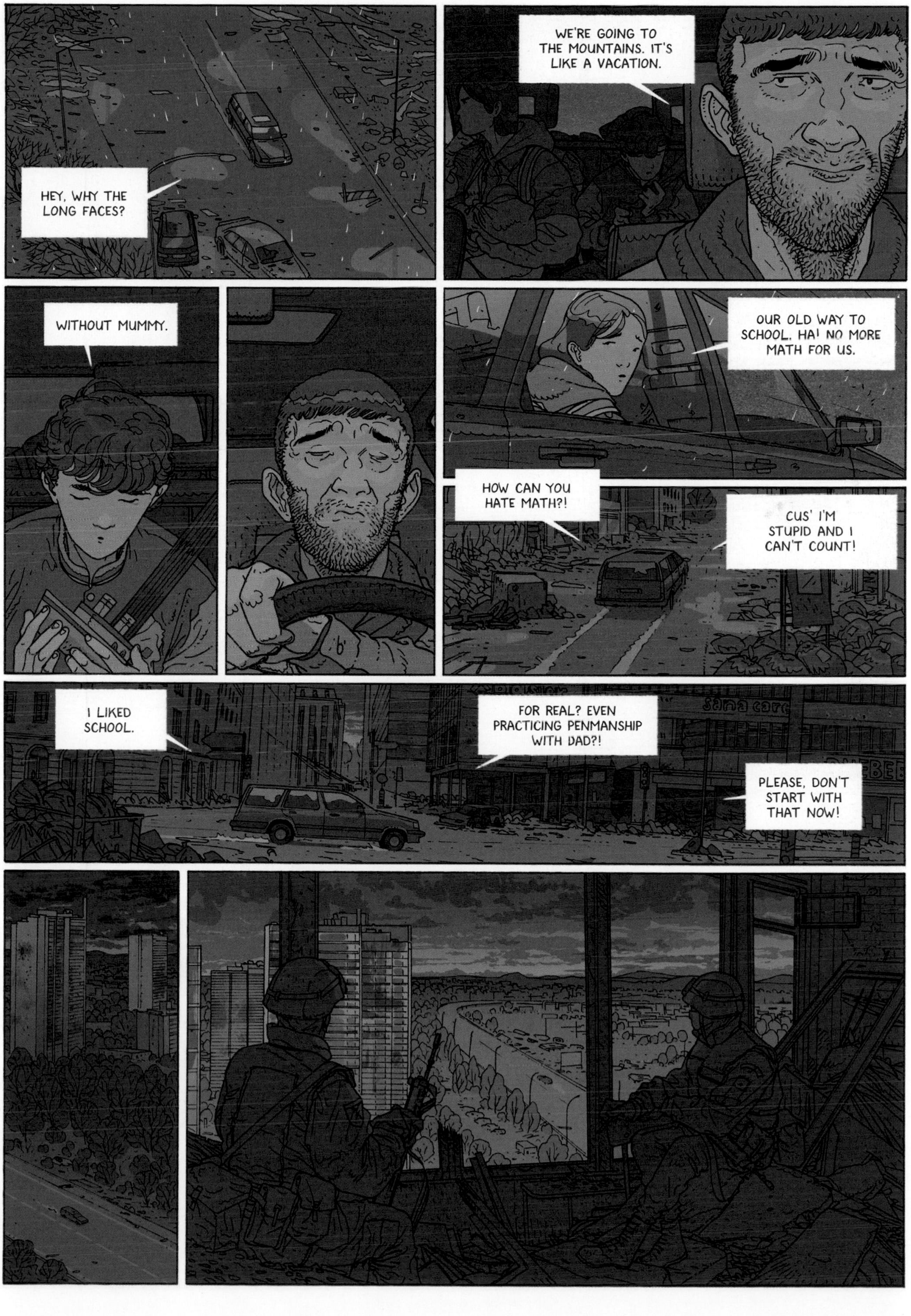
HEY, WHY THE LONG FACES?
WE'RE GOING TO THE MOUNTAINS. IT'S LIKE A VACATION.
WITHOUT MUMMY.
OUR OLD WAY TO SCHOOL. HA! NO MORE MATH FOR US.
HOW CAN YOU HATE MATH?!
CUS' I'M STUPID AND I CAN'T COUNT!
I LIKED SCHOOL.
FOR REAL? EVEN PRACTICING PENMANSHIP WITH DAD?!
PLEASE, DON'T START WITH THAT NOW!

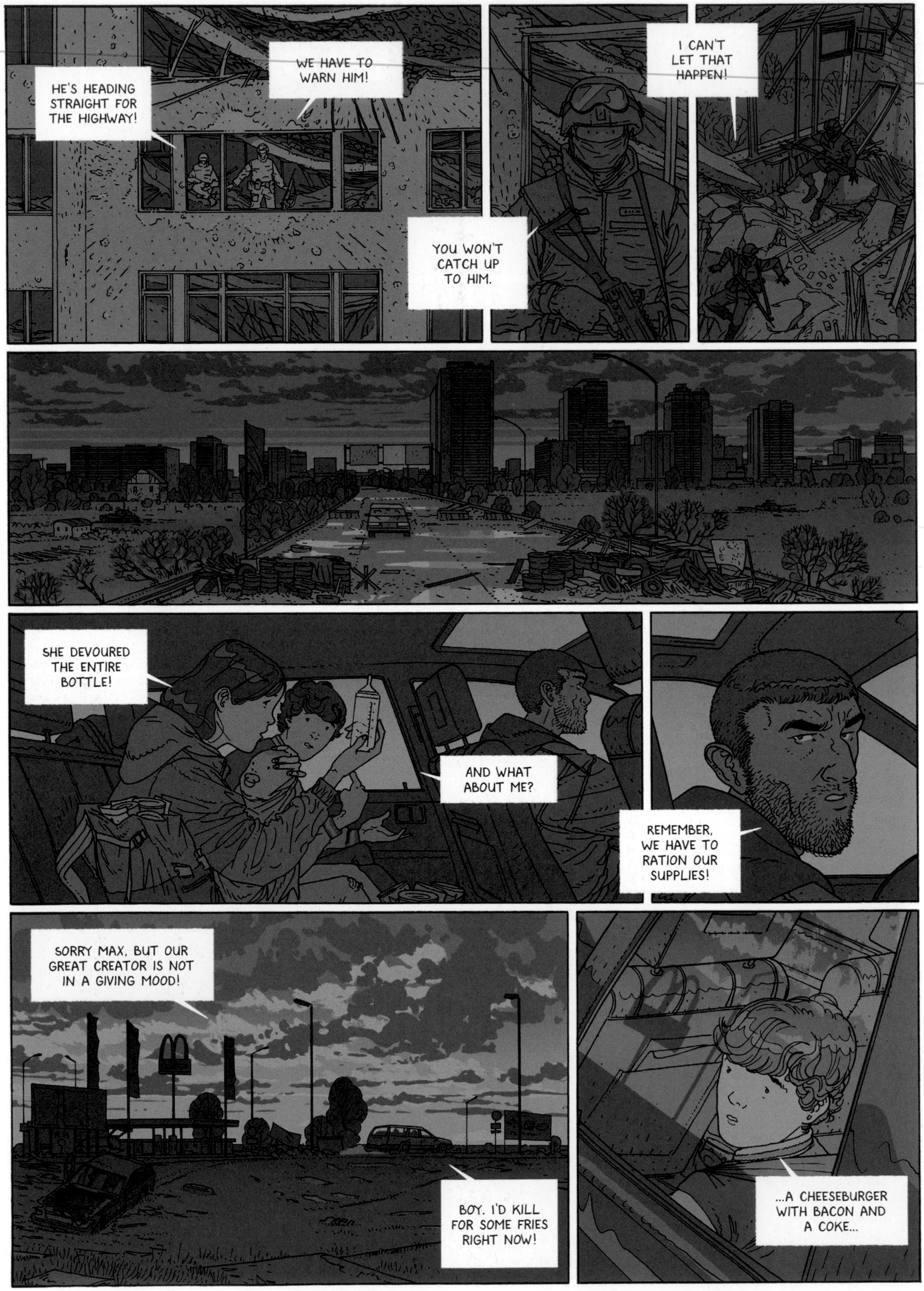
HE'S HEADING STRAIGHT FOR THE HIGHWAY!
WE HAVE TO WARN HIM!
YOU WON'T CATCH UP TO HIM.
I CAN'T LET THAT HAPPEN!
SHE DEVOURED THE ENTIRE BOTTLE!
AND WHAT ABOUT ME?
REMEMBER, WE HAVE TO RATION OUR SUPPLIES!
SORRY MAX, BUT OUR GREAT CREATOR IS NOT IN A GIVING MOOD!
BOY. I'D KILL FOR SOME FRIES RIGHT NOW!
...A CHEESEBURGER WITH BACON AND A COKE...

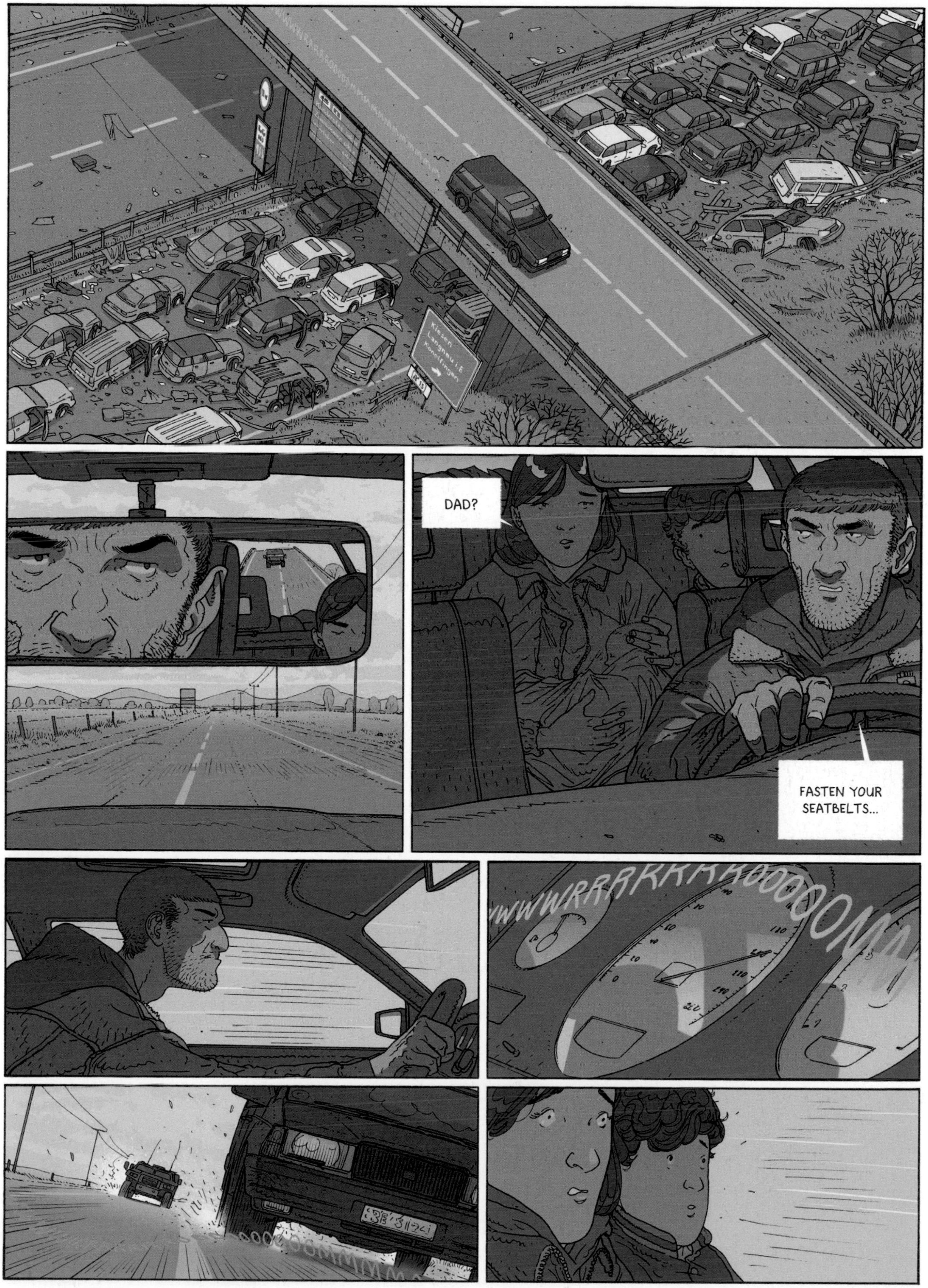
DAD?
FASTEN YOUR SEATBELTS...

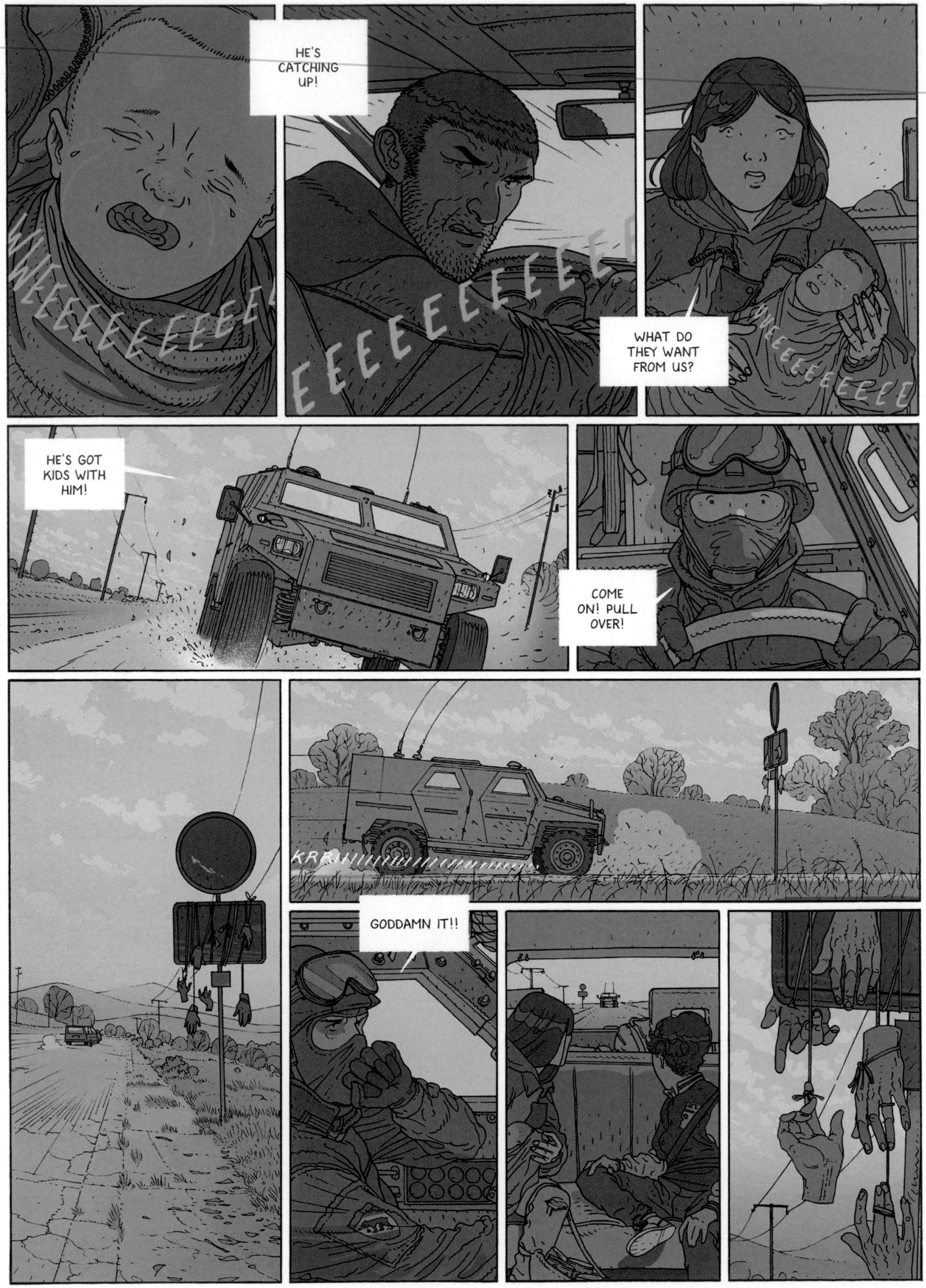
WHEEEEEEEEEEE
HE'S CATCHING UP!
EEEEEEEEEEEE
WHAT DO THEY WANT FROM US?
HE'S GOT KIDS WITH HIM!
COME ON! PULL OVER!
KRRNIIIIIIIIII
GODDAMN IT!!

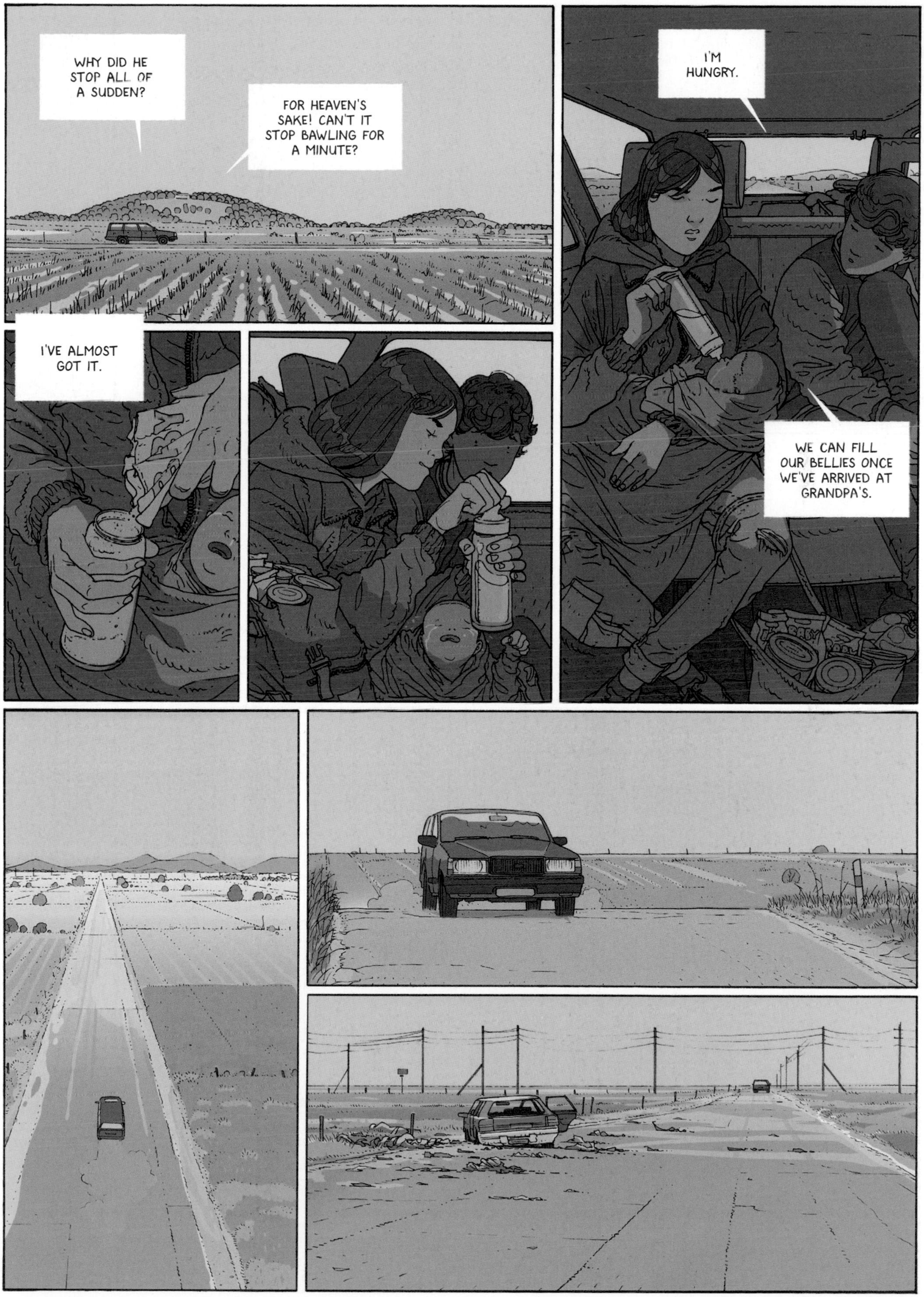
WHY DID HE STOP ALL OF A SUDDEN?
FOR HEAVEN'S SAKE! CAN'T IT STOP BAWLING FOR A MINUTE?
I'M HUNGRY.
WE CAN FILL OUR BELLIES ONCE WE'VE ARRIVED AT GRANDPA'S.
I'VE ALMOST GOT IT.

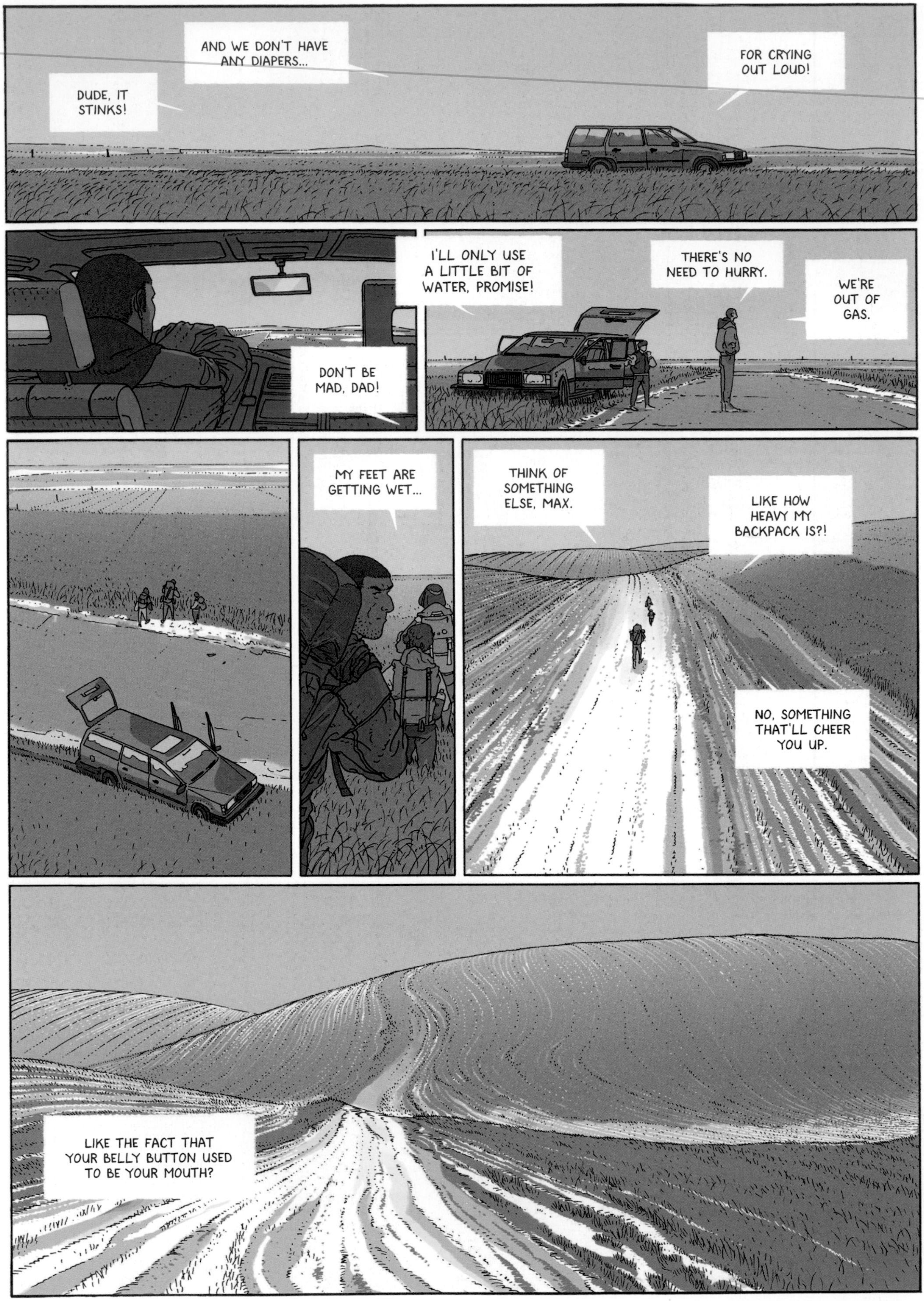
DUDE, IT STINKS!
AND WE DON'T HAVE ANY DIAPERS...
FOR CRYING OUT LOUD!
DON'T BE MAD, DAD!
I'LL ONLY USE A LITTLE BIT OF WATER, PROMISE!
THERE'S NO NEED TO HURRY.
WE'RE OUT OF GAS.
MY FEET ARE GETTING WET...
THINK OF SOMETHING ELSE, MAX.
LIKE HOW HEAVY MY BACKPACK IS?!
NO, SOMETHING THAT'LL CHEER YOU UP.
LIKE THE FACT THAT YOUR BELLY BUTTON USED TO BE YOUR MOUTH?

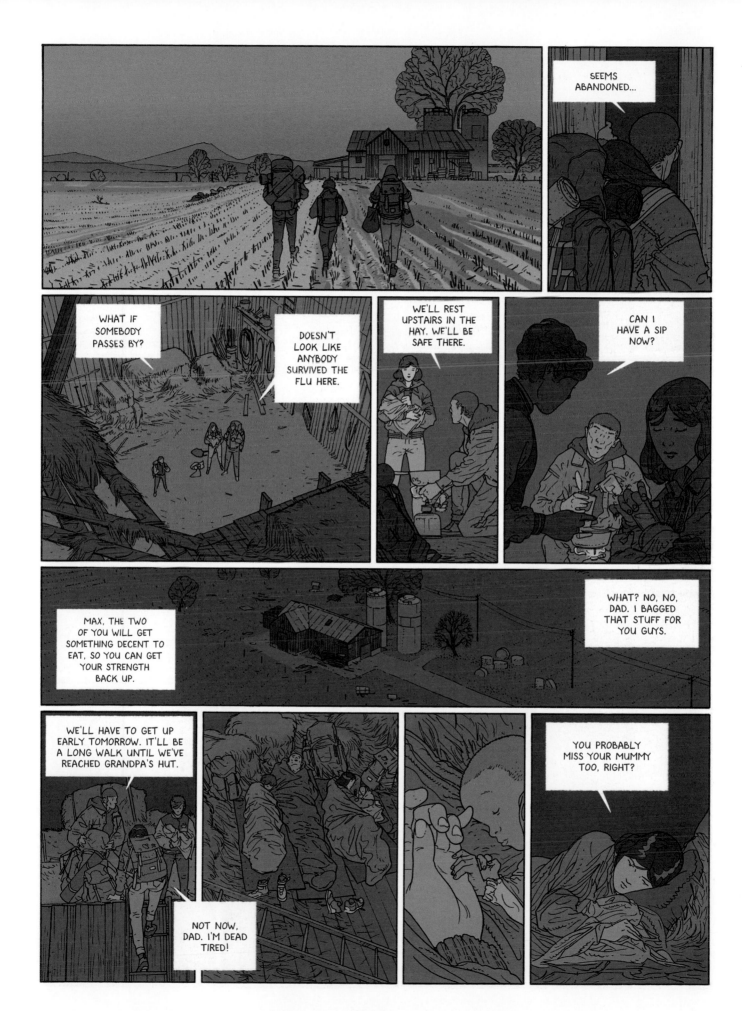

SEEMS ABANDONED...

WHAT IF SOMEBODY PASSES BY?

DOESN'T LOOK LIKE ANYBODY SURVIVED THE FLU HERE.

WE'LL REST UPSTAIRS IN THE HAY. WE'LL BE SAFE THERE.

CAN I HAVE A SIP NOW?

MAX, THE TWO OF YOU WILL GET SOMETHING DECENT TO EAT, SO YOU CAN GET YOUR STRENGTH BACK UP.

WHAT? NO, NO, DAD. I BAGGED THAT STUFF FOR YOU GUYS.

WE'LL HAVE TO GET UP EARLY TOMORROW. IT'LL BE A LONG WALK UNTIL WE'VE REACHED GRANDPA'S HUT.

NOT NOW, DAD. I'M DEAD TIRED!

YOU PROBABLY MISS YOUR MUMMY TOO, RIGHT?

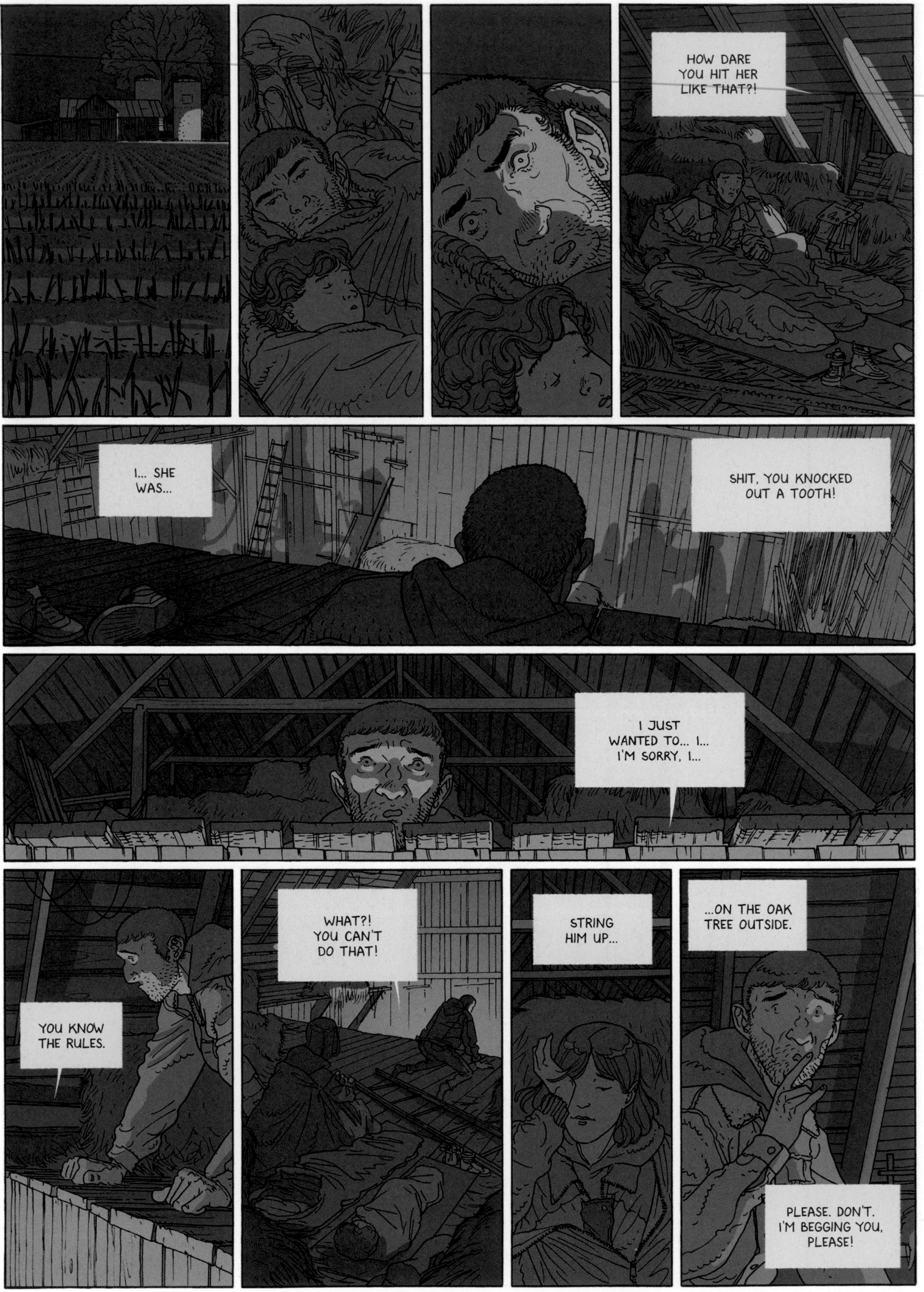
HOW DARE YOU HIT HER LIKE THAT?!
I... SHE WAS...
SHIT, YOU KNOCKED OUT A TOOTH!
I JUST WANTED TO... I... I'M SORRY, I...
YOU KNOW THE RULES.
WHAT?! YOU CAN'T DO THAT!
STRING HIM UP...
...ON THE OAK TREE OUTSIDE.
PLEASE. DON'T. I'M BEGGING YOU, PLEASE!

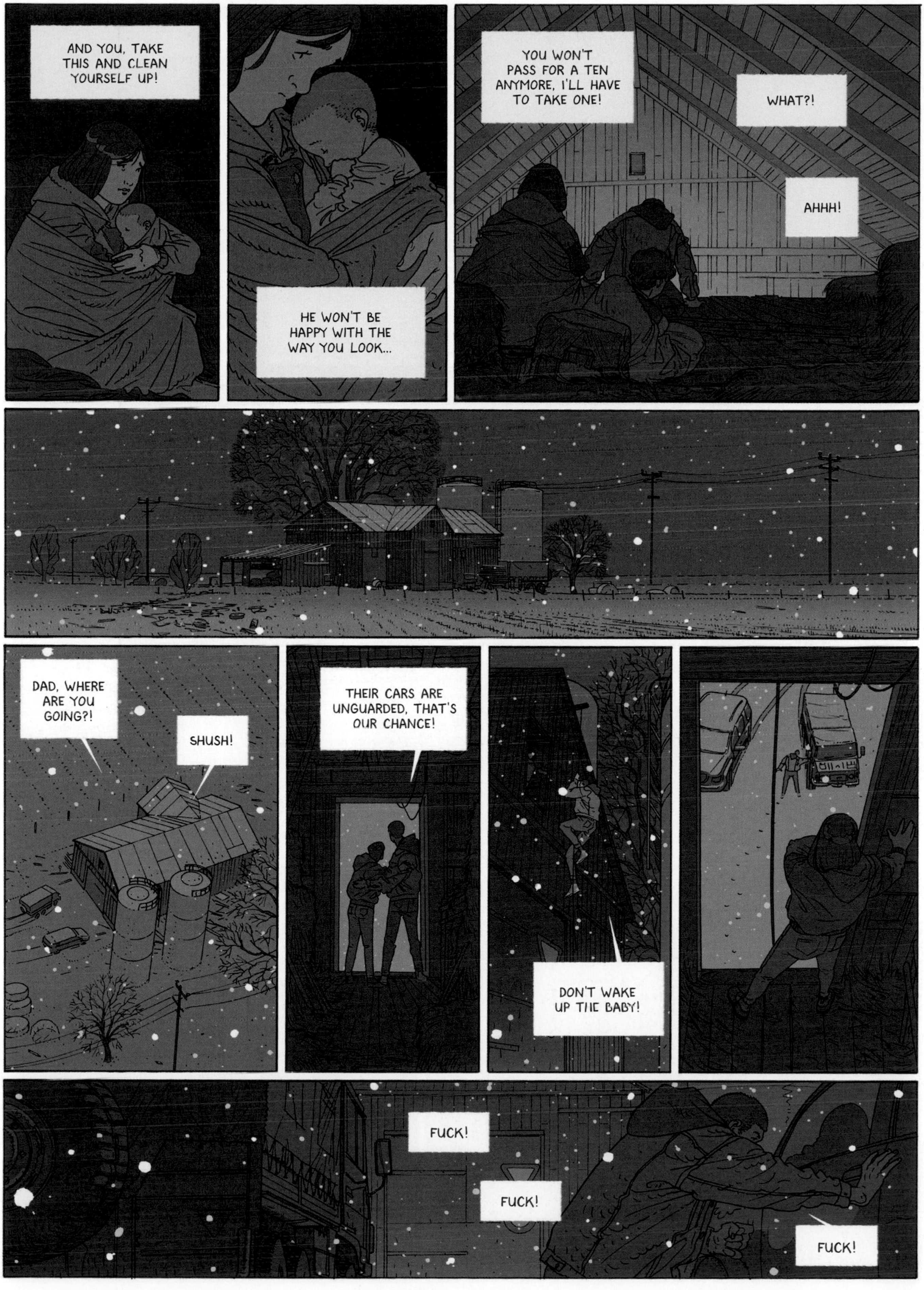
AND YOU, TAKE THIS AND CLEAN YOURSELF UP!
HE WON'T BE HAPPY WITH THE WAY YOU LOOK...
YOU WON'T PASS FOR A TEN ANYMORE, I'LL HAVE TO TAKE ONE!
WHAT?!
AHHH!
DAD, WHERE ARE YOU GOING?!
SHUSH!
THEIR CARS ARE UNGUARDED, THAT'S OUR CHANCE!
DON'T WAKE UP THE BABY!
FUCK!
FUCK!
FUCK!

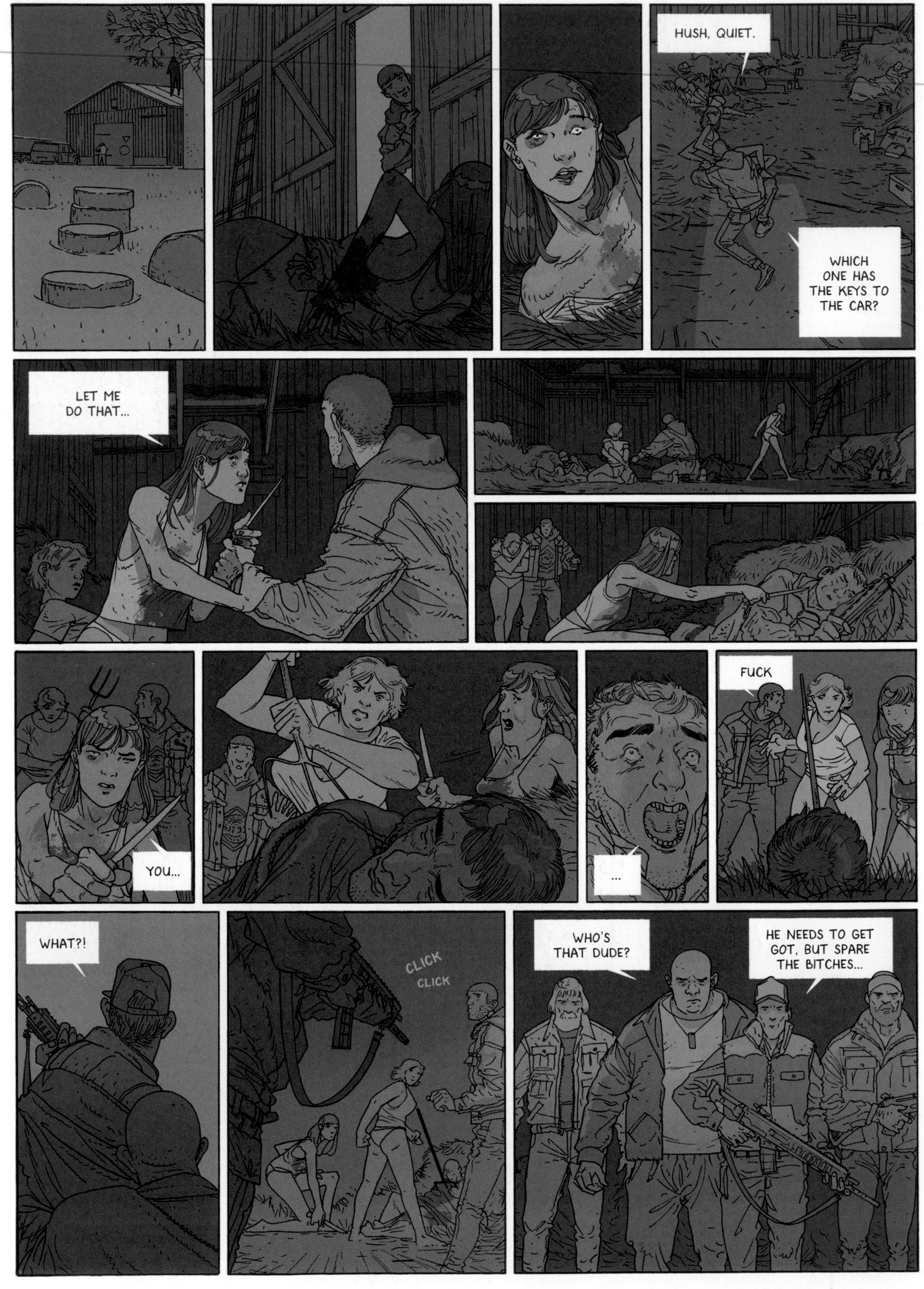
HUSH, QUIET.
WHICH ONE HAS THE KEYS TO THE CAR?
LET ME DO THAT...
YOU...
...
FUCK
WHAT?!
CLICK
CLICK
WHO'S THAT DUDE?
HE NEEDS TO GET GOT, BUT SPARE THE BITCHES...

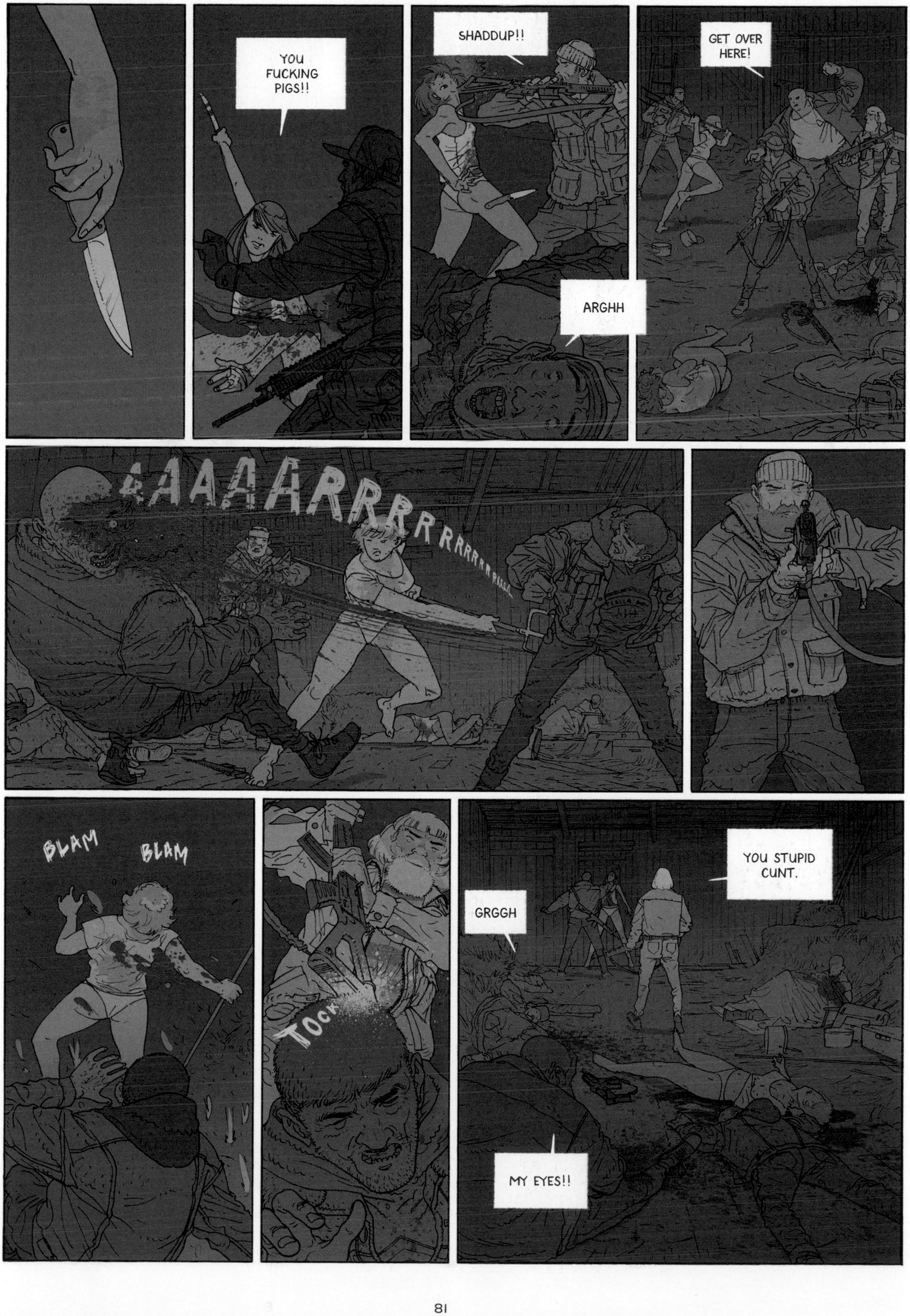
YOU FUCKING PIGS!!
SHADDUP!!
ARGHH
GET OVER HERE!
AAAAARRRRRrrrrrrrr
BLAM
BLAM
TOCK
YOU STUPID CUNT.
GRGGH
MY EYES!!

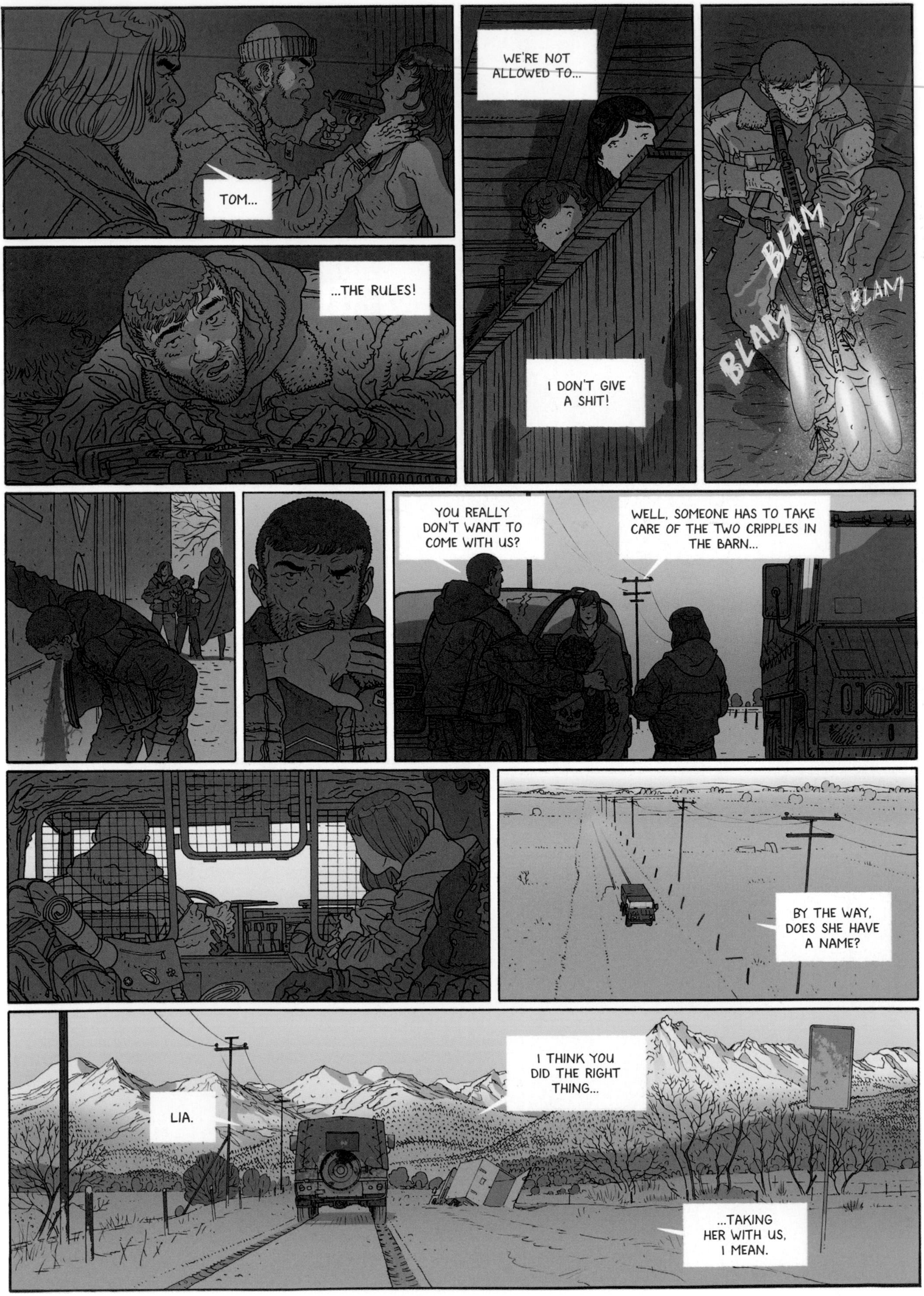

TOM...
...THE RULES!
WE'RE NOT ALLOWED TO...
I DON'T GIVE A SHIT!
BLAM
BLAM
BLAM
YOU REALLY DON'T WANT TO COME WITH US?
WELL, SOMEONE HAS TO TAKE CARE OF THE TWO CRIPPLES IN THE BARN...
BY THE WAY, DOES SHE HAVE A NAME?
LIA.
I THINK YOU DID THE RIGHT THING...
...TAKING HER WITH US, I MEAN.

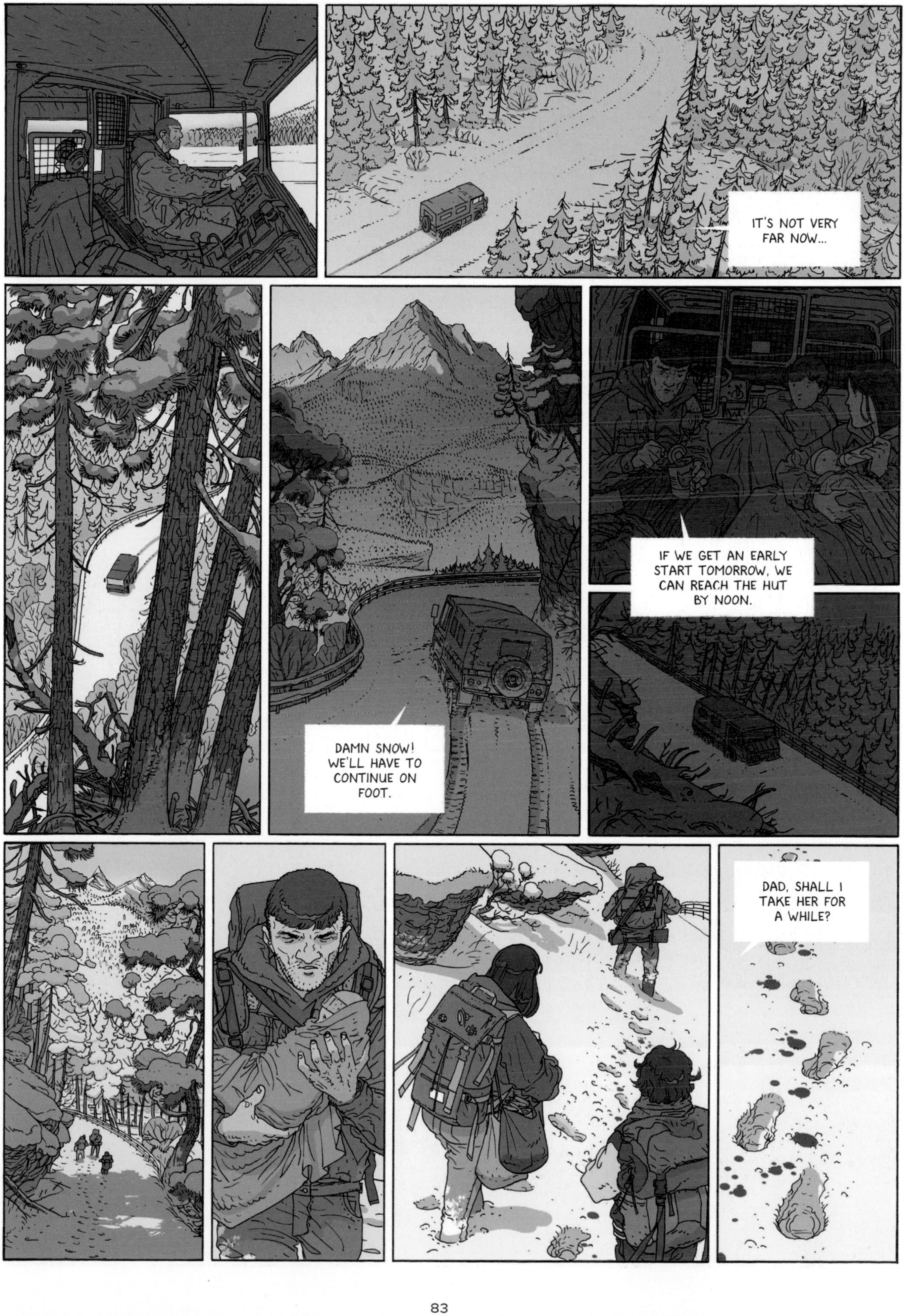
IT'S NOT VERY FAR NOW...
DAMN SNOW! WE'LL HAVE TO CONTINUE ON FOOT.
IF WE GET AN EARLY START TOMORROW, WE CAN REACH THE HUT BY NOON.
DAD, SHALL I TAKE HER FOR A WHILE?

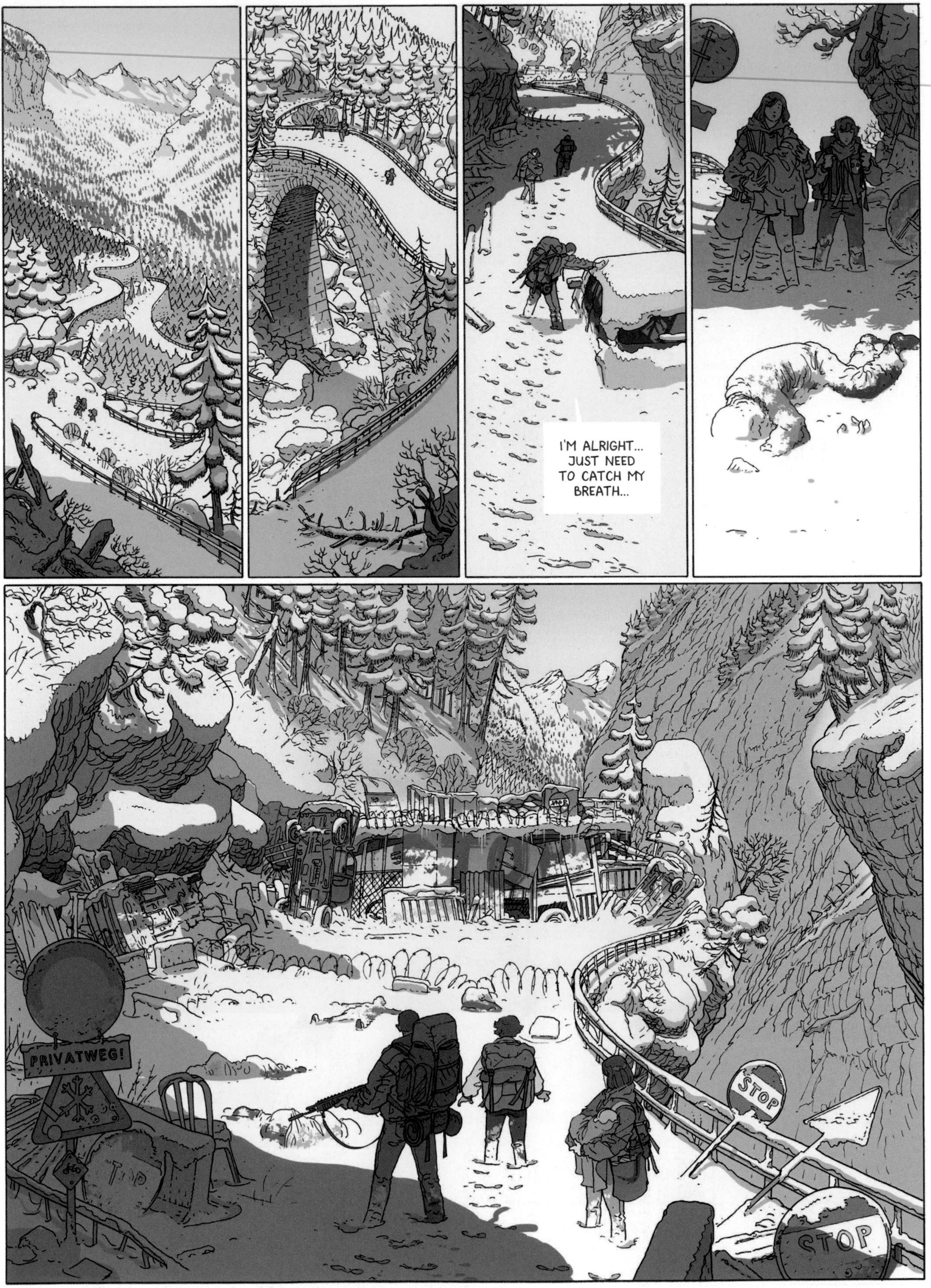
I'M ALRIGHT... JUST NEED TO CATCH MY BREATH...
PRIVATWEG!
STOP
STOP

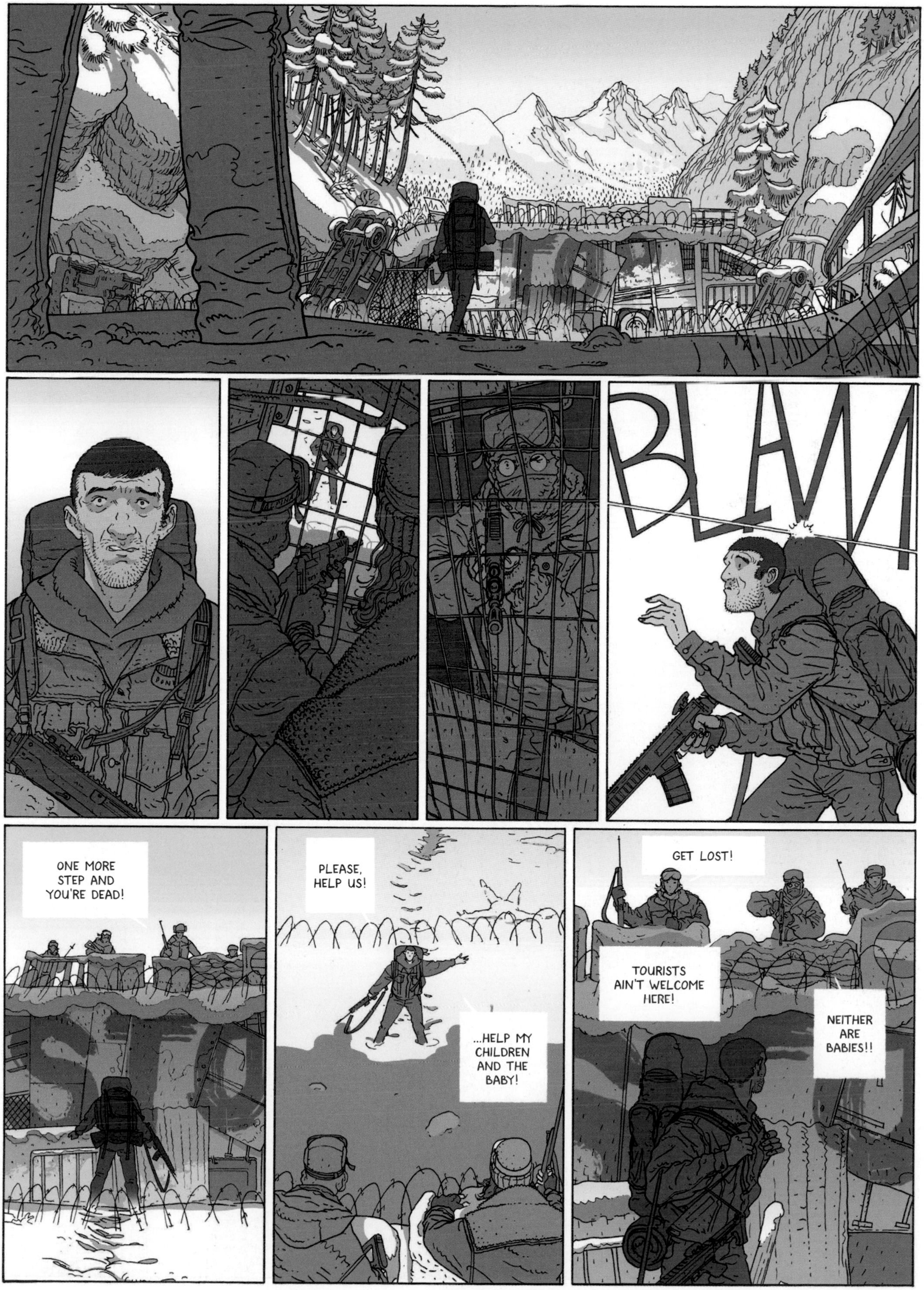
BLAM
ONE MORE STEP AND YOU'RE DEAD!
PLEASE, HELP US!
...HELP MY CHILDREN AND THE BABY!
GET LOST!
TOURISTS AIN'T WELCOME HERE!
NEITHER ARE BABIES!!

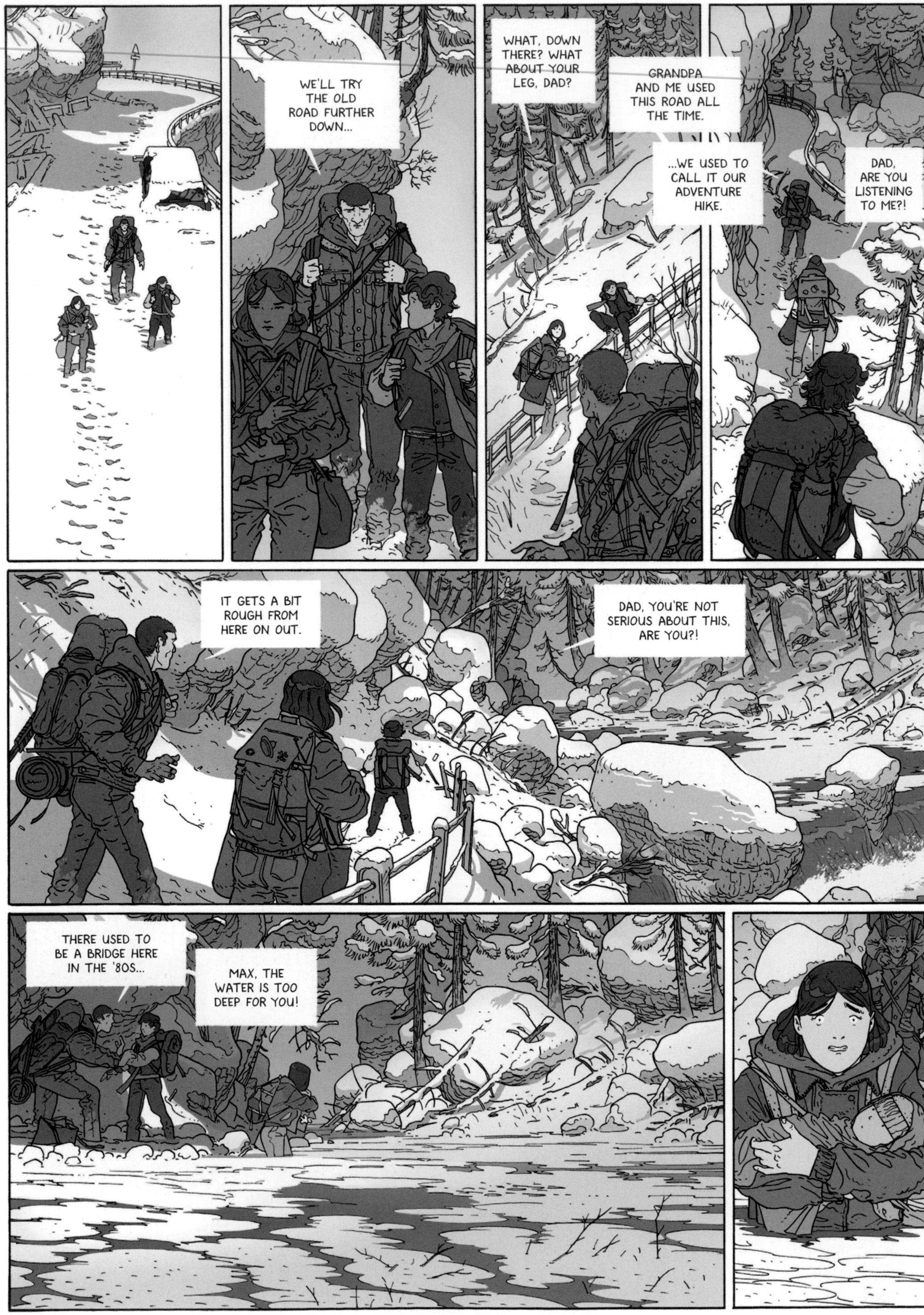
WE'LL TRY THE OLD ROAD FURTHER DOWN...
WHAT, DOWN THERE? WHAT ABOUT YOUR LEG, DAD?
GRANDPA AND ME USED THIS ROAD ALL THE TIME.
...WE USED TO CALL IT OUR ADVENTURE HIKE.
DAD, ARE YOU LISTENING TO ME?!
IT GETS A BIT ROUGH FROM HERE ON OUT.
DAD, YOU'RE NOT SERIOUS ABOUT THIS, ARE YOU?!
THERE USED TO BE A BRIDGE HERE IN THE '80S...
MAX, THE WATER IS TOO DEEP FOR YOU!

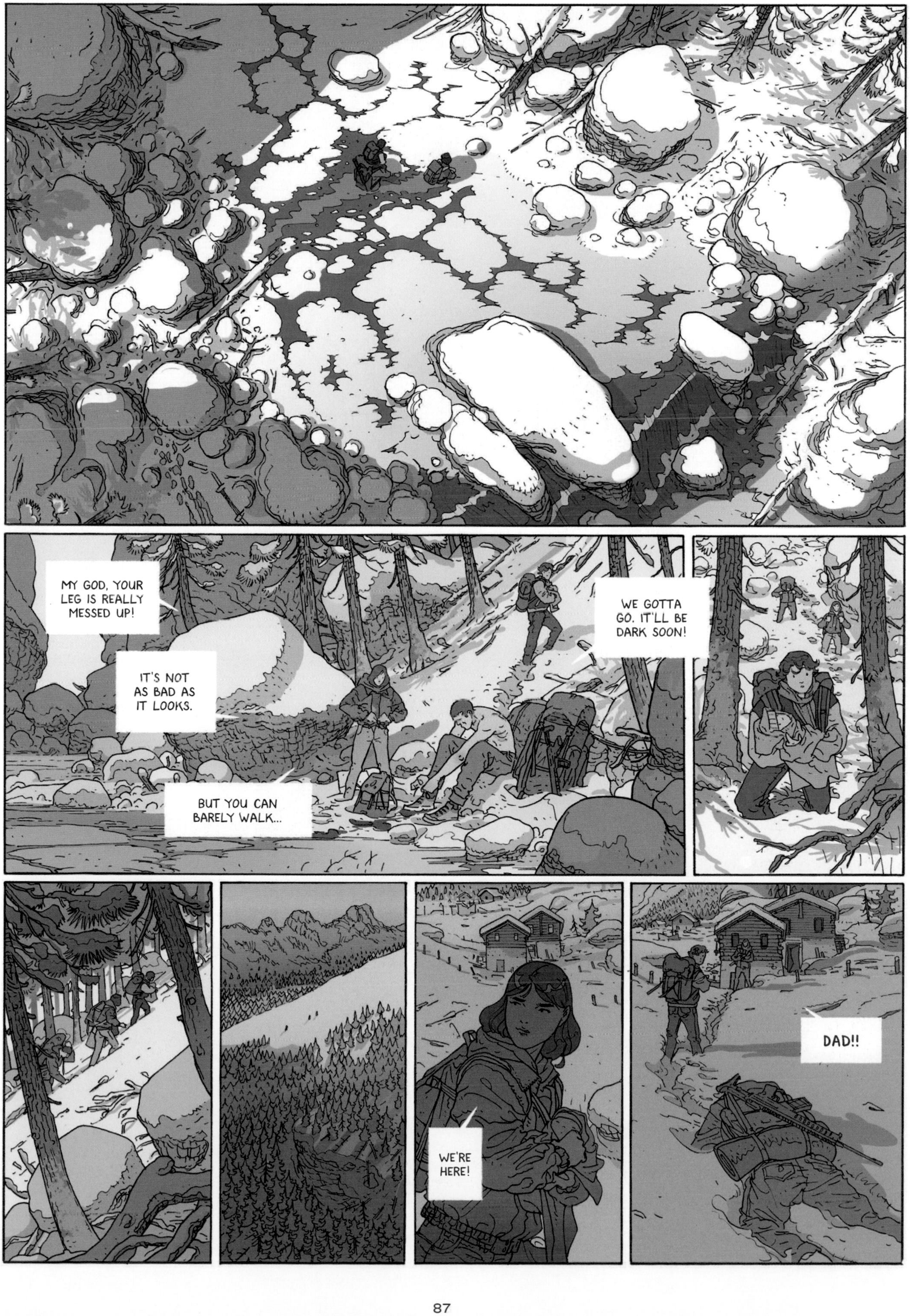
MY GOD, YOUR LEG IS REALLY MESSED UP!
IT'S NOT AS BAD AS IT LOOKS.
BUT YOU CAN BARELY WALK...
WE GOTTA GO. IT'LL BE DARK SOON!
WE'RE HERE!
DAD!!

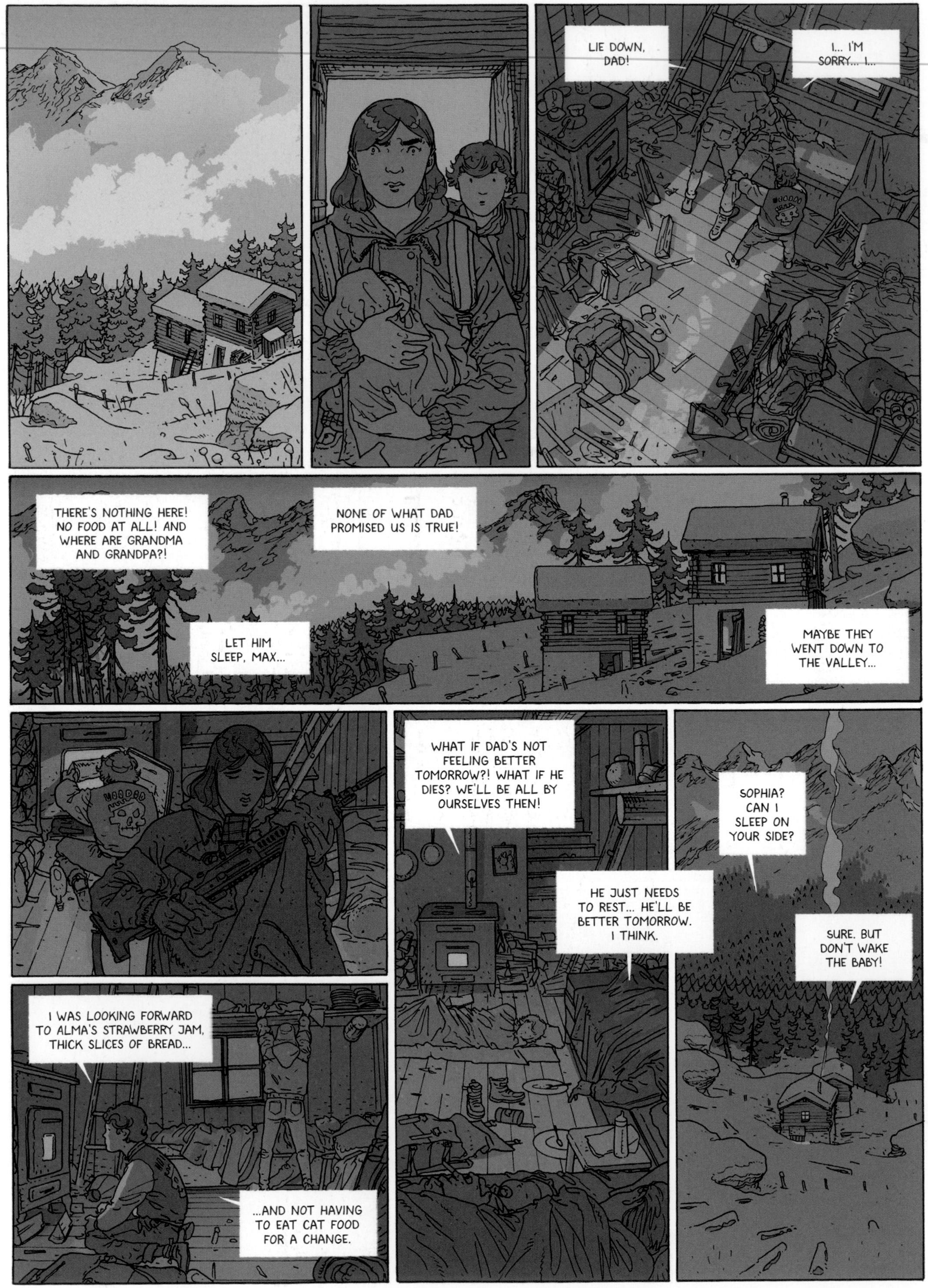
LIE DOWN, DAD!
I... I'M SORRY... I...
THERE'S NOTHING HERE! NO FOOD AT ALL! AND WHERE ARE GRANDMA AND GRANDPA?!
NONE OF WHAT DAD PROMISED US IS TRUE!
LET HIM SLEEP, MAX...
MAYBE THEY WENT DOWN TO THE VALLEY...
I WAS LOOKING FORWARD TO ALMA'S STRAWBERRY JAM, THICK SLICES OF BREAD...
...AND NOT HAVING TO EAT CAT FOOD FOR A CHANGE.
WHAT IF DAD'S NOT FEELING BETTER TOMORROW?! WHAT IF HE DIES? WE'LL BE ALL BY OURSELVES THEN!
HE JUST NEEDS TO REST... HE'LL BE BETTER TOMORROW. I THINK.
SOPHIA? CAN I SLEEP ON YOUR SIDE?
SURE. BUT DON'T WAKE THE BABY!

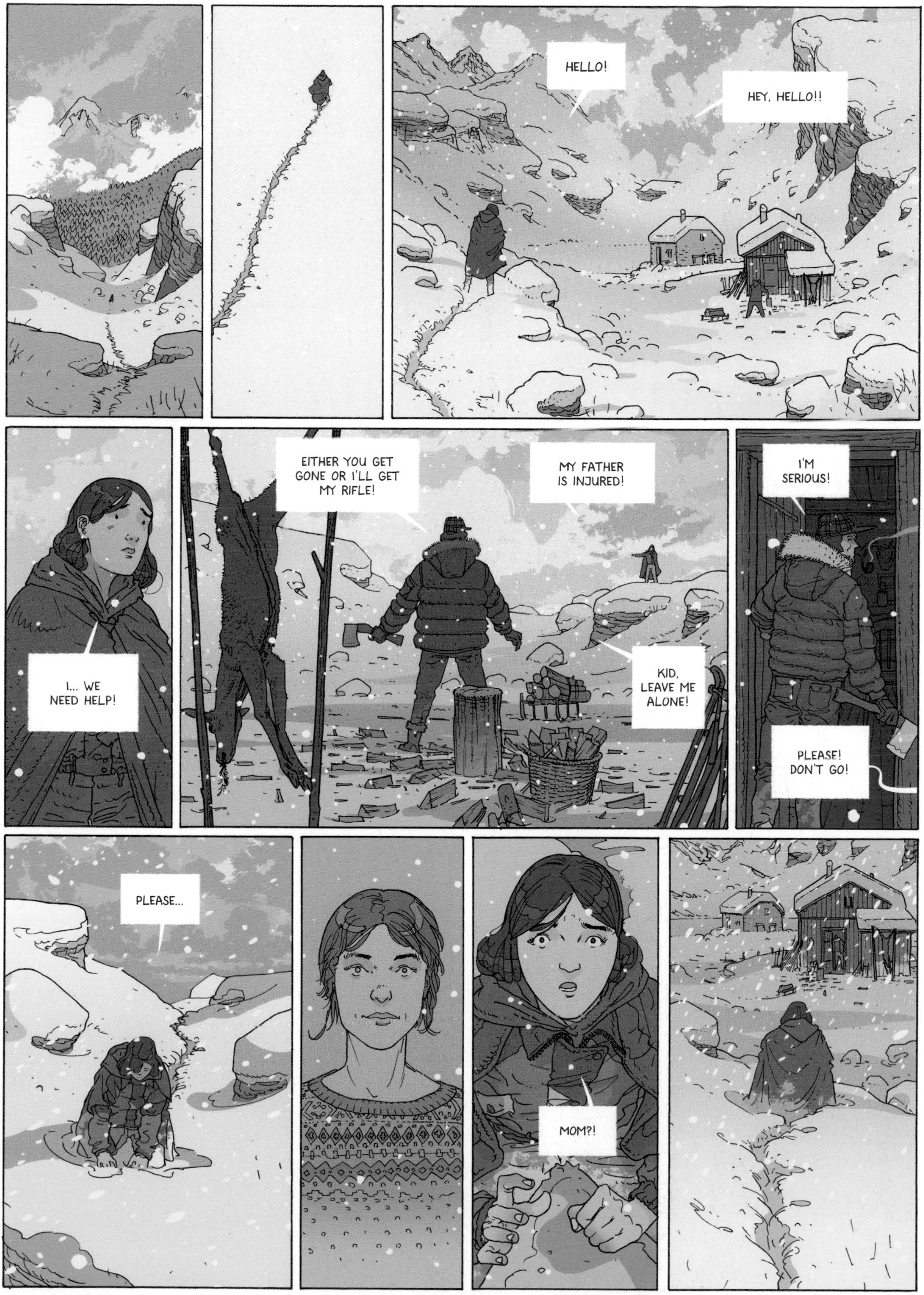
HELLO!
HEY, HELLO!!
I... WE NEED HELP!
EITHER YOU GET GONE OR I'LL GET MY RIFLE!
MY FATHER IS INJURED!
KID, LEAVE ME ALONE!
I'M SERIOUS!
PLEASE! DON'T GO!
PLEASE...
MOM?!

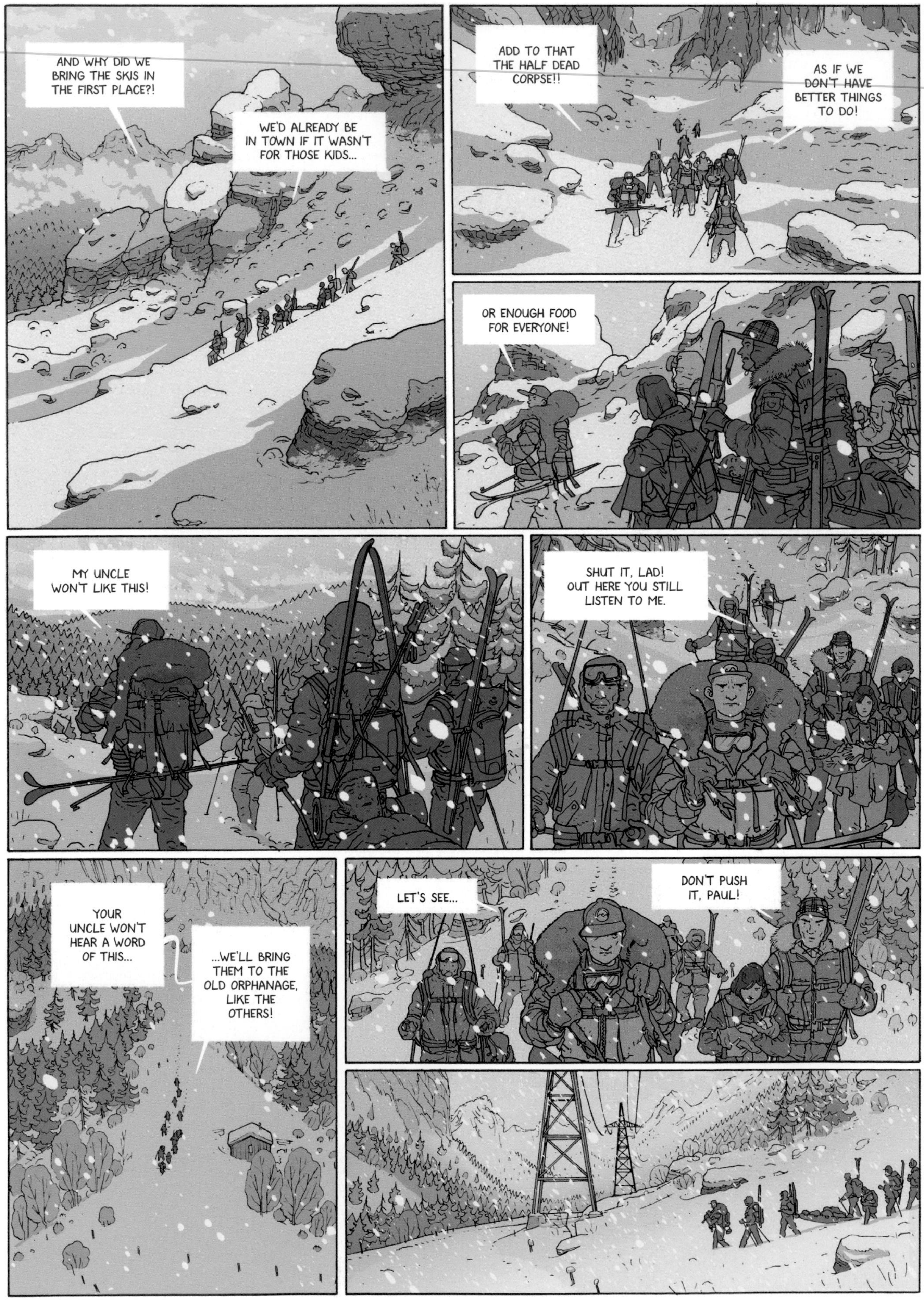
AND WHY DID WE BRING THE SKIS IN THE FIRST PLACE?!
WE'D ALREADY BE IN TOWN IF IT WASN'T FOR THOSE KIDS...
ADD TO THAT THE HALF DEAD CORPSE!!
AS IF WE DON'T HAVE BETTER THINGS TO DO!
OR ENOUGH FOOD FOR EVERYONE!
MY UNCLE WON'T LIKE THIS!
SHUT IT, LAD! OUT HERE YOU STILL LISTEN TO ME.
YOUR UNCLE WON'T HEAR A WORD OF THIS...
...WE'LL BRING THEM TO THE OLD ORPHANAGE, LIKE THE OTHERS!
LET'S SEE...
DON'T PUSH IT, PAUL!

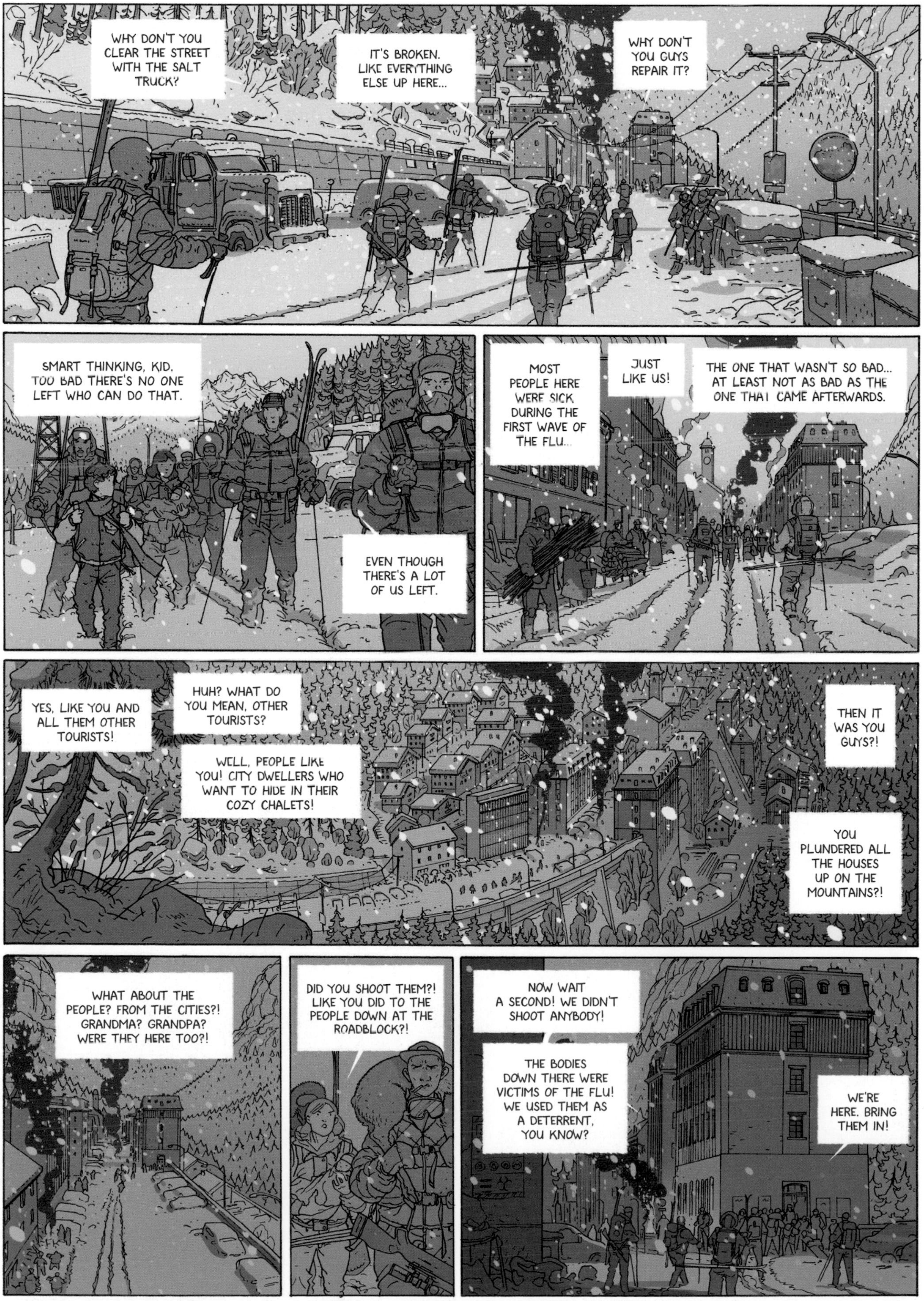

WHY DON'T YOU CLEAR THE STREET WITH THE SALT TRUCK?
IT'S BROKEN. LIKE EVERYTHING ELSE UP HERE...
WHY DON'T YOU GUYS REPAIR IT?
SMART THINKING, KID. TOO BAD THERE'S NO ONE LEFT WHO CAN DO THAT.
EVEN THOUGH THERE'S A LOT OF US LEFT.
MOST PEOPLE HERE WERE SICK DURING THE FIRST WAVE OF THE FLU...
JUST LIKE US!
THE ONE THAT WASN'T SO BAD... AT LEAST NOT AS BAD AS THE ONE THAT CAME AFTERWARDS.
YES, LIKE YOU AND ALL THEM OTHER TOURISTS!
HUH? WHAT DO YOU MEAN, OTHER TOURISTS?
WELL, PEOPLE LIKE YOU! CITY DWELLERS WHO WANT TO HIDE IN THEIR COZY CHALETS!
THEN IT WAS YOU GUYS?!
YOU PLUNDERED ALL THE HOUSES UP ON THE MOUNTAINS?!
WHAT ABOUT THE PEOPLE? FROM THE CITIES?! GRANDMA? GRANDPA? WERE THEY HERE TOO?!
DID YOU SHOOT THEM?! LIKE YOU DID TO THE PEOPLE DOWN AT THE ROADBLOCK?!
NOW WAIT A SECOND! WE DIDN'T SHOOT ANYBODY!
THE BODIES DOWN THERE WERE VICTIMS OF THE FLU! WE USED THEM AS A DETERRENT, YOU KNOW?
WE'RE HERE. BRING THEM IN!

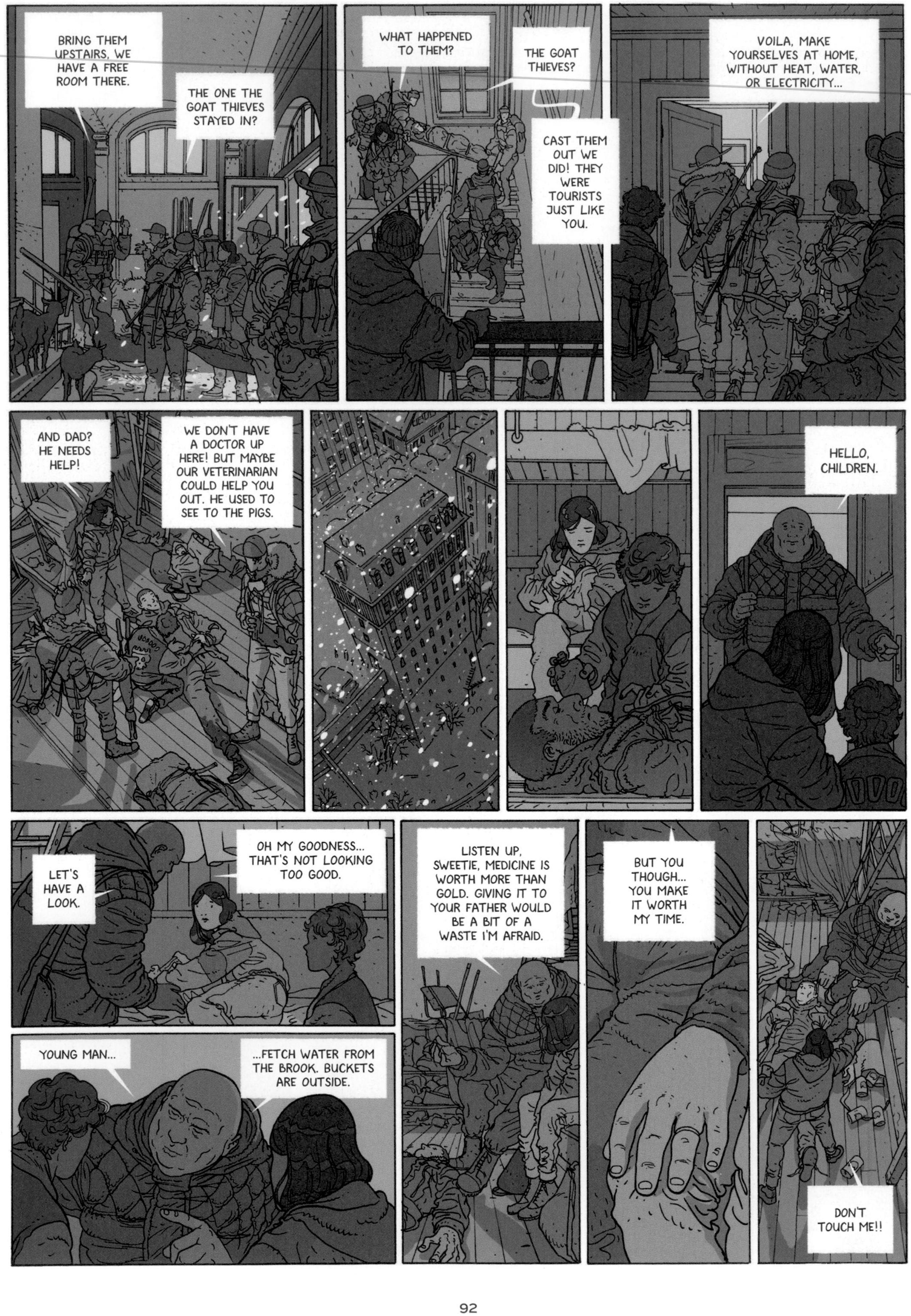

BRING THEM UPSTAIRS, WE HAVE A FREE ROOM THERE.
THE ONE THE GOAT THIEVES STAYED IN?
WHAT HAPPENED TO THEM?
THE GOAT THIEVES?
CAST THEM OUT WE DID! THEY WERE TOURISTS JUST LIKE YOU.
VOILA, MAKE YOURSELVES AT HOME, WITHOUT HEAT, WATER, OR ELECTRICITY...
AND DAD? HE NEEDS HELP!
WE DON'T HAVE A DOCTOR UP HERE! BUT MAYBE OUR VETERINARIAN COULD HELP YOU OUT. HE USED TO SEE TO THE PIGS.
HELLO, CHILDREN.
LET'S HAVE A LOOK.
OH MY GOODNESS... THAT'S NOT LOOKING TOO GOOD.
YOUNG MAN...
...FETCH WATER FROM THE BROOK. BUCKETS ARE OUTSIDE.
LISTEN UP, SWEETIE, MEDICINE IS WORTH MORE THAN GOLD. GIVING IT TO YOUR FATHER WOULD BE A BIT OF A WASTE I'M AFRAID.
BUT YOU THOUGH... YOU MAKE IT WORTH MY TIME.
DON'T TOUCH ME!!

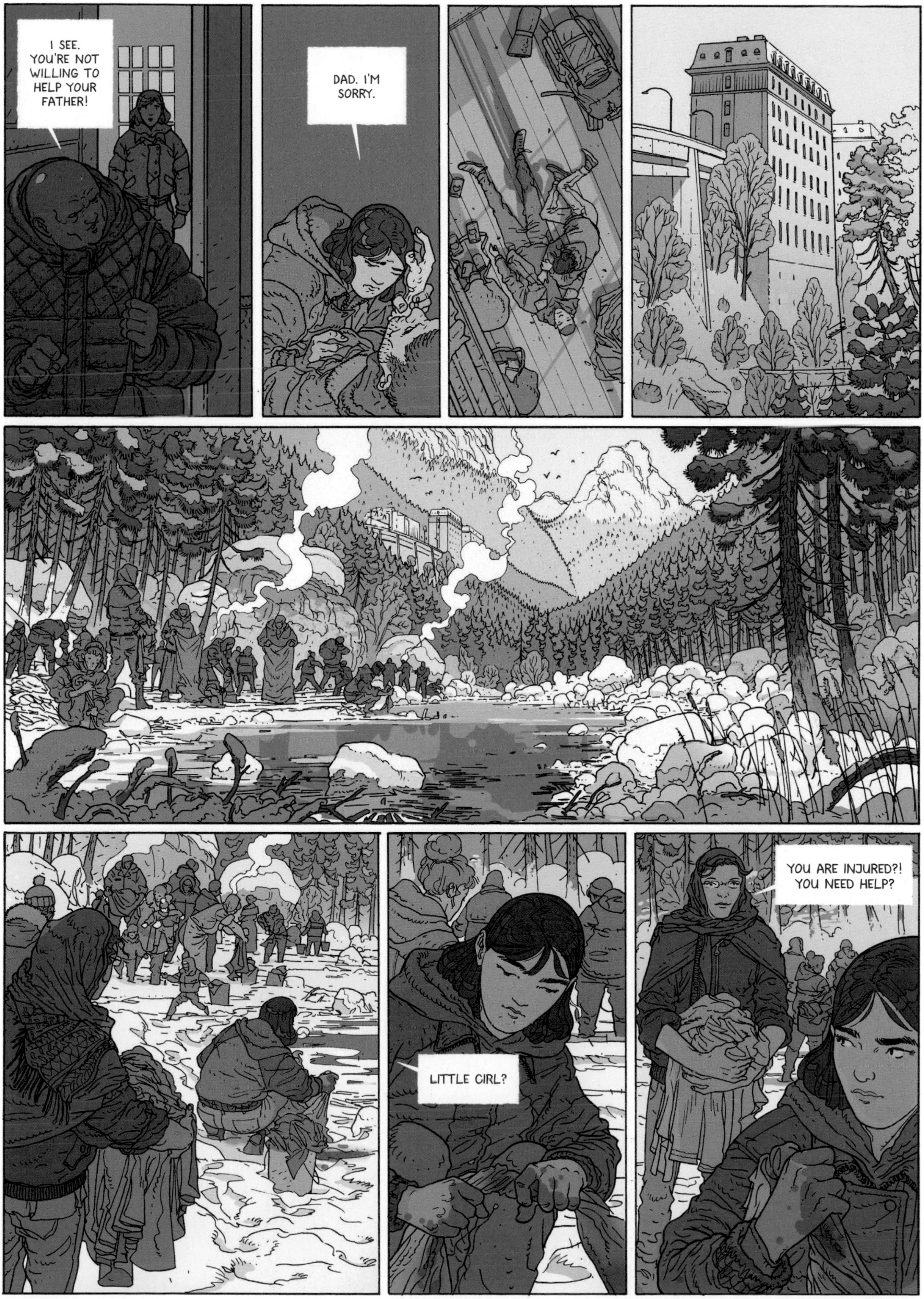
I SEE. YOU'RE NOT WILLING TO HELP YOUR FATHER!
DAD. I'M SORRY.
LITTLE GIRL?
YOU ARE INJURED?! YOU NEED HELP?

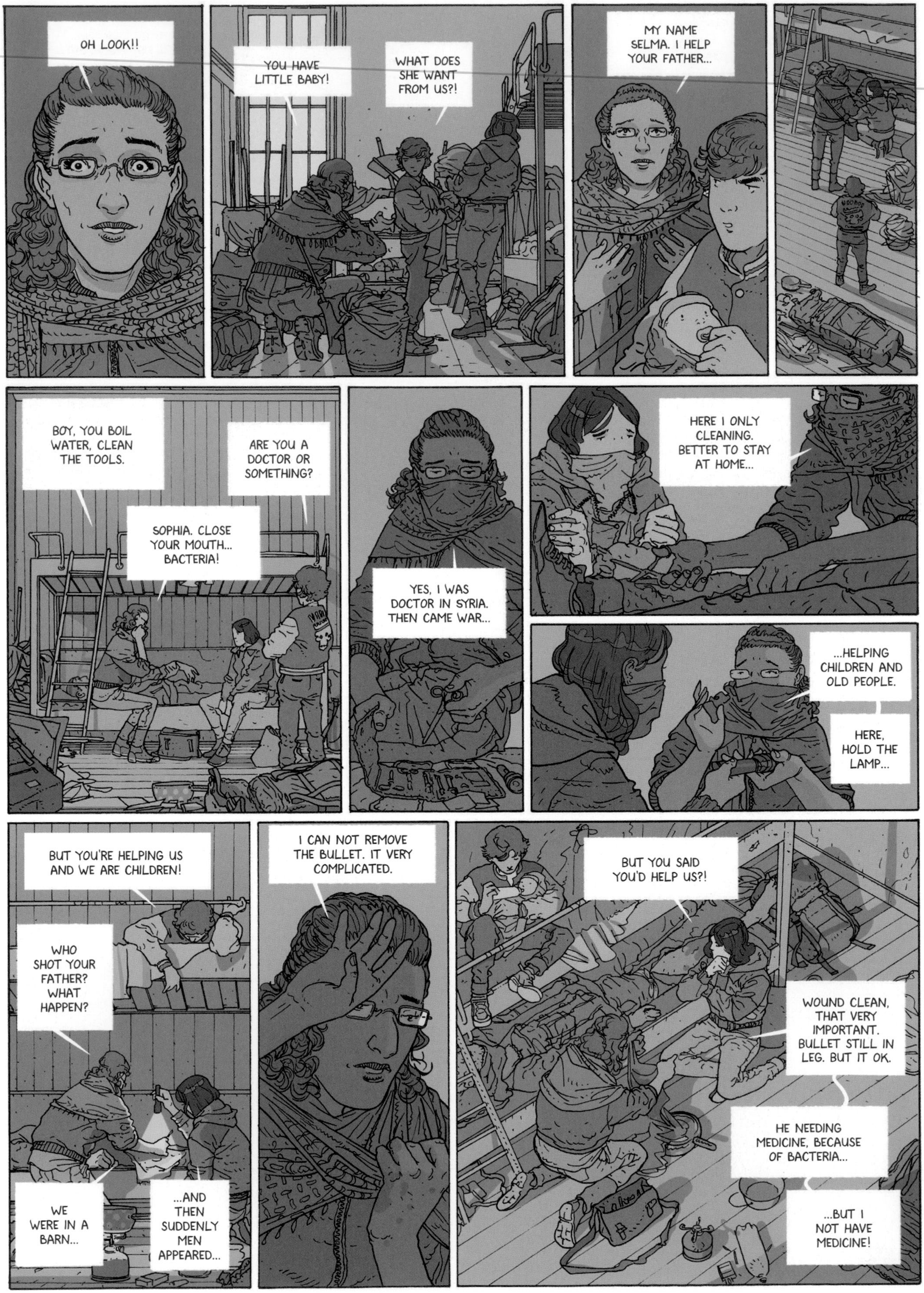
OH LOOK!!
YOU HAVE LITTLE BABY!
WHAT DOES SHE WANT FROM US?!
MY NAME SELMA. I HELP YOUR FATHER...
BOY, YOU BOIL WATER, CLEAN THE TOOLS.
SOPHIA. CLOSE YOUR MOUTH... BACTERIA!
ARE YOU A DOCTOR OR SOMETHING?
YES, I WAS DOCTOR IN SYRIA. THEN CAME WAR...
HERE I ONLY CLEANING. BETTER TO STAY AT HOME...
...HELPING CHILDREN AND OLD PEOPLE.
HERE, HOLD THE LAMP...
BUT YOU'RE HELPING US AND WE ARE CHILDREN!
WHO SHOT YOUR FATHER? WHAT HAPPEN?
WE WERE IN A BARN...
...AND THEN SUDDENLY MEN APPEARED...
I CAN NOT REMOVE THE BULLET. IT VERY COMPLICATED.
BUT YOU SAID YOU'D HELP US?!
WOUND CLEAN, THAT VERY IMPORTANT. BULLET STILL IN LEG. BUT IT OK.
HE NEEDING MEDICINE, BECAUSE OF BACTERIA...
...BUT I NOT HAVE MEDICINE!

THE VET! HE'S GOTTA HAVE MEDICINE!

ANTIBIOTICS AND ALL THAT!

YES, ANTIBIOTICS, YOU NEED. BUT DOCTOR VERY DANGEROUS MAN.

HERE, FOR YOU. IT'S NOT MUCH, BUT...

THANK YOU, DEAR! BUT IT TOO MUCH...

FOOD VERY SCARCE!

IT'S ALRIGHT! JUST TELL ME WHERE THAT VET IS STAYING!

WEEEEEE WEEEEE

SHE'S HUNGRY AGAIN. AND I BET HER DIAPER'S FULL TOO!

HOW AM I SUPPOSED TO DO ALL THIS?!

GOATS DOWNSTAIRS. MILK GOOD FOR BABY... LITTLE BROTHER MUST HELP.

CHANGE BANDAGES DAILY. BOIL IN HOT WATER.

HE LIVE AT END OF STREET...

...BUT NOW HE IN THE RIFUGIO. EVERYONE IN THE RIFUGIO AT THIS HOUR.

YOU TAKE CARE, LITTLE ONE! DOCTOR VERY EVIL MAN!!

DON'T KEEP IT ALL BOTTLED IN MAN. I KNOW YOU DO THAT.

IT'S OK TO LET IT OUT, SO DON'T FORGET TO DO IT ONCE IN A WHILE.

Y'ALL TALKING 'BOUT BREAKING WIND OR WHAT?

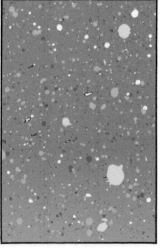

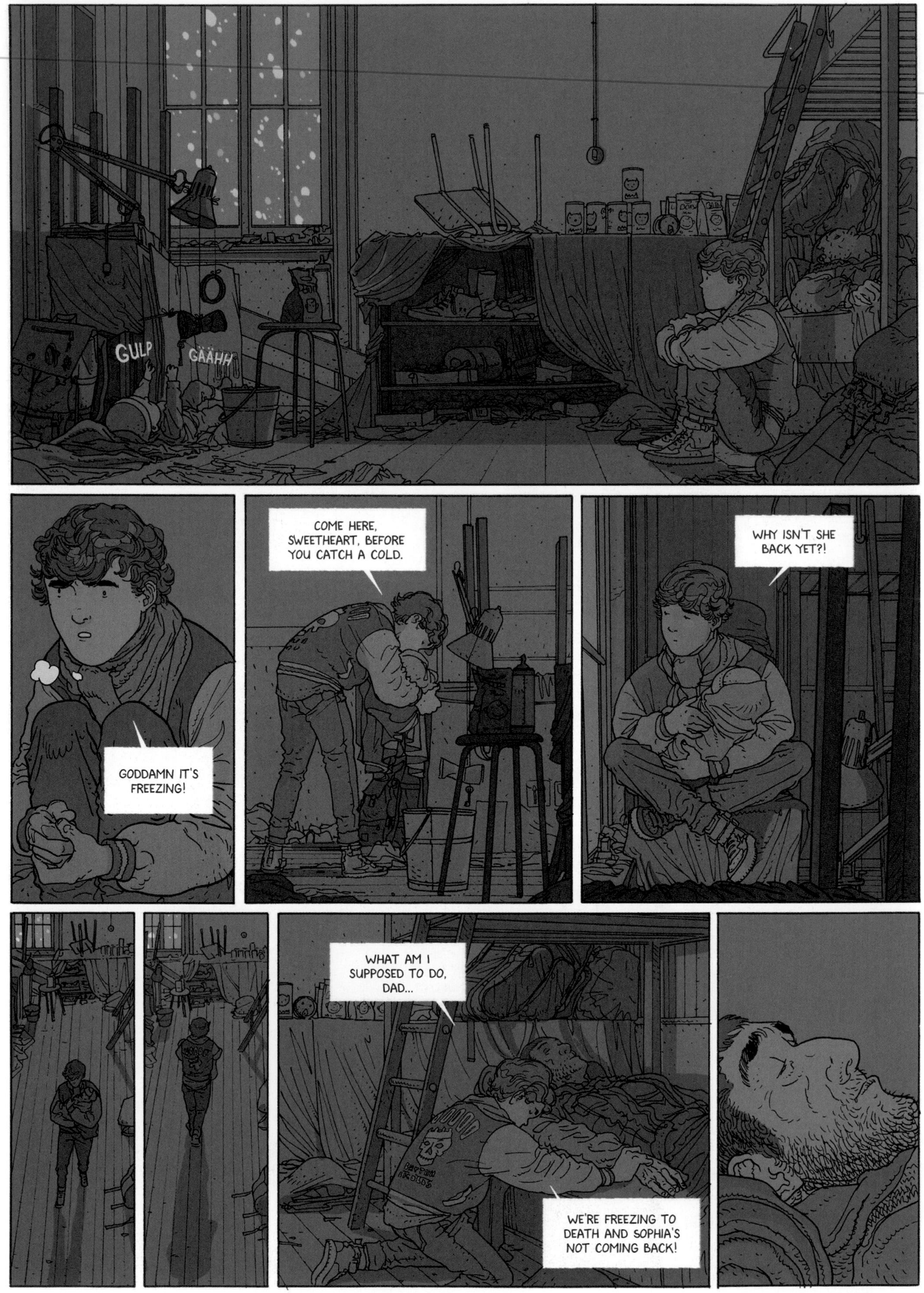
GULP
GÄÄHH
GODDAMN IT'S FREEZING!
COME HERE, SWEETHEART, BEFORE YOU CATCH A COLD.
WHY ISN'T SHE BACK YET?!
WHAT AM I SUPPOSED TO DO, DAD...
WE'RE FREEZING TO DEATH AND SOPHIA'S NOT COMING BACK!

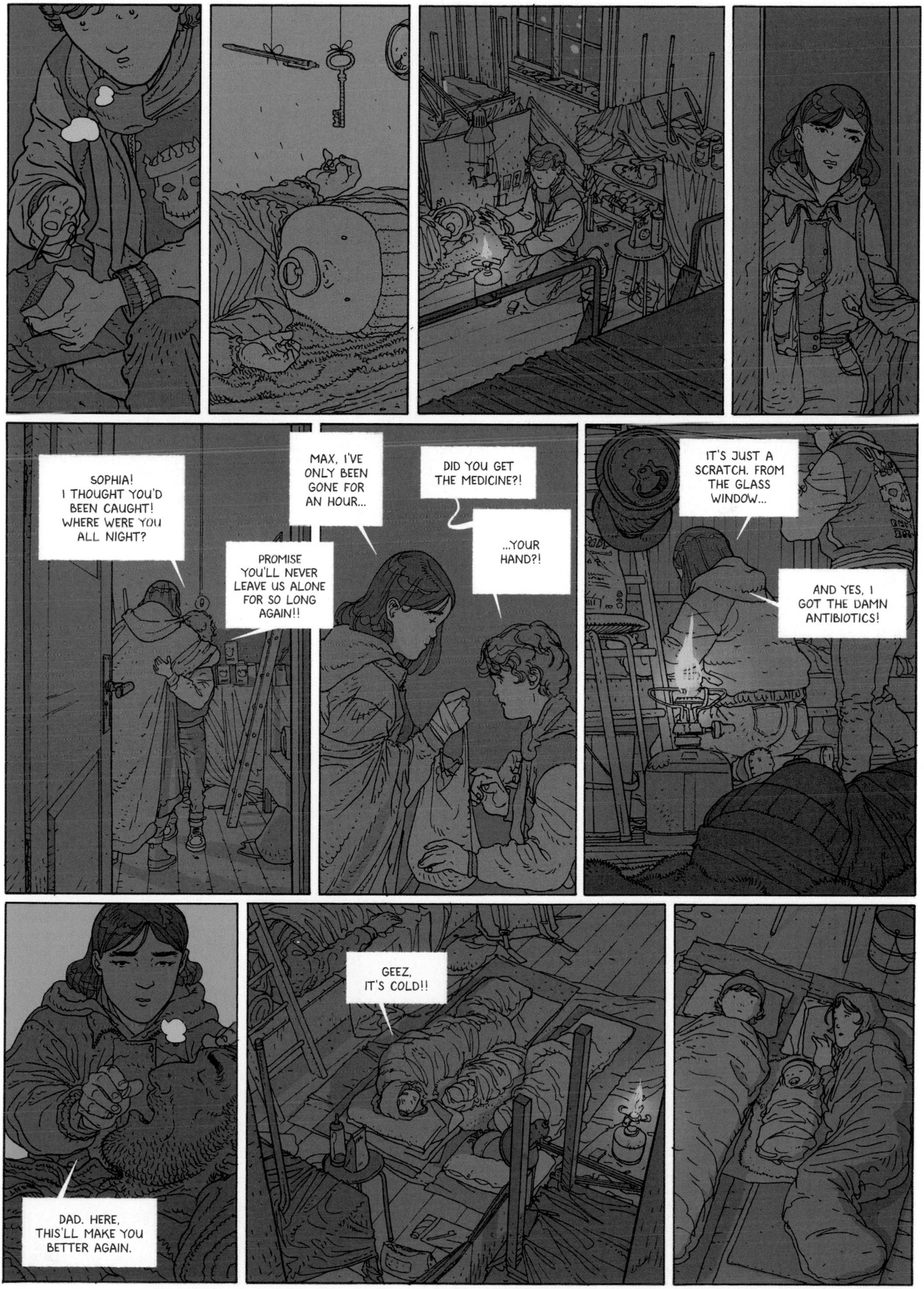
SOPHIA! I THOUGHT YOU'D BEEN CAUGHT! WHERE WERE YOU ALL NIGHT?
PROMISE YOU'LL NEVER LEAVE US ALONE FOR SO LONG AGAIN!!
MAX, I'VE ONLY BEEN GONE FOR AN HOUR...
DID YOU GET THE MEDICINE?!
...YOUR HAND?!
IT'S JUST A SCRATCH. FROM THE GLASS WINDOW...
AND YES, I GOT THE DAMN ANTIBIOTICS!
DAD. HERE, THIS'LL MAKE YOU BETTER AGAIN.
GEEZ, IT'S COLD!!

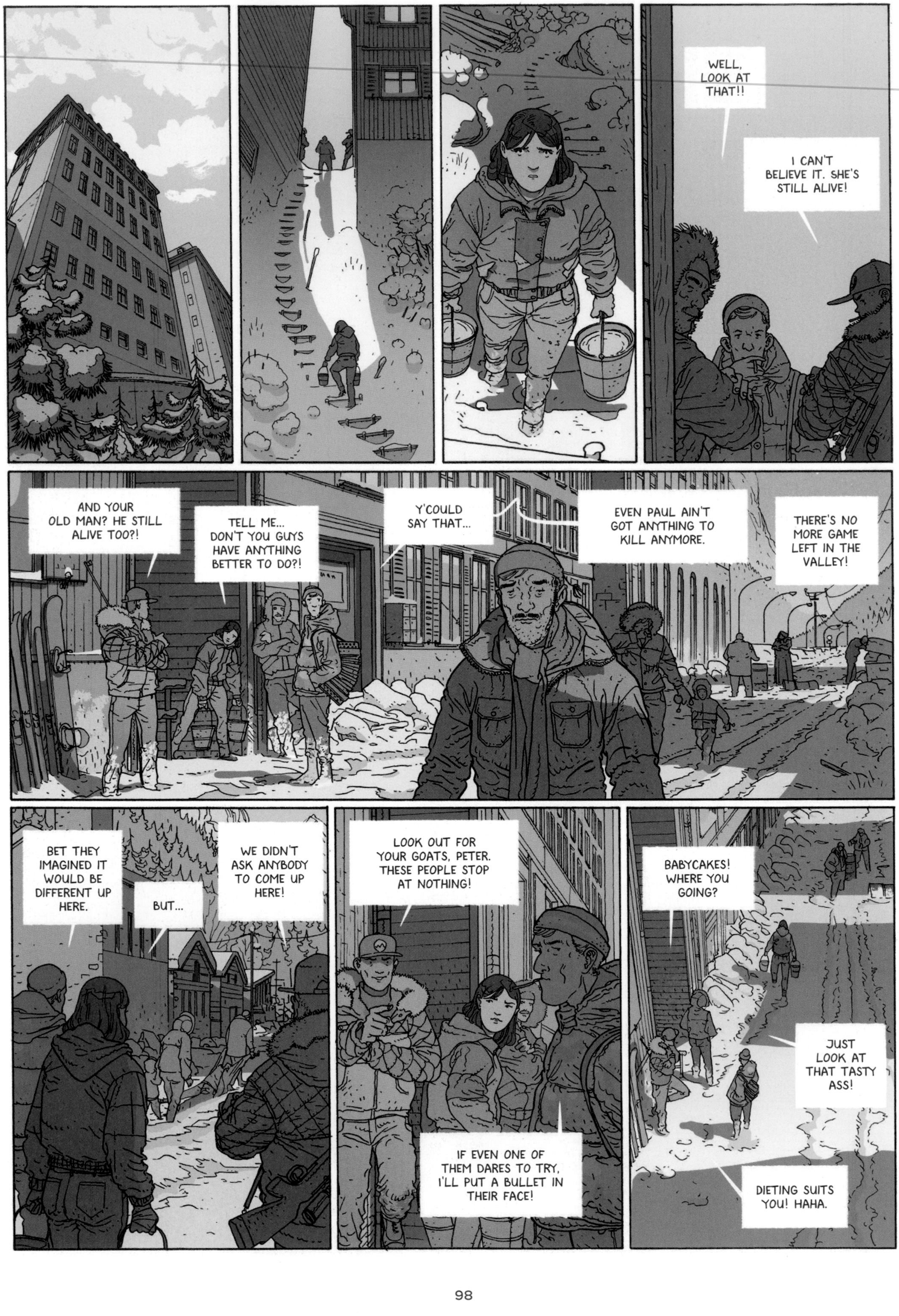

WELL, LOOK AT THAT!!
I CAN'T BELIEVE IT. SHE'S STILL ALIVE!
AND YOUR OLD MAN? HE STILL ALIVE TOO?!
TELL ME... DON'T YOU GUYS HAVE ANYTHING BETTER TO DO?!
Y'COULD SAY THAT...
EVEN PAUL AIN'T GOT ANYTHING TO KILL ANYMORE.
THERE'S NO MORE GAME LEFT IN THE VALLEY!
BET THEY IMAGINED IT WOULD BE DIFFERENT UP HERE.
BUT...
WE DIDN'T ASK ANYBODY TO COME UP HERE!
LOOK OUT FOR YOUR GOATS, PETER. THESE PEOPLE STOP AT NOTHING!
IF EVEN ONE OF THEM DARES TO TRY, I'LL PUT A BULLET IN THEIR FACE!
BABYCAKES! WHERE YOU GOING?
JUST LOOK AT THAT TASTY ASS!
DIETING SUITS YOU! HAHA.

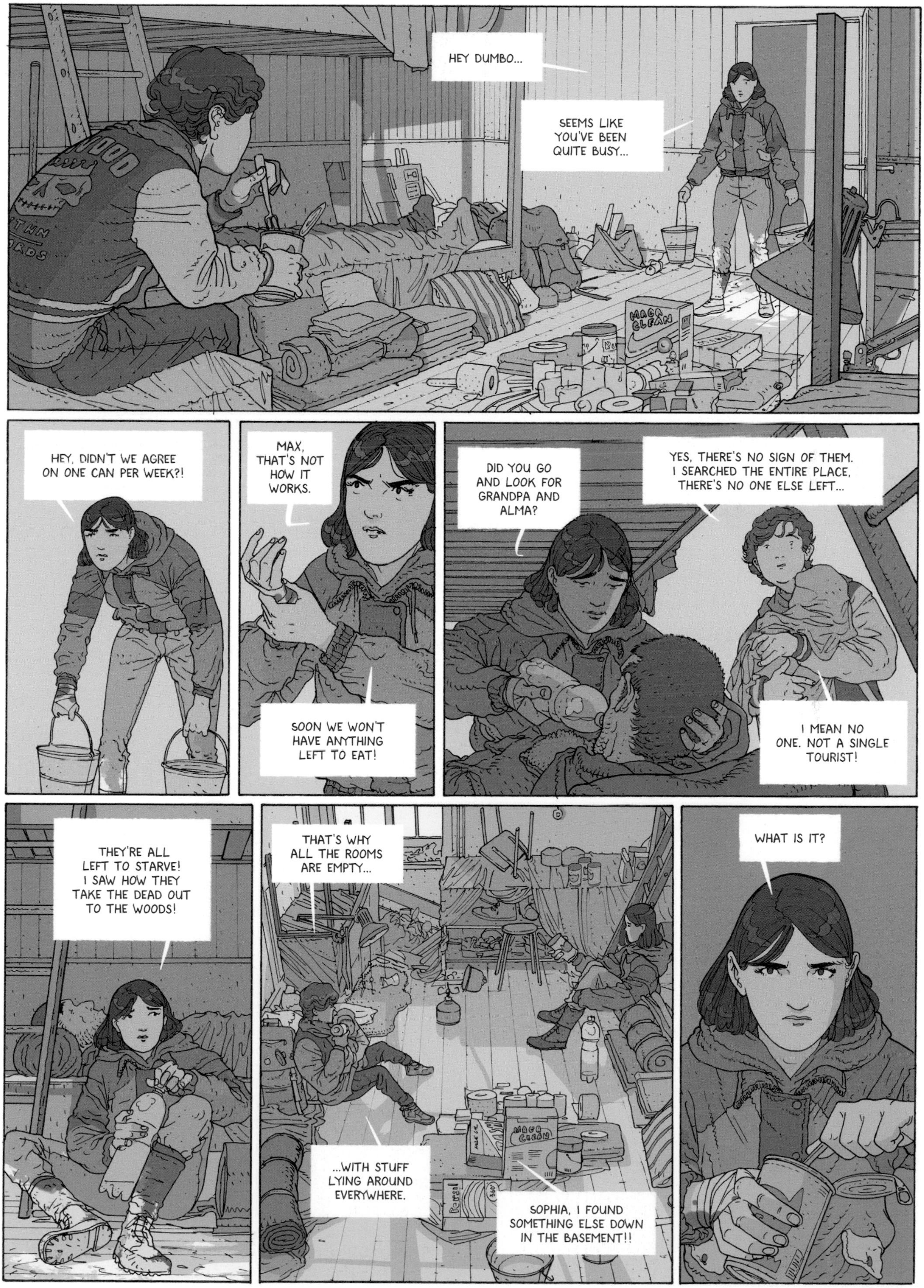
HEY DUMBO...
SEEMS LIKE YOU'VE BEEN QUITE BUSY...
HEY, DIDN'T WE AGREE ON ONE CAN PER WEEK?!
MAX, THAT'S NOT HOW IT WORKS.
SOON WE WON'T HAVE ANYTHING LEFT TO EAT!
DID YOU GO AND LOOK FOR GRANDPA AND ALMA?
YES, THERE'S NO SIGN OF THEM. I SEARCHED THE ENTIRE PLACE, THERE'S NO ONE ELSE LEFT...
I MEAN NO ONE. NOT A SINGLE TOURIST!
THEY'RE ALL LEFT TO STARVE! I SAW HOW THEY TAKE THE DEAD OUT TO THE WOODS!
THAT'S WHY ALL THE ROOMS ARE EMPTY...
...WITH STUFF LYING AROUND EVERYWHERE.
SOPHIA, I FOUND SOMETHING ELSE DOWN IN THE BASEMENT!!
WHAT IS IT?

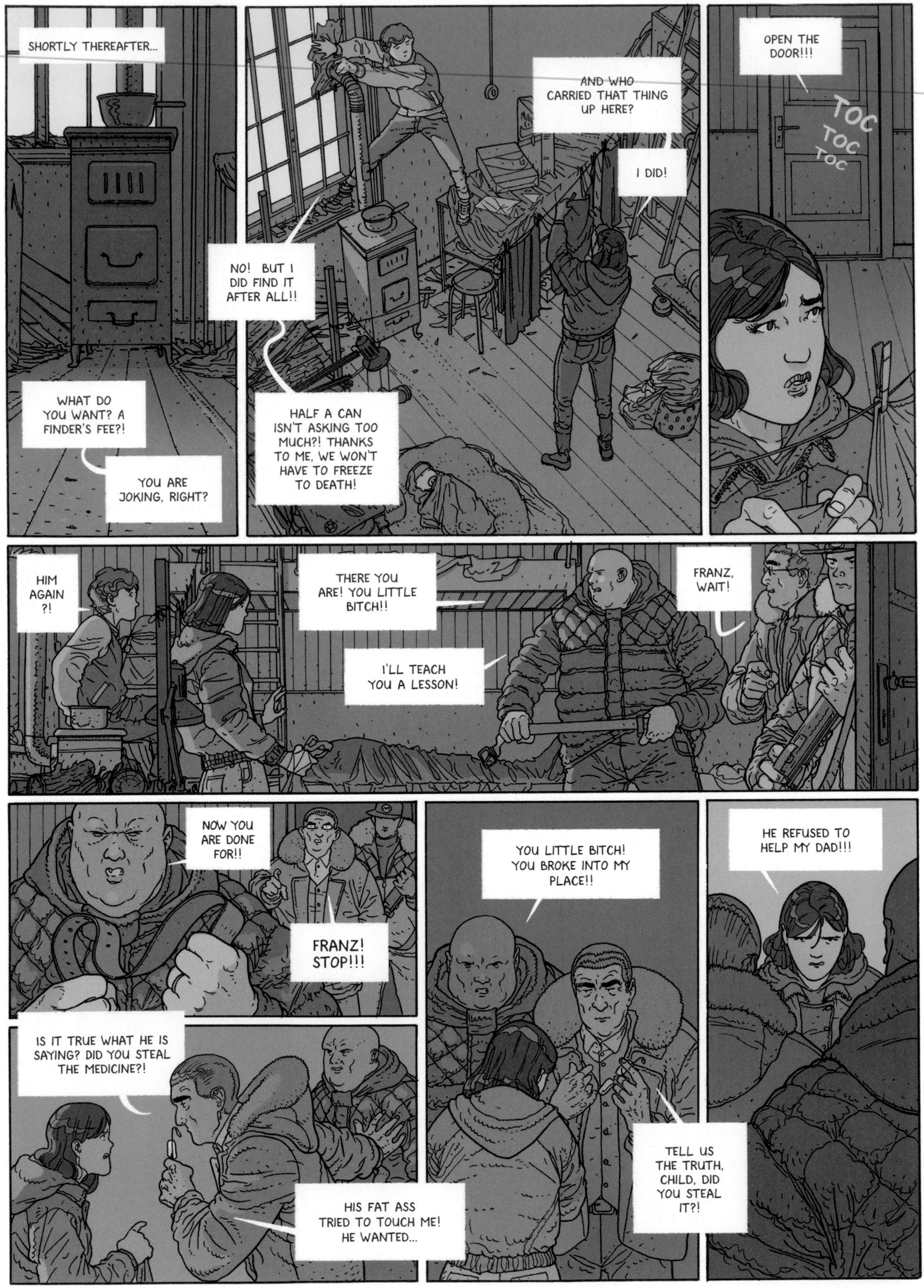
SHORTLY THEREAFTER...
WHAT DO YOU WANT? A FINDER'S FEE?!
YOU ARE JOKING, RIGHT?
NO! BUT I DID FIND IT AFTER ALL!!
HALF A CAN ISN'T ASKING TOO MUCH?! THANKS TO ME, WE WON'T HAVE TO FREEZE TO DEATH!
AND WHO CARRIED THAT THING UP HERE?
I DID!
OPEN THE DOOR!!!
TOC TOC TOC
HIM AGAIN ?!
THERE YOU ARE! YOU LITTLE BITCH!!
I'LL TEACH YOU A LESSON!
FRANZ, WAIT!
NOW YOU ARE DONE FOR!!
FRANZ! STOP!!!
IS IT TRUE WHAT HE IS SAYING? DID YOU STEAL THE MEDICINE?!
HIS FAT ASS TRIED TO TOUCH ME! HE WANTED...
YOU LITTLE BITCH! YOU BROKE INTO MY PLACE!!
TELL US THE TRUTH, CHILD, DID YOU STEAL IT?!
HE REFUSED TO HELP MY DAD!!!

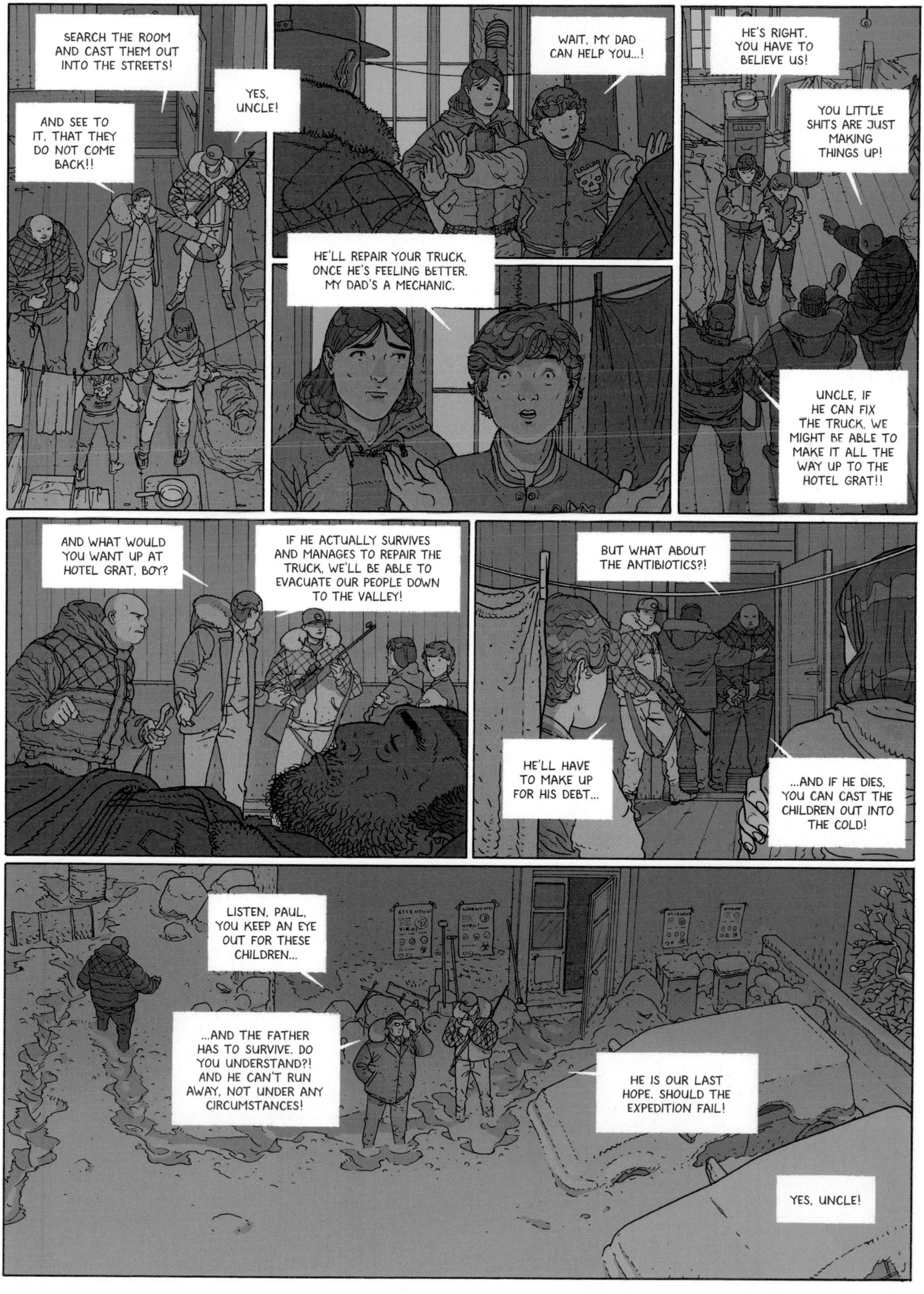
SEARCH THE ROOM AND CAST THEM OUT INTO THE STREETS!
AND SEE TO IT, THAT THEY DO NOT COME BACK!!
YES, UNCLE!
WAIT, MY DAD CAN HELP YOU...!
HE'LL REPAIR YOUR TRUCK, ONCE HE'S FEELING BETTER. MY DAD'S A MECHANIC.
HE'S RIGHT. YOU HAVE TO BELIEVE US!
YOU LITTLE SHITS ARE JUST MAKING THINGS UP!
UNCLE, IF HE CAN FIX THE TRUCK, WE MIGHT BE ABLE TO MAKE IT ALL THE WAY UP TO THE HOTEL GRAT!!
AND WHAT WOULD YOU WANT UP AT HOTEL GRAT, BOY?
IF HE ACTUALLY SURVIVES AND MANAGES TO REPAIR THE TRUCK, WE'LL BE ABLE TO EVACUATE OUR PEOPLE DOWN TO THE VALLEY!
BUT WHAT ABOUT THE ANTIBIOTICS?!
HE'LL HAVE TO MAKE UP FOR HIS DEBT...
...AND IF HE DIES, YOU CAN CAST THE CHILDREN OUT INTO THE COLD!
LISTEN, PAUL, YOU KEEP AN EYE OUT FOR THESE CHILDREN...
...AND THE FATHER HAS TO SURVIVE. DO YOU UNDERSTAND?! AND HE CAN'T RUN AWAY, NOT UNDER ANY CIRCUMSTANCES!
HE IS OUR LAST HOPE. SHOULD THE EXPEDITION FAIL!
YES, UNCLE!

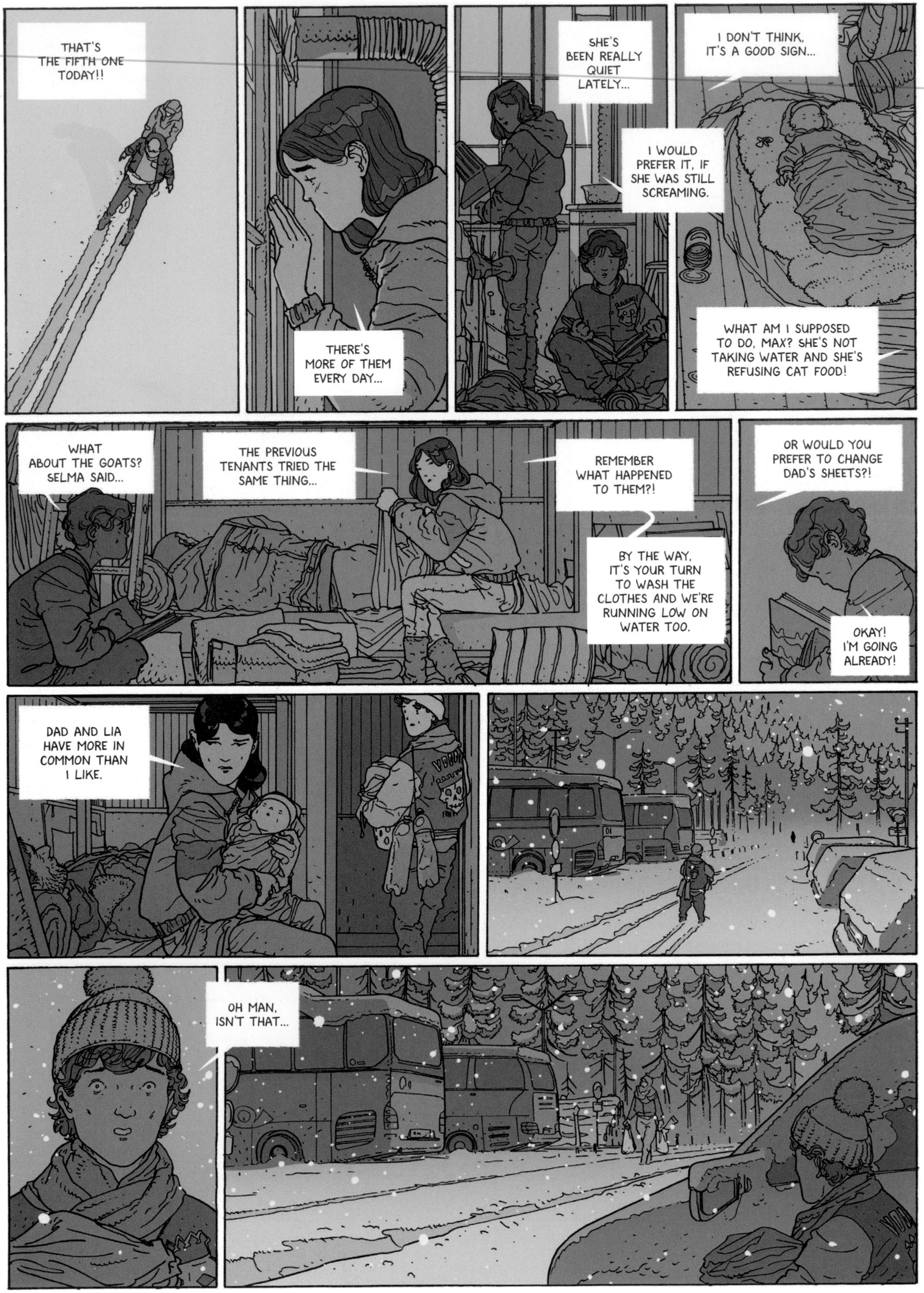
THAT'S THE FIFTH ONE TODAY!!
THERE'S MORE OF THEM EVERY DAY...
SHE'S BEEN REALLY QUIET LATELY...
I WOULD PREFER IT, IF SHE WAS STILL SCREAMING.
I DON'T THINK, IT'S A GOOD SIGN...
WHAT AM I SUPPOSED TO DO, MAX? SHE'S NOT TAKING WATER AND SHE'S REFUSING CAT FOOD!
WHAT ABOUT THE GOATS? SELMA SAID...
THE PREVIOUS TENANTS TRIED THE SAME THING...
REMEMBER WHAT HAPPENED TO THEM?!
BY THE WAY, IT'S YOUR TURN TO WASH THE CLOTHES AND WE'RE RUNNING LOW ON WATER TOO.
OR WOULD YOU PREFER TO CHANGE DAD'S SHEETS?!
OKAY! I'M GOING ALREADY!
DAD AND LIA HAVE MORE IN COMMON THAN I LIKE.
OH MAN, ISN'T THAT...

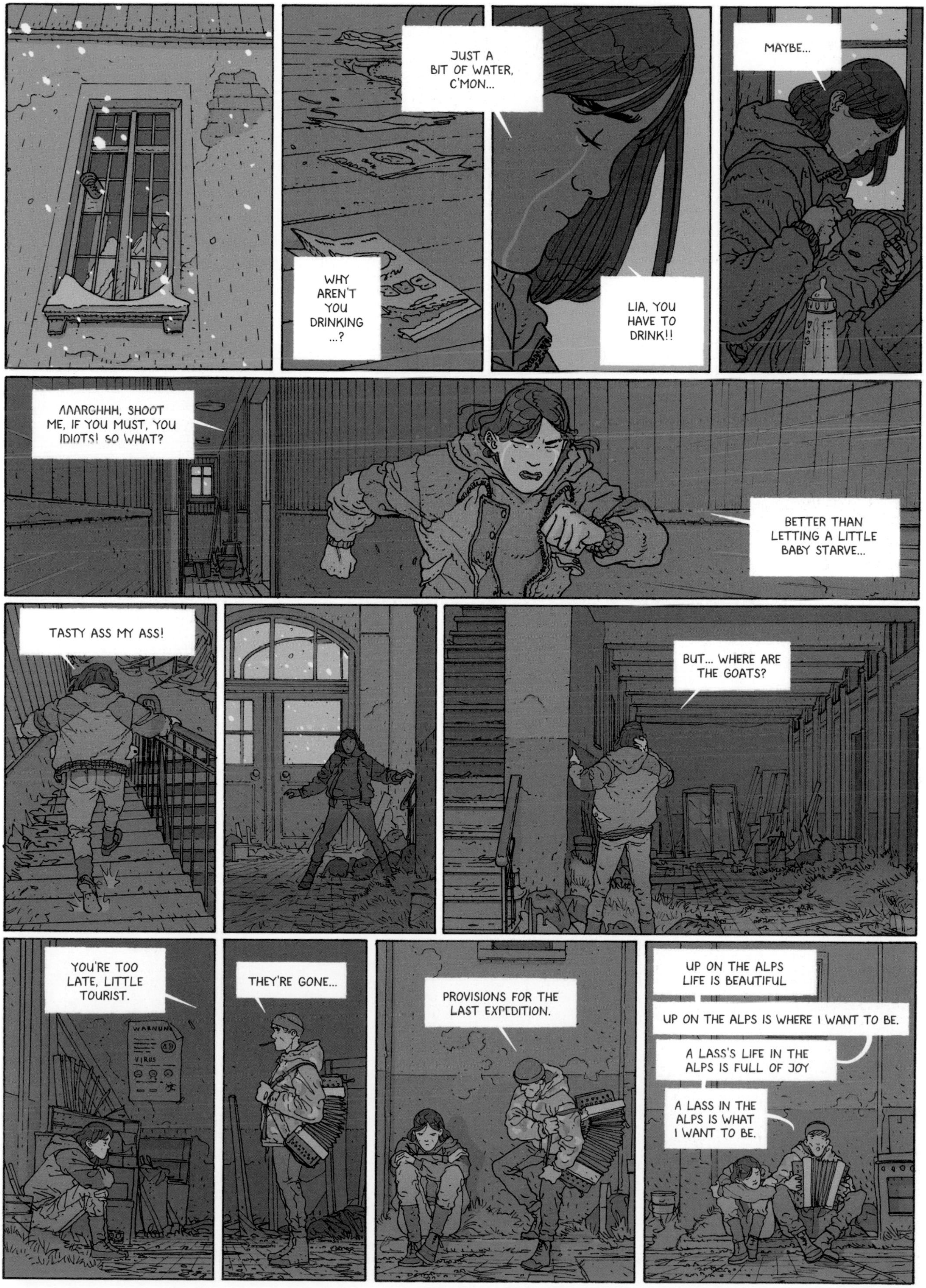
JUST A BIT OF WATER, C'MON...
WHY AREN'T YOU DRINKING ...?
LIA, YOU HAVE TO DRINK!!
MAYBE...
AAARGHHH, SHOOT ME, IF YOU MUST, YOU IDIOTS! SO WHAT?
BETTER THAN LETTING A LITTLE BABY STARVE...
TASTY ASS MY ASS!
BUT... WHERE ARE THE GOATS?
YOU'RE TOO LATE, LITTLE TOURIST.
WARNUNG
VIRUS
THEY'RE GONE...
PROVISIONS FOR THE LAST EXPEDITION.
UP ON THE ALPS LIFE IS BEAUTIFUL
UP ON THE ALPS IS WHERE I WANT TO BE.
A LASS'S LIFE IN THE ALPS IS FULL OF JOY
A LASS IN THE ALPS IS WHAT I WANT TO BE.

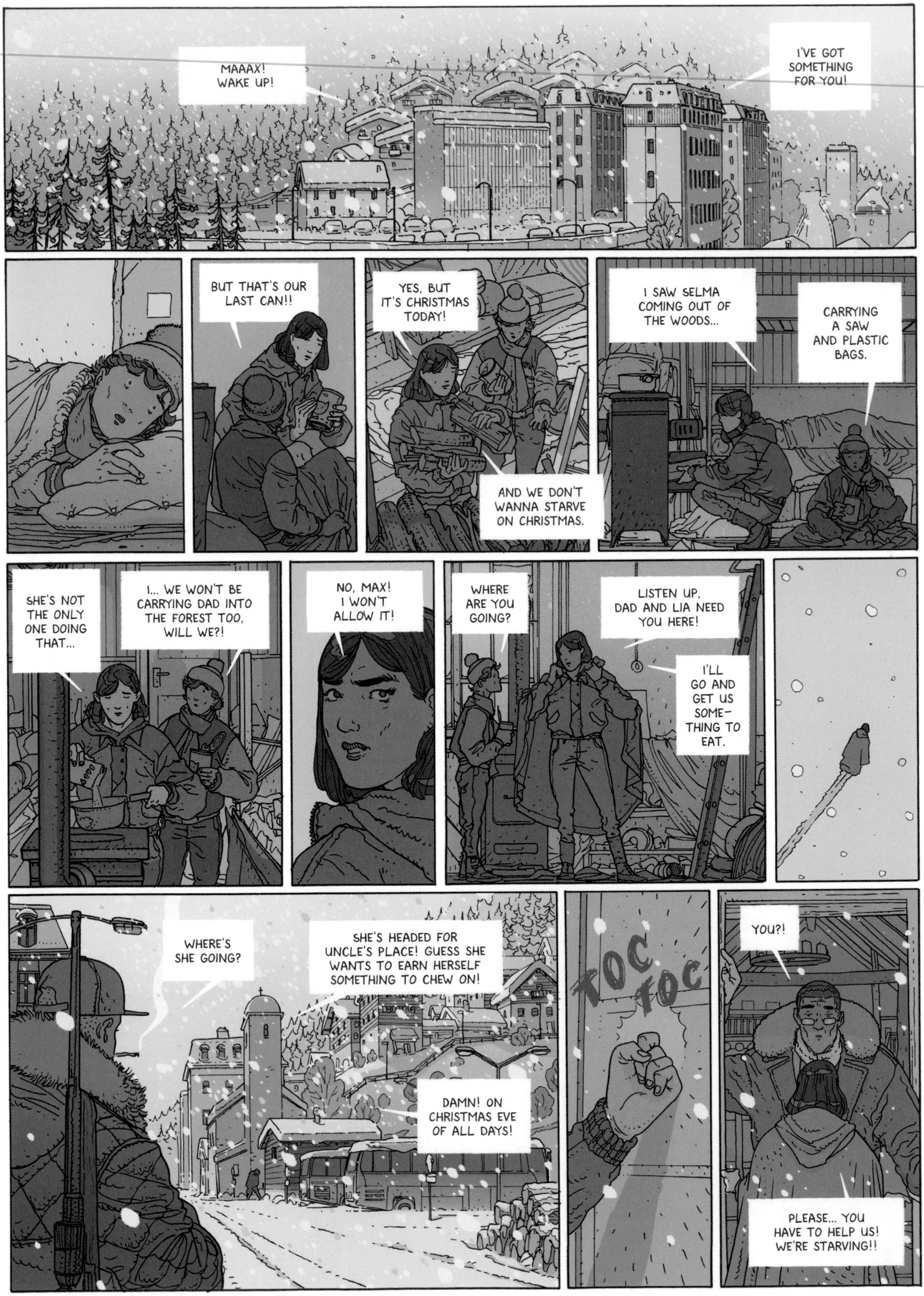
MAAAX! WAKE UP!
I'VE GOT SOMETHING FOR YOU!
BUT THAT'S OUR LAST CAN!!
YES, BUT IT'S CHRISTMAS TODAY!
AND WE DON'T WANNA STARVE ON CHRISTMAS.
I SAW SELMA COMING OUT OF THE WOODS...
CARRYING A SAW AND PLASTIC BAGS.
SHE'S NOT THE ONLY ONE DOING THAT...
I... WE WON'T BE CARRYING DAD INTO THE FOREST TOO, WILL WE?!
NO, MAX! I WON'T ALLOW IT!
WHERE ARE YOU GOING?
LISTEN UP, DAD AND LIA NEED YOU HERE!
I'LL GO AND GET US SOME-THING TO EAT.
WHERE'S SHE GOING?
SHE'S HEADED FOR UNCLE'S PLACE! GUESS SHE WANTS TO EARN HERSELF SOMETHING TO CHEW ON!
DAMN! ON CHRISTMAS EVE OF ALL DAYS!
TOC TOC
YOU?!
PLEASE... YOU HAVE TO HELP US! WE'RE STARVING!!

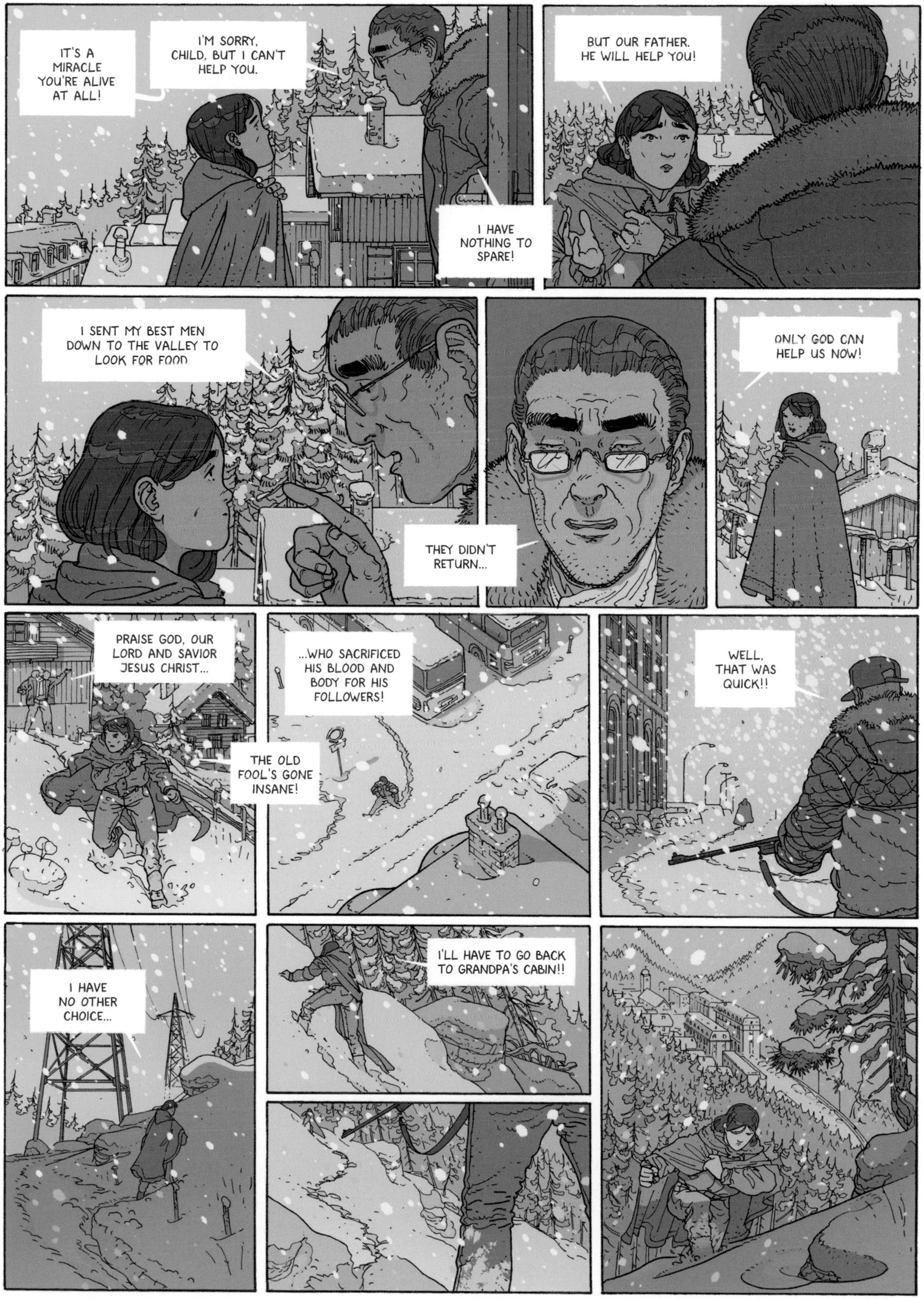
IT'S A MIRACLE YOU'RE ALIVE AT ALL!
I'M SORRY, CHILD, BUT I CAN'T HELP YOU.
I HAVE NOTHING TO SPARE!
BUT OUR FATHER. HE WILL HELP YOU!
I SENT MY BEST MEN DOWN TO THE VALLEY TO LOOK FOR FOOD.
THEY DIDN'T RETURN...
ONLY GOD CAN HELP US NOW!
PRAISE GOD, OUR LORD AND SAVIOR JESUS CHRIST...
THE OLD FOOL'S GONE INSANE!
...WHO SACRIFICED HIS BLOOD AND BODY FOR HIS FOLLOWERS!
WELL, THAT WAS QUICK!!
I HAVE NO OTHER CHOICE...
I'LL HAVE TO GO BACK TO GRANDPA'S CABIN!!

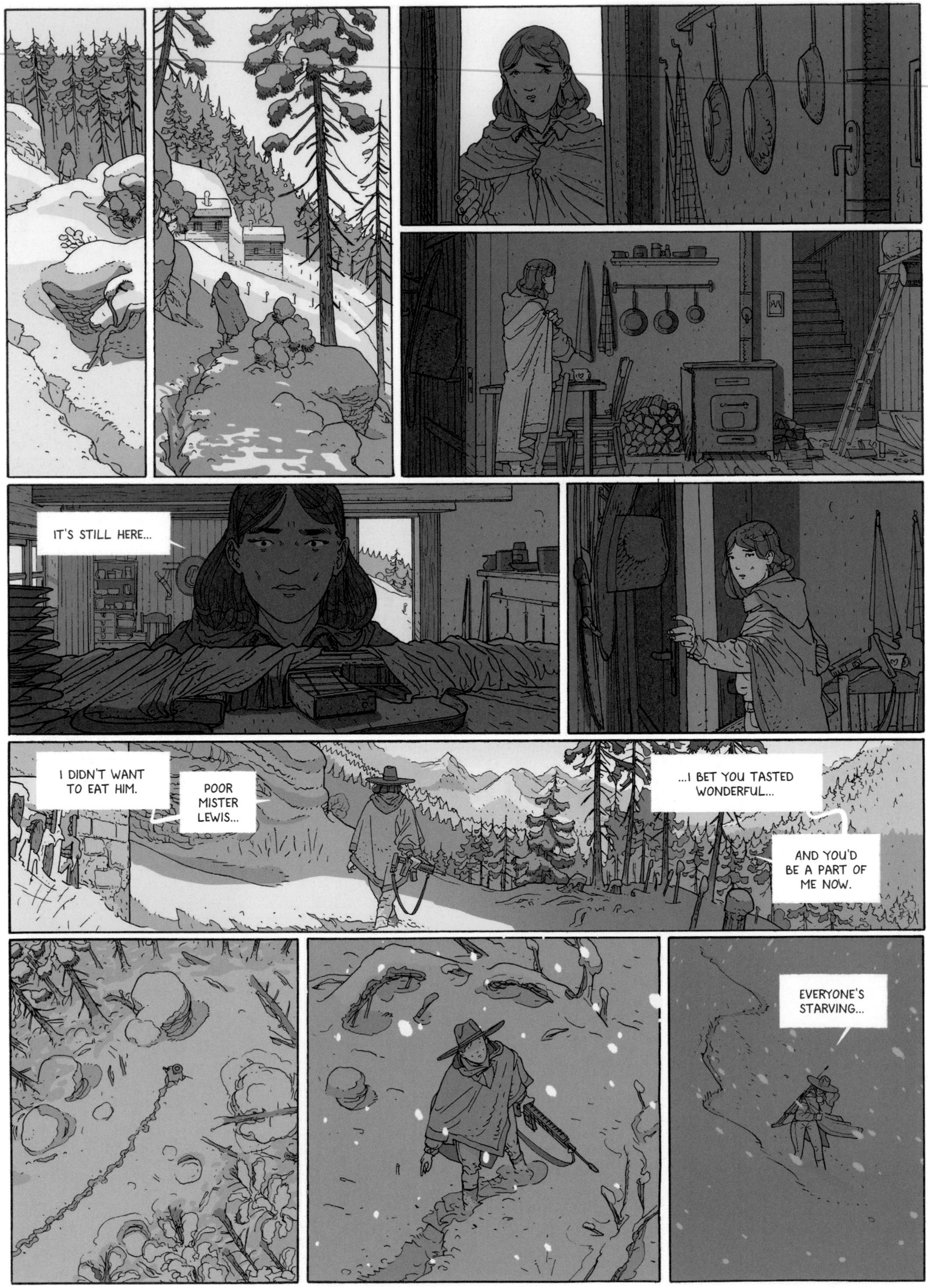
IT'S STILL HERE...
I DIDN'T WANT TO EAT HIM.
POOR MISTER LEWIS...
...I BET YOU TASTED WONDERFUL...
AND YOU'D BE A PART OF ME NOW.
EVERYONE'S STARVING...

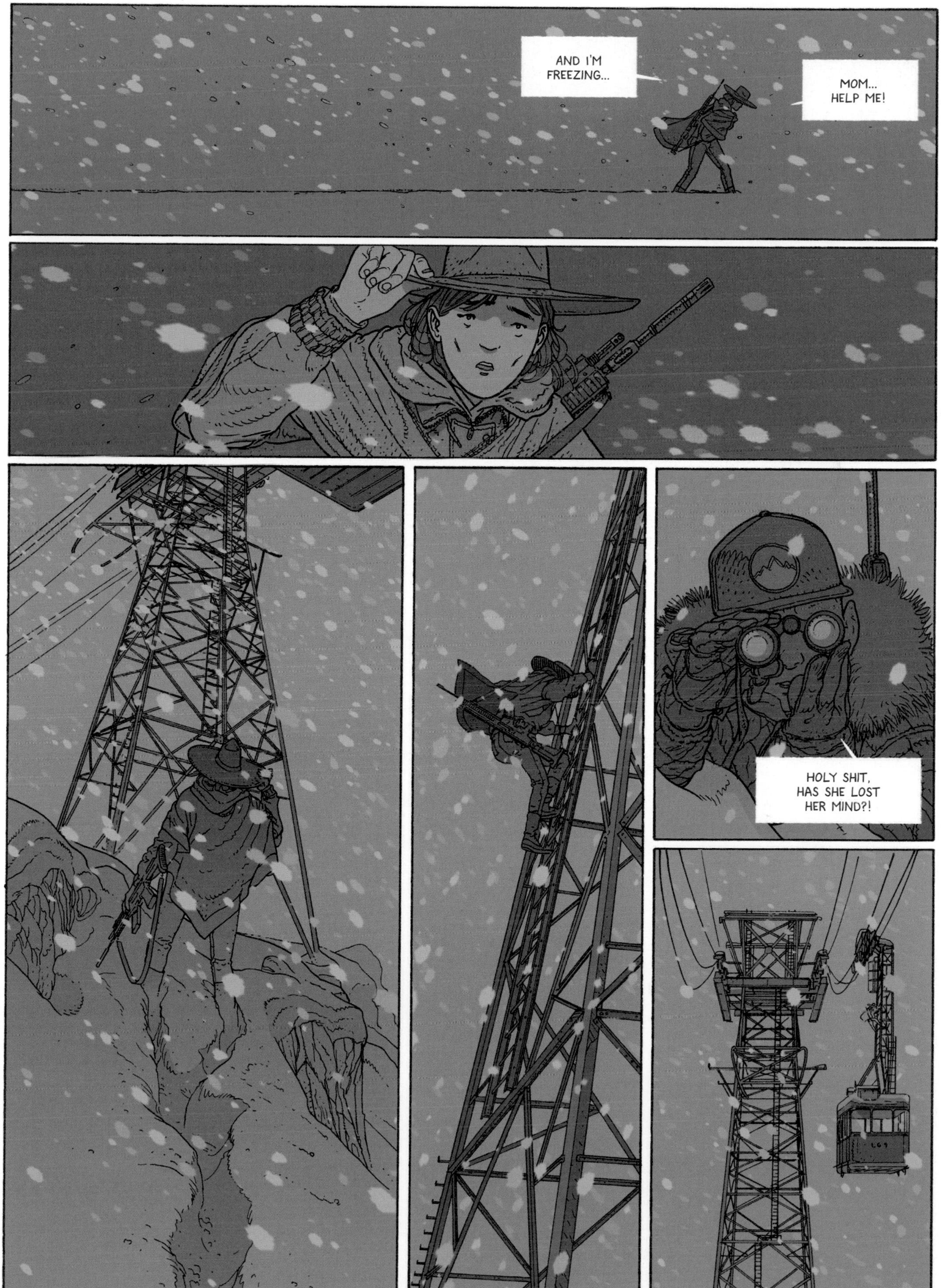
AND I'M FREEZING...
MOM... HELP ME!
HOLY SHIT, HAS SHE LOST HER MIND?!

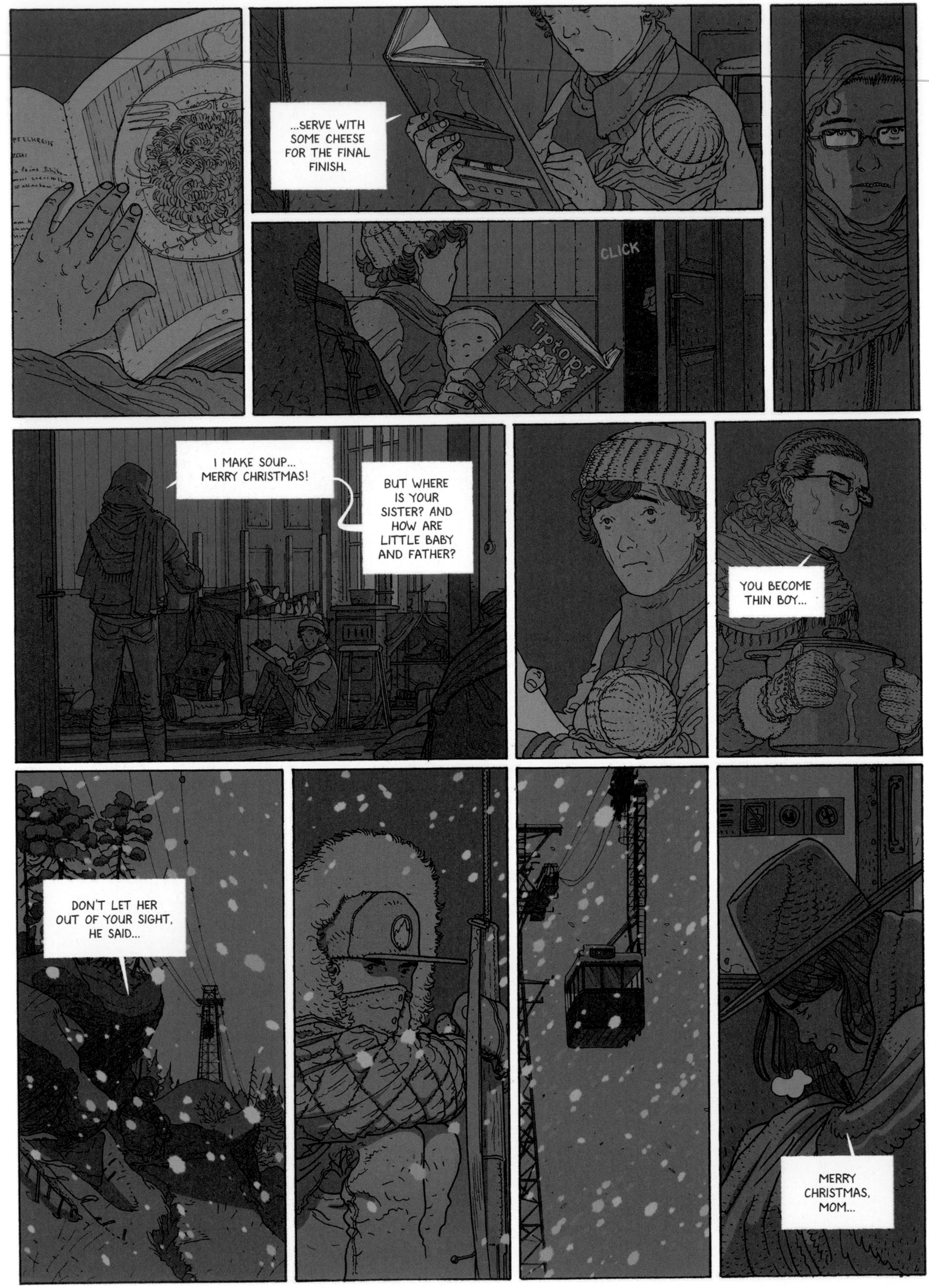
...SERVE WITH SOME CHEESE FOR THE FINAL FINISH.
Tiptopf
CLICK
I MAKE SOUP... MERRY CHRISTMAS!
BUT WHERE IS YOUR SISTER? AND HOW ARE LITTLE BABY AND FATHER?
YOU BECOME THIN BOY...
DON'T LET HER OUT OF YOUR SIGHT, HE SAID...
MERRY CHRISTMAS, MOM...

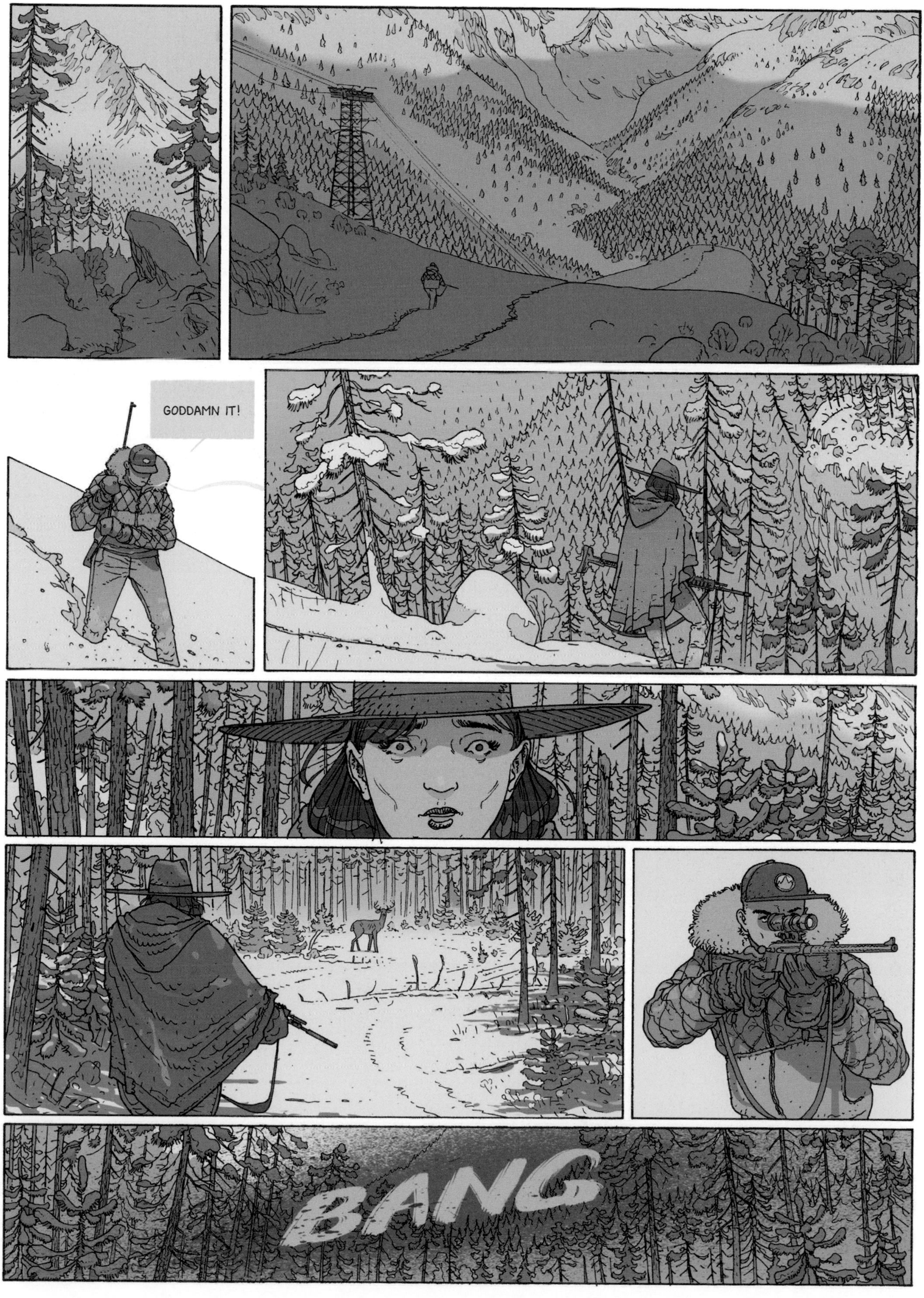
GODDAMN IT!
BANG

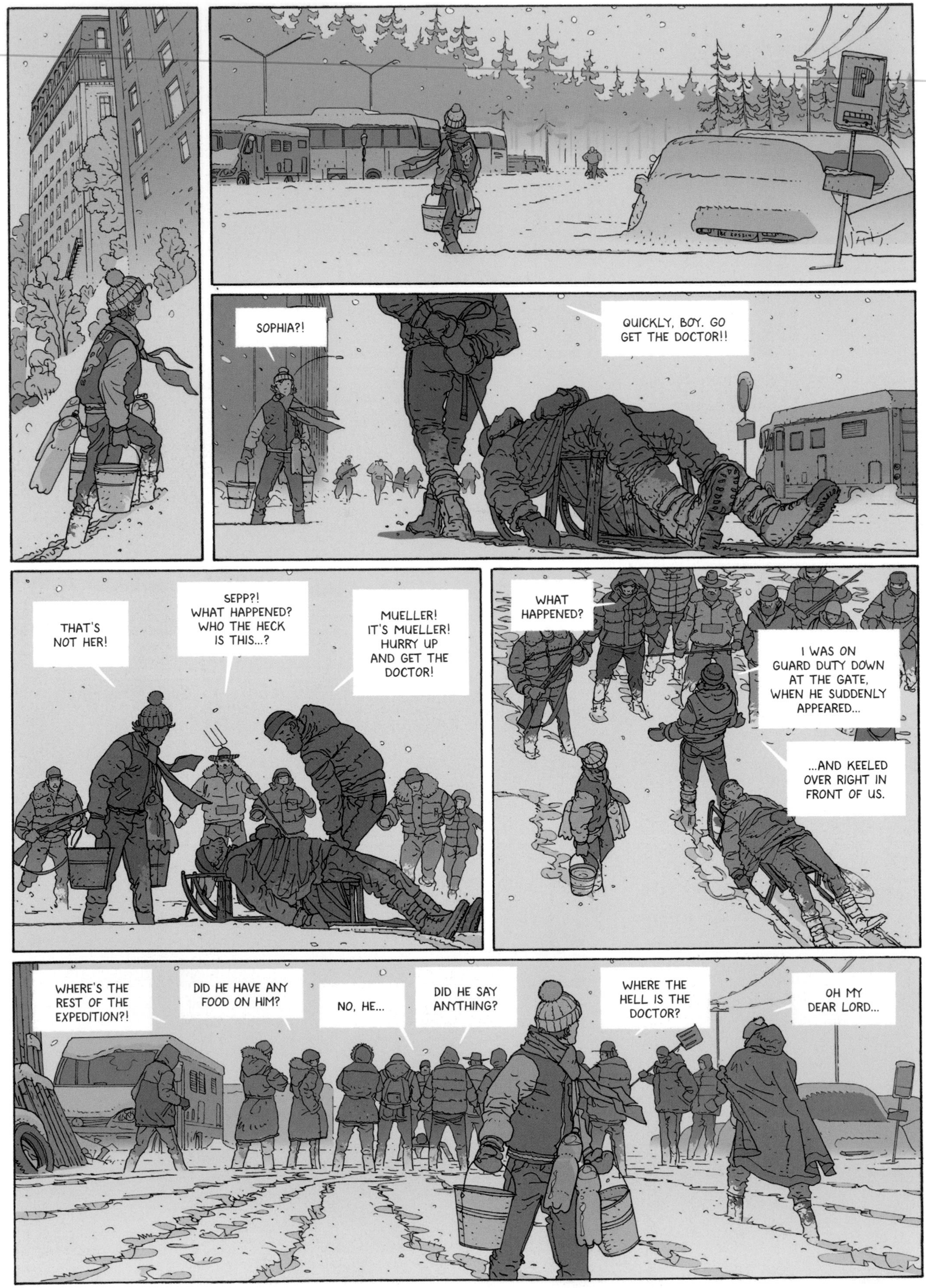

SOPHIA?!
QUICKLY, BOY. GO GET THE DOCTOR!!
THAT'S NOT HER!
SEPP?! WHAT HAPPENED? WHO THE HECK IS THIS...?
MUELLER! IT'S MUELLER! HURRY UP AND GET THE DOCTOR!
WHAT HAPPENED?
I WAS ON GUARD DUTY DOWN AT THE GATE, WHEN HE SUDDENLY APPEARED...
...AND KEELED OVER RIGHT IN FRONT OF US.
WHERE'S THE REST OF THE EXPEDITION?!
DID HE HAVE ANY FOOD ON HIM?
NO, HE...
DID HE SAY ANYTHING?
WHERE THE HELL IS THE DOCTOR?
OH MY DEAR LORD...

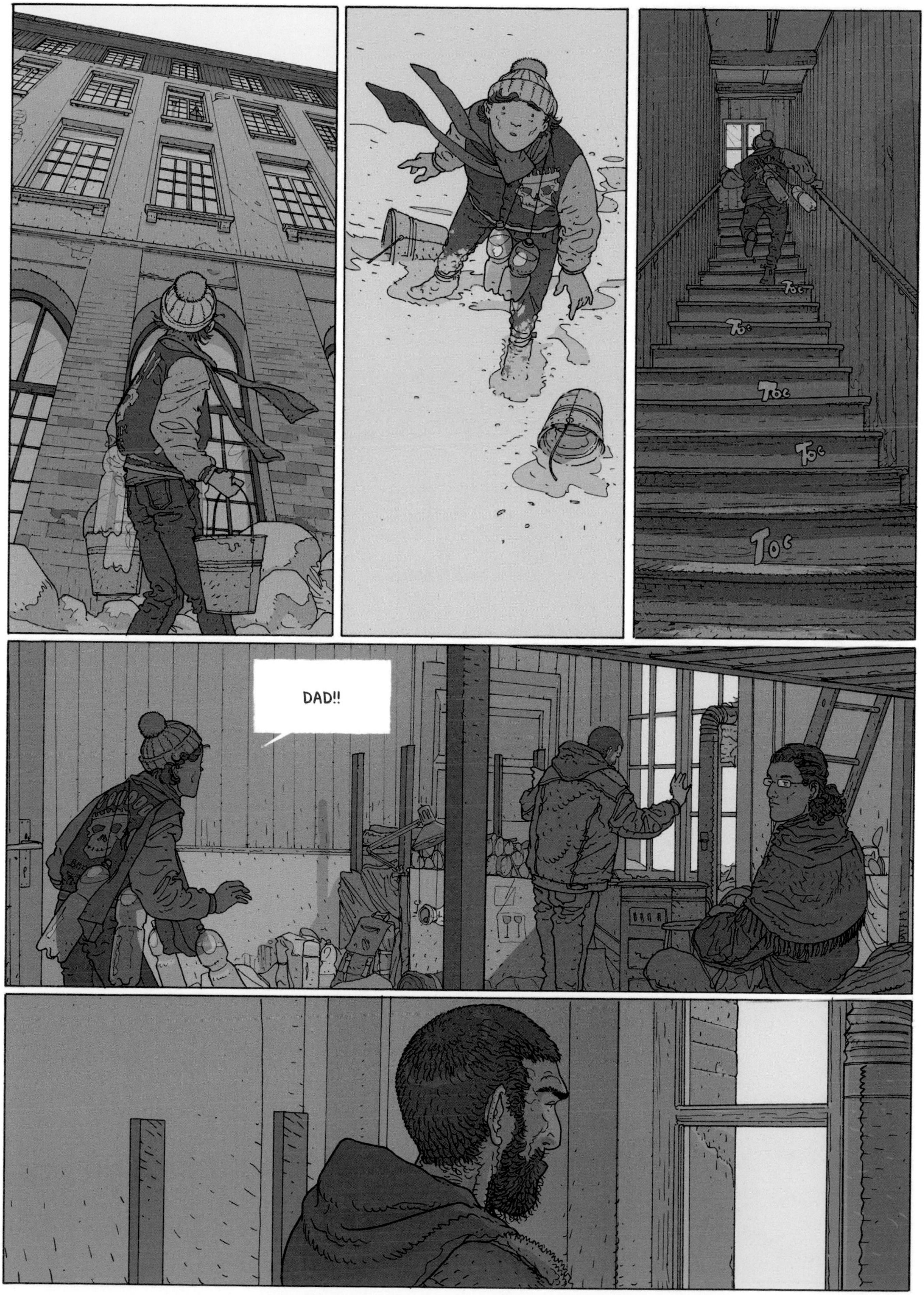
TOC
TOC
TOC
TOC
TOC
DAD!!

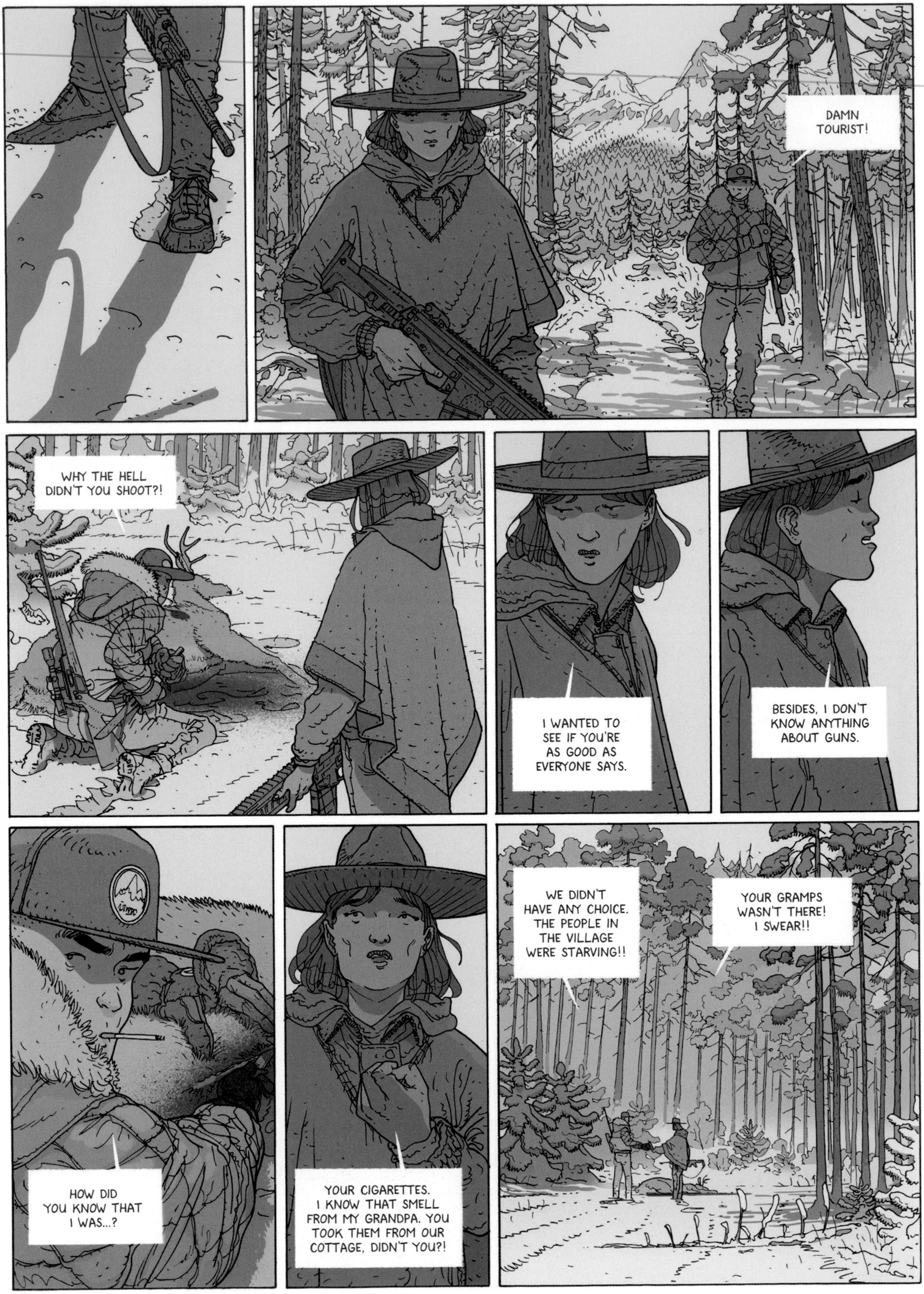
DAMN TOURIST!
WHY THE HELL DIDN'T YOU SHOOT?!
I WANTED TO SEE IF YOU'RE AS GOOD AS EVERYONE SAYS.
BESIDES, I DON'T KNOW ANYTHING ABOUT GUNS.
HOW DID YOU KNOW THAT I WAS...?
YOUR CIGARETTES. I KNOW THAT SMELL FROM MY GRANDPA. YOU TOOK THEM FROM OUR COTTAGE, DIDN'T YOU?!
WE DIDN'T HAVE ANY CHOICE. THE PEOPLE IN THE VILLAGE WERE STARVING!!
YOUR GRAMPS WASN'T THERE! I SWEAR!!

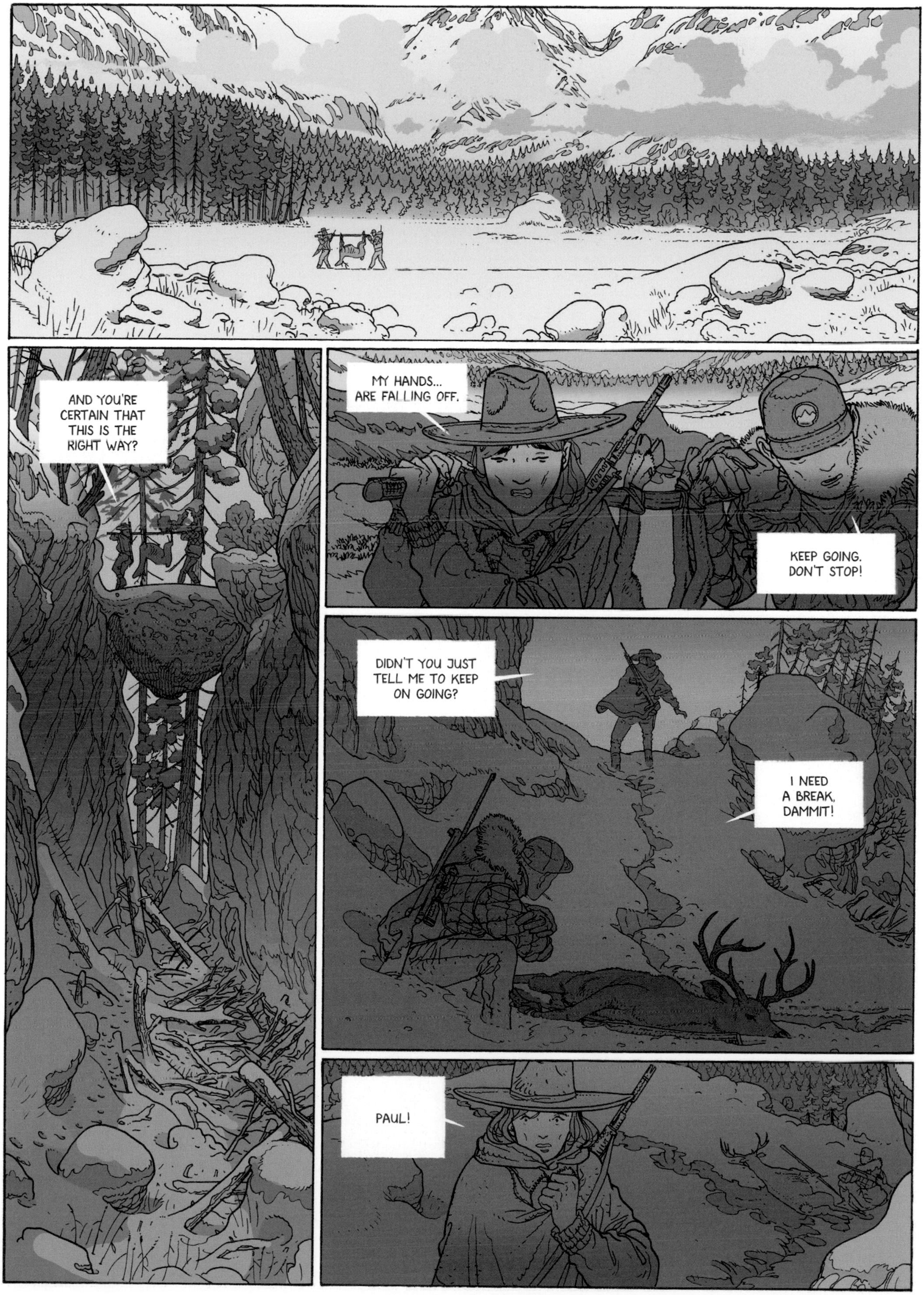
AND YOU'RE CERTAIN THAT THIS IS THE RIGHT WAY?
MY HANDS... ARE FALLING OFF.
KEEP GOING. DON'T STOP!
DIDN'T YOU JUST TELL ME TO KEEP ON GOING?
I NEED A BREAK, DAMMIT!
PAUL!

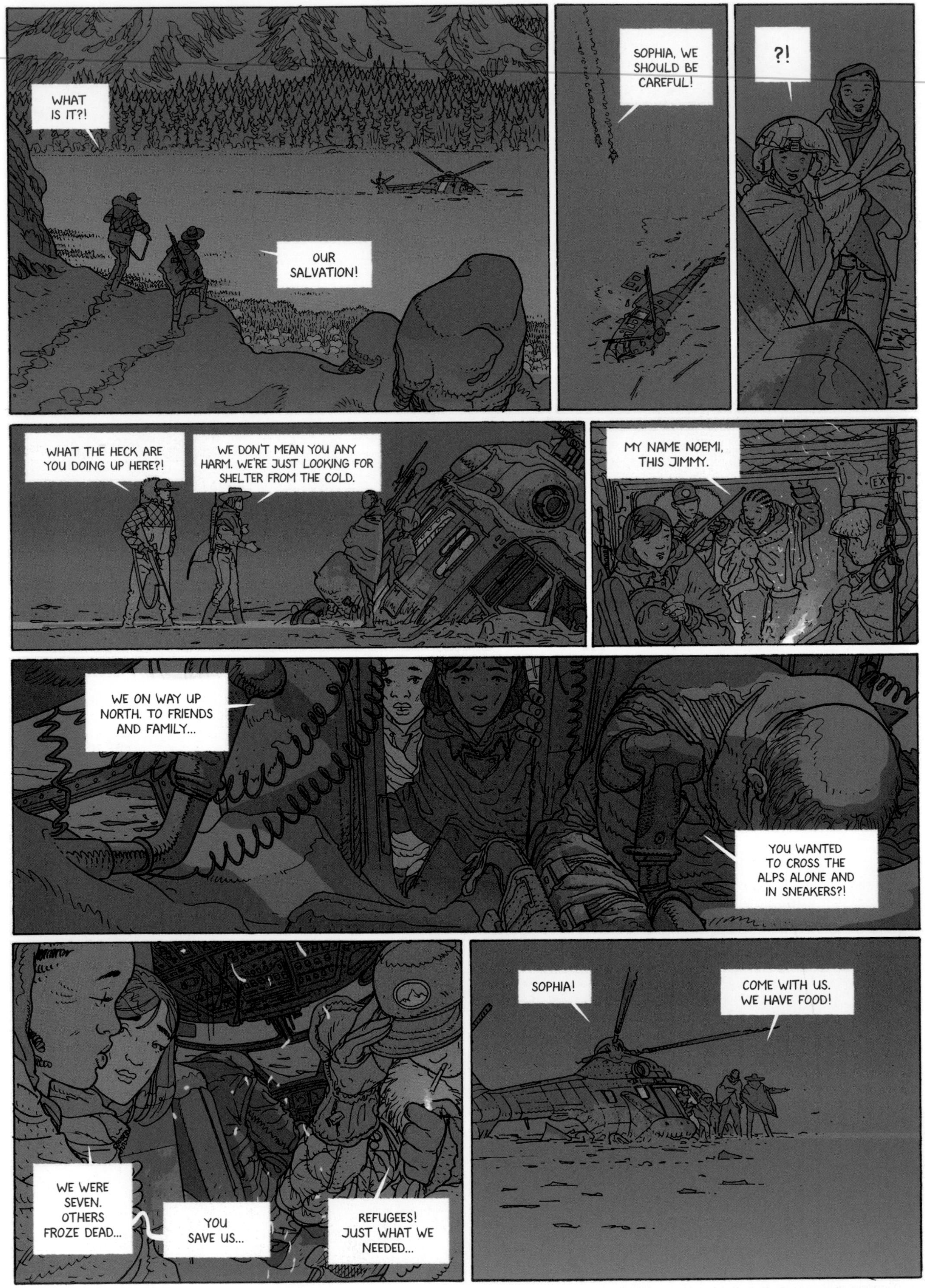
WHAT IS IT?!
OUR SALVATION!
SOPHIA, WE SHOULD BE CAREFUL!
?!
WHAT THE HECK ARE YOU DOING UP HERE?!
WE DON'T MEAN YOU ANY HARM. WE'RE JUST LOOKING FOR SHELTER FROM THE COLD.
MY NAME NOEMI, THIS JIMMY.
EXIT
WE ON WAY UP NORTH. TO FRIENDS AND FAMILY...
YOU WANTED TO CROSS THE ALPS ALONE AND IN SNEAKERS?!
WE WERE SEVEN. OTHERS FROZE DEAD...
YOU SAVE US...
REFUGEES! JUST WHAT WE NEEDED...
SOPHIA!
COME WITH US. WE HAVE FOOD!

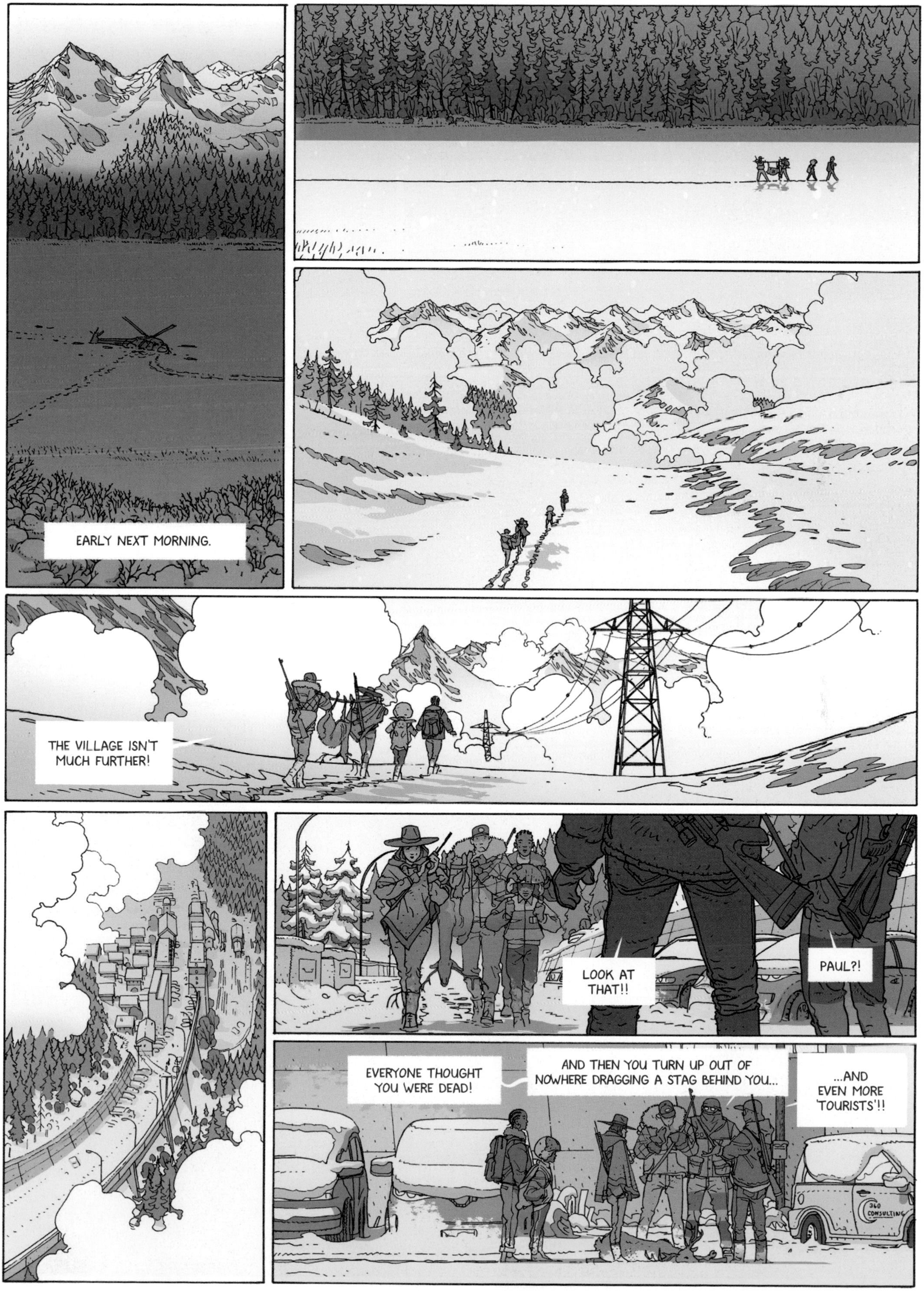
EARLY NEXT MORNING.
THE VILLAGE ISN'T MUCH FURTHER!
LOOK AT THAT!!
PAUL?!
EVERYONE THOUGHT YOU WERE DEAD!
AND THEN YOU TURN UP OUT OF NOWHERE DRAGGING A STAG BEHIND YOU...
...AND EVEN MORE 'TOURISTS'!!
360 CONSULTING

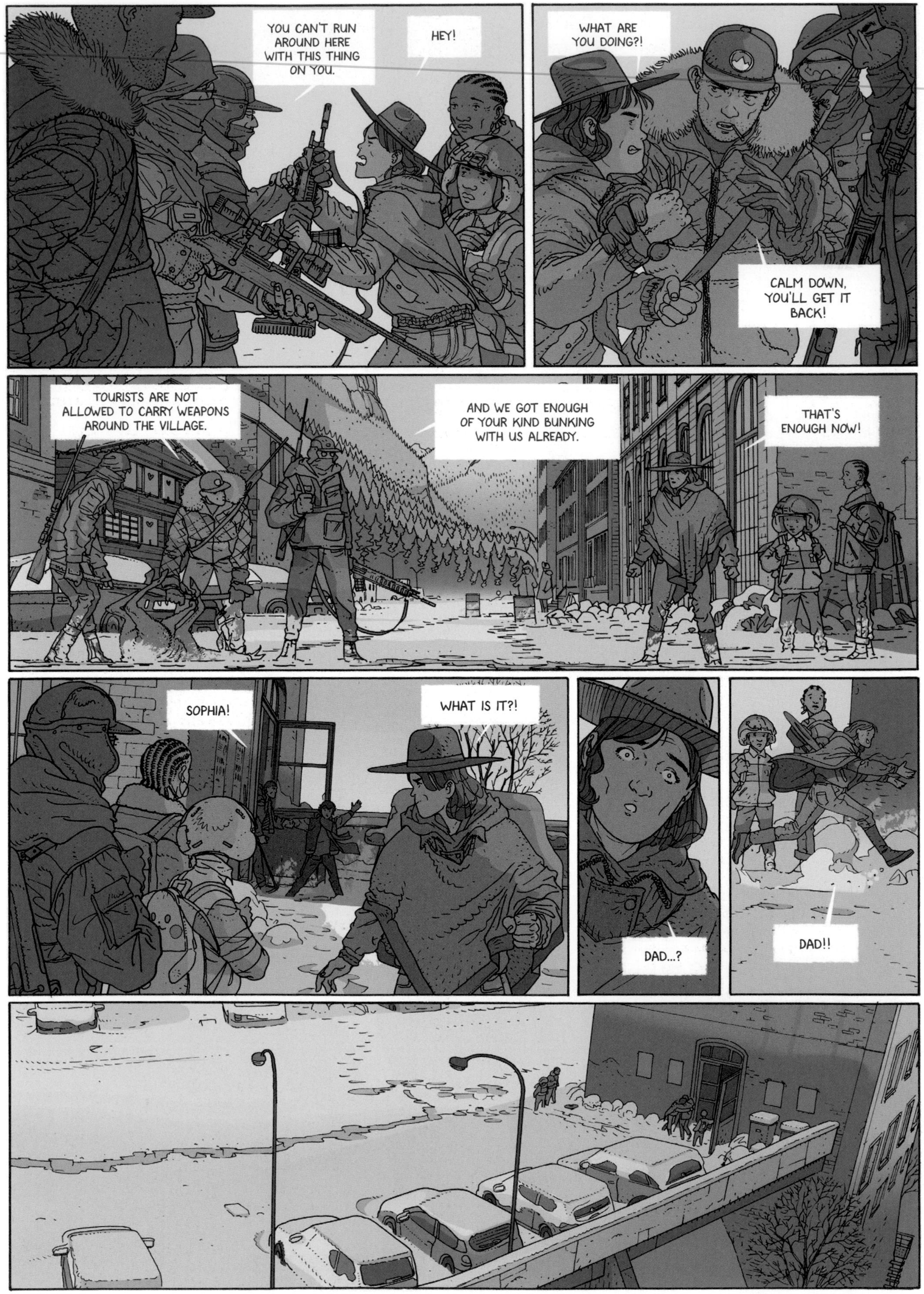
YOU CAN'T RUN AROUND HERE WITH THIS THING ON YOU.
HEY!
WHAT ARE YOU DOING?!
CALM DOWN, YOU'LL GET IT BACK!
TOURISTS ARE NOT ALLOWED TO CARRY WEAPONS AROUND THE VILLAGE.
AND WE GOT ENOUGH OF YOUR KIND BUNKING WITH US ALREADY.
THAT'S ENOUGH NOW!
SOPHIA!
WHAT IS IT?!
DAD...?
DAD!!

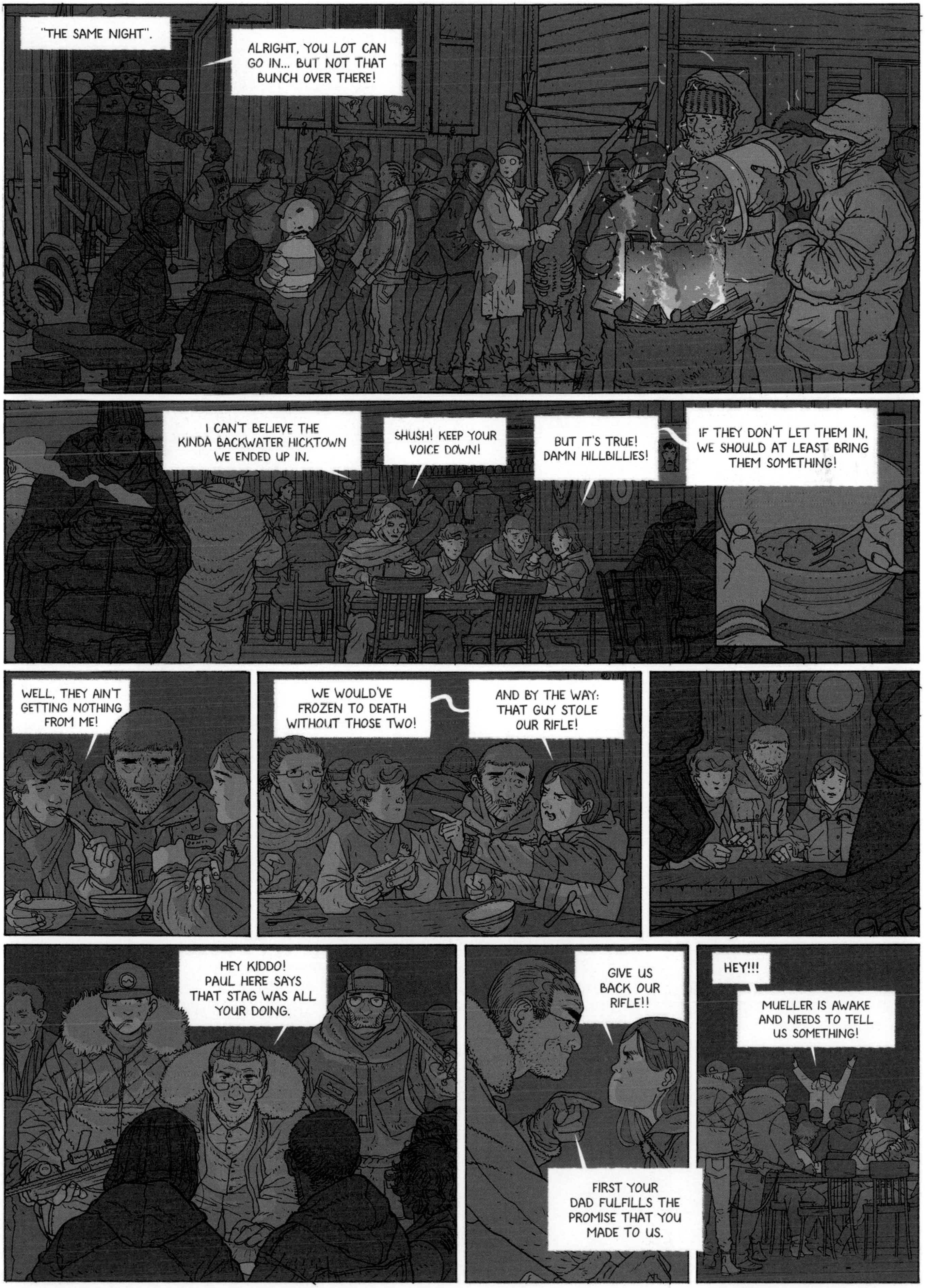
"THE SAME NIGHT".
ALRIGHT, YOU LOT CAN GO IN... BUT NOT THAT BUNCH OVER THERE!
I CAN'T BELIEVE THE KINDA BACKWATER HICKTOWN WE ENDED UP IN.
SHUSH! KEEP YOUR VOICE DOWN!
BUT IT'S TRUE! DAMN HILLBILLIES!
IF THEY DON'T LET THEM IN, WE SHOULD AT LEAST BRING THEM SOMETHING!
WELL, THEY AIN'T GETTING NOTHING FROM ME!
WE WOULD'VE FROZEN TO DEATH WITHOUT THOSE TWO!
AND BY THE WAY: THAT GUY STOLE OUR RIFLE!
HEY KIDDO! PAUL HERE SAYS THAT STAG WAS ALL YOUR DOING.
GIVE US BACK OUR RIFLE!!
FIRST YOUR DAD FULFILLS THE PROMISE THAT YOU MADE TO US.
HEY!!!
MUELLER IS AWAKE AND NEEDS TO TELL US SOMETHING!

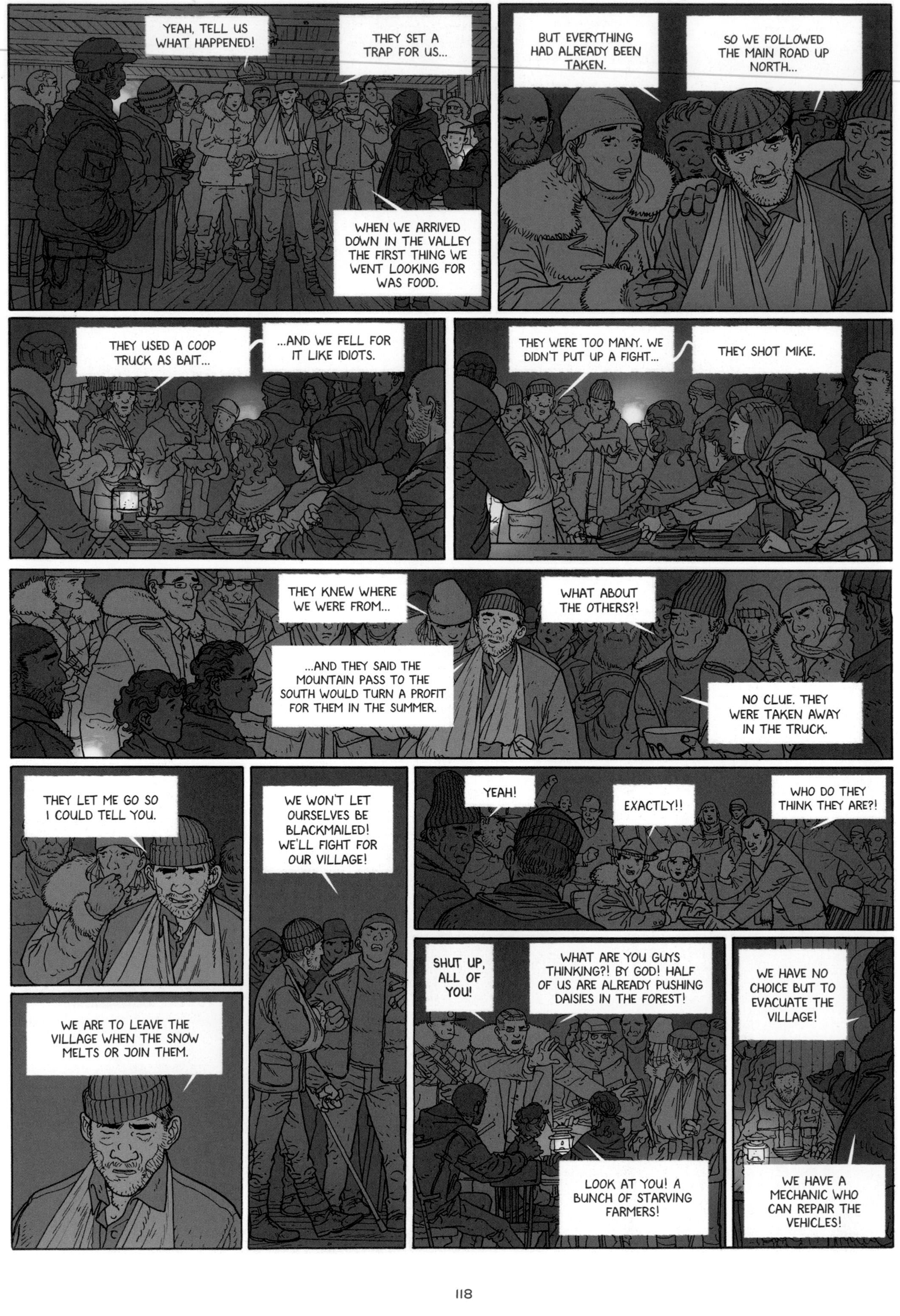

YEAH, TELL US WHAT HAPPENED!
THEY SET A TRAP FOR US...
WHEN WE ARRIVED DOWN IN THE VALLEY THE FIRST THING WE WENT LOOKING FOR WAS FOOD.
BUT EVERYTHING HAD ALREADY BEEN TAKEN.
SO WE FOLLOWED THE MAIN ROAD UP NORTH...
THEY USED A COOP TRUCK AS BAIT...
...AND WE FELL FOR IT LIKE IDIOTS.
THEY WERE TOO MANY. WE DIDN'T PUT UP A FIGHT...
THEY SHOT MIKE.
THEY KNEW WHERE WE WERE FROM...
...AND THEY SAID THE MOUNTAIN PASS TO THE SOUTH WOULD TURN A PROFIT FOR THEM IN THE SUMMER.
WHAT ABOUT THE OTHERS?!
NO CLUE. THEY WERE TAKEN AWAY IN THE TRUCK.
THEY LET ME GO SO I COULD TELL YOU.
WE ARE TO LEAVE THE VILLAGE WHEN THE SNOW MELTS OR JOIN THEM.
WE WON'T LET OURSELVES BE BLACKMAILED! WE'LL FIGHT FOR OUR VILLAGE!
YEAH!
EXACTLY!!
WHO DO THEY THINK THEY ARE?!
SHUT UP, ALL OF YOU!
WHAT ARE YOU GUYS THINKING?! BY GOD! HALF OF US ARE ALREADY PUSHING DAISIES IN THE FOREST!
LOOK AT YOU! A BUNCH OF STARVING FARMERS!
WE HAVE NO CHOICE BUT TO EVACUATE THE VILLAGE!
WE HAVE A MECHANIC WHO CAN REPAIR THE VEHICLES!

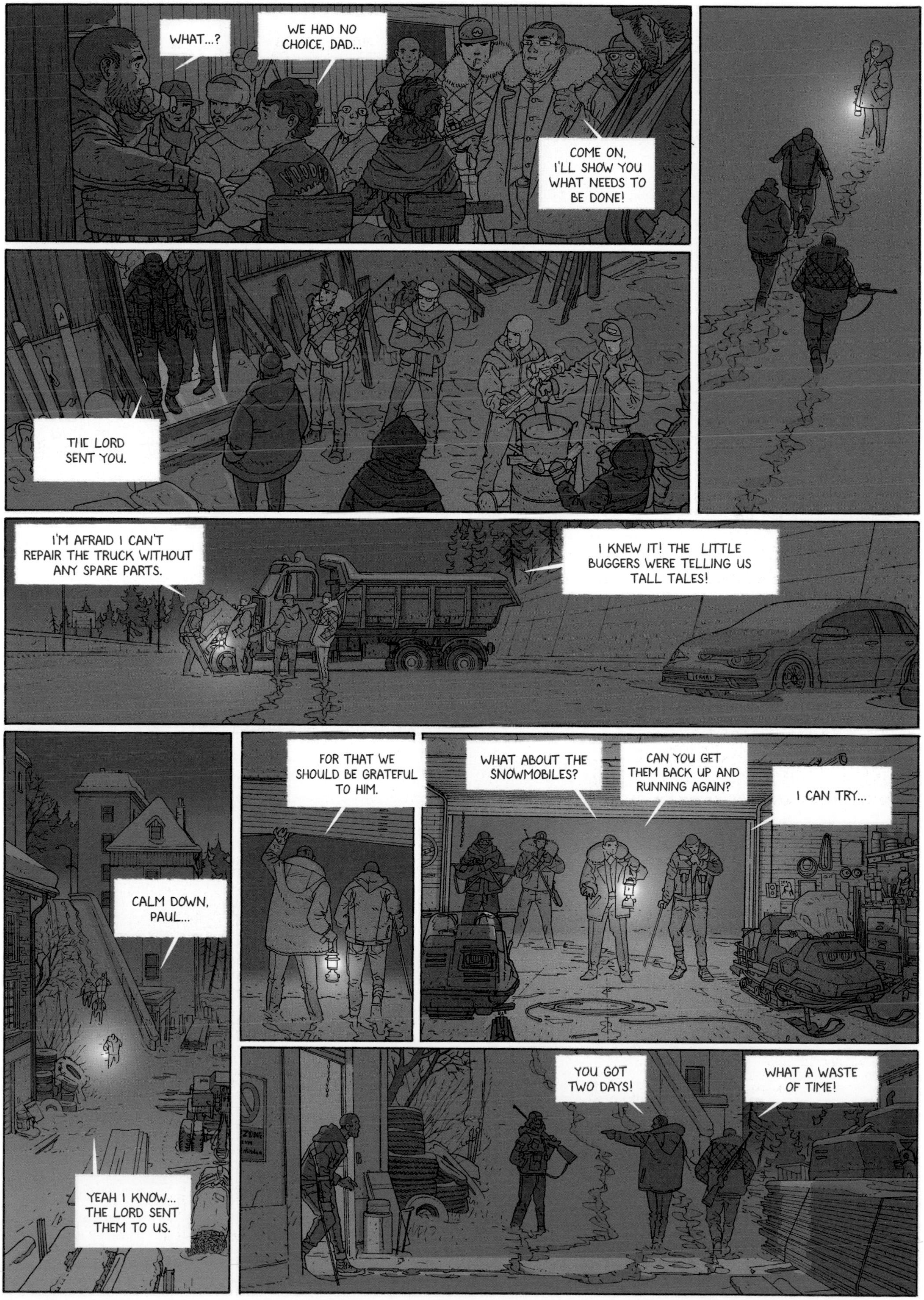
WHAT...?
WE HAD NO CHOICE, DAD...
COME ON, I'LL SHOW YOU WHAT NEEDS TO BE DONE!
THE LORD SENT YOU.
I'M AFRAID I CAN'T REPAIR THE TRUCK WITHOUT ANY SPARE PARTS.
I KNEW IT! THE LITTLE BUGGERS WERE TELLING US TALL TALES!
CALM DOWN, PAUL...
YEAH I KNOW... THE LORD SENT THEM TO US.
FOR THAT WE SHOULD BE GRATEFUL TO HIM.
WHAT ABOUT THE SNOWMOBILES?
CAN YOU GET THEM BACK UP AND RUNNING AGAIN?
I CAN TRY...
YOU GOT TWO DAYS!
WHAT A WASTE OF TIME!

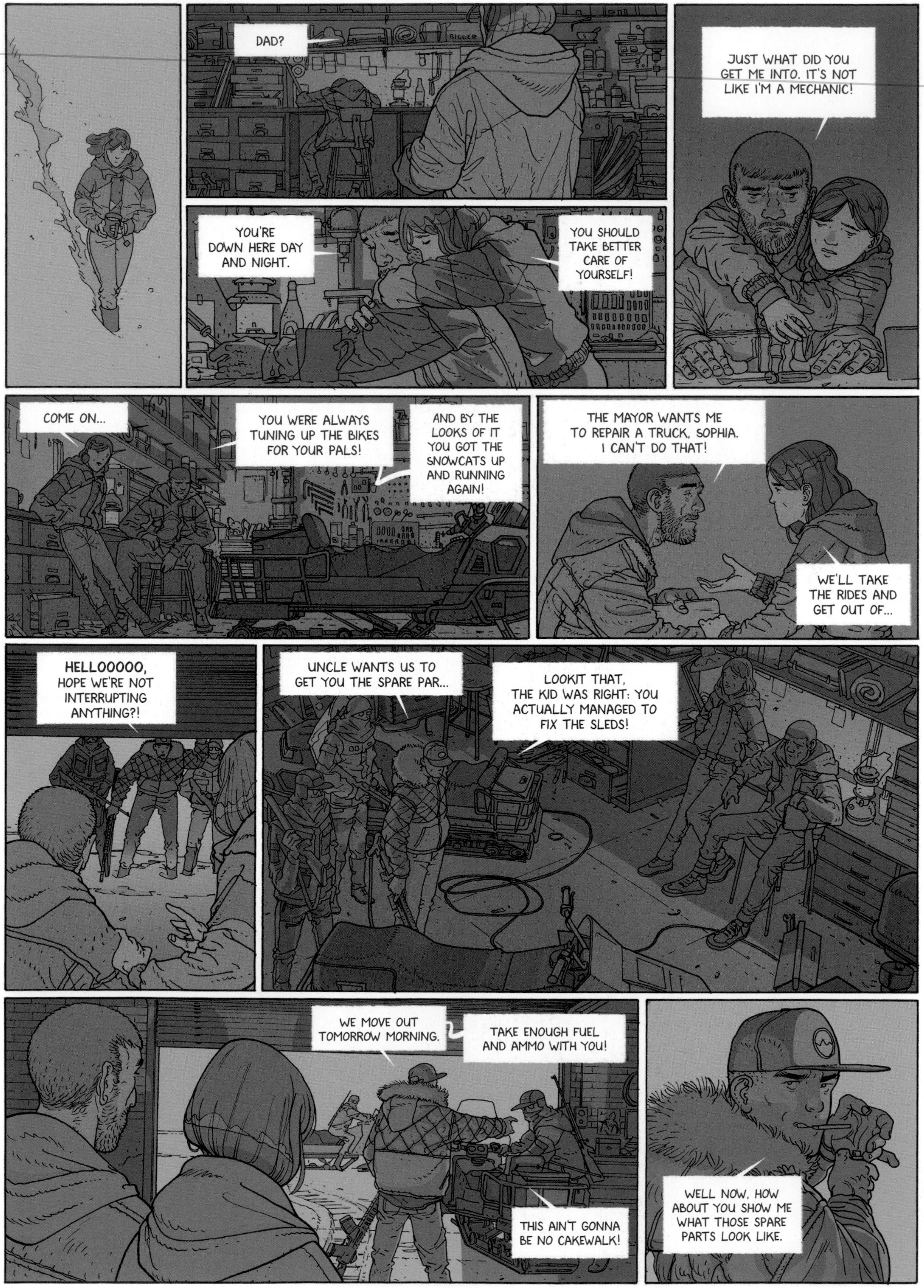

DAD?
YOU'RE DOWN HERE DAY AND NIGHT.
YOU SHOULD TAKE BETTER CARE OF YOURSELF!
JUST WHAT DID YOU GET ME INTO. IT'S NOT LIKE I'M A MECHANIC!
COME ON...
YOU WERE ALWAYS TUNING UP THE BIKES FOR YOUR PALS!
AND BY THE LOOKS OF IT YOU GOT THE SNOWCATS UP AND RUNNING AGAIN!
THE MAYOR WANTS ME TO REPAIR A TRUCK, SOPHIA. I CAN'T DO THAT!
WE'LL TAKE THE RIDES AND GET OUT OF...
HELLOOOOO, HOPE WE'RE NOT INTERRUPTING ANYTHING?!
UNCLE WANTS US TO GET YOU THE SPARE PAR...
LOOKIT THAT, THE KID WAS RIGHT: YOU ACTUALLY MANAGED TO FIX THE SLEDS!
WE MOVE OUT TOMORROW MORNING.
TAKE ENOUGH FUEL AND AMMO WITH YOU!
THIS AIN'T GONNA BE NO CAKEWALK!
WELL NOW, HOW ABOUT YOU SHOW ME WHAT THOSE SPARE PARTS LOOK LIKE.

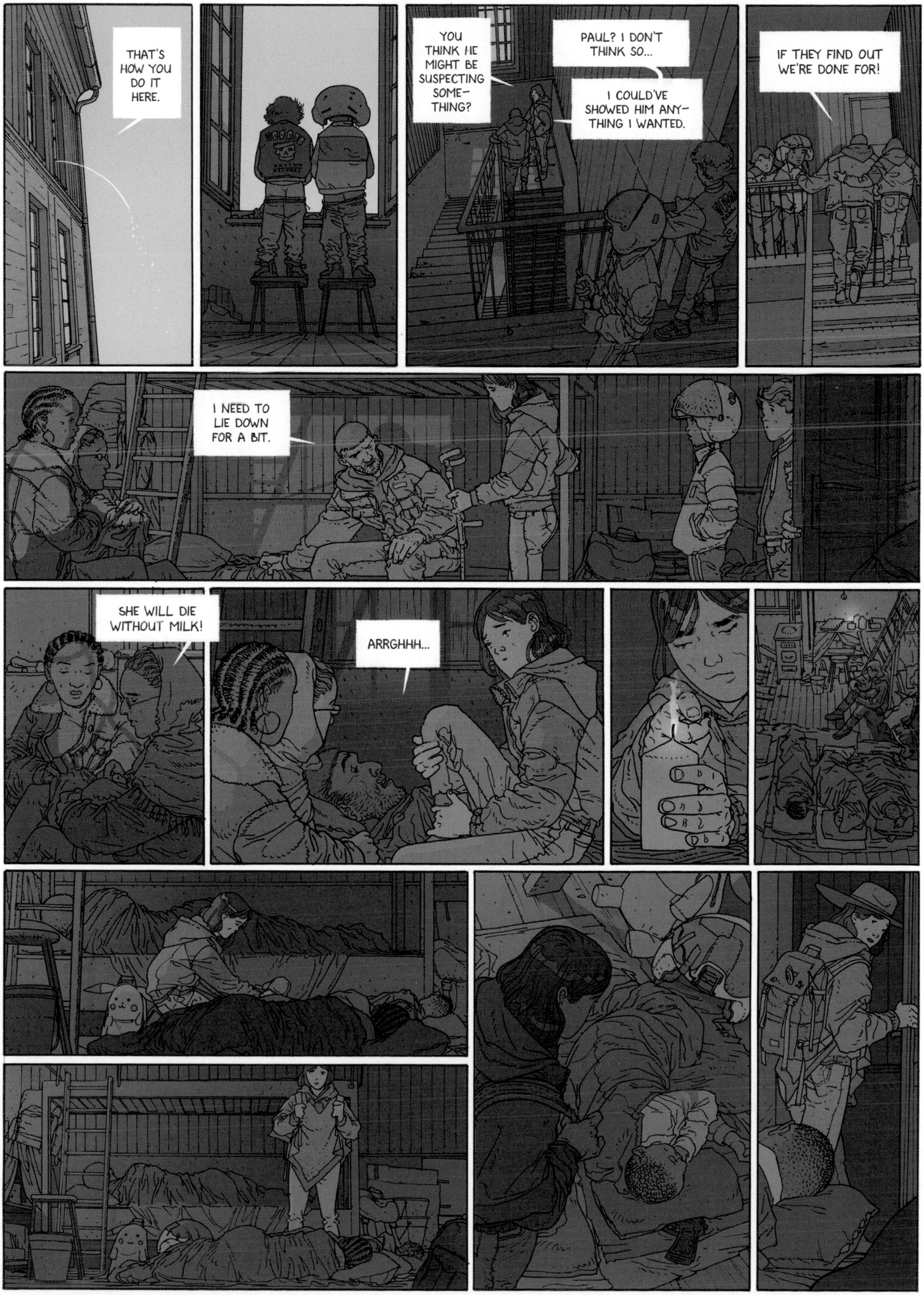
THAT'S HOW YOU DO IT HERE.
YOU THINK HE MIGHT BE SUSPECTING SOME-THING?
PAUL? I DON'T THINK SO...
I COULD'VE SHOWED HIM ANY-THING I WANTED.
IF THEY FIND OUT WE'RE DONE FOR!
I NEED TO LIE DOWN FOR A BIT.
SHE WILL DIE WITHOUT MILK!
ARRGHHH...

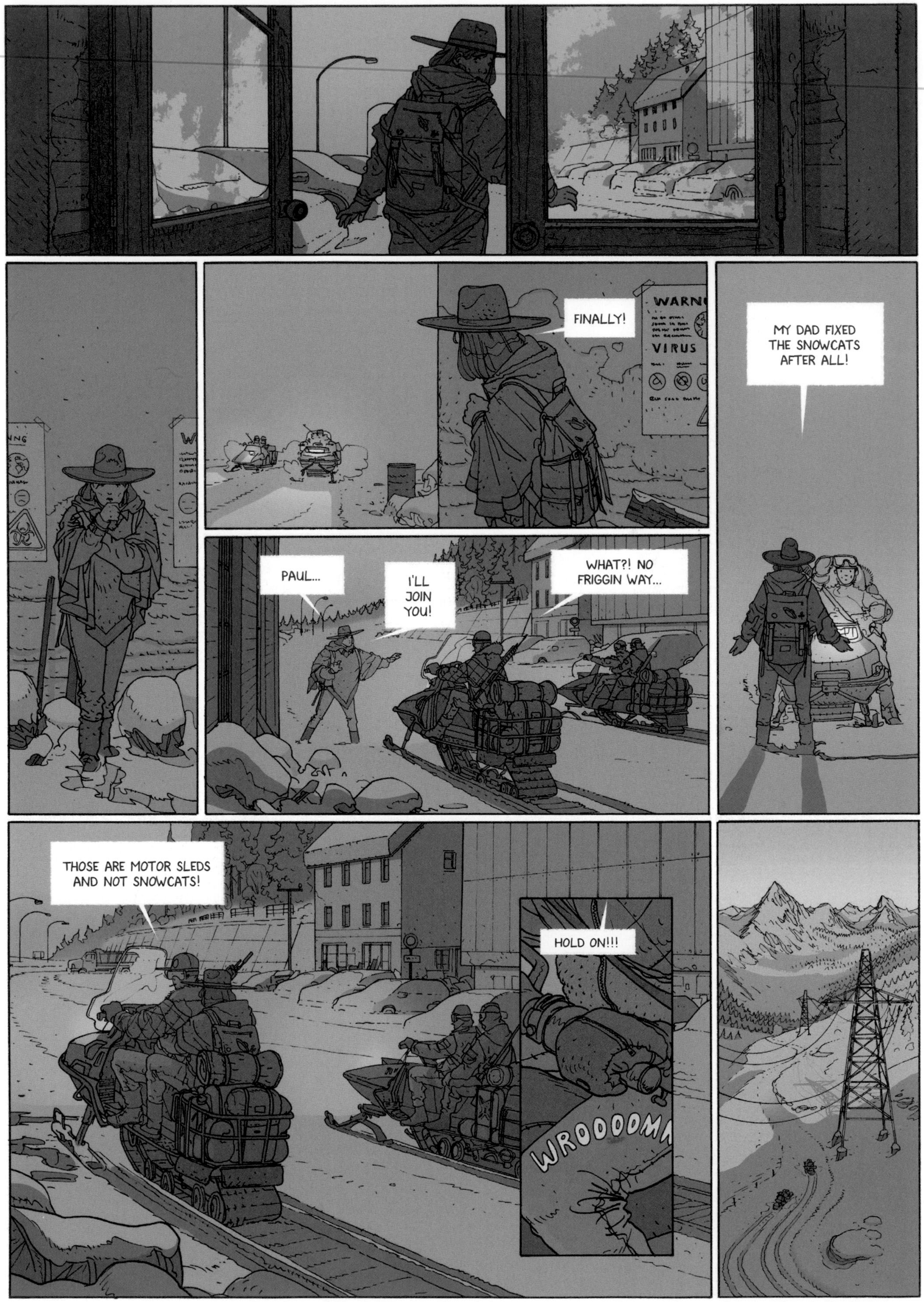

FINALLY!
MY DAD FIXED THE SNOWCATS AFTER ALL!
PAUL...
I'LL JOIN YOU!
WHAT?! NO FRIGGIN WAY...
THOSE ARE MOTOR SLEDS AND NOT SNOWCATS!
HOLD ON!!!
WROOOOMM

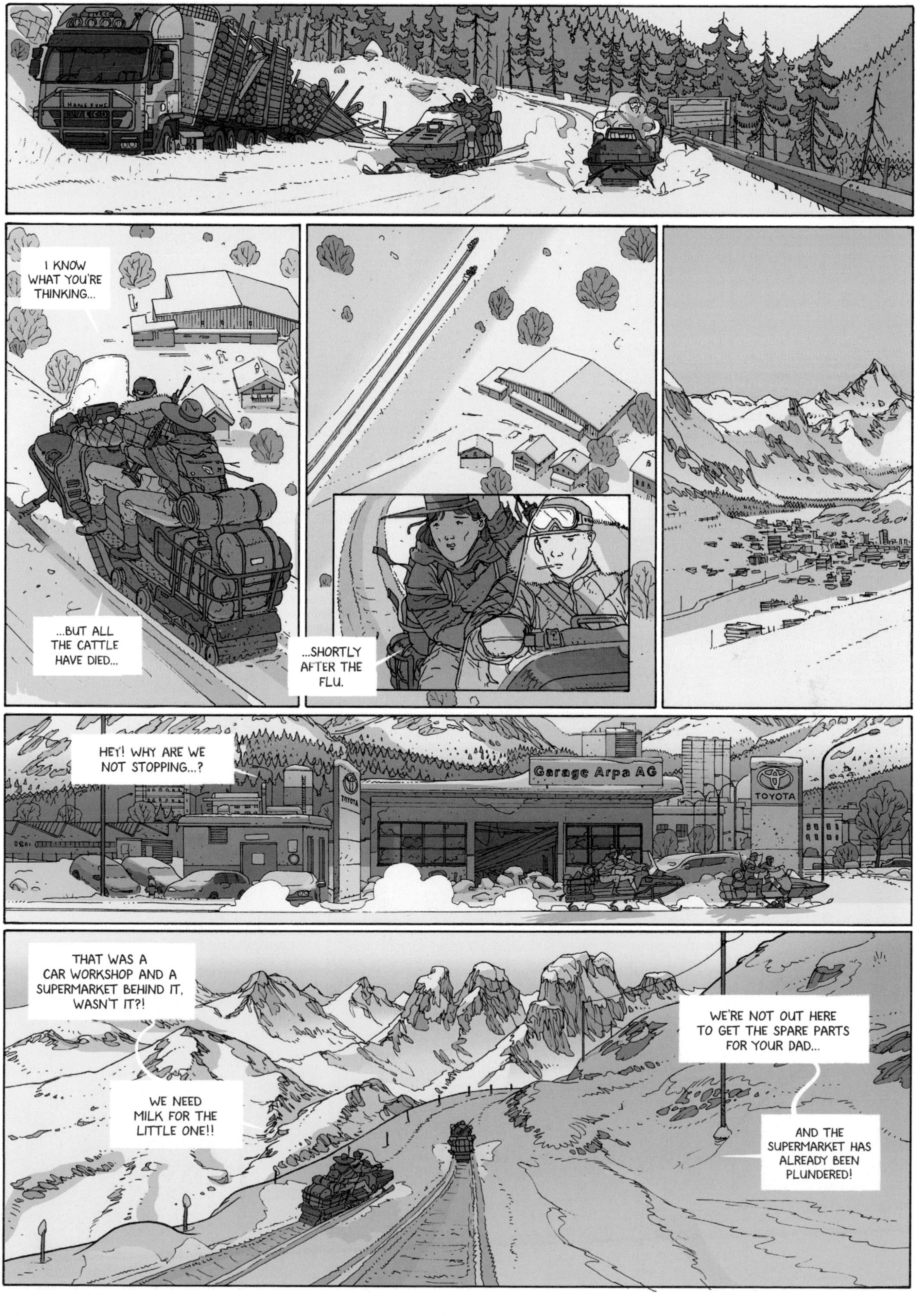
I KNOW WHAT YOU'RE THINKING...
...BUT ALL THE CATTLE HAVE DIED...
...SHORTLY AFTER THE FLU.
HEY! WHY ARE WE NOT STOPPING...?
Garage Arpa AG
TOYOTA
TOYOTA
THAT WAS A CAR WORKSHOP AND A SUPERMARKET BEHIND IT, WASN'T IT?!
WE NEED MILK FOR THE LITTLE ONE!!
WE'RE NOT OUT HERE TO GET THE SPARE PARTS FOR YOUR DAD...
AND THE SUPERMARKET HAS ALREADY BEEN PLUNDERED!

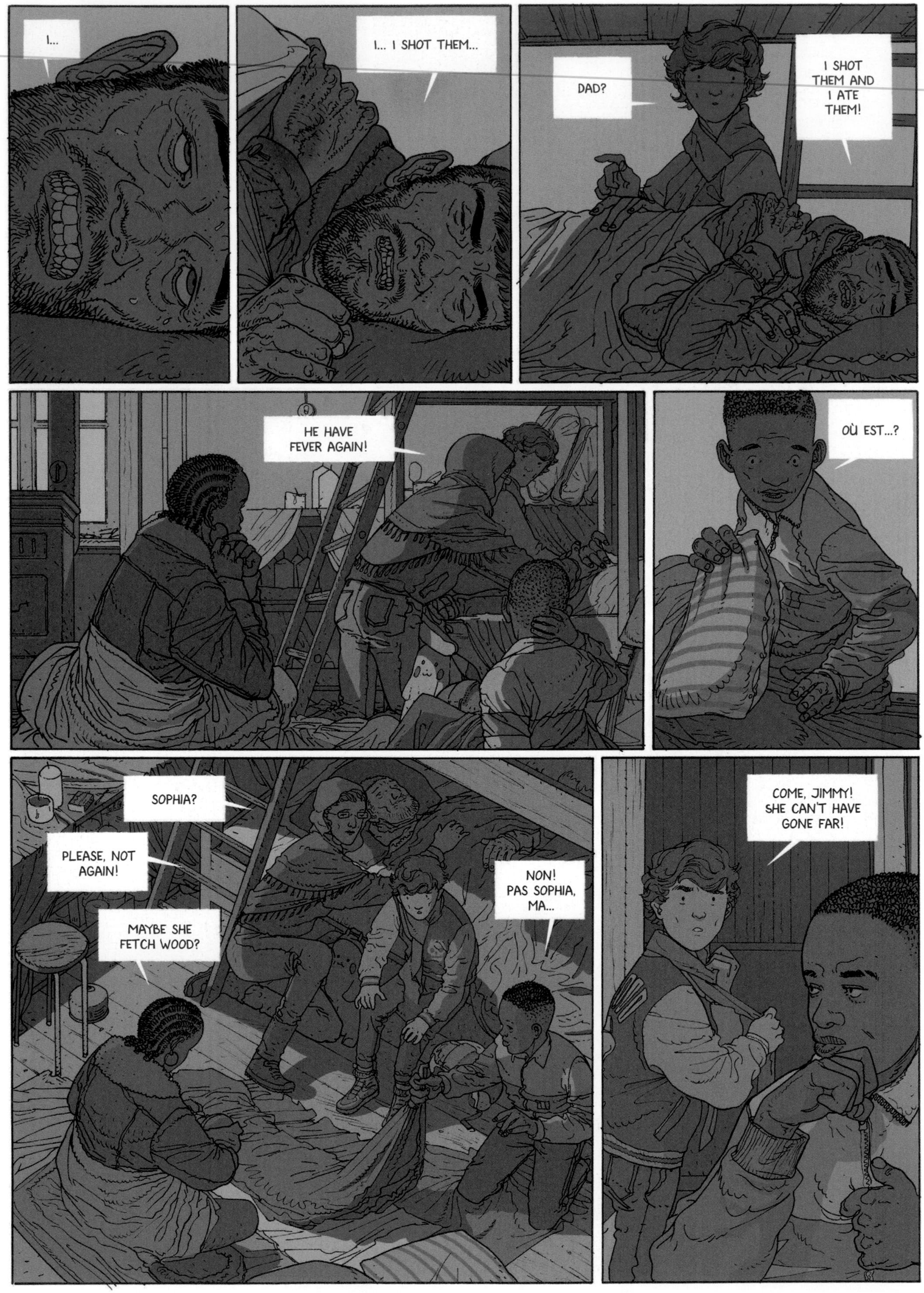
I...
I... I SHOT THEM...
DAD?
I SHOT THEM AND I ATE THEM!
HE HAVE FEVER AGAIN!
OÙ EST...?
SOPHIA?
PLEASE, NOT AGAIN!
MAYBE SHE FETCH WOOD?
NON! PAS SOPHIA, MA...
COME, JIMMY! SHE CAN'T HAVE GONE FAR!

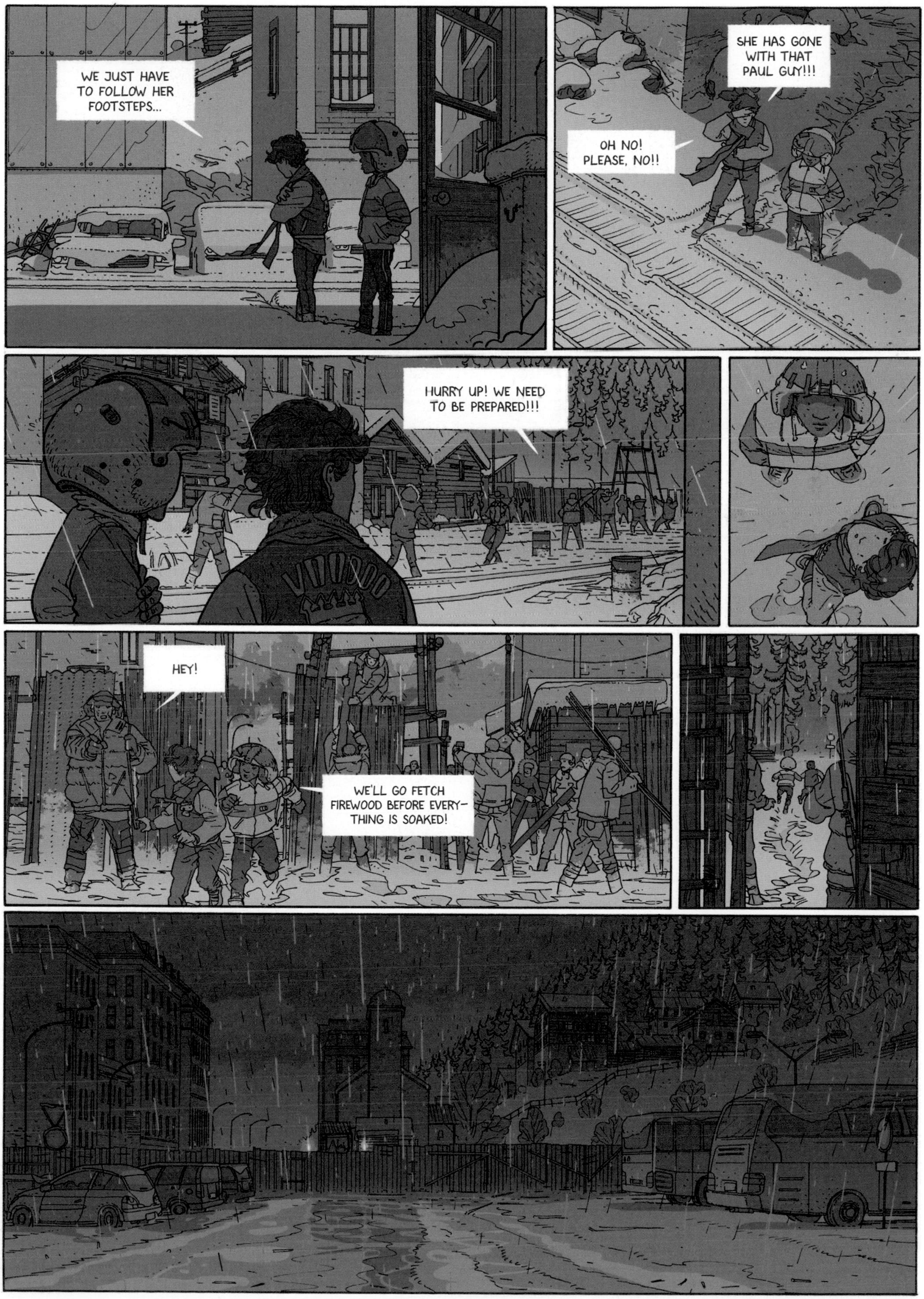
WE JUST HAVE TO FOLLOW HER FOOTSTEPS...
SHE HAS GONE WITH THAT PAUL GUY!!!
OH NO! PLEASE, NO!!
HURRY UP! WE NEED TO BE PREPARED!!!
HEY!
WE'LL GO FETCH FIREWOOD BEFORE EVERY-THING IS SOAKED!

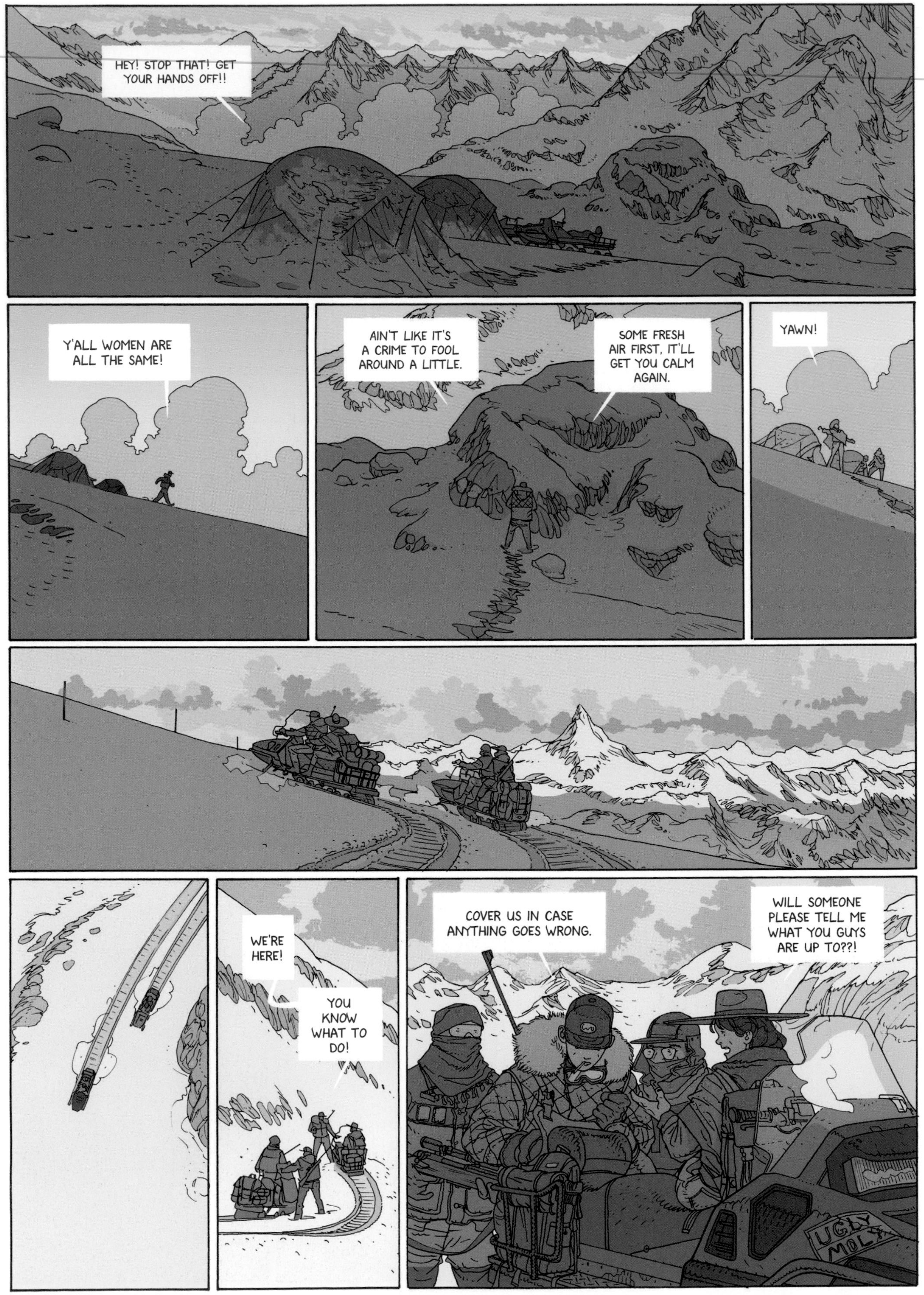
HEY! STOP THAT! GET YOUR HANDS OFF!!
Y'ALL WOMEN ARE ALL THE SAME!
AIN'T LIKE IT'S A CRIME TO FOOL AROUND A LITTLE.
SOME FRESH AIR FIRST, IT'LL GET YOU CALM AGAIN.
YAWN!
WE'RE HERE!
YOU KNOW WHAT TO DO!
COVER US IN CASE ANYTHING GOES WRONG.
WILL SOMEONE PLEASE TELL ME WHAT YOU GUYS ARE UP TO??!

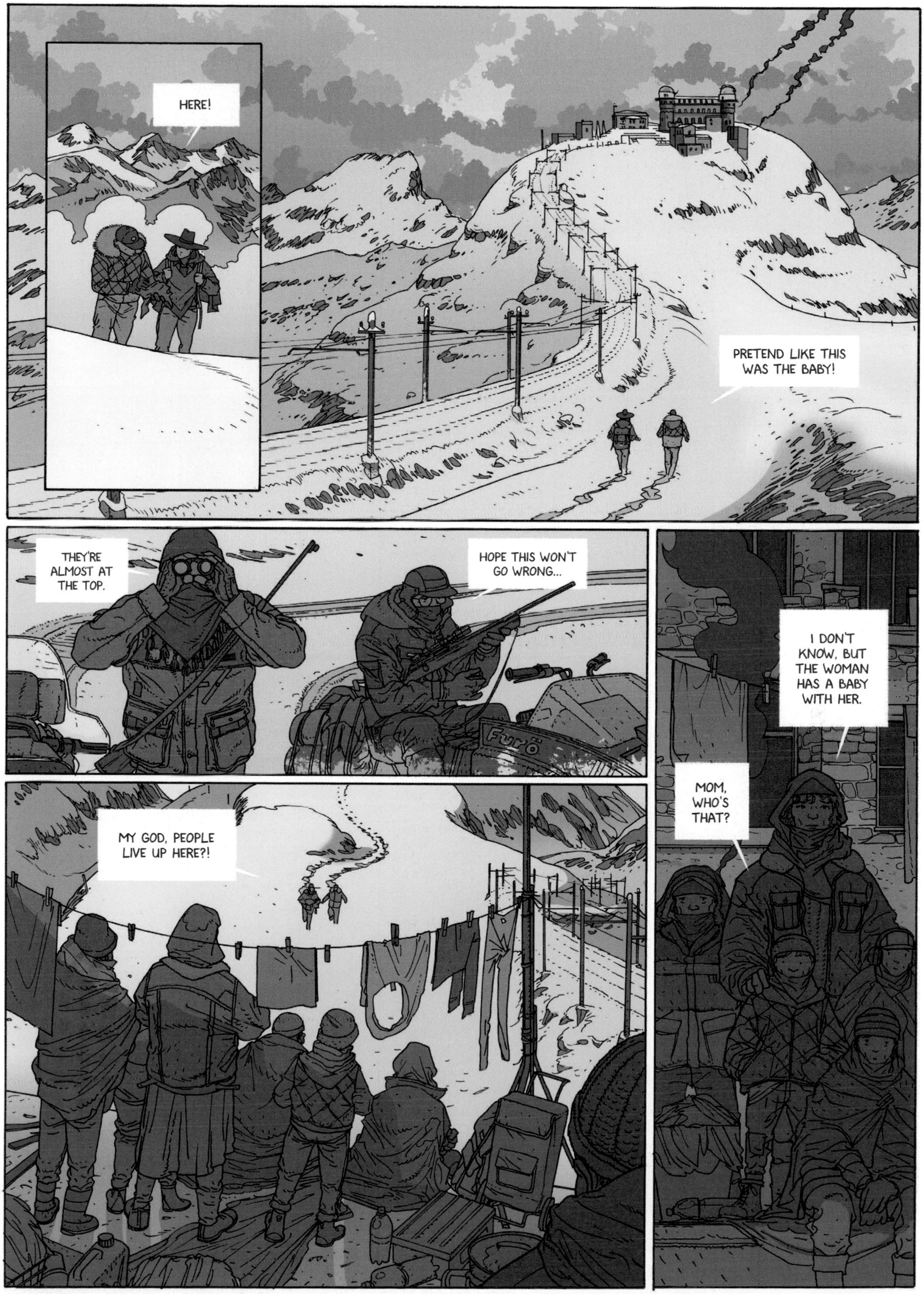
HERE!
PRETEND LIKE THIS WAS THE BABY!
THEY'RE ALMOST AT THE TOP.
HOPE THIS WON'T GO WRONG...
Furö
I DON'T KNOW, BUT THE WOMAN HAS A BABY WITH HER.
MOM, WHO'S THAT?
MY GOD, PEOPLE LIVE UP HERE?!

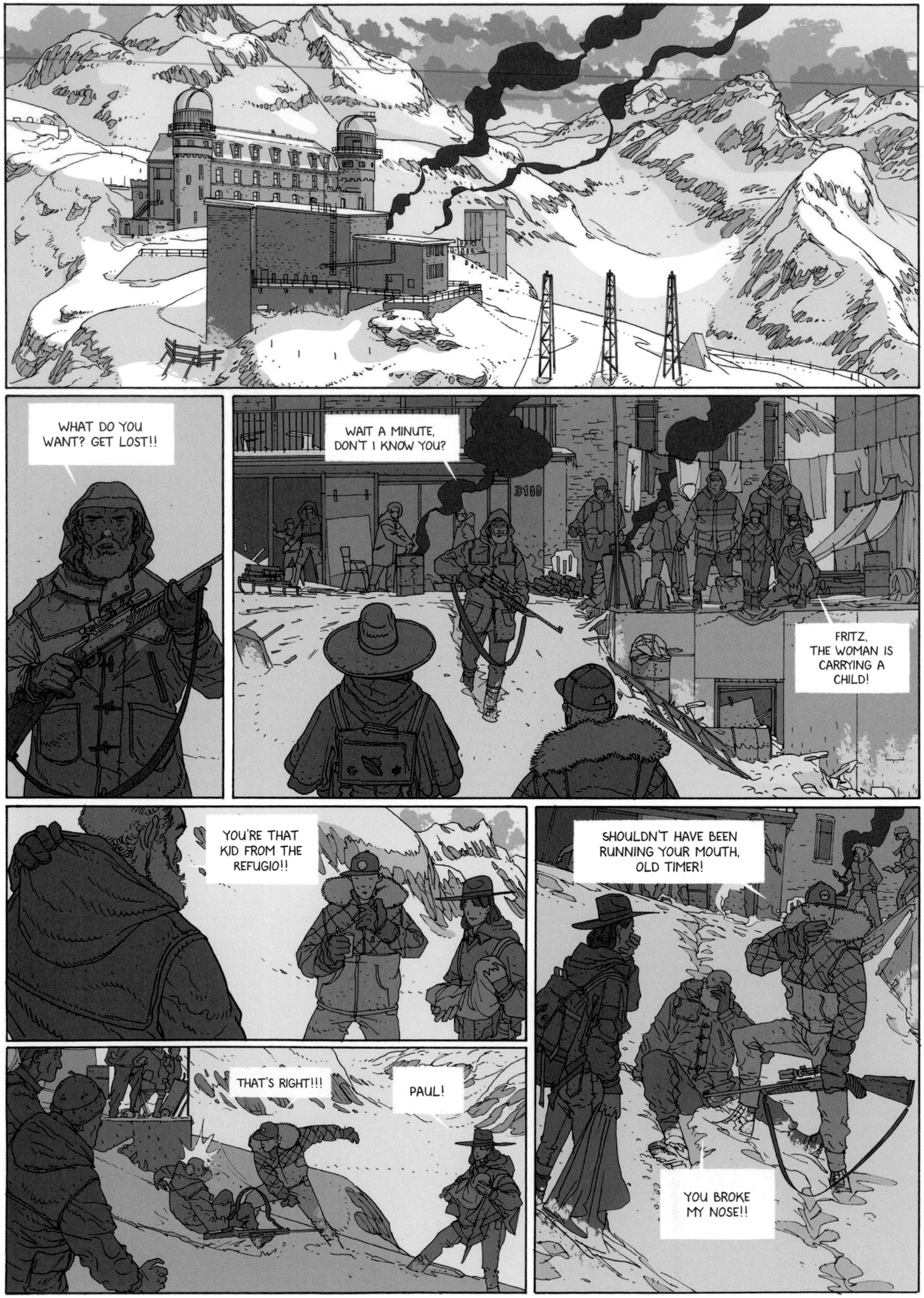
WHAT DO YOU WANT? GET LOST!!
WAIT A MINUTE, DON'T I KNOW YOU?
3100
FRITZ, THE WOMAN IS CARRYING A CHILD!
YOU'RE THAT KID FROM THE REFUGIO!!
THAT'S RIGHT!!!
PAUL!
SHOULDN'T HAVE BEEN RUNNING YOUR MOUTH, OLD TIMER!
YOU BROKE MY NOSE!!

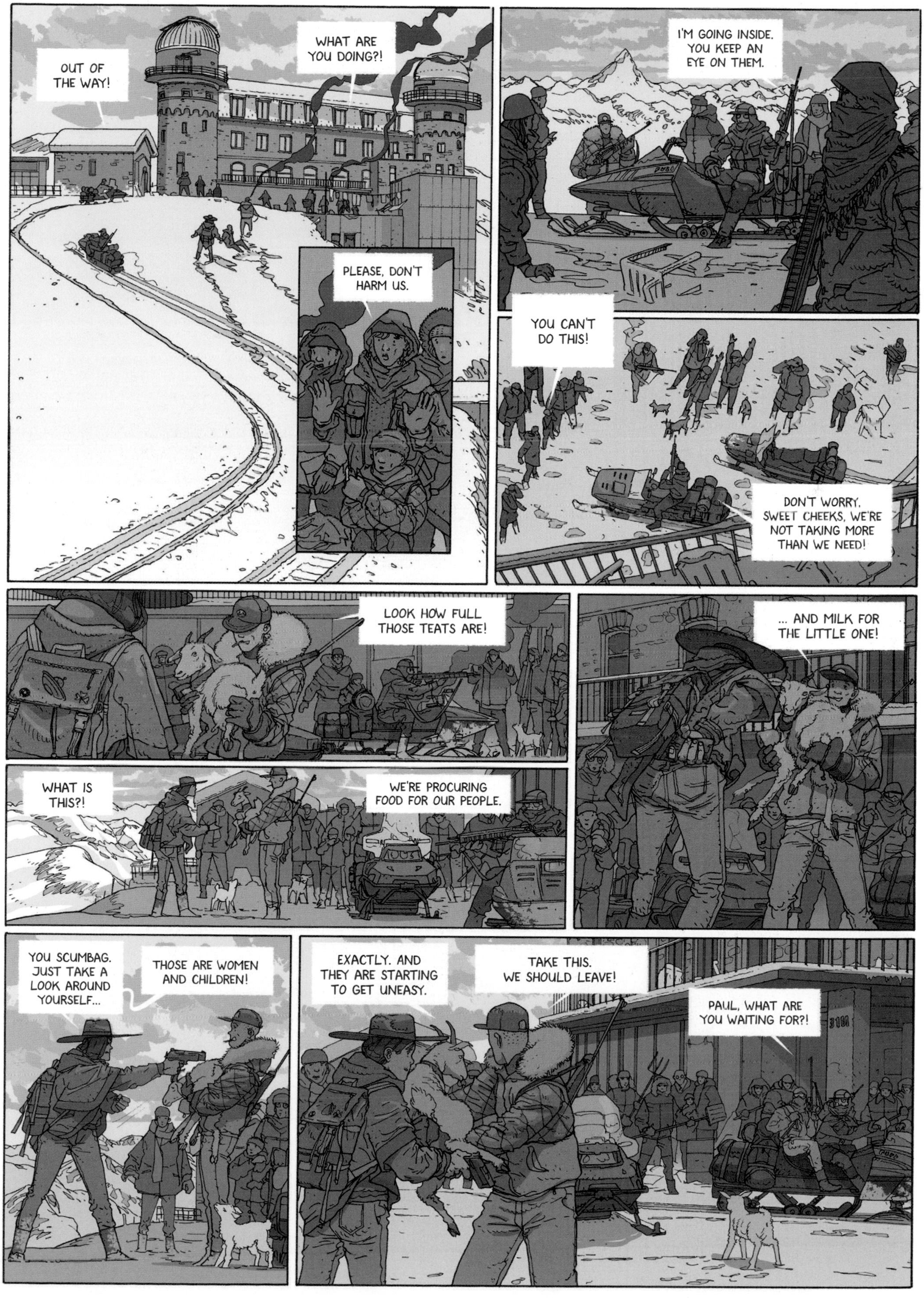
OUT OF THE WAY!
WHAT ARE YOU DOING?!
PLEASE, DON'T HARM US.
I'M GOING INSIDE. YOU KEEP AN EYE ON THEM.
YOU CAN'T DO THIS!
DON'T WORRY, SWEET CHEEKS, WE'RE NOT TAKING MORE THAN WE NEED!
LOOK HOW FULL THOSE TEATS ARE!
WHAT IS THIS?!
WE'RE PROCURING FOOD FOR OUR PEOPLE.
... AND MILK FOR THE LITTLE ONE!
YOU SCUMBAG. JUST TAKE A LOOK AROUND YOURSELF...
THOSE ARE WOMEN AND CHILDREN!
EXACTLY. AND THEY ARE STARTING TO GET UNEASY.
TAKE THIS. WE SHOULD LEAVE!
PAUL, WHAT ARE YOU WAITING FOR?!

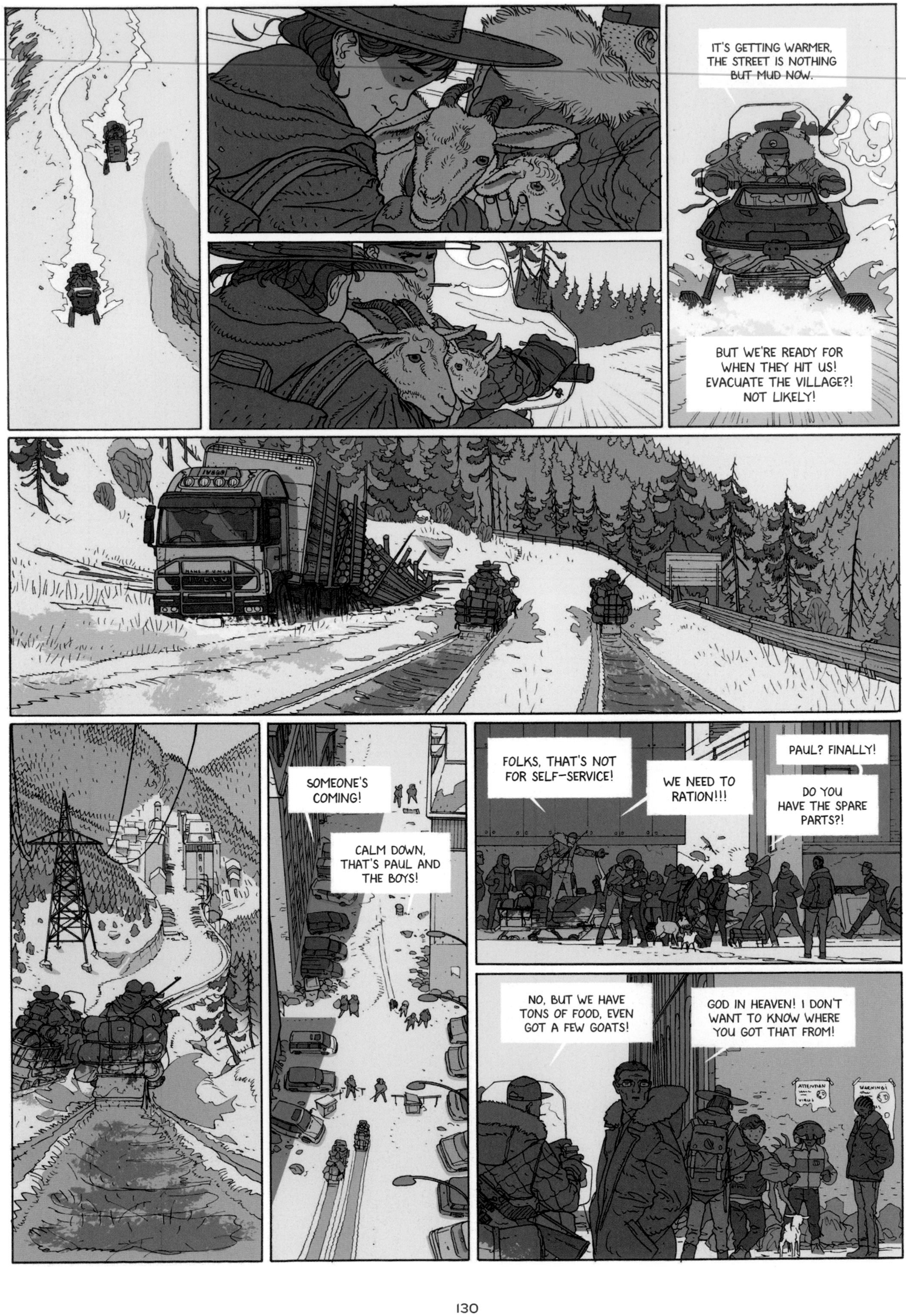
IT'S GETTING WARMER, THE STREET IS NOTHING BUT MUD NOW.
BUT WE'RE READY FOR WHEN THEY HIT US! EVACUATE THE VILLAGE?! NOT LIKELY!
SOMEONE'S COMING!
CALM DOWN, THAT'S PAUL AND THE BOYS!
FOLKS, THAT'S NOT FOR SELF-SERVICE!
WE NEED TO RATION!!!
PAUL? FINALLY!
DO YOU HAVE THE SPARE PARTS?!
NO, BUT WE HAVE TONS OF FOOD, EVEN GOT A FEW GOATS!
GOD IN HEAVEN! I DON'T WANT TO KNOW WHERE YOU GOT THAT FROM!

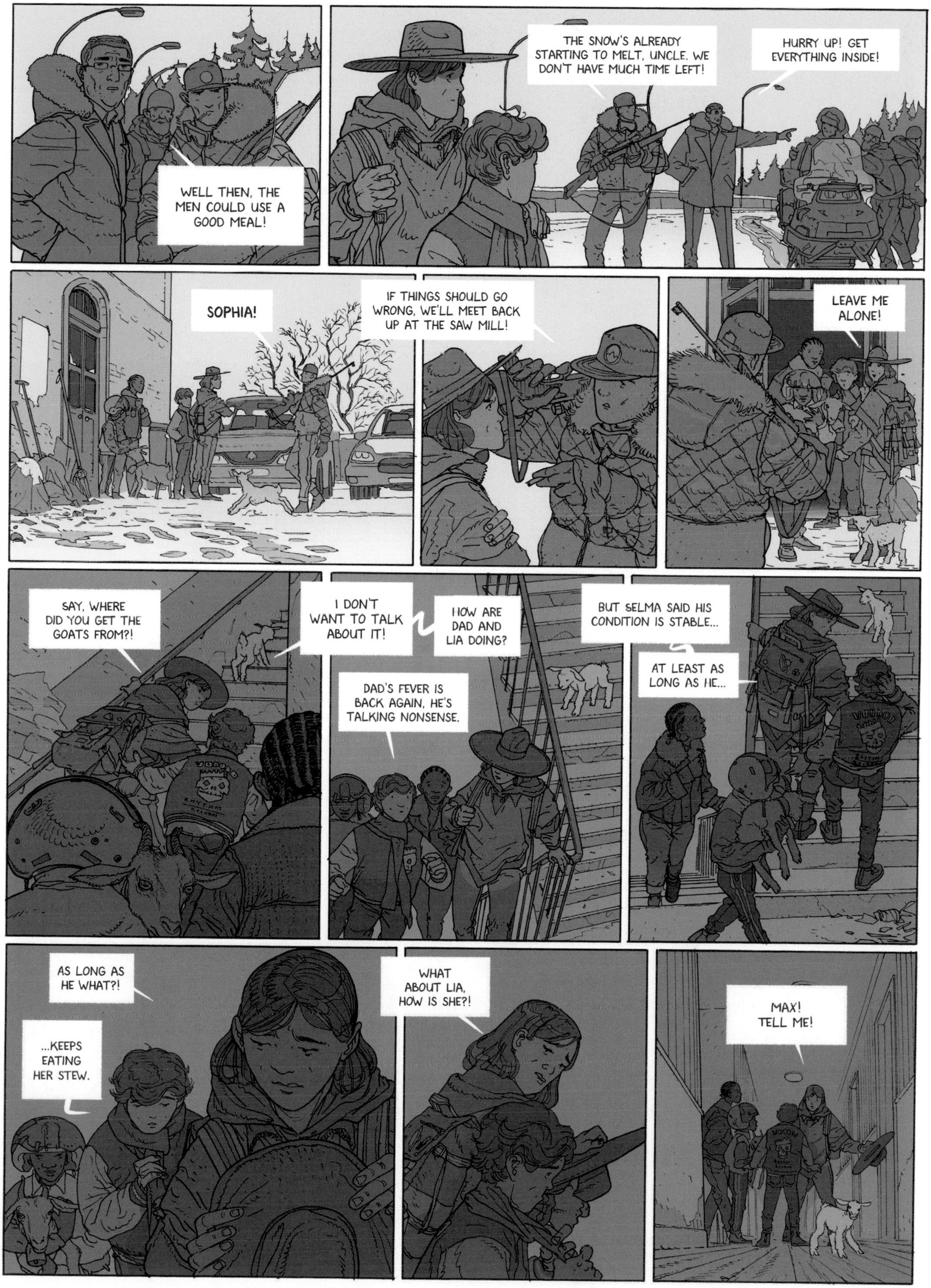

WELL THEN, THE MEN COULD USE A GOOD MEAL!
THE SNOW'S ALREADY STARTING TO MELT, UNCLE. WE DON'T HAVE MUCH TIME LEFT!
HURRY UP! GET EVERYTHING INSIDE!
SOPHIA!
IF THINGS SHOULD GO WRONG, WE'LL MEET BACK UP AT THE SAW MILL!
LEAVE ME ALONE!
SAY, WHERE DID YOU GET THE GOATS FROM?!
I DON'T WANT TO TALK ABOUT IT!
HOW ARE DAD AND LIA DOING?
DAD'S FEVER IS BACK AGAIN, HE'S TALKING NONSENSE.
BUT SELMA SAID HIS CONDITION IS STABLE...
AT LEAST AS LONG AS HE...
AS LONG AS HE WHAT?!
...KEEPS EATING HER STEW.
WHAT ABOUT LIA, HOW IS SHE?!
MAX! TELL ME!

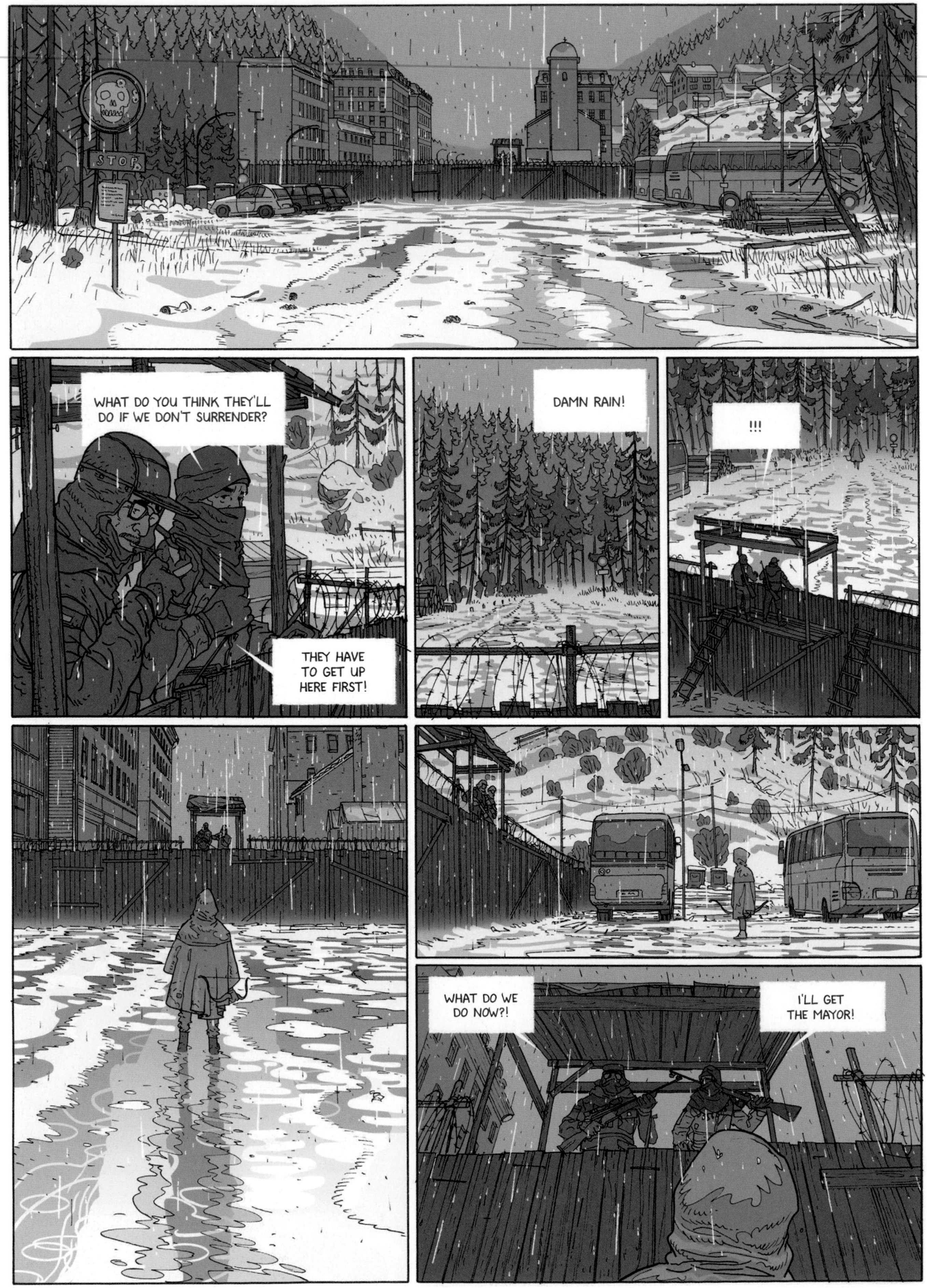
STOP
WHAT DO YOU THINK THEY'LL DO IF WE DON'T SURRENDER?
THEY HAVE TO GET UP HERE FIRST!
DAMN RAIN!
!!!
WHAT DO WE DO NOW?!
I'LL GET THE MAYOR!

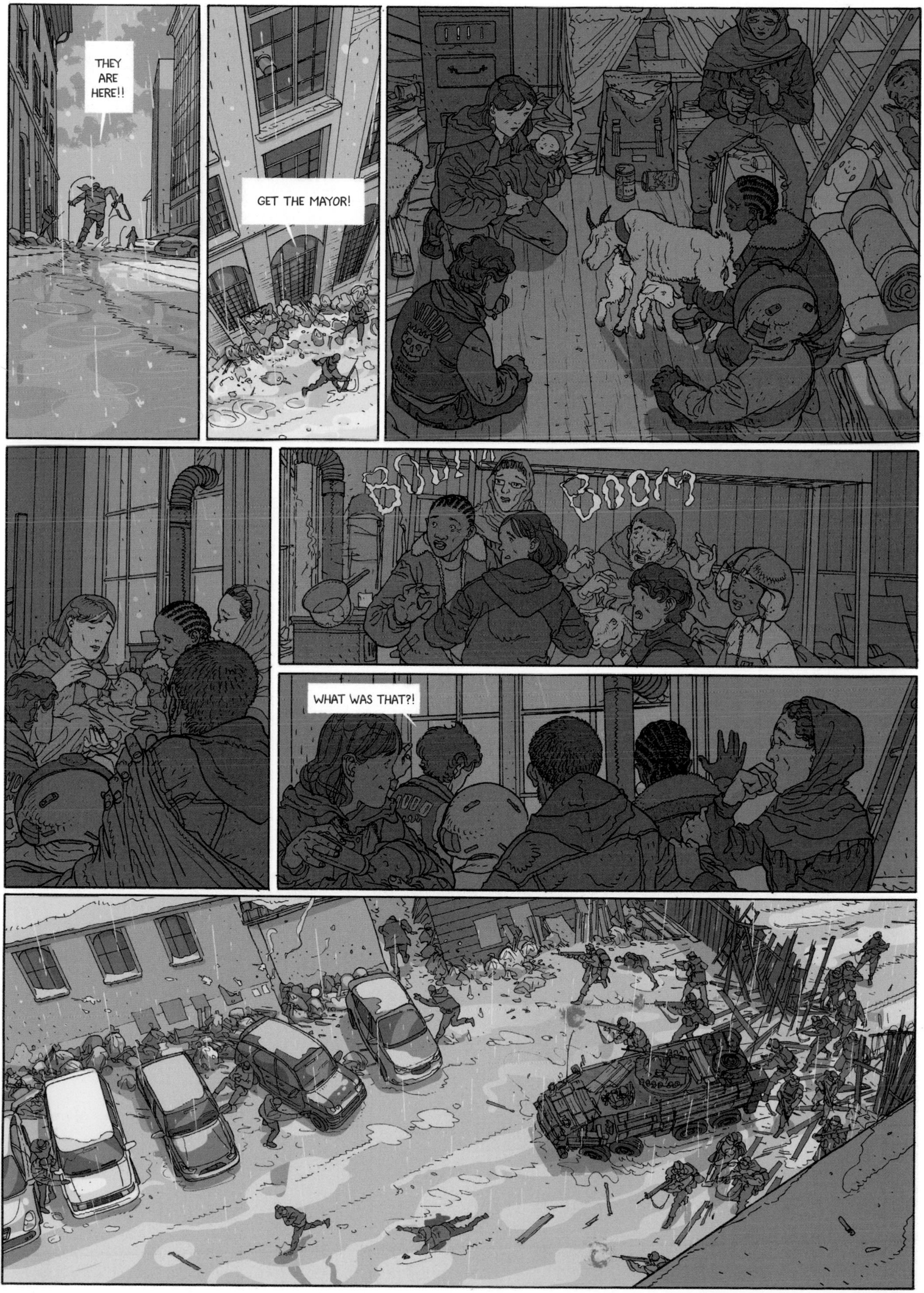
THEY ARE HERE!!
GET THE MAYOR!
BOOM
WHAT WAS THAT?!

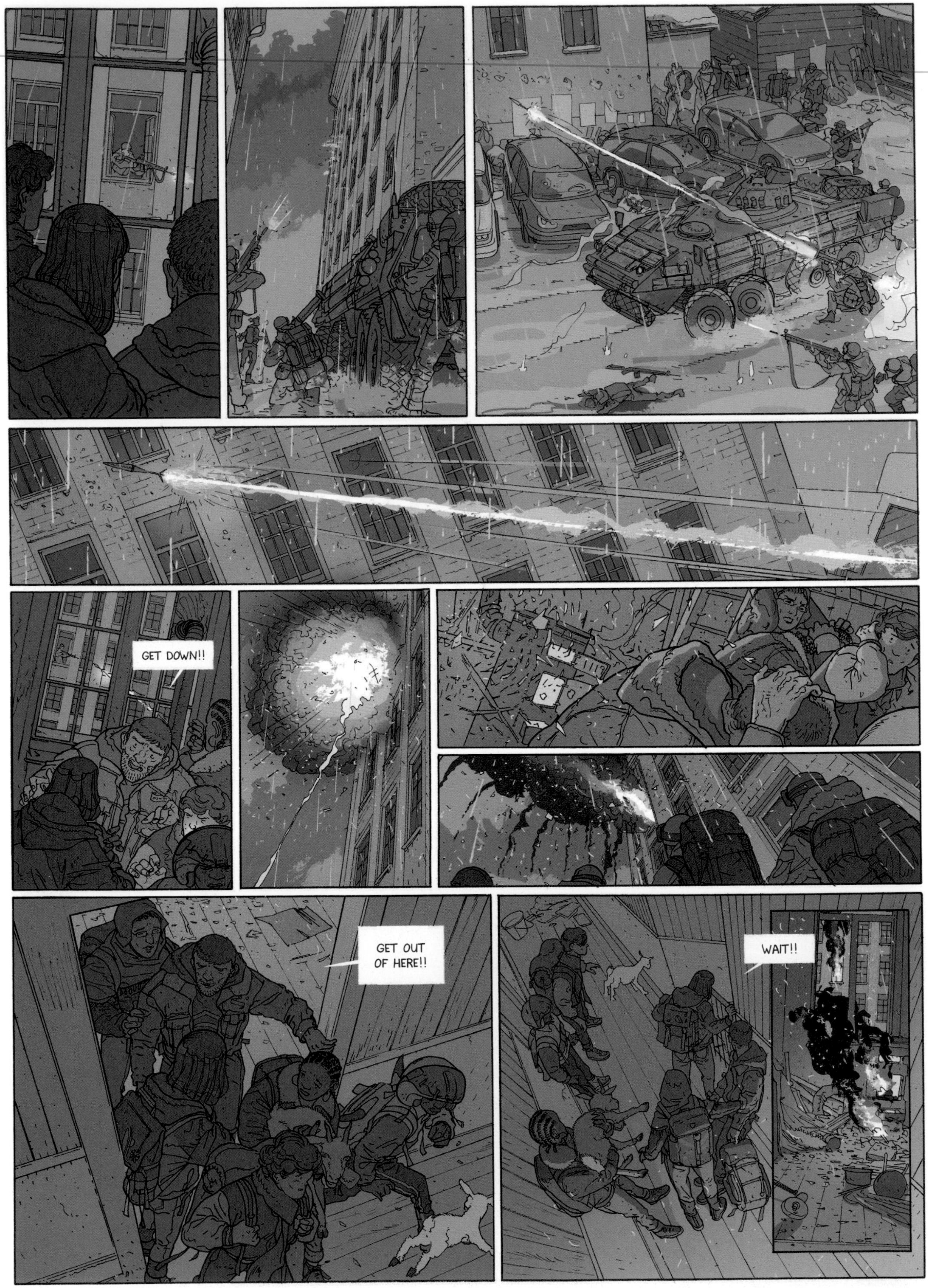
GET DOWN!!
GET OUT OF HERE!!
WAIT!!

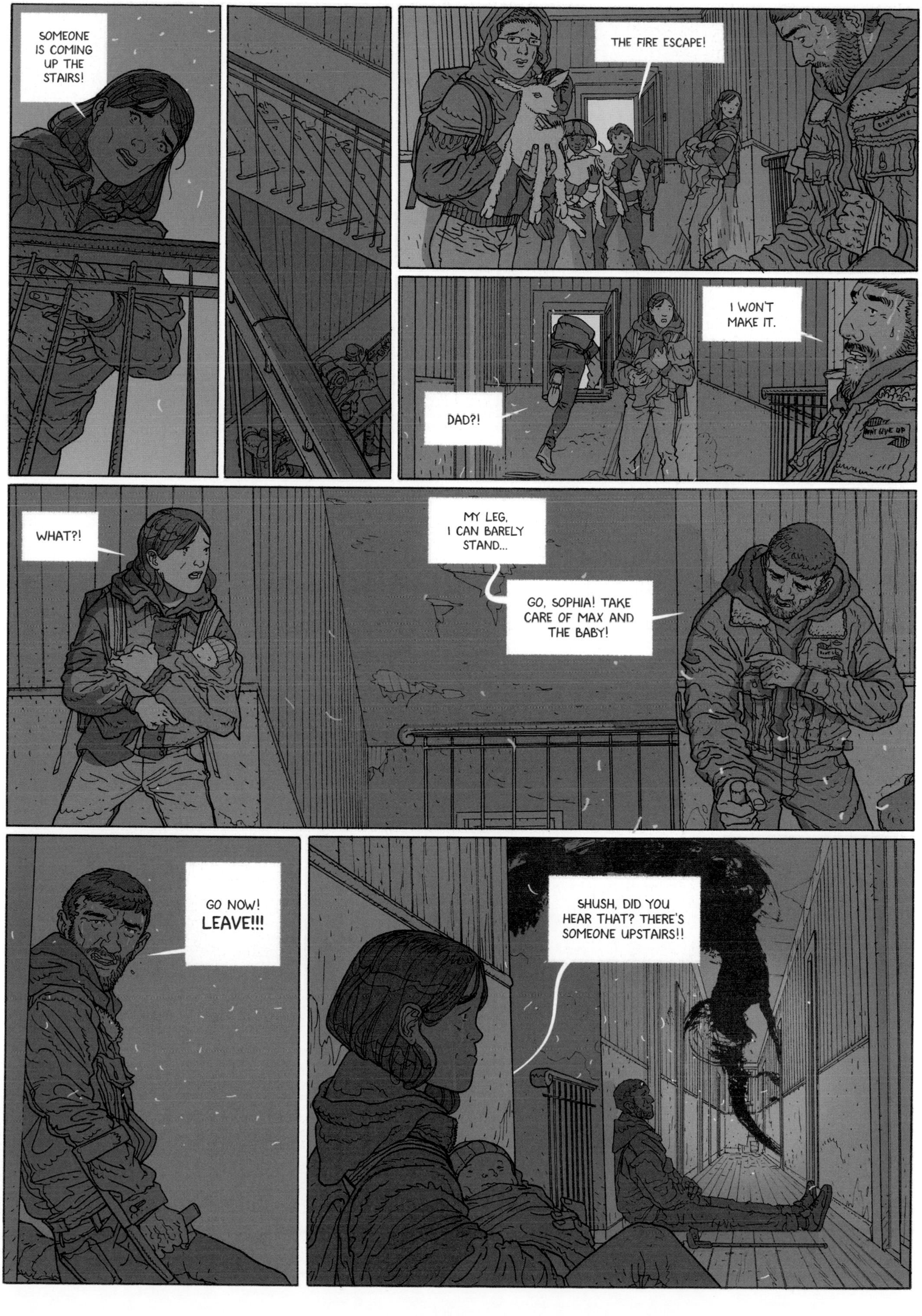
SOMEONE IS COMING UP THE STAIRS!
THE FIRE ESCAPE!
I WON'T MAKE IT.
DAD?!
WHAT?!
MY LEG, I CAN BARELY STAND...
GO, SOPHIA! TAKE CARE OF MAX AND THE BABY!
GO NOW! **LEAVE!!!**
SHUSH, DID YOU HEAR THAT? THERE'S SOMEONE UPSTAIRS!!

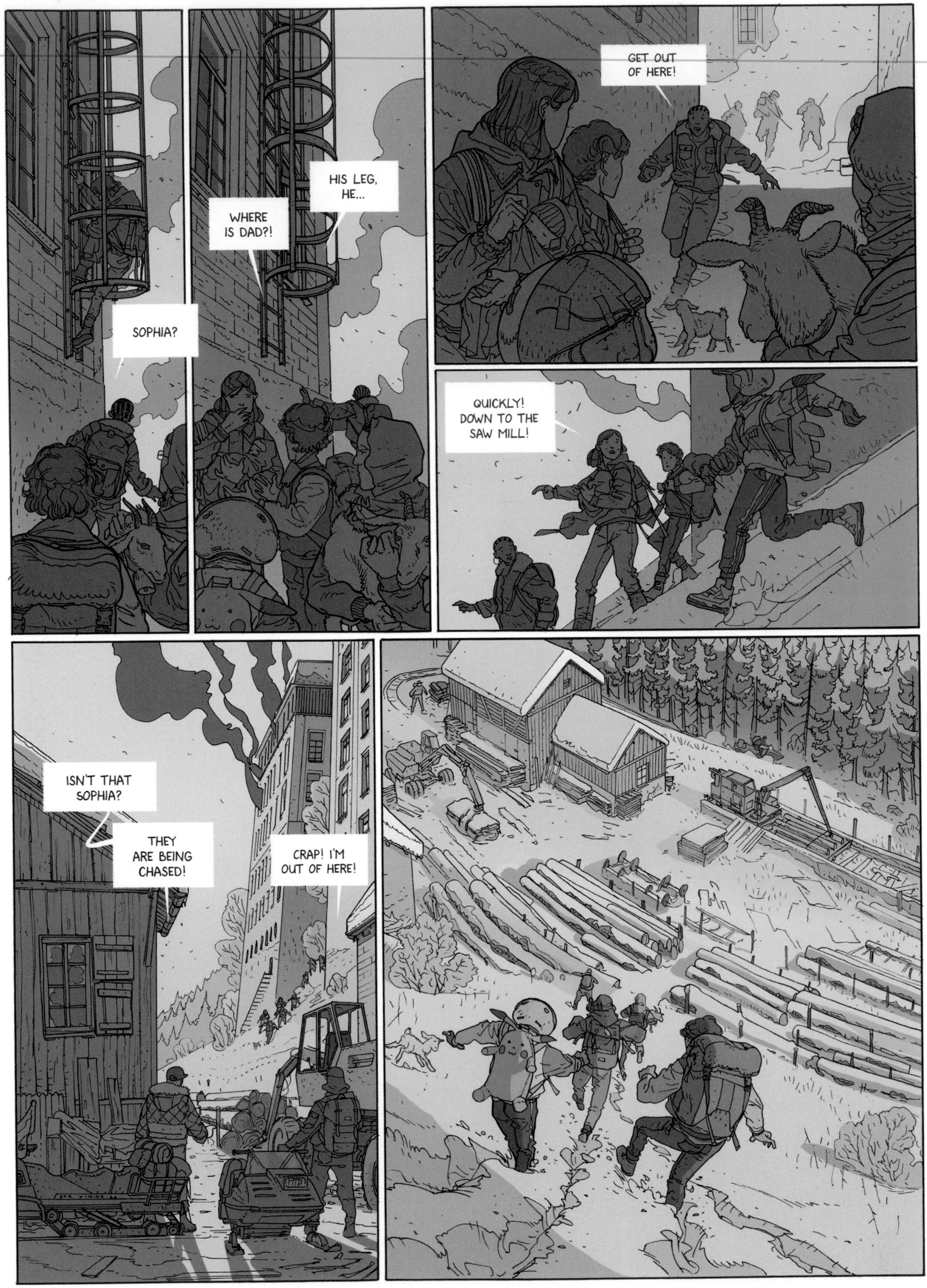
SOPHIA?
WHERE IS DAD?!
HIS LEG, HE...
GET OUT OF HERE!
QUICKLY! DOWN TO THE SAW MILL!
ISN'T THAT SOPHIA?
THEY ARE BEING CHASED!
CRAP! I'M OUT OF HERE!

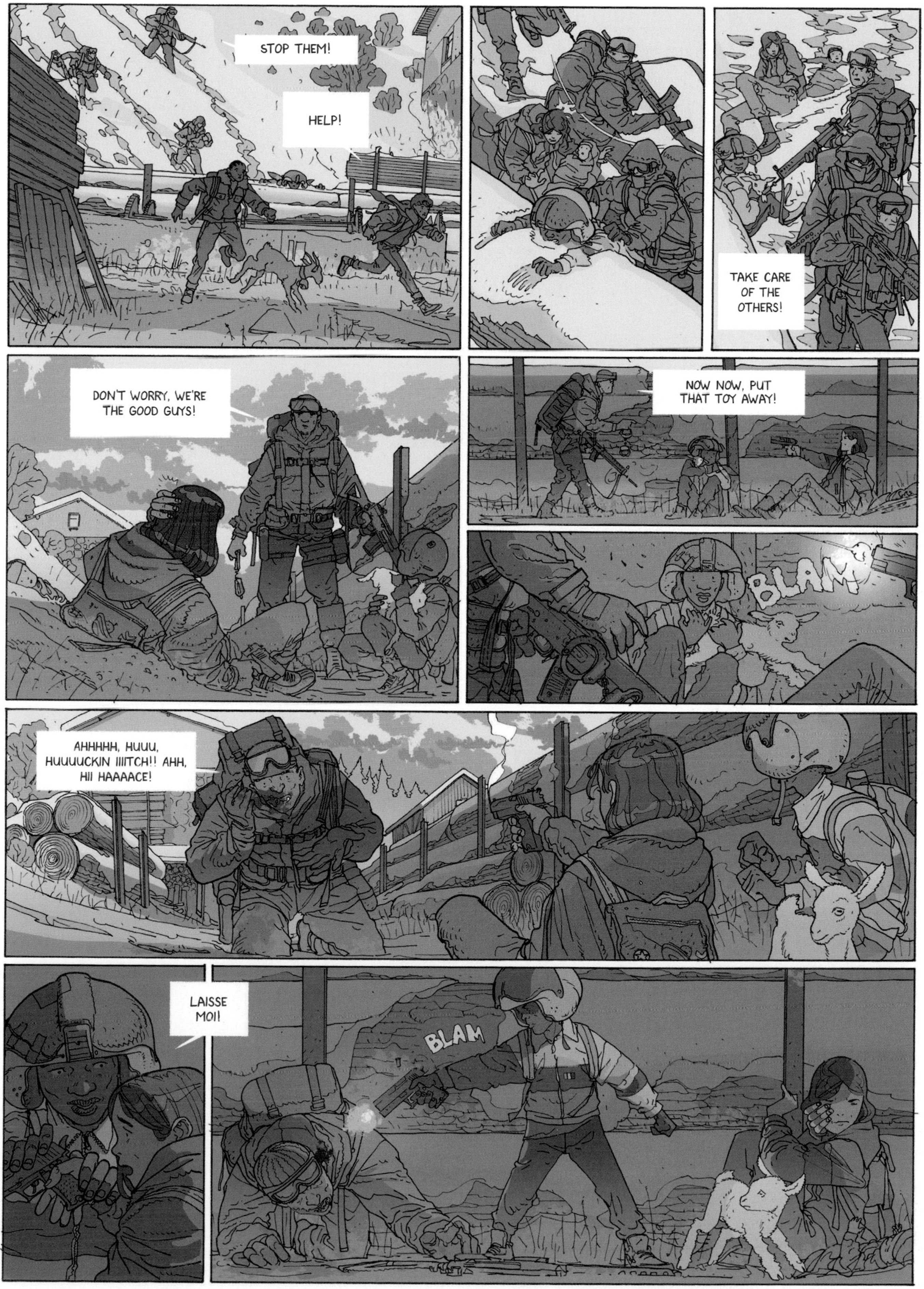
STOP THEM!
HELP!
TAKE CARE OF THE OTHERS!
DON'T WORRY, WE'RE THE GOOD GUYS!
NOW NOW, PUT THAT TOY AWAY!
BLAM
AHHHHH, HUUU, HUUUUCKIN IIIITCH!! AHH, HII HAAAACE!
LAISSE MOI!
BLAM

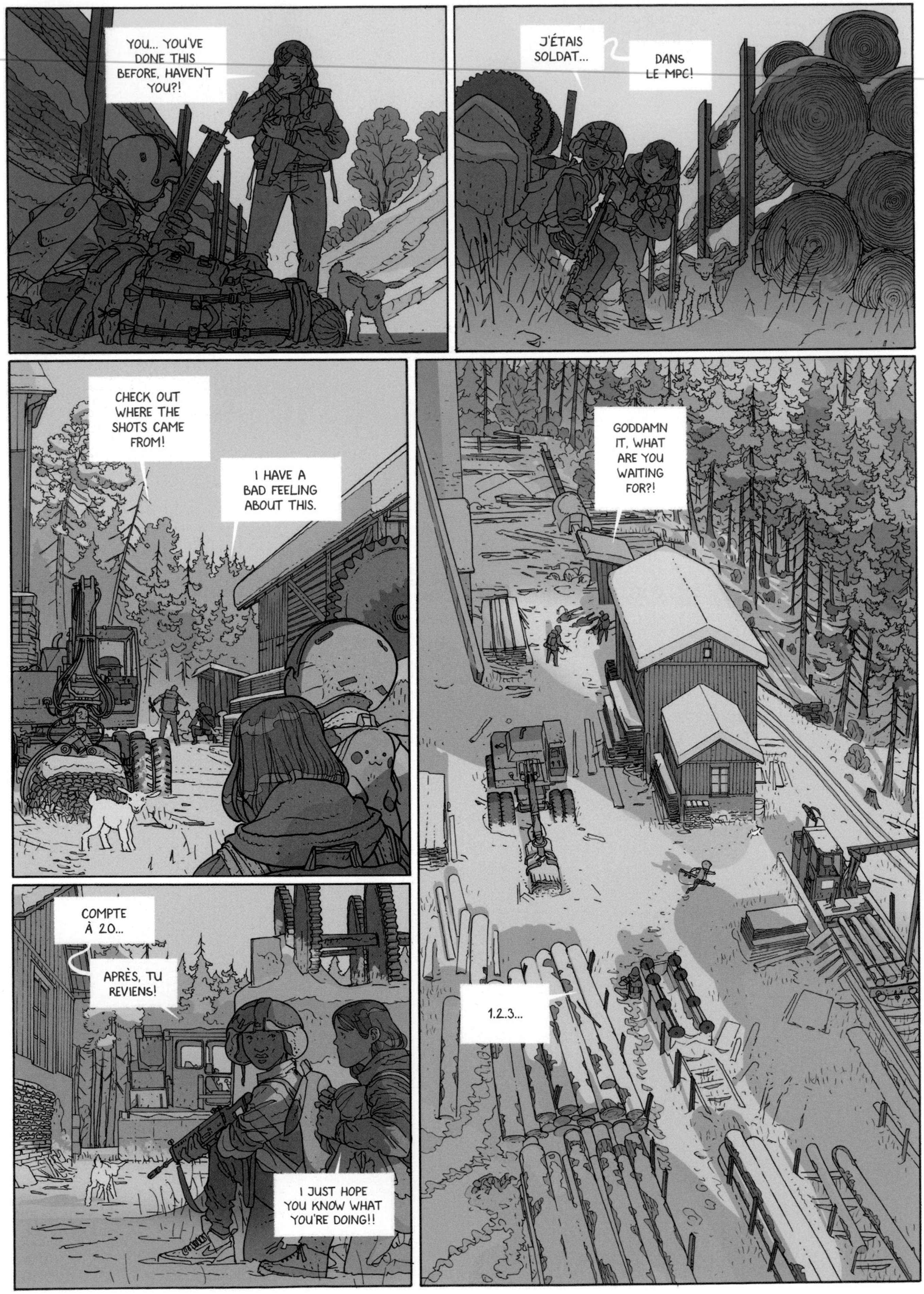
YOU... YOU'VE DONE THIS BEFORE, HAVEN'T YOU?!
J'ÉTAIS SOLDAT...
DANS LE MPC!
CHECK OUT WHERE THE SHOTS CAME FROM!
I HAVE A BAD FEELING ABOUT THIS.
COMPTE À 20...
APRÈS, TU REVIENS!
I JUST HOPE YOU KNOW WHAT YOU'RE DOING!!
GODDAMN IT, WHAT ARE YOU WAITING FOR?!
1.2.3...

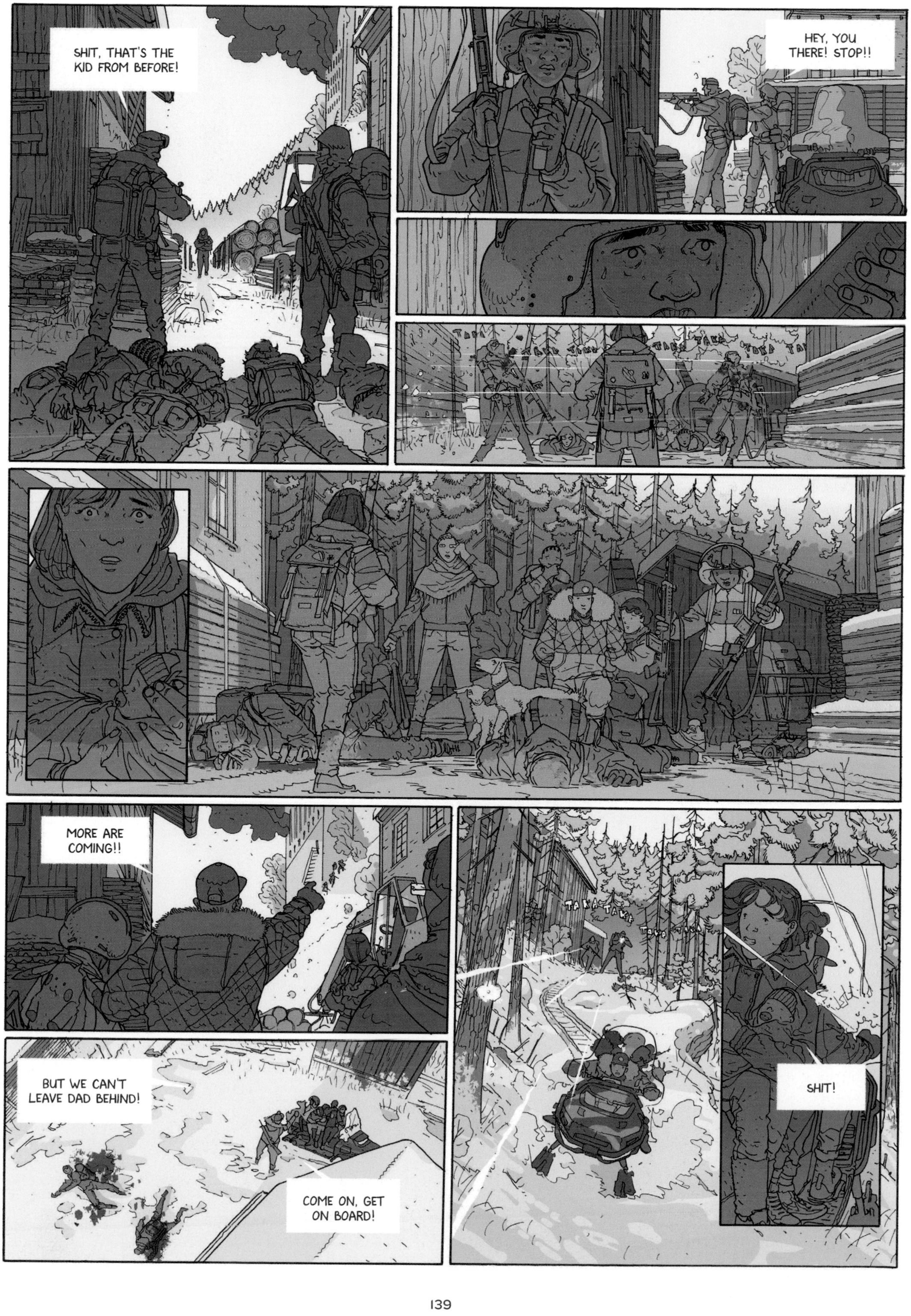
SHIT, THAT'S THE KID FROM BEFORE!
HEY, YOU THERE! STOP!!
MORE ARE COMING!!
BUT WE CAN'T LEAVE DAD BEHIND!
COME ON, GET ON BOARD!
SHIT!

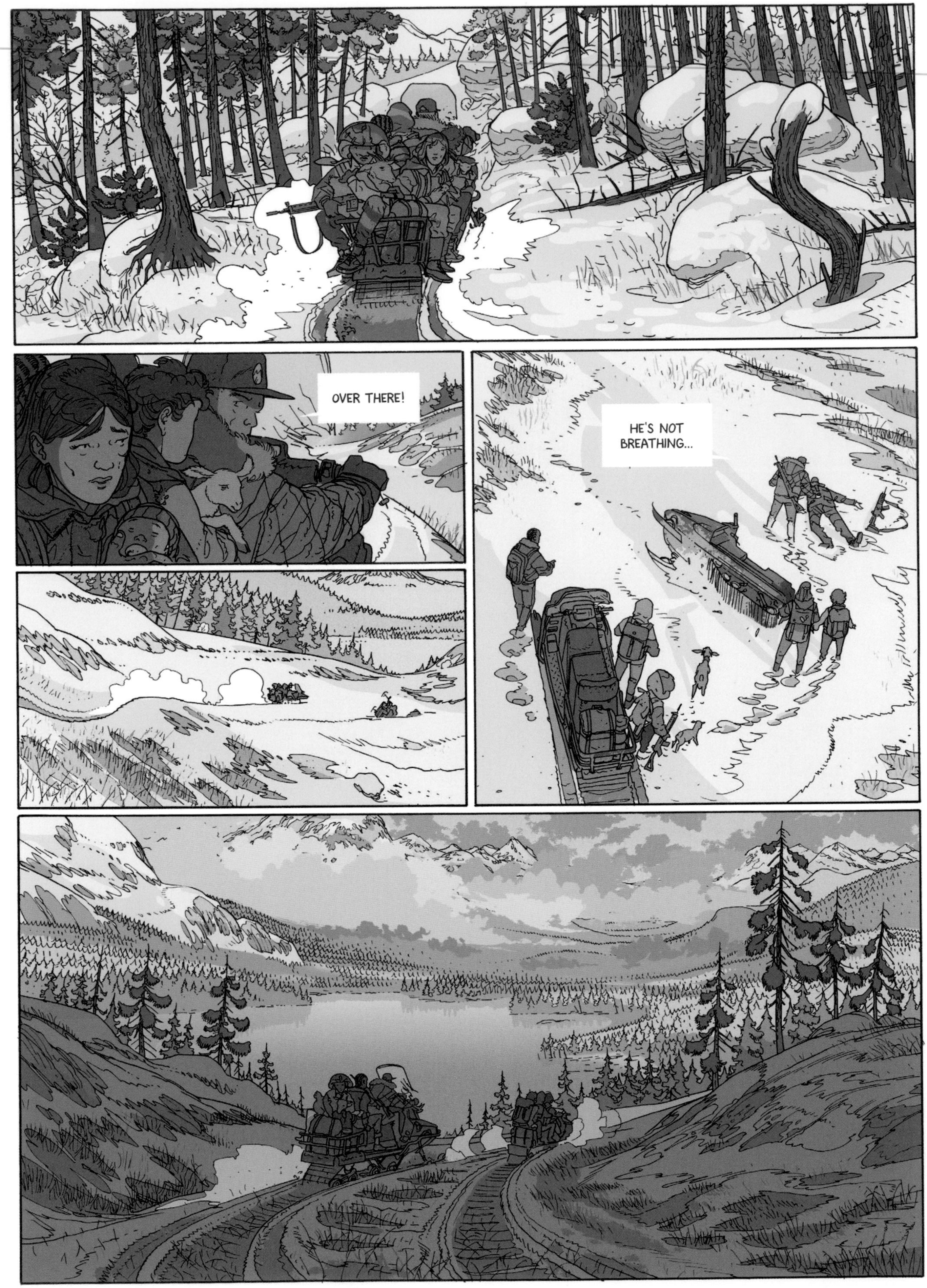
OVER THERE!
HE'S NOT BREATHING...

TO BE CONTINUED...

Interview with Jared Muralt

Jared Muralt, you have created a bleak setting and show us how a civilization starts to fall apart by showcasing it on your hometown of Bern, Why?

I actually wanted to tell a story which was set in a postapocalyptic world. But then I noticed how that wouldn't suffice and that I also wanted to tell the tale of how it even got to this apocalypse at all. The world which I have created for my comic book is not set that that far apart from our world. I have simply over exaggerated a few things. But the root causes already exist to some extent, like for example environmental problems or economic crises. The society in «The Fall» is also under attack from a virus, the danger of which is not fully recognized in the beginning.

In what sense has that which you have drawn three years ago come true with the arrival of the Coronavirus?

There are obvious parallels like the virus or panic buying. But the virus in «The Fall» is far more aggressive than the Corona Virus and kills way more people. Another difference is that a global economic crisis and recession already run rampant, even before the arrival of the virus. Since both the people and the economy are suffering, it is harder for adequate countermeasures to be implemented due to a lack of resources. This is why the system completely breaks down in «The Fall». The dead are not retrieved from their homes anymore, marauding gangs roam the streets and people are fleeing the cities. But luckily, we're not that far along yet.

Which other inspirations do you draw on from the real world?

When continuing the story current events always have an influence. That's why my protagonists meet a doctor from Syria in the wintery Grand Hotel and a child soldier from the Central African Republic. And when I see on the news, how refugees try to cross the alps in sneakers made from cloth, then being rescued under the most dire of situations by French citizens, which then in turn are being dragged to court, then that situation just seems so absurd to me, that I can't help but work it into my comic book in some form or another.

What is it about the postapocalyptic setting that fascinates you?

I ponder the question, which forms of society emerge, when the overarching structure, and by that I mean civilization as an element of order, no longer exists. Humans will always gather together in groups since they are more fit for survival in groups. New groups first need to define power structures and a balance of power, for themselves but also in relation to other groups. Different approaches, positions, views and ideologies then clash. These proceedings are of interest to me as well as the question, which values will be adopted in the new world and which will be lost.

A small family or rather a father and his two children are at the core of «The Fall». You yourself have become a father of twins during the production of «The Fall». Has this event had any kind of impact on your story?

It has had an impact insofar as that the first fifty

Jared Muralt (*1982) is a Bern based comic book artist. After a preliminary year at the School of Design Bern, he trained as a decorator while secretly spending his time with anatomical studies. He soon started freelancing as an illustrator, founded a graphic design collective with three friends in 2009 and and has been focusing on his comic book career full time since 2016, starting with the release of "THE FALL - VOL I" in 2018. The French translation "La Chute" (Futuropolis) won the Atomium Prize "Le Soir Prize for News Report Comics" in 2020.

pages were mostly created sometime during the night between 11 p.m. and 4 a.m. I also believe that me becoming a father has had a positive impact on how the character of the father was depicted. He became more realistic since I can now better define what a father is, what he isn't and what is able to do or not.

The first volume of «The Fall» is quite dark. Why?

It is a matter of fact, that my characters are going through a really shitty rough patch. Sometimes I almost pity them. But for dramatic reasons they have to hit rock bottom first, before things can take a turn for the better again. And it will happen. I promise. I'm also interested in the question of how one can preserve their humanity in a world as dark as this, a world no one really wants to be living in.

Your plan is to release ongoing single issues of about 24 pages. Your goal was to release a chapter like this every 6 months. Isn't that a bit too ambitious?

Yes it is, especially since I'm a lone wolf and have to do virtually everything by myself. But for me personally I found that it helps to set tight deadlines. If I have too much time I will start going over old pages, correcting or even redrawing them and that in turn is about the worst thing a comic book artist can do, since you won't be able to move forward at all.

How many issues is the entire series planned for?

That's still written in the stars. I might have an overarching arc in mind, but for how long I will stretch it, we'll have to see. I want to model it after the example set by television shows. If my story appeals to people, then it will be extended and get a longer run. Of course, this is very alluring artistically speaking since I'll be able to show how locations go through changes if my story takes place over a longer period of time. But more importantly I can experiment with how new forms of civilization could rise from the ruins of the old world or which elements from those old civilizations will be adopted by the new ones and which won't. I can have buildings decay and illustrate how nature reclaims its space.

Interview: Gisela Feuz

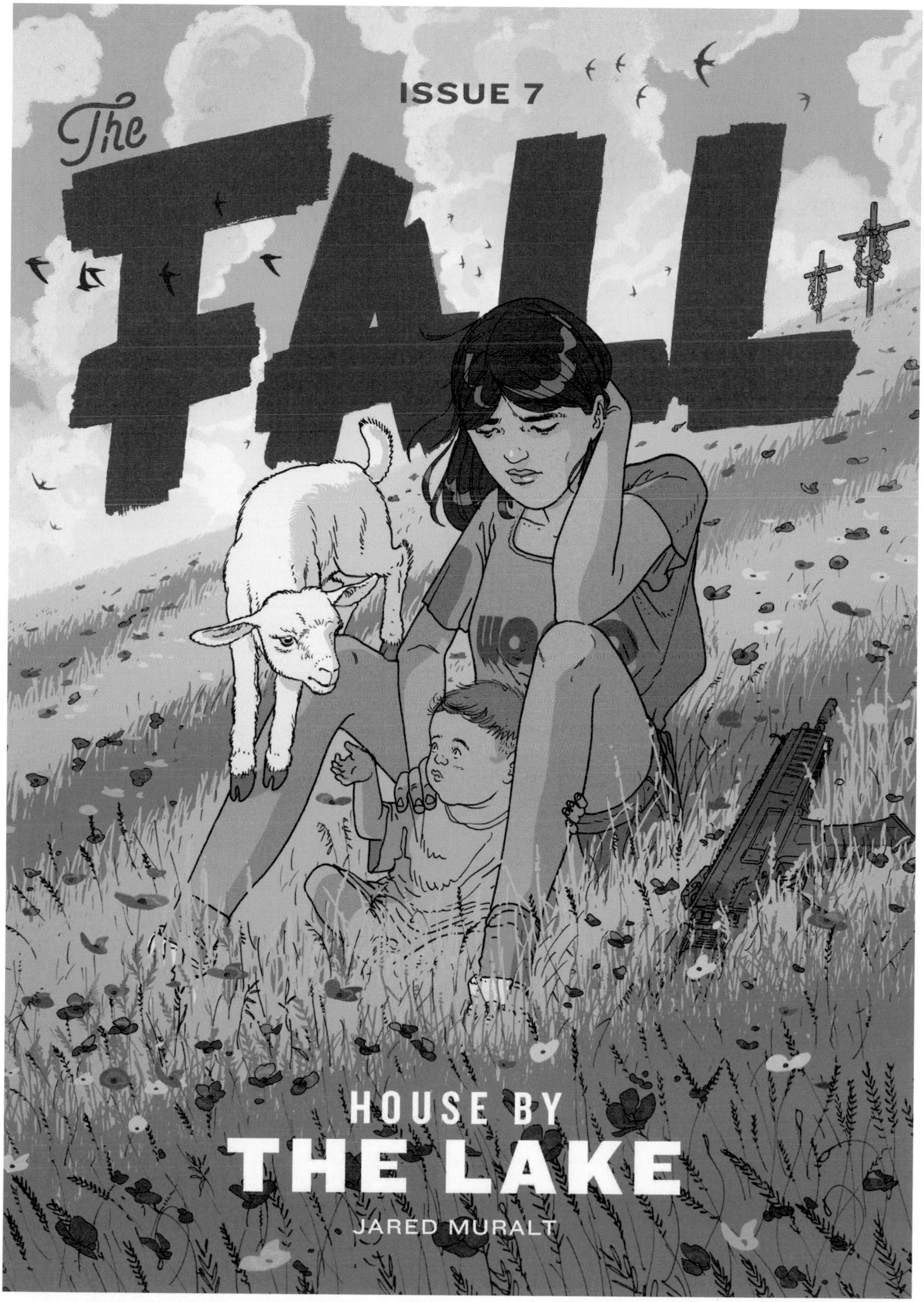
ISSUE 7
The FALL
HOUSE BY
THE LAKE
JARED MURALT

The story of The Fall will be continued in Issue 7: "House By The Lake" (published by Tintenkilby).
AVAILABLE ON SHOP.BLACKYARD.CH

THOUGHTS

Drawing comics: truly a disaster.

I hadn't even finished drawing "Hellship", my first real comic book, when my thoughts turned to my next project. Even though working on my first comic was a proper nightmare in hindsight.

Back when I first started working on "Hellship" ten years ago, I usually worked on it in segments of three weeks at a time. I alternated between working a couple of weeks on commissioned work and a couple of weeks on the comic.
Depending on how many commissions I had, sometimes the finished pages of "Hellship" spent months hidden in a drawer. And every time I forced myself to take these pages out of their drawer, all I could see was all the mistakes I had made. So, I would often end up drawing these pages anew, instead of just continuing the story.

And so, this pattern continued for almost seven years. In the end, I had to completely rewrite the ending of the story, because I honestly hadn't put enough thought into it in the beginning. When I had finally finished it, I promised myself to either never draw another comic ever again or to fully plan the whole story and draw the comic in one go, no interruptions.

The beginning of "The Fall"

I started writing the story of "The Fall" the moment I had finally published "Hellship" in 2016. I had learned a lot during my work on "Hellship" after all. A lot, but not nearly enough as it turned out. I spent a long time collecting material for "The Fall". I finished writing the first three issues and had enough ideas for a sequel. The balance in my bank account had also recovered enough to survive as a comic book artist for a couple of months.

Euphorically I began to sketch the first three chapters in one go, then the pencil drawings, followed by the outlining in ink and finally coloring. I soon realized how little time I had taken to flesh out the characters. Their appearance kept changing: the farther I got with the story, the clearer they came to me. I soon had to revise all the faces I had drawn in the first couple of pages. I also started to seriously doubt the storyline.

For the following three issues I wanted to invest a lot more time into writing the story. I used the time while coloring the previous chapters to listen to countless podcasts and interviews of famous screenwriters and this is when I started to really doubt myself. It didn't make sense to only spend two months writing the story when it took me almost two years to draw the whole thing.

But it was too late - all I could do was try to save the dialogue. I really didn't want to start all over again, as I had finally finished drawing all the pages. But I had learned another valuable lesson. And I will keep on learning with every new issue. Or so I hope.

THE UNOFFICIAL SOUNDTRACK ON SPOTIFY!
Listen to the songs Jared listened to while he was drawing and writing THE FALL while you are reading THE FALL.

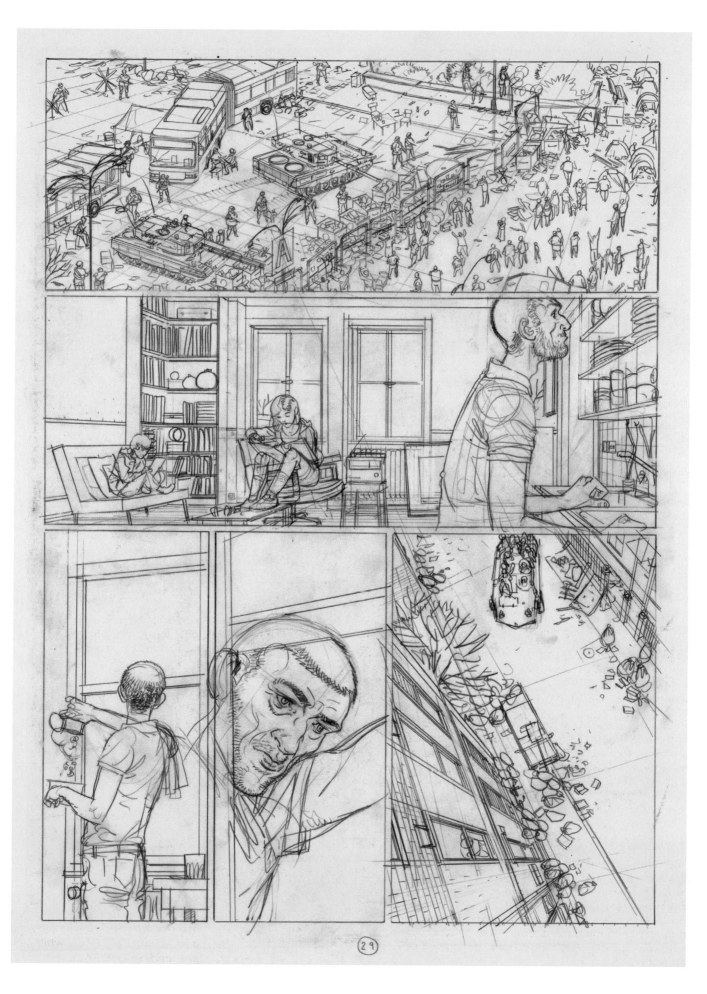

29

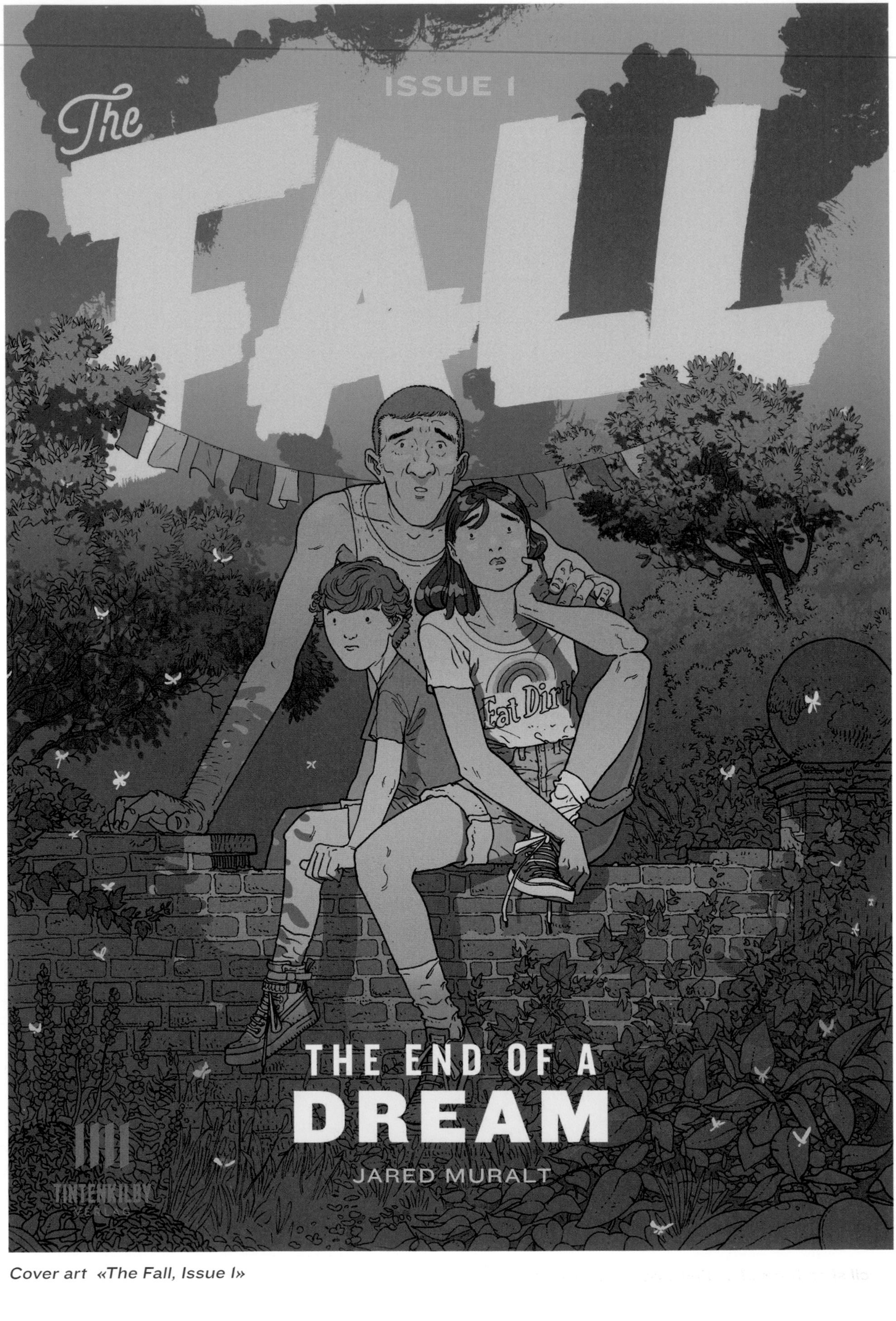
ISSUE I
The
FALL
Eat Dirt
THE END OF A
DREAM
JARED MURALT
TINTENKILBY
VERLAG

Cover art «The Fall, Issue I»

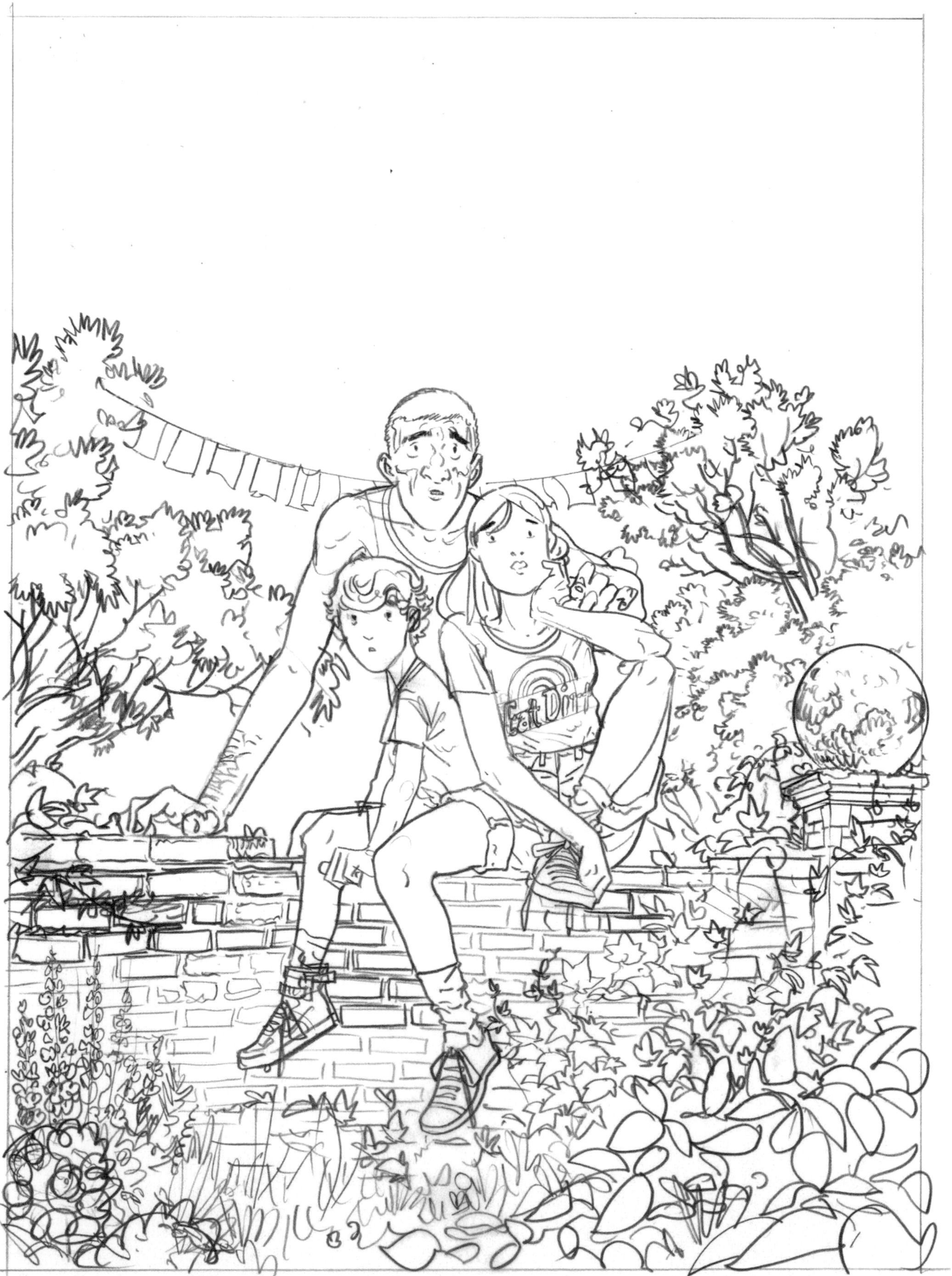
Eat Dirt

Pencil sketch for «The Fall, Issue I» cover art.

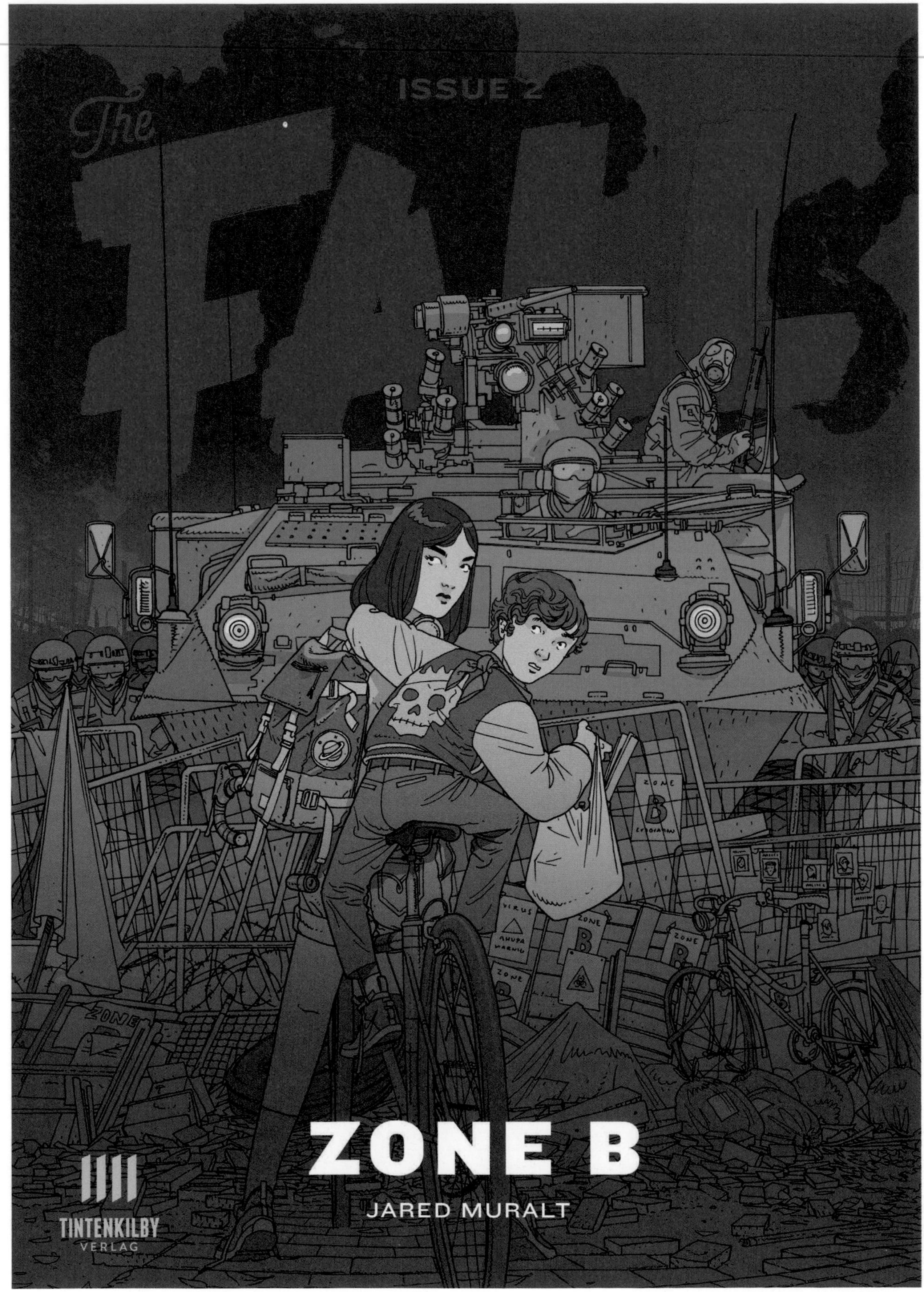
The
ISSUE 2
FALL
ZONE B
JARED MURALT
TINTENKILBY
VERLAG

Cover art «The Fall, Issue 2»

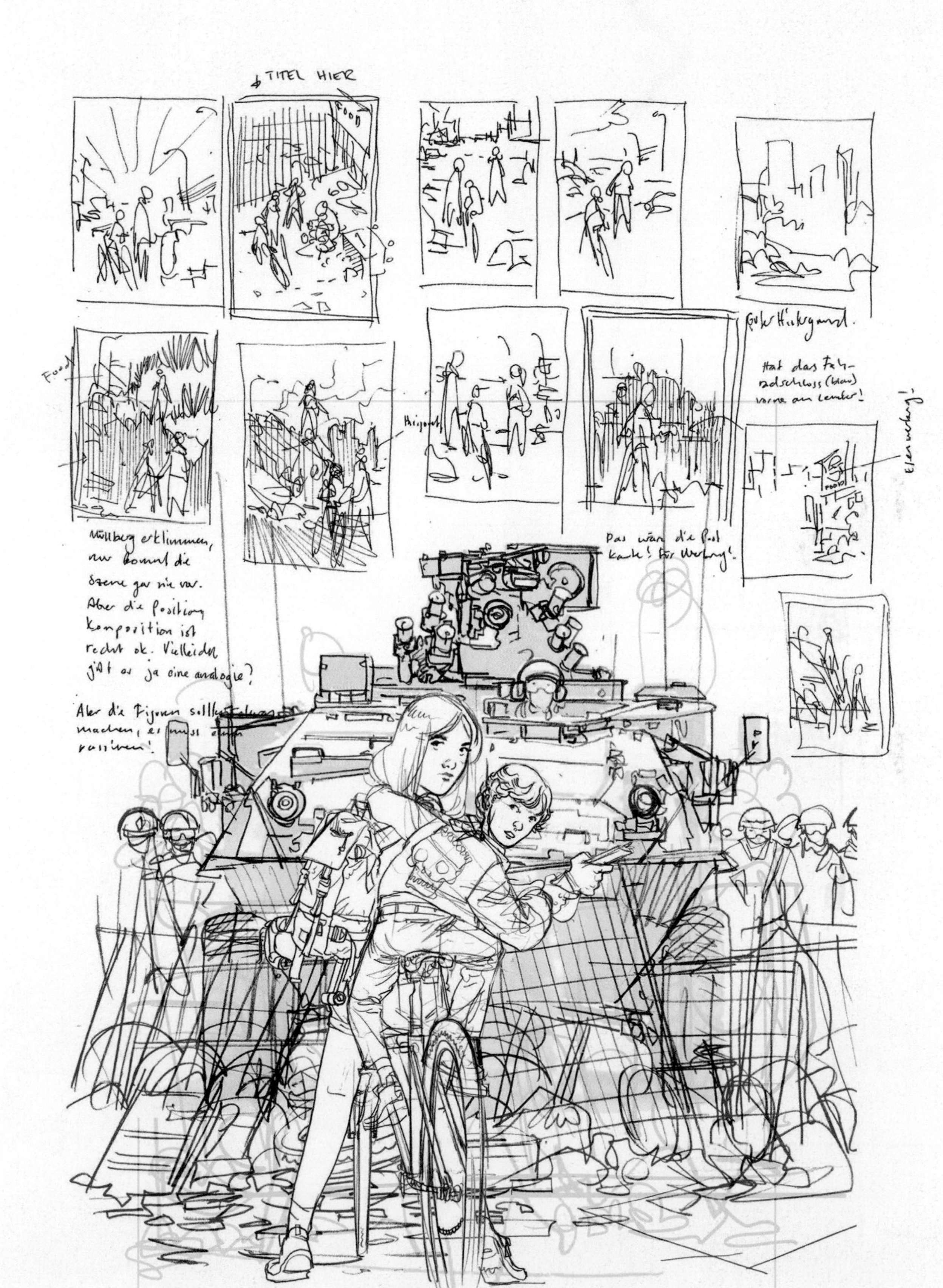
TITEL HIER
FOOD
Müllberg erklimmen, nur kommt die Szene gar nie vor. Aber die Position Komposition ist recht ok. Vielleicht gibt es ja eine analogie?
Das wär die Post karte! Für Werbung!
Guter Hintergrund.
Hat das Fahrradschloss (blau) vorne am Lenker!

Fineliner thumbnails, pencil sketches & notes for «The Fall, Issue 2» cover art.

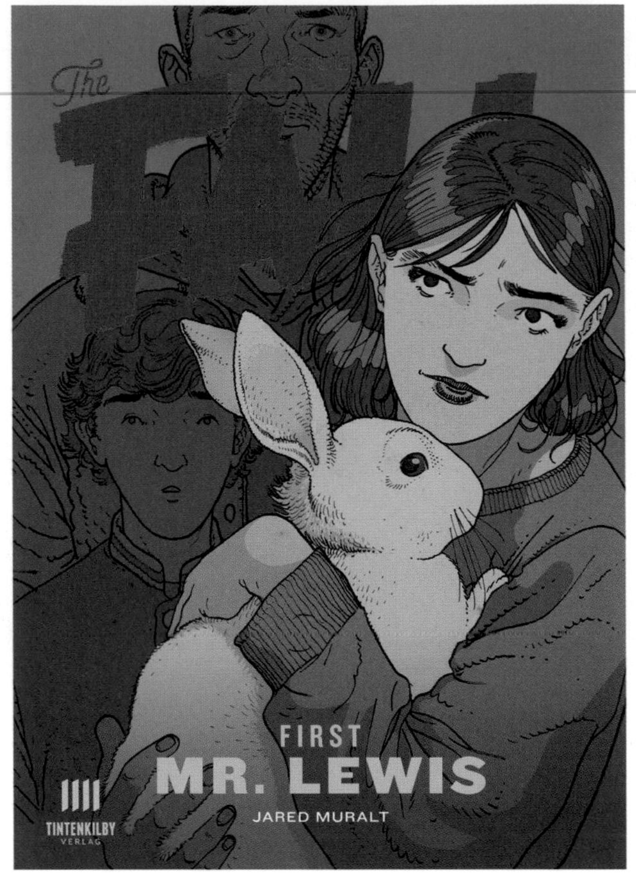
The
FALL
FIRST
MR. LEWIS
JARED MURALT
TINTENKILBY
VERLAG

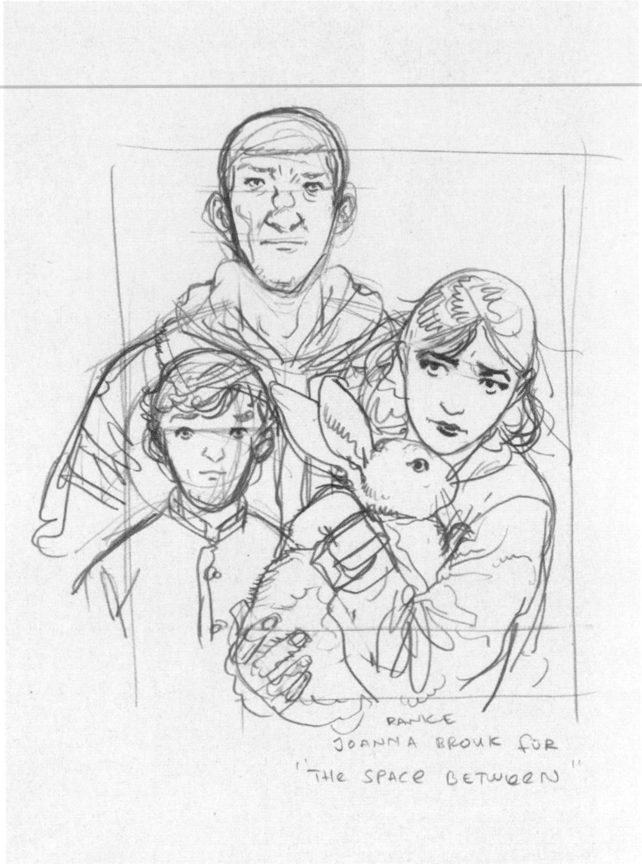
RANKE
JOANNA BROUK FÜR
"THE SPACE BETWEEN"

Cover art and pencil sketch for «The Fall, Issue 3»

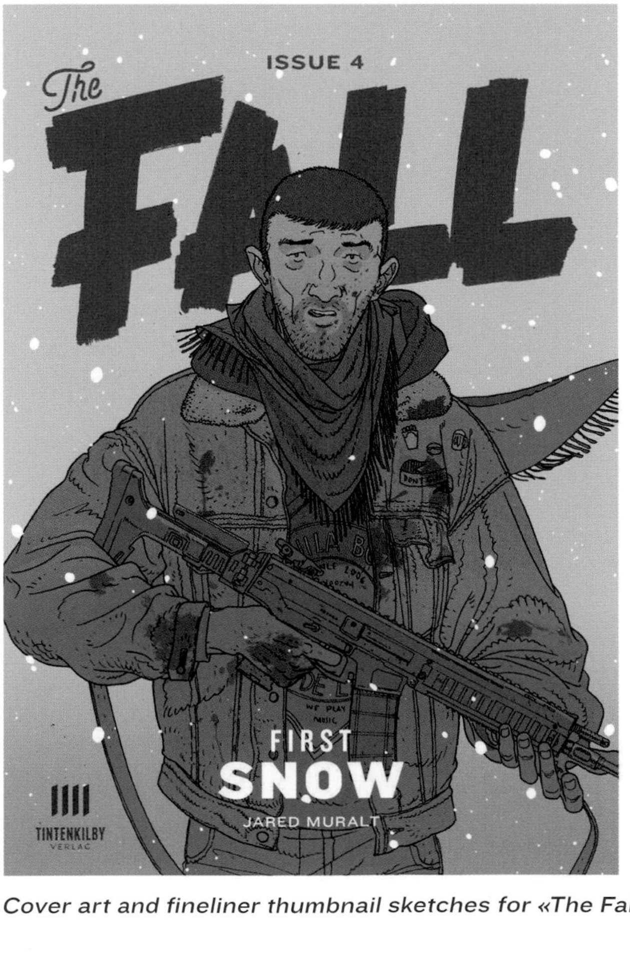
ISSUE 4
The
FALL
FIRST
SNOW
JARED MURALT
TINTENKILBY
VERLAG

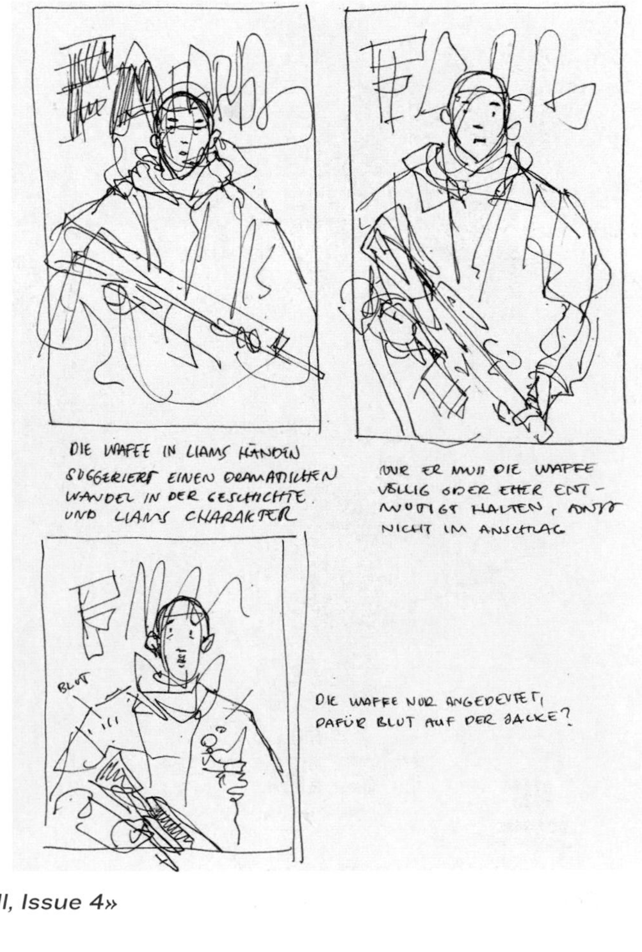
DIE WAFFE IN LIAMS HÄNDEN
SUGGERIERT EINEN DRAMATICHEN
WANDEL IN DER GESCHICHTE
UND LIAMS CHARAKTER
NUR ER MUSS DIE WAFFE
VÖLLIG ODER EHER ENT-
MUTIGT HALTEN,
NICHT IM ANSCHLAG
BLUT
DIE WAFFE NUR ANGEDEUTET,
DAFÜR BLUT AUF DER JACKE?

Cover art and fineliner thumbnail sketches for «The Fall, Issue 4»

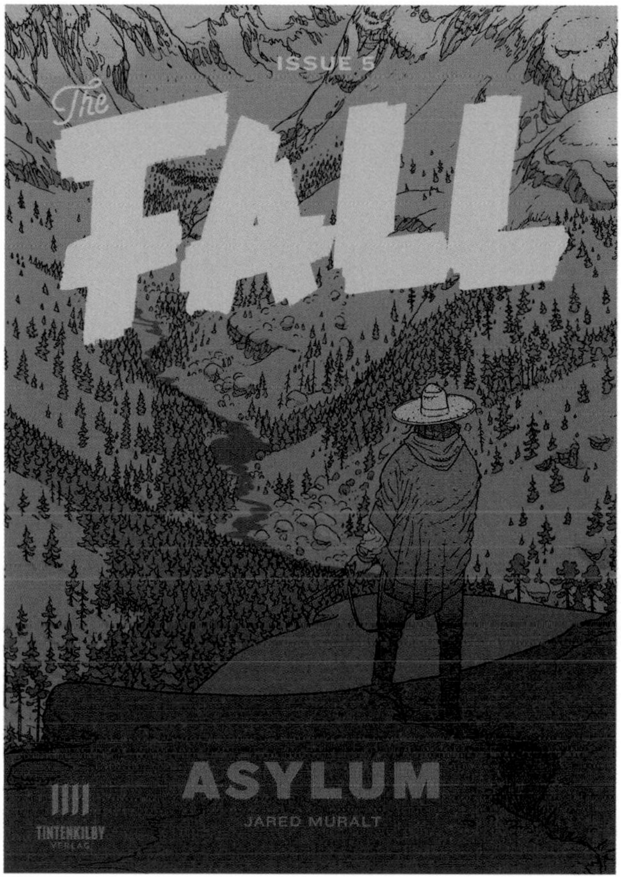
ISSUE 5
The
FALL
ASYLUM
JARED MURALT
TINTENKILBY
VERLAG

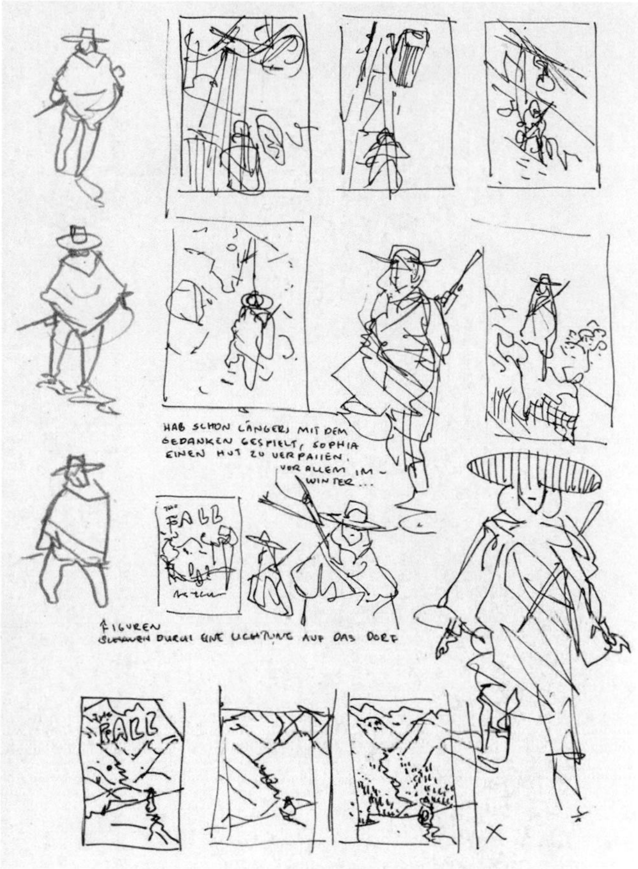
HAB SCHON LÄNGER/ MIT DEM GEDANKEN GESPIELT, SOPHIA EINEN HUT ZU VERPASSEN.
VOR ALLEM IM WINTER...
FIGUREN
SCHAUEN DURCH EINE LICHTUNG AUF DAS DORF

Cover art, pencil studies and fineliner thumbnails for «The Fall, Issue 5»

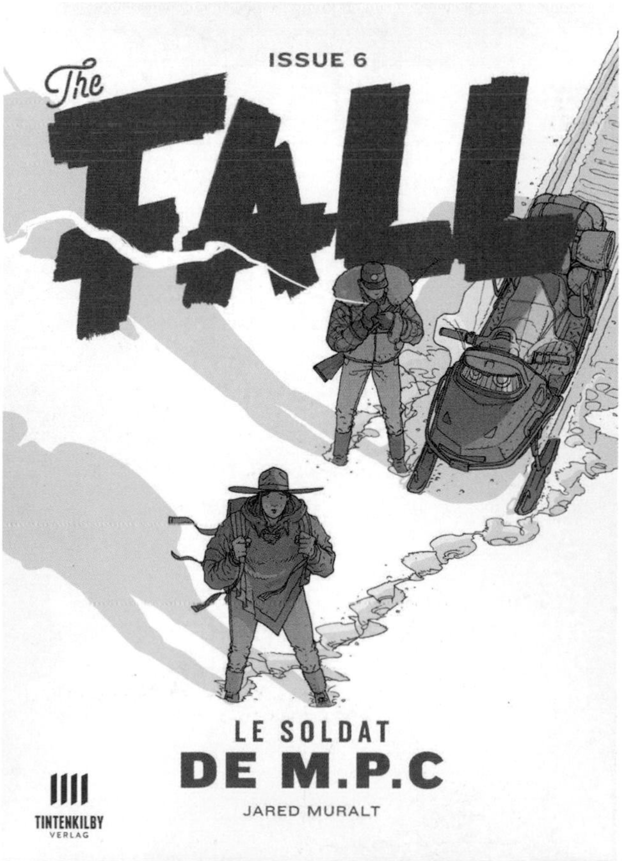
ISSUE 6
The
FALL
LE SOLDAT
DE M.P.C
JARED MURALT
TINTENKILBY
VERLAG

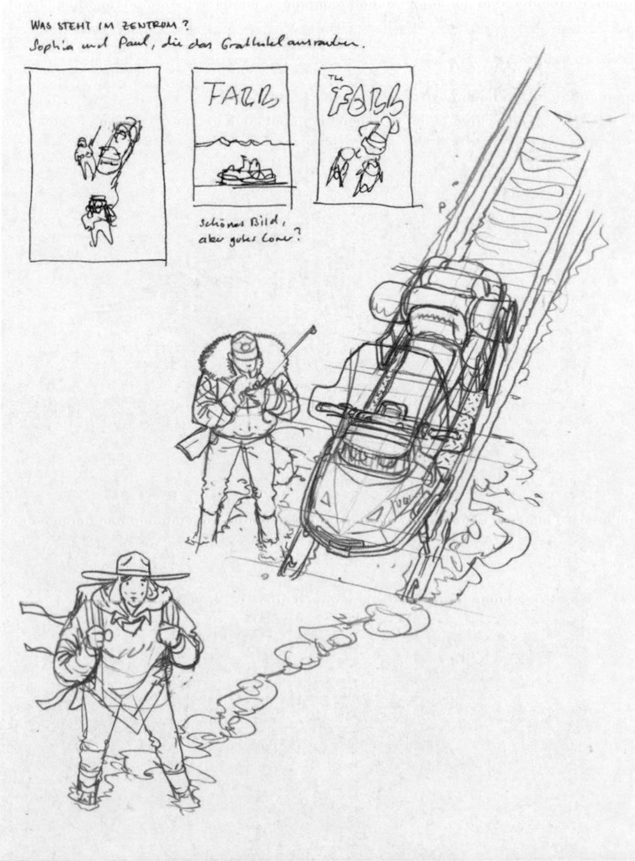
WAS STEHT IM ZENTRUM ?
Schönes Bild, aber gutes Cover?

Cover art, pencil pre-drawing & fineliner thumbnails for «The Fall, Issue 6»

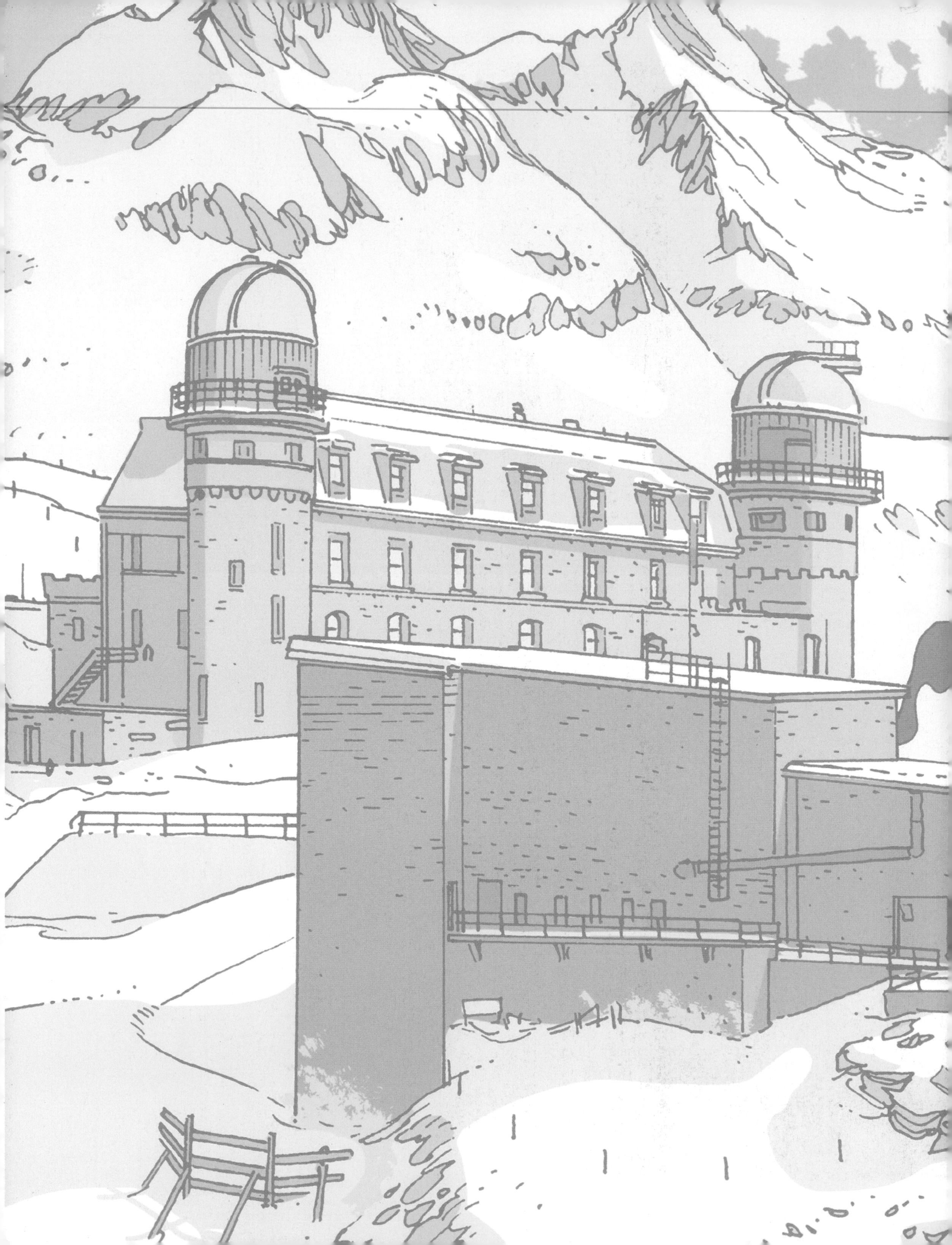